"Just because you're known for one thing doesn't mean you can't *hiccup* be something different if you choose."

- Drunk Gert super-fan, Maddie,
who died moments after this quote.

REGULAR EDITION ISBN: 978-1-5343-0330-0
FORBIDDEN PLANET/BIG BANG COMICS
EXCLUSIVE EDITION ISBN: 978-1-5343-0620-2

I HATE FAIRYLAND, VOL. 3: GOOD GIRL. First Printing. October 2017.
Published by Image Comics, Inc. Office of publication: 2701 NW
Vaughn St., Suite 780, Portland, OR 97210. Copyright © 2017
Skottie Young. All rights reserved. Contains material originally
published in single magazine form as I HATE FAIRYLAND #11-15.
"I HATE FAIRYLAND," its logos, and the likenesses of all
characters herein are trademarks of Skottie Young, unless
otherwise noted. "Image" and the Image Comics logos are
registered trademarks of Image Comics, Inc. No part of this
publication may be reproduced or transmitted, in any form or
by any means (except for short excerpts for journalistic or
review purposes), without the express written permission of
Skottie Young, or Image Comics, Inc. All names, characters,
events, and locales in this publication are entirely fictional.
Any resemblance to actual persons (living or dead), events, or
places, without satiric intent, is coincidental. Printed in the USA.
For information regarding the CPSIA on this printed material
call: 203-595-3636 and provide reference #RICH-764780. For
international rights, contact: foreignlicensing@imagecomics.com

Written and Drawn by
SKOTTIE YOUNG

Coloring by
JEAN-FRANCOIS BEAULIEU

Additional Art in Chapter Thirteen by
DEAN RANKINE

Lettering & Design by
NATE PIEKOS OF BLAMBOT®

Edited by
KENT WAGENSCHUTZ

Volume Three Book Design by
VINCENT KUKUA

Logo Design by
RIAN HUGHES

VOLUME THREE:

OOD GIRL

IMAGE COMICS, INC.
Robert Kirkman — Chief Operating Officer
Erik Larsen — Chief Financial Officer
Todd McFarlane — President
Marc Silvestri — Chief Executive Officer
Jim Valentino — Vice President
Eric Stephenson — Publisher
Corey Murphy — Director of Sales
Jeff Boison — Director of Publishing
Planning & Book Trade Sales
Chris Ross — Director of Digital Sales
Jeff Stang — Director of Specialty Sales
Kat Salazar — Director of PR & Marketing
Branwyn Bigglestone — Controller
Kali Dugan — Senior Accounting Manager
Sue Korpela — Accounting & HR Manager
Drew Gill — Art Director
Heather Doornink — Production Director
Leigh Thomas — Print Manager
Tricia Ramos — Traffic Manager
Briah Skelly — Publicist

IMAGECOMICS.COM
Aly Hoffman — Events & Conventions
Coordinator
Sasha Head — Sales & Marketing
Production Designer
David Brothers — Branding Manager
Melissa Gifford — Content Manager
Drew Fitzgerald — Publicity Assistant
Vincent Kukua — Production Artist
Erika Schnatz — Production Artist
Ryan Brewer — Production Artist
Shanna Matuszak — Production Artist
Carey Hall — Production Artist
Esther Kim — Direct Market Sales
Representative
Emilio Bautista — Digital Sales
Representative
Leanna Caunter — Accounting Analyst
Chloe Ramos-Peterson — Library Market
Sales Representative
Marla Eizik — Administrative Assistant

ELEVEN

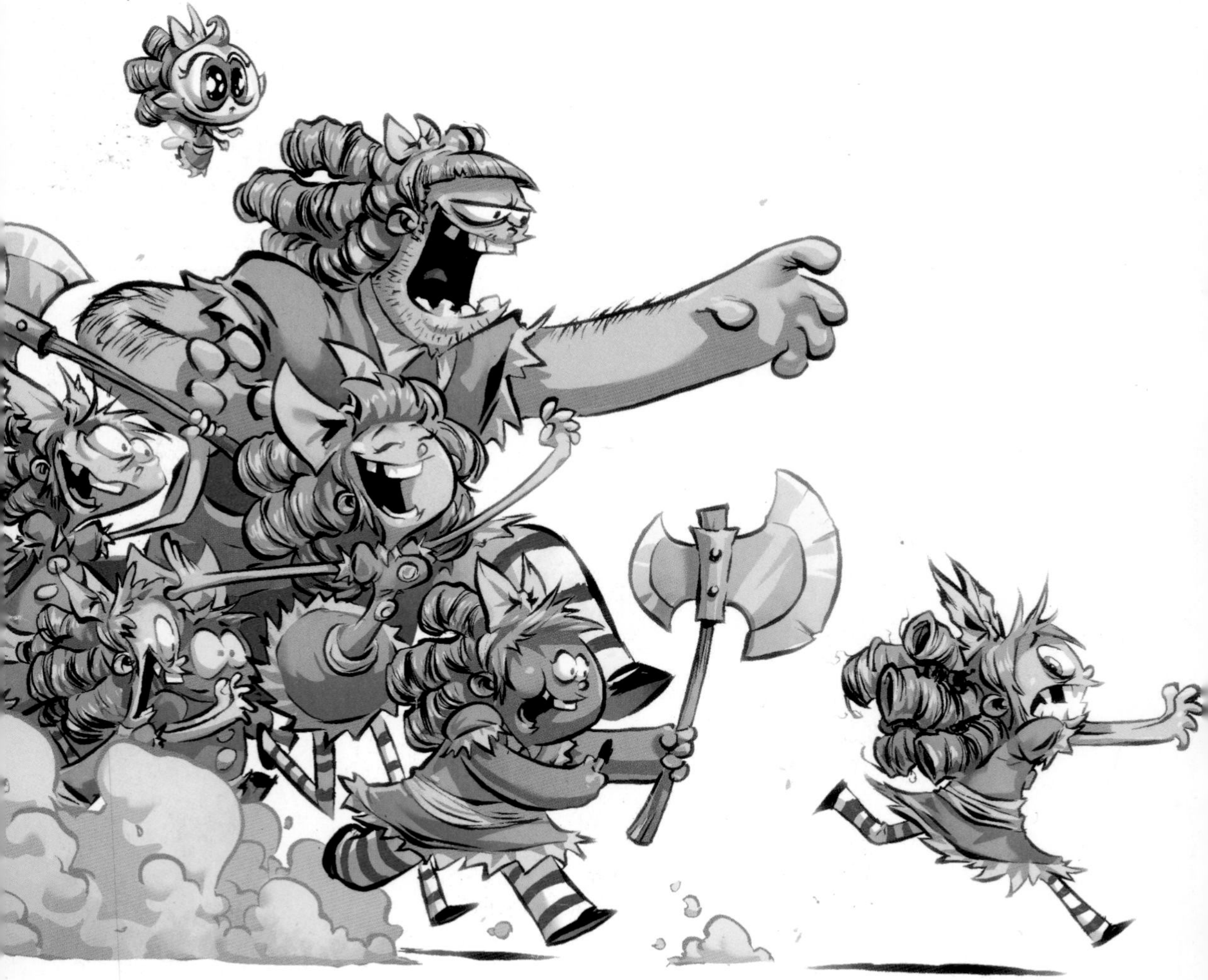

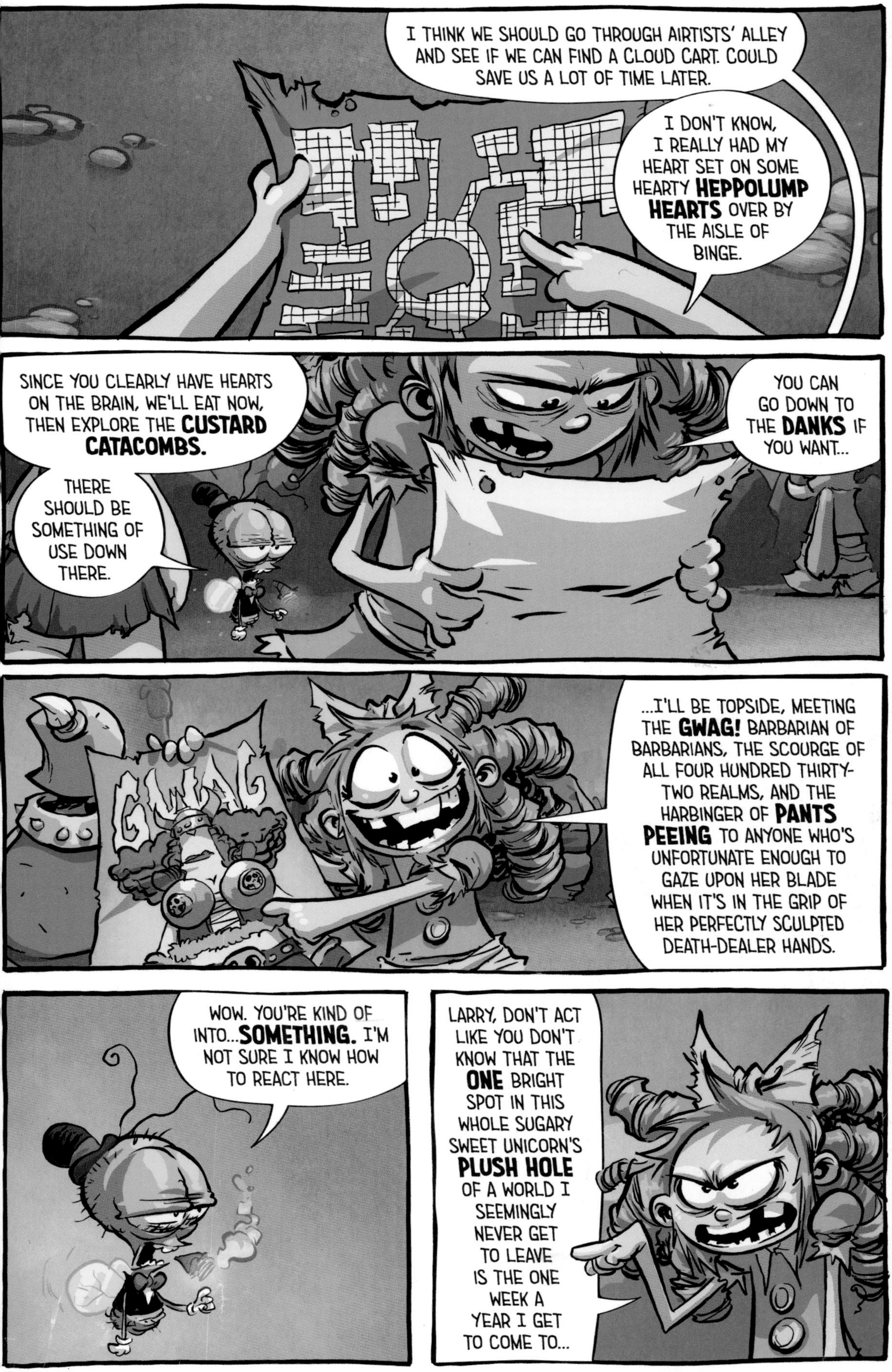

I THINK WE SHOULD GO THROUGH AIRTISTS' ALLEY AND SEE IF WE CAN FIND A CLOUD CART. COULD SAVE US A LOT OF TIME LATER.
I DON'T KNOW, I REALLY HAD MY HEART SET ON SOME HEARTY **HEPPOLUMP HEARTS** OVER BY THE AISLE OF BINGE.
SINCE YOU CLEARLY HAVE HEARTS ON THE BRAIN, WE'LL EAT NOW, THEN EXPLORE THE **CUSTARD CATACOMBS.**
THERE SHOULD BE SOMETHING OF USE DOWN THERE.
YOU CAN GO DOWN TO THE **DANKS** IF YOU WANT...
GWAG
...I'LL BE TOPSIDE, MEETING THE **GWAG!** BARBARIAN OF BARBARIANS, THE SCOURGE OF ALL FOUR HUNDRED THIRTY-TWO REALMS, AND THE HARBINGER OF **PANTS PEEING** TO ANYONE WHO'S UNFORTUNATE ENOUGH TO GAZE UPON HER BLADE WHEN IT'S IN THE GRIP OF HER PERFECTLY SCULPTED DEATH-DEALER HANDS.
WOW. YOU'RE KIND OF INTO...**SOMETHING.** I'M NOT SURE I KNOW HOW TO REACT HERE.
LARRY, DON'T ACT LIKE YOU DON'T KNOW THAT THE **ONE** BRIGHT SPOT IN THIS WHOLE SUGARY SWEET UNICORN'S **PLUSH HOLE** OF A WORLD I SEEMINGLY NEVER GET TO LEAVE IS THE ONE WEEK A YEAR I GET TO COME TO...

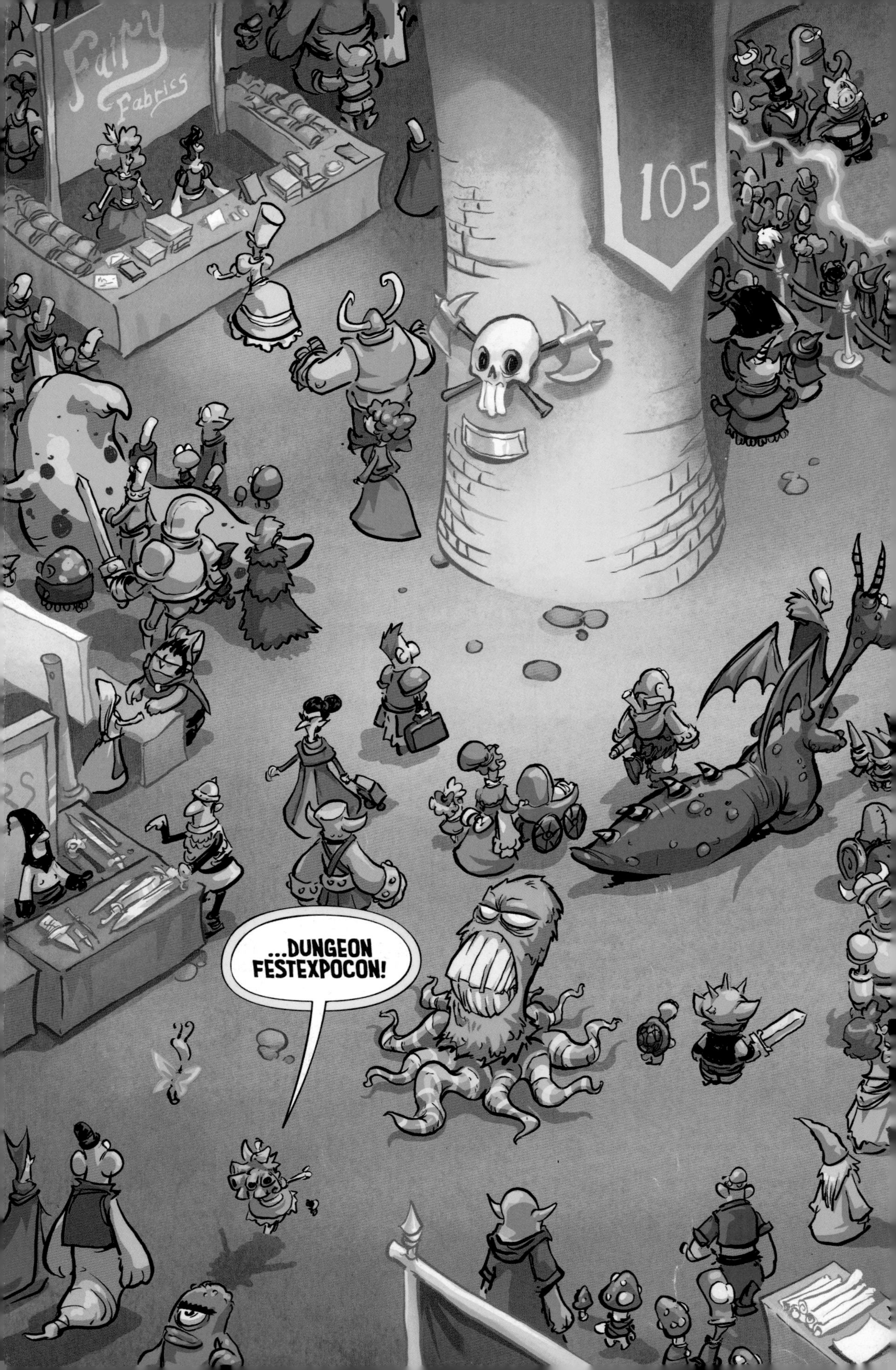
Fairy Fabrics
105
...DUNGEON FESTEXPOCON!

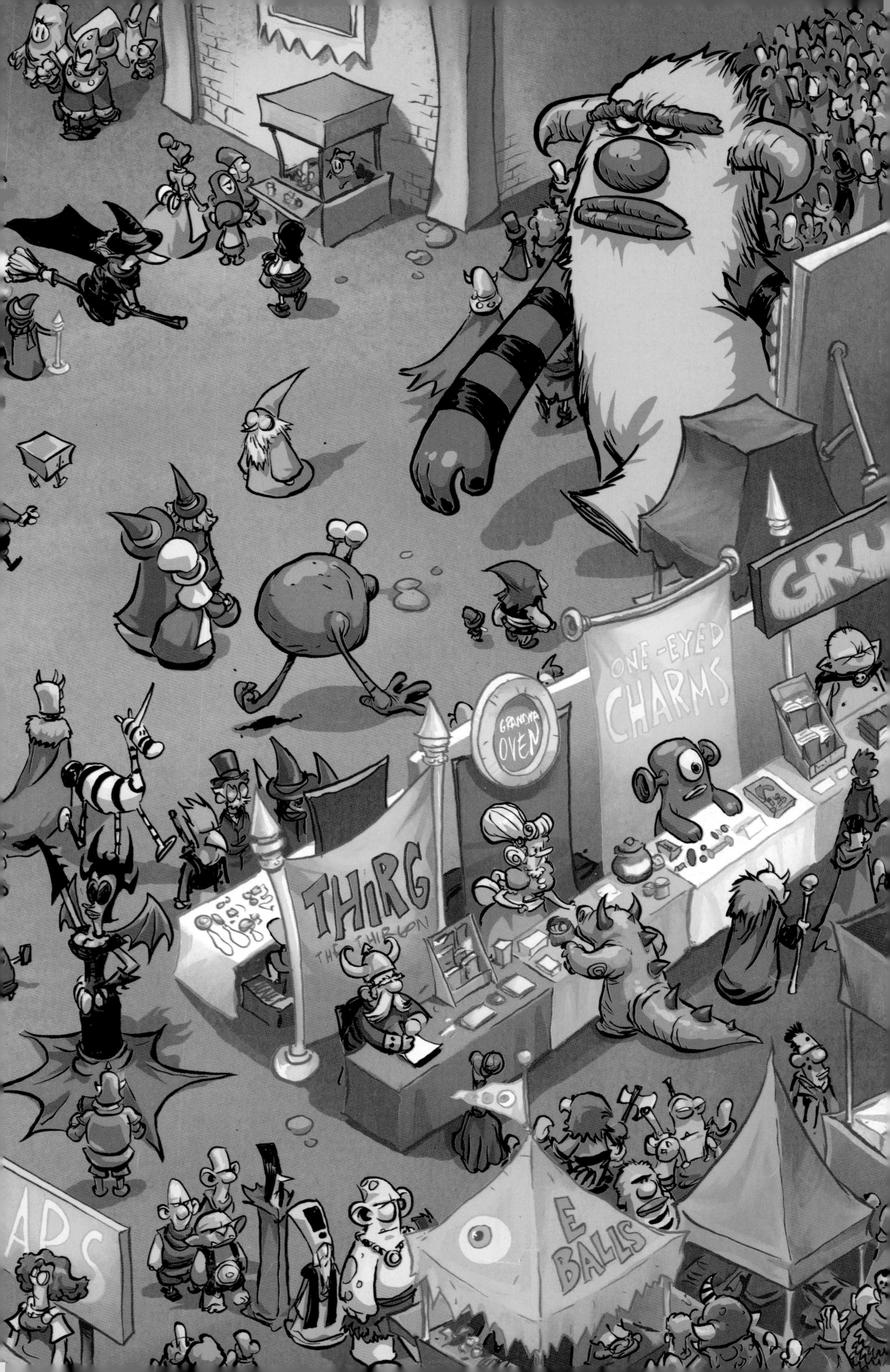
GRU
ONE-EYED CHARMS
GRANDMA OVEN
THIRG
THE THIRGON
APS
E BALLS

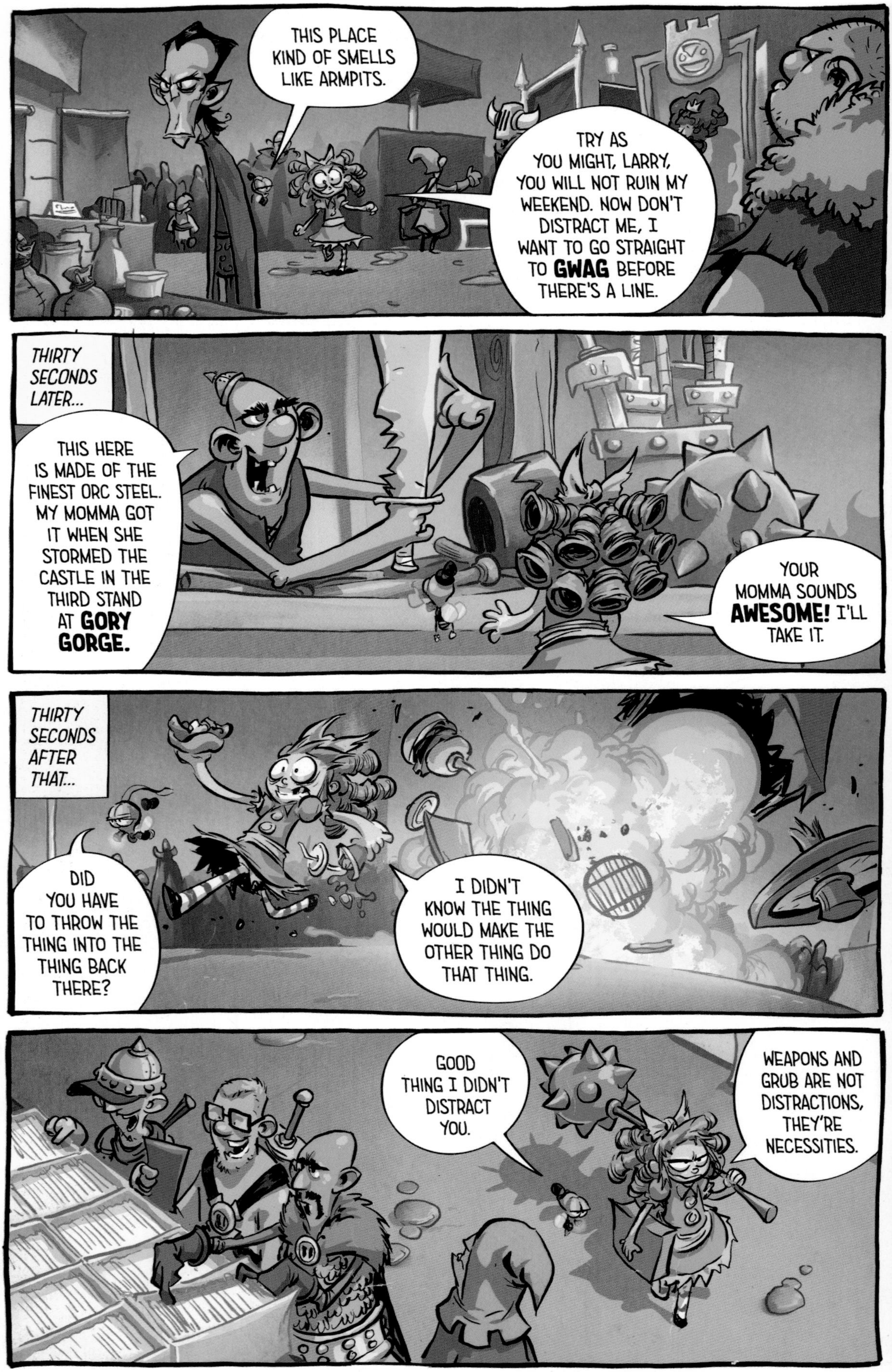
THIS PLACE KIND OF SMELLS LIKE ARMPITS.
TRY AS YOU MIGHT, LARRY, YOU WILL NOT RUIN MY WEEKEND. NOW DON'T DISTRACT ME, I WANT TO GO STRAIGHT TO **GWAG** BEFORE THERE'S A LINE.
THIRTY SECONDS LATER...
THIS HERE IS MADE OF THE FINEST ORC STEEL. MY MOMMA GOT IT WHEN SHE STORMED THE CASTLE IN THE THIRD STAND AT **GORY GORGE.**
YOUR MOMMA SOUNDS **AWESOME!** I'LL TAKE IT.
THIRTY SECONDS AFTER THAT...
DID YOU HAVE TO THROW THE THING INTO THE THING BACK THERE?
I DIDN'T KNOW THE THING WOULD MAKE THE OTHER THING DO THAT THING.
GOOD THING I DIDN'T DISTRACT YOU.
WEAPONS AND GRUB ARE NOT DISTRACTIONS, THEY'RE NECESSITIES.

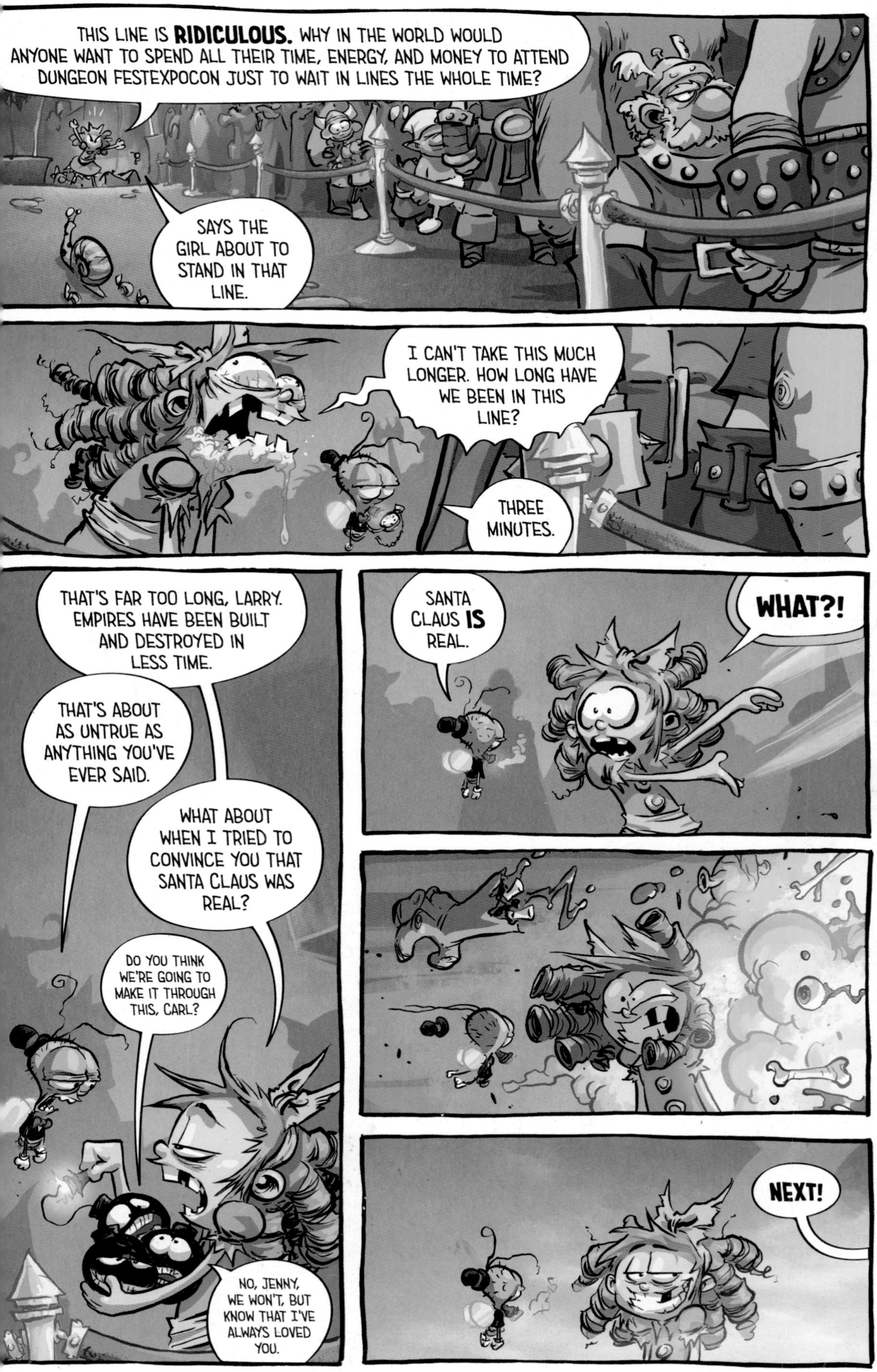
THIS LINE IS **RIDICULOUS.** WHY IN THE WORLD WOULD ANYONE WANT TO SPEND ALL THEIR TIME, ENERGY, AND MONEY TO ATTEND DUNGEON FESTEXPOCON JUST TO WAIT IN LINES THE WHOLE TIME?
SAYS THE GIRL ABOUT TO STAND IN THAT LINE.
I CAN'T TAKE THIS MUCH LONGER. HOW LONG HAVE WE BEEN IN THIS LINE?
THREE MINUTES.
THAT'S FAR TOO LONG, LARRY. EMPIRES HAVE BEEN BUILT AND DESTROYED IN LESS TIME.
THAT'S ABOUT AS UNTRUE AS ANYTHING YOU'VE EVER SAID.
WHAT ABOUT WHEN I TRIED TO CONVINCE YOU THAT SANTA CLAUS WAS REAL?
DO YOU THINK WE'RE GOING TO MAKE IT THROUGH THIS, CARL?
NO, JENNY, WE WON'T, BUT KNOW THAT I'VE ALWAYS LOVED YOU.
SANTA CLAUS **IS** REAL.
WHAT?!
NEXT!

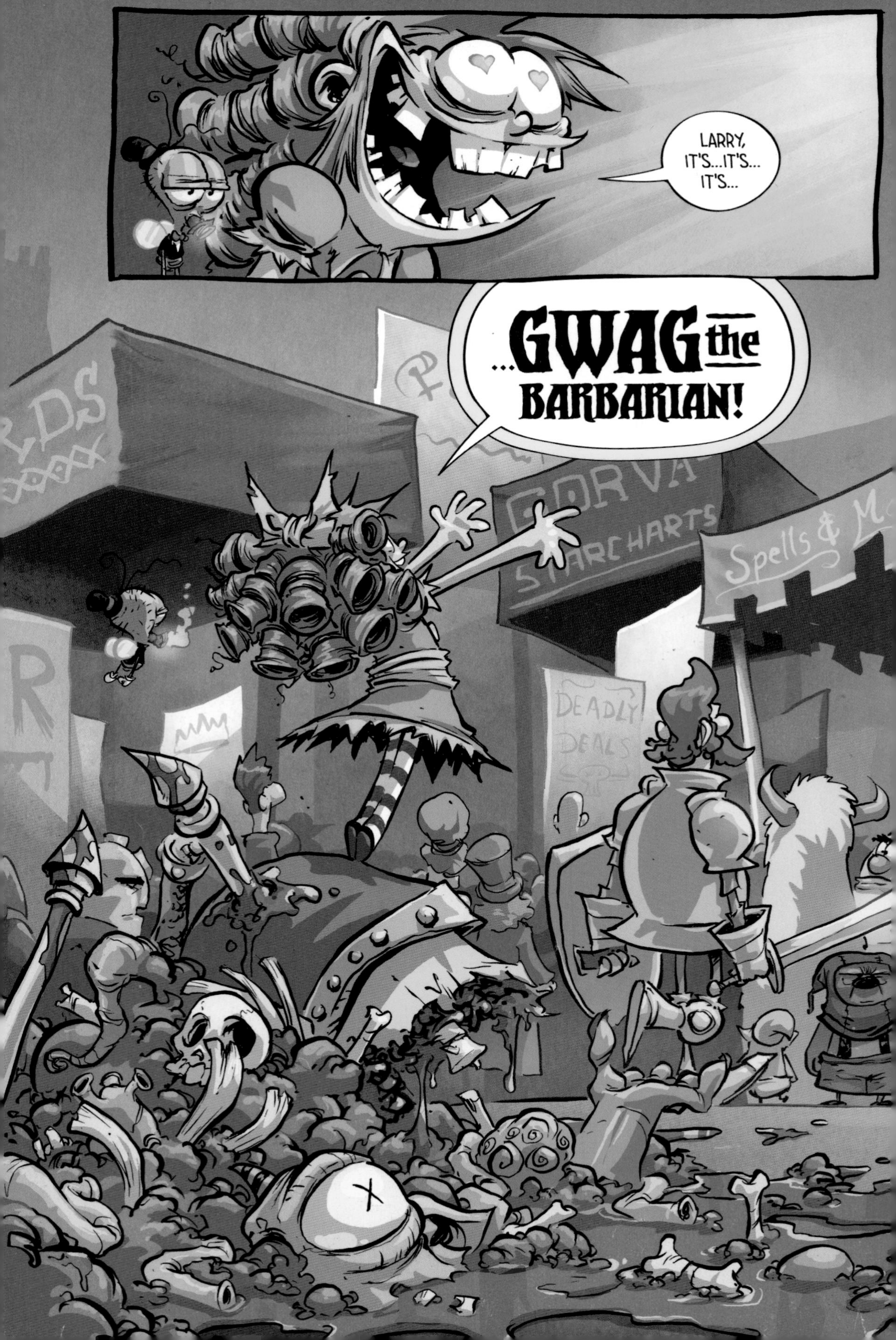

LARRY, IT'S...IT'S... IT'S...
...GWAG the BARBARIAN!
Spells & M
GORVA
STARCHARTS
DEADLY DEALS

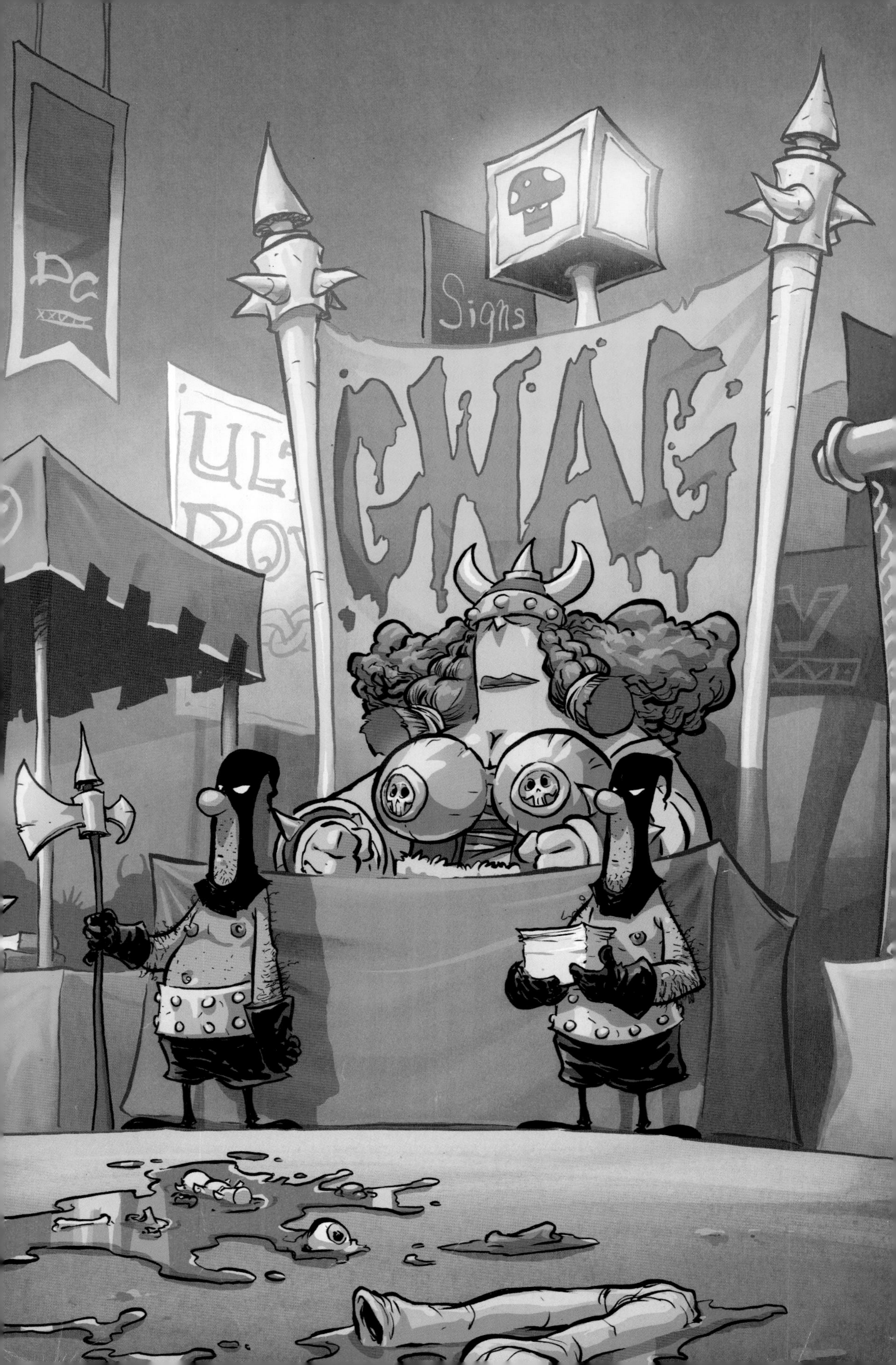
DC
Signs

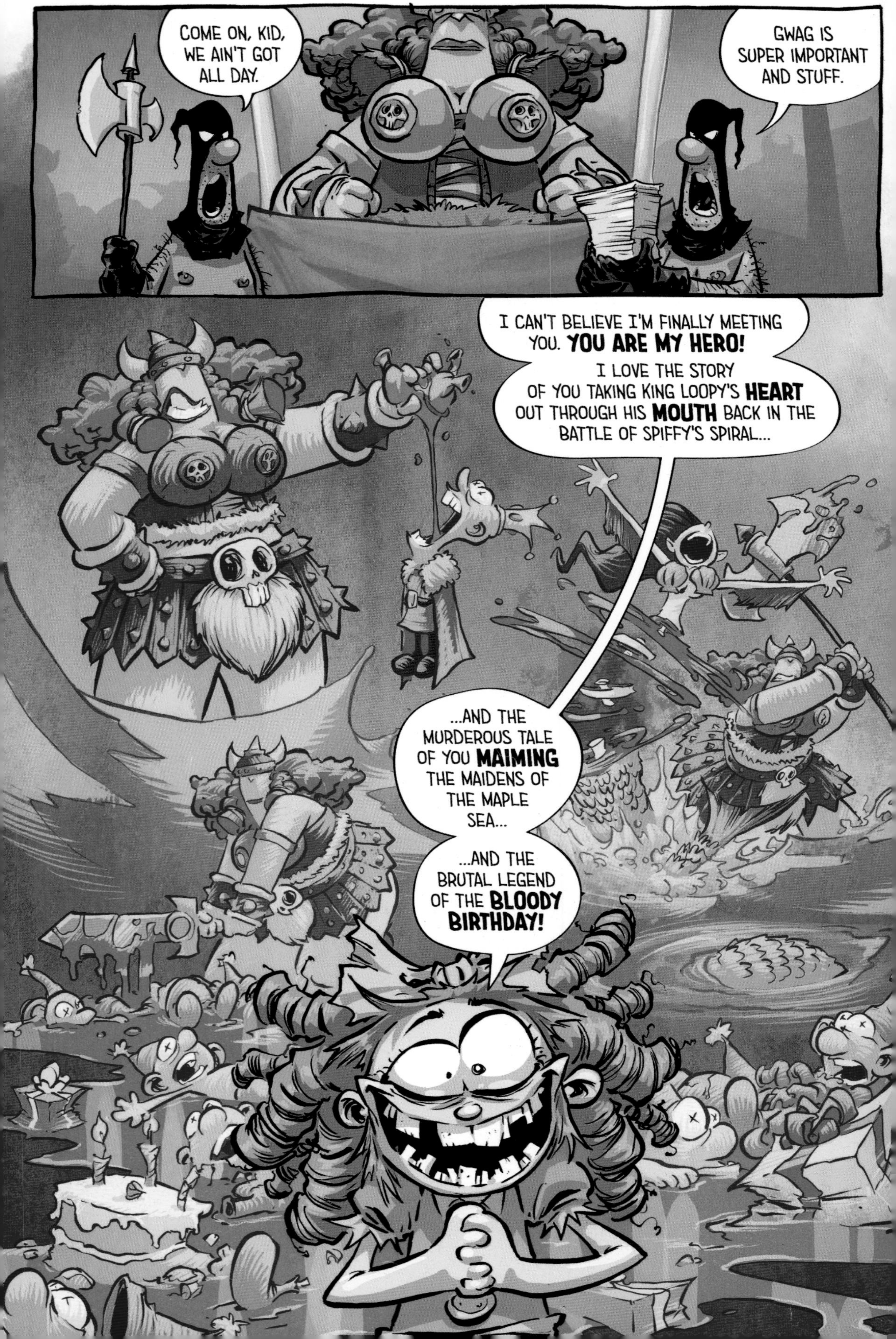
COME ON, KID, WE AIN'T GOT ALL DAY.
GWAG IS SUPER IMPORTANT AND STUFF.
I CAN'T BELIEVE I'M FINALLY MEETING YOU. YOU ARE MY HERO!
I LOVE THE STORY OF YOU TAKING KING LOOPY'S HEART OUT THROUGH HIS MOUTH BACK IN THE BATTLE OF SPIFFY'S SPIRAL...
...AND THE MURDEROUS TALE OF YOU MAIMING THE MAIDENS OF THE MAPLE SEA...
...AND THE BRUTAL LEGEND OF THE BLOODY BIRTHDAY!

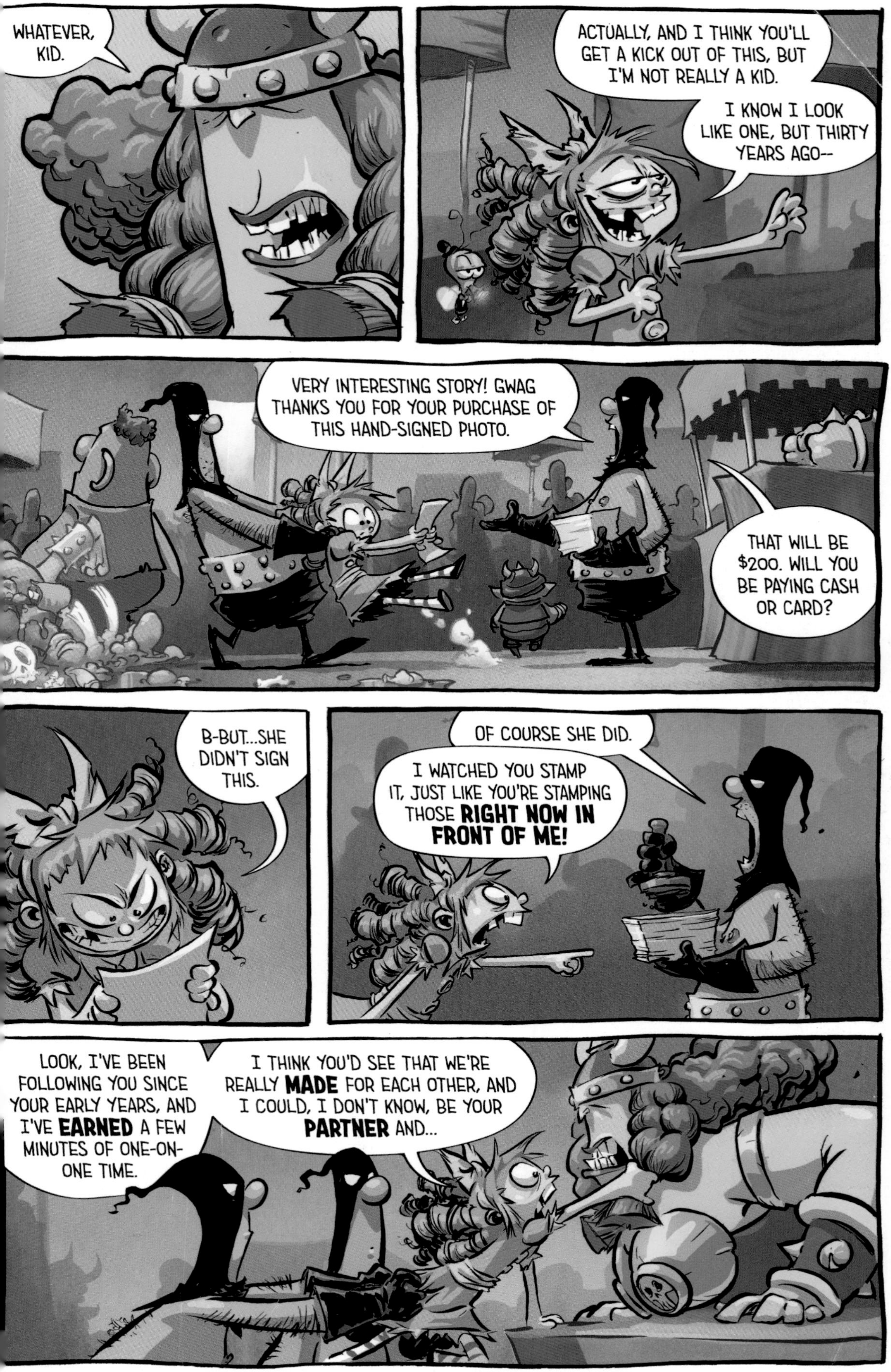
WHATEVER, KID.
ACTUALLY, AND I THINK YOU'LL GET A KICK OUT OF THIS, BUT I'M NOT REALLY A KID.
I KNOW I LOOK LIKE ONE, BUT THIRTY YEARS AGO--
VERY INTERESTING STORY! GWAG THANKS YOU FOR YOUR PURCHASE OF THIS HAND-SIGNED PHOTO.
THAT WILL BE $200. WILL YOU BE PAYING CASH OR CARD?
B-BUT...SHE DIDN'T SIGN THIS.
OF COURSE SHE DID.
I WATCHED YOU STAMP IT, JUST LIKE YOU'RE STAMPING THOSE **RIGHT NOW IN FRONT OF ME!**
LOOK, I'VE BEEN FOLLOWING YOU SINCE YOUR EARLY YEARS, AND I'VE **EARNED** A FEW MINUTES OF ONE-ON-ONE TIME.
I THINK YOU'D SEE THAT WE'RE REALLY **MADE** FOR EACH OTHER, AND I COULD, I DON'T KNOW, BE YOUR **PARTNER** AND...

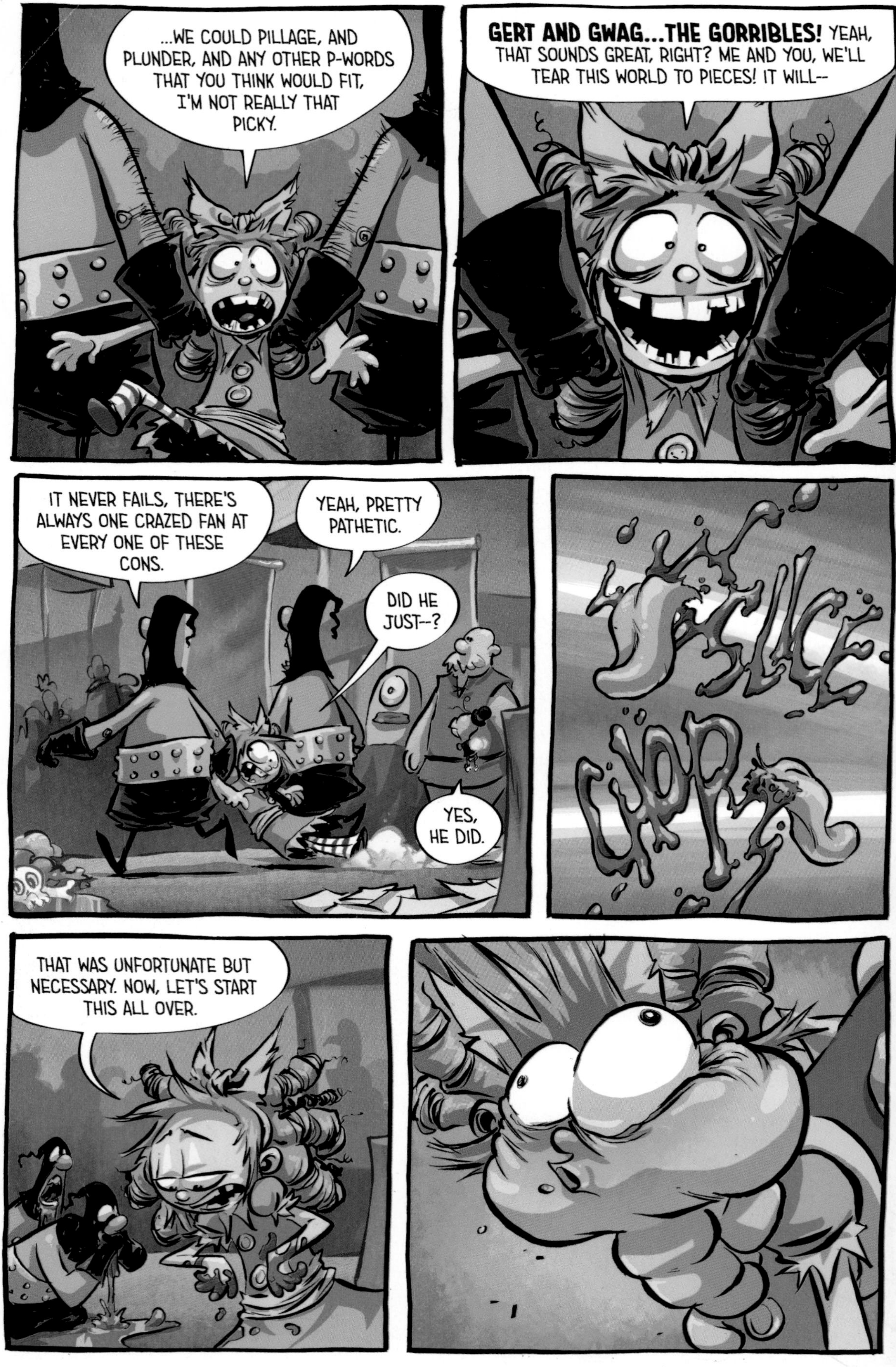
...WE COULD PILLAGE, AND PLUNDER, AND ANY OTHER P-WORDS THAT YOU THINK WOULD FIT, I'M NOT REALLY THAT PICKY.
GERT AND GWAG...THE GORRIBLES! YEAH, THAT SOUNDS GREAT, RIGHT? ME AND YOU, WE'LL TEAR THIS WORLD TO PIECES! IT WILL--
IT NEVER FAILS, THERE'S ALWAYS ONE CRAZED FAN AT EVERY ONE OF THESE CONS.
YEAH, PRETTY PATHETIC.
DID HE JUST--?
YES, HE DID.
SLICE
CHOP
THAT WAS UNFORTUNATE BUT NECESSARY. NOW, LET'S START THIS ALL OVER.

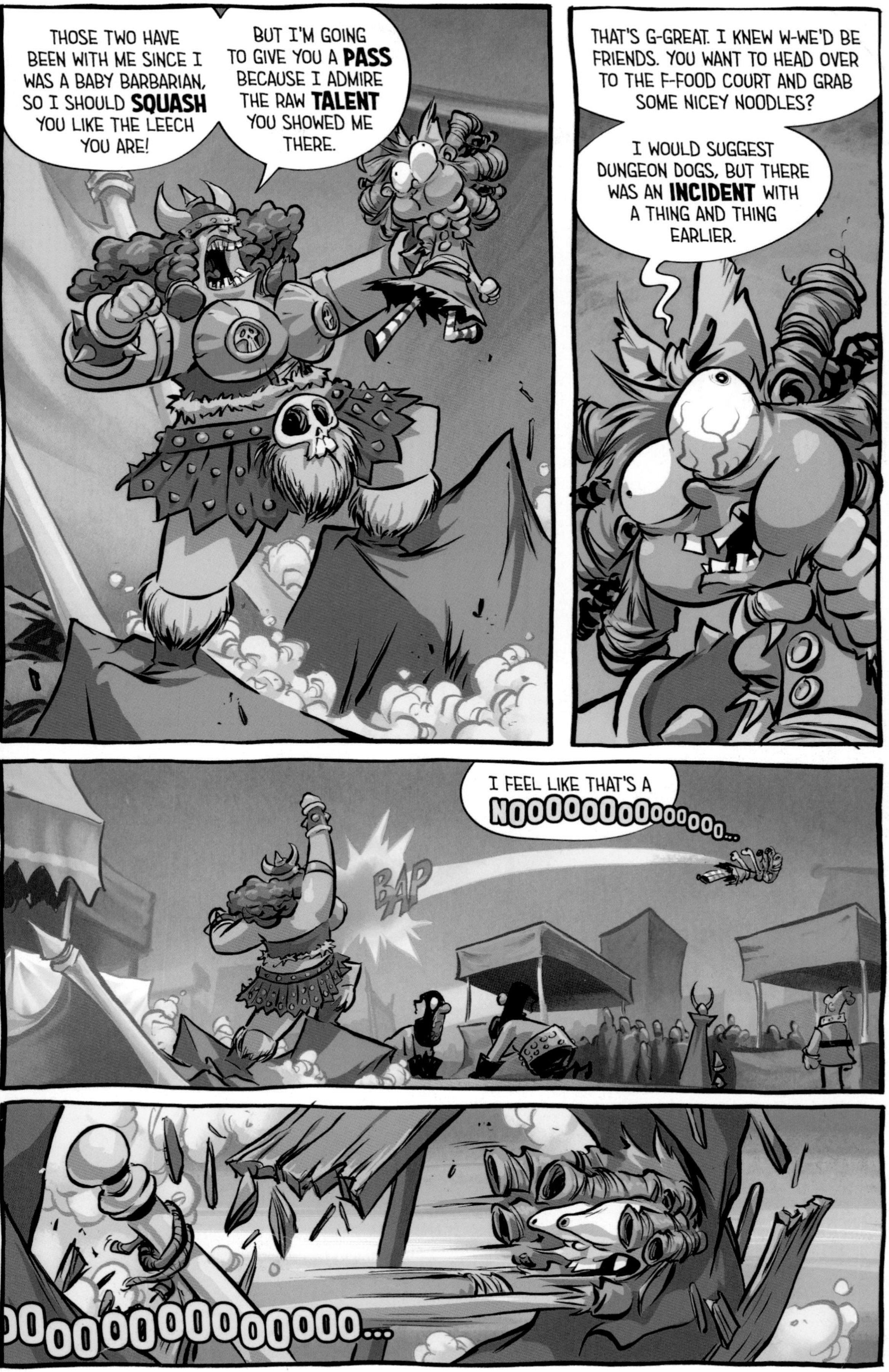
THOSE TWO HAVE BEEN WITH ME SINCE I WAS A BABY BARBARIAN, SO I SHOULD **SQUASH** YOU LIKE THE LEECH YOU ARE!
BUT I'M GOING TO GIVE YOU A **PASS** BECAUSE I ADMIRE THE RAW **TALENT** YOU SHOWED ME THERE.
THAT'S G-GREAT. I KNEW W-WE'D BE FRIENDS. YOU WANT TO HEAD OVER TO THE F-FOOD COURT AND GRAB SOME NICEY NOODLES?
I WOULD SUGGEST DUNGEON DOGS, BUT THERE WAS AN **INCIDENT** WITH A THING AND THING EARLIER.
I FEEL LIKE THAT'S A
NOOOOOOOOOOOOOOO...
BAP
OOOOOOOOOOOOOOOO...

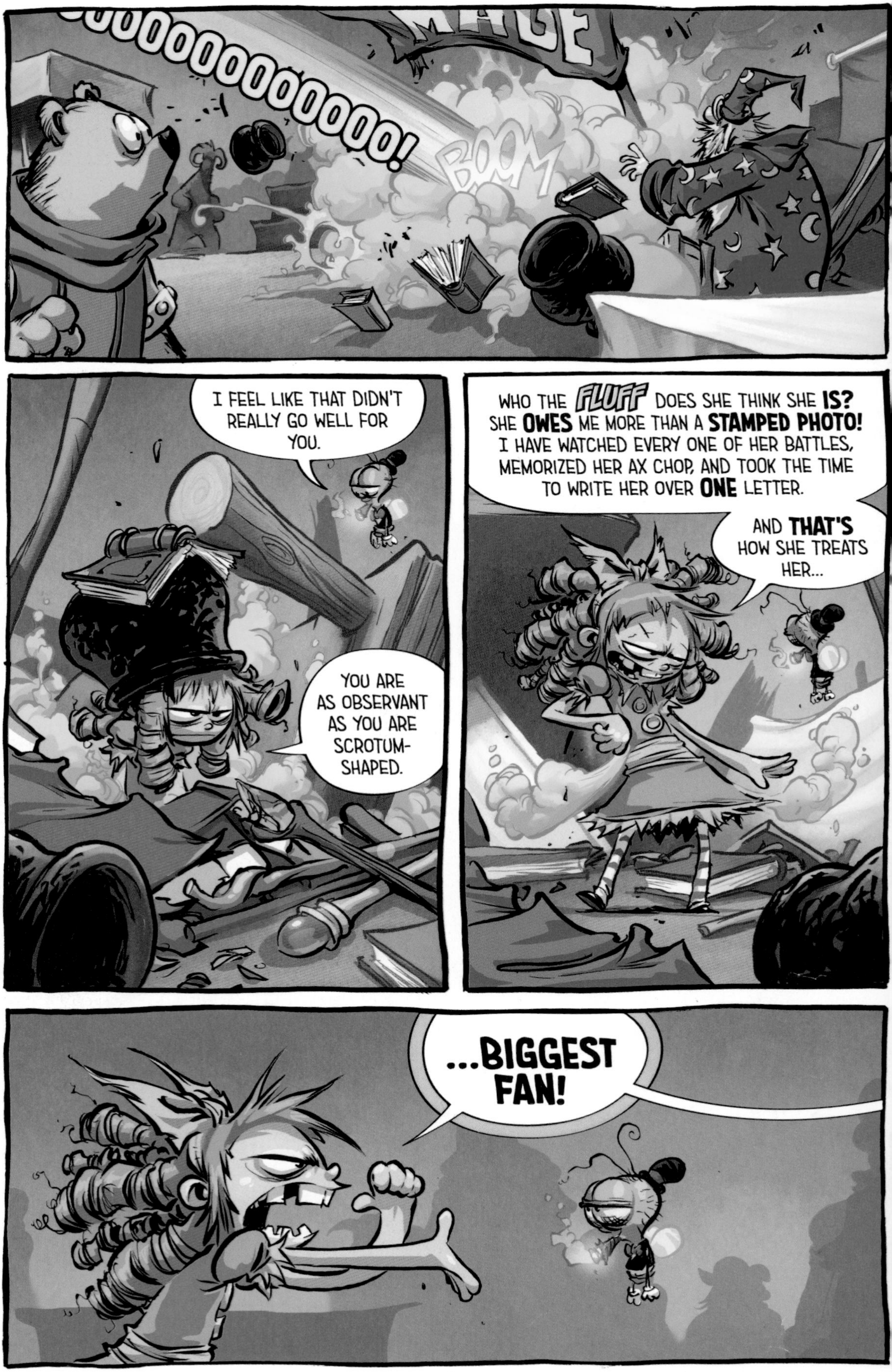

OOOOOOOOOOOOOO!
BOOM
I FEEL LIKE THAT DIDN'T REALLY GO WELL FOR YOU.
YOU ARE AS OBSERVANT AS YOU ARE SCROTUM-SHAPED.
WHO THE FLUFF DOES SHE THINK SHE IS? SHE OWES ME MORE THAN A STAMPED PHOTO! I HAVE WATCHED EVERY ONE OF HER BATTLES, MEMORIZED HER AX CHOP, AND TOOK THE TIME TO WRITE HER OVER ONE LETTER.
AND THAT'S HOW SHE TREATS HER...
...BIGGEST FAN!

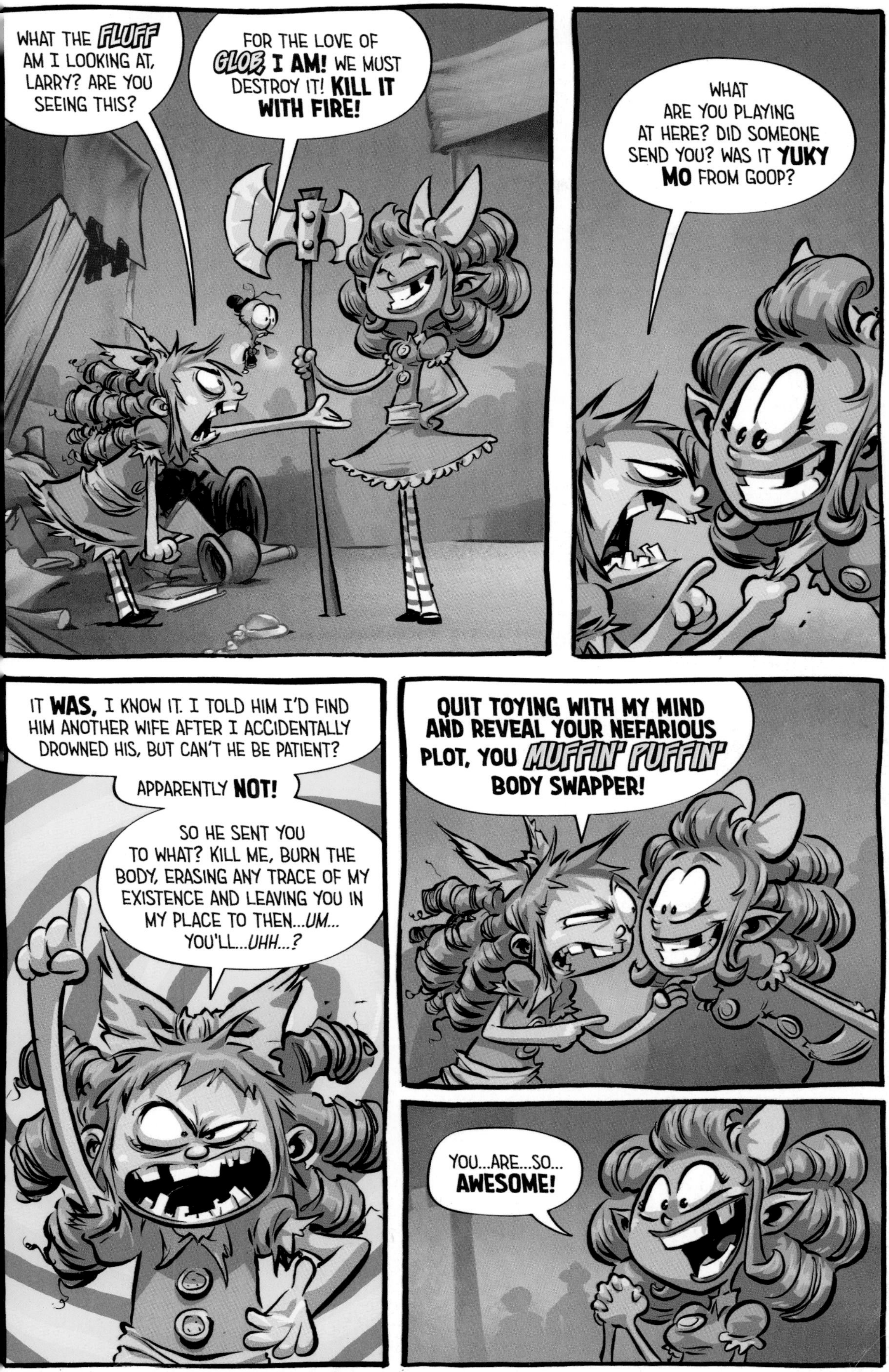
WHAT THE FLUFF AM I LOOKING AT, LARRY? ARE YOU SEEING THIS?
FOR THE LOVE OF GLOB, I AM! WE MUST DESTROY IT! KILL IT WITH FIRE!
WHAT ARE YOU PLAYING AT HERE? DID SOMEONE SEND YOU? WAS IT YUKY MO FROM GOOP?
IT WAS, I KNOW IT. I TOLD HIM I'D FIND HIM ANOTHER WIFE AFTER I ACCIDENTALLY DROWNED HIS, BUT CAN'T HE BE PATIENT?
APPARENTLY NOT!
SO HE SENT YOU TO WHAT? KILL ME, BURN THE BODY, ERASING ANY TRACE OF MY EXISTENCE AND LEAVING YOU IN MY PLACE TO THEN...UM... YOU'LL...UHH...?
QUIT TOYING WITH MY MIND AND REVEAL YOUR NEFARIOUS PLOT, YOU MUFFIN' PUFFIN' BODY SWAPPER!
YOU...ARE...SO... AWESOME!

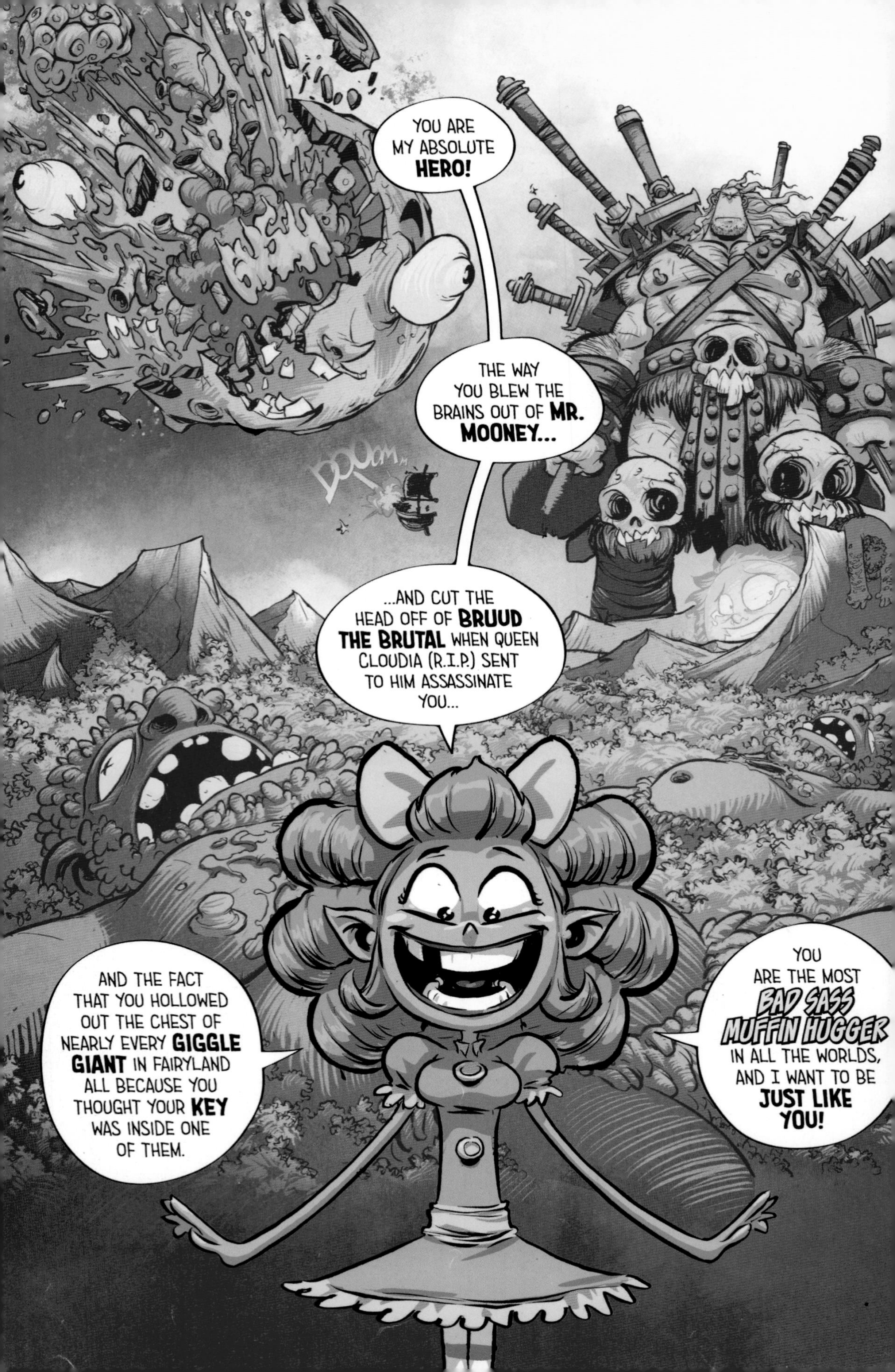
YOU ARE MY ABSOLUTE HERO!
THE WAY YOU BLEW THE BRAINS OUT OF MR. MOONEY...
DOOOM
...AND CUT THE HEAD OFF OF BRUUD THE BRUTAL WHEN QUEEN CLOUDIA (R.I.P.) SENT TO HIM ASSASSINATE YOU...
AND THE FACT THAT YOU HOLLOWED OUT THE CHEST OF NEARLY EVERY GIGGLE GIANT IN FAIRYLAND ALL BECAUSE YOU THOUGHT YOUR KEY WAS INSIDE ONE OF THEM.
YOU ARE THE MOST BAD SASS MUFFIN HUGGER IN ALL THE WORLDS, AND I WANT TO BE JUST LIKE YOU!

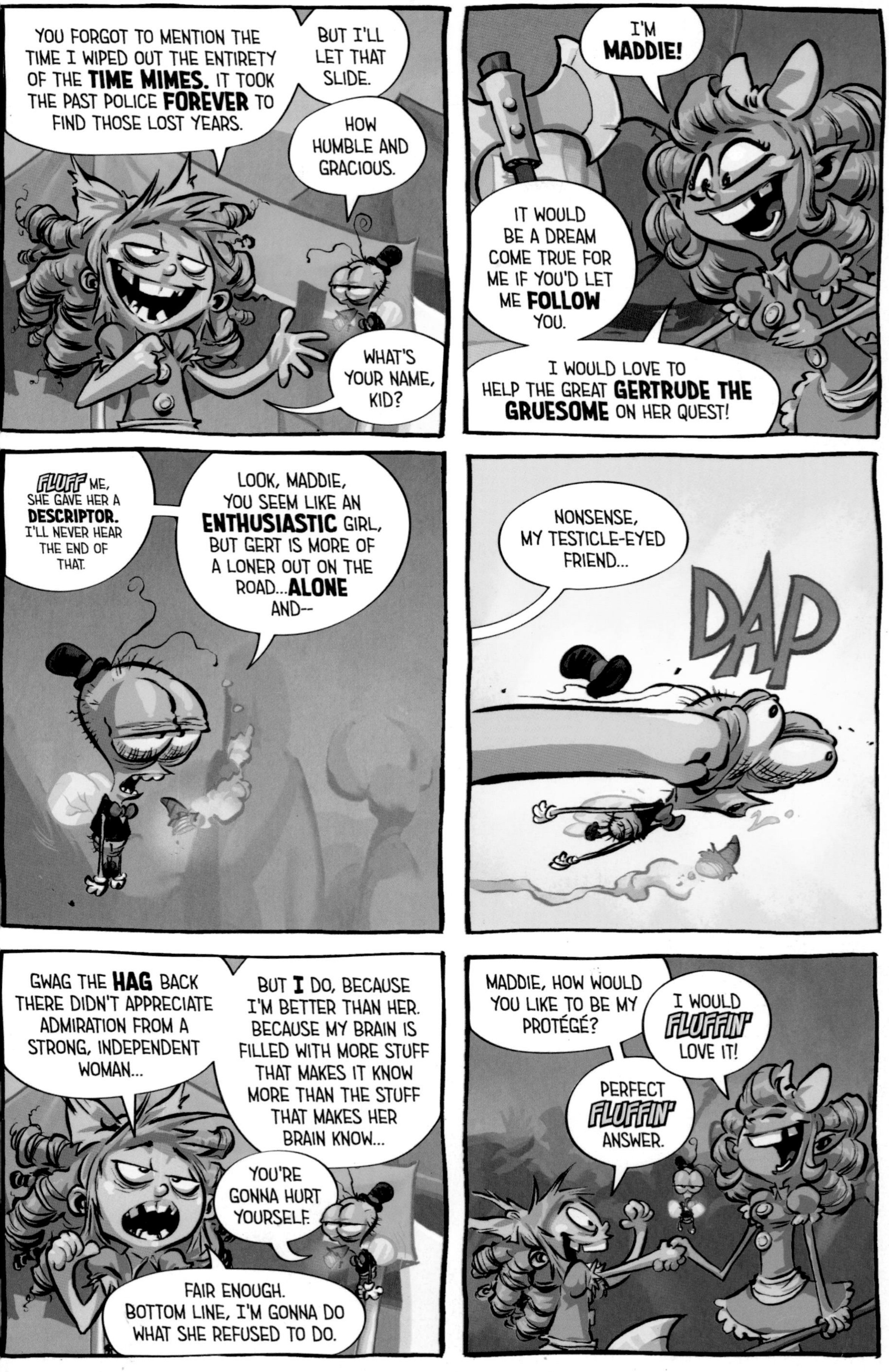
YOU FORGOT TO MENTION THE TIME I WIPED OUT THE ENTIRETY OF THE **TIME MIMES.** IT TOOK THE PAST POLICE **FOREVER** TO FIND THOSE LOST YEARS.
BUT I'LL LET THAT SLIDE.
HOW HUMBLE AND GRACIOUS.
WHAT'S YOUR NAME, KID?
I'M **MADDIE!**
IT WOULD BE A DREAM COME TRUE FOR ME IF YOU'D LET ME **FOLLOW** YOU.
I WOULD LOVE TO HELP THE GREAT **GERTRUDE THE GRUESOME** ON HER QUEST!
FLUFF ME, SHE GAVE HER A **DESCRIPTOR.** I'LL NEVER HEAR THE END OF THAT.
LOOK, MADDIE, YOU SEEM LIKE AN **ENTHUSIASTIC** GIRL, BUT GERT IS MORE OF A LONER OUT ON THE ROAD...**ALONE** AND--
NONSENSE, MY TESTICLE-EYED FRIEND...
DAP
GWAG THE **HAG** BACK THERE DIDN'T APPRECIATE ADMIRATION FROM A STRONG, INDEPENDENT WOMAN...
BUT **I** DO, BECAUSE I'M BETTER THAN HER. BECAUSE MY BRAIN IS FILLED WITH MORE STUFF THAT MAKES IT KNOW MORE THAN THE STUFF THAT MAKES HER BRAIN KNOW...
YOU'RE GONNA HURT YOURSELF.
FAIR ENOUGH. BOTTOM LINE, I'M GONNA DO WHAT SHE REFUSED TO DO.
MADDIE, HOW WOULD YOU LIKE TO BE MY PROTÉGÉ?
I WOULD FLUFFIN' LOVE IT!
PERFECT FLUFFIN' ANSWER.

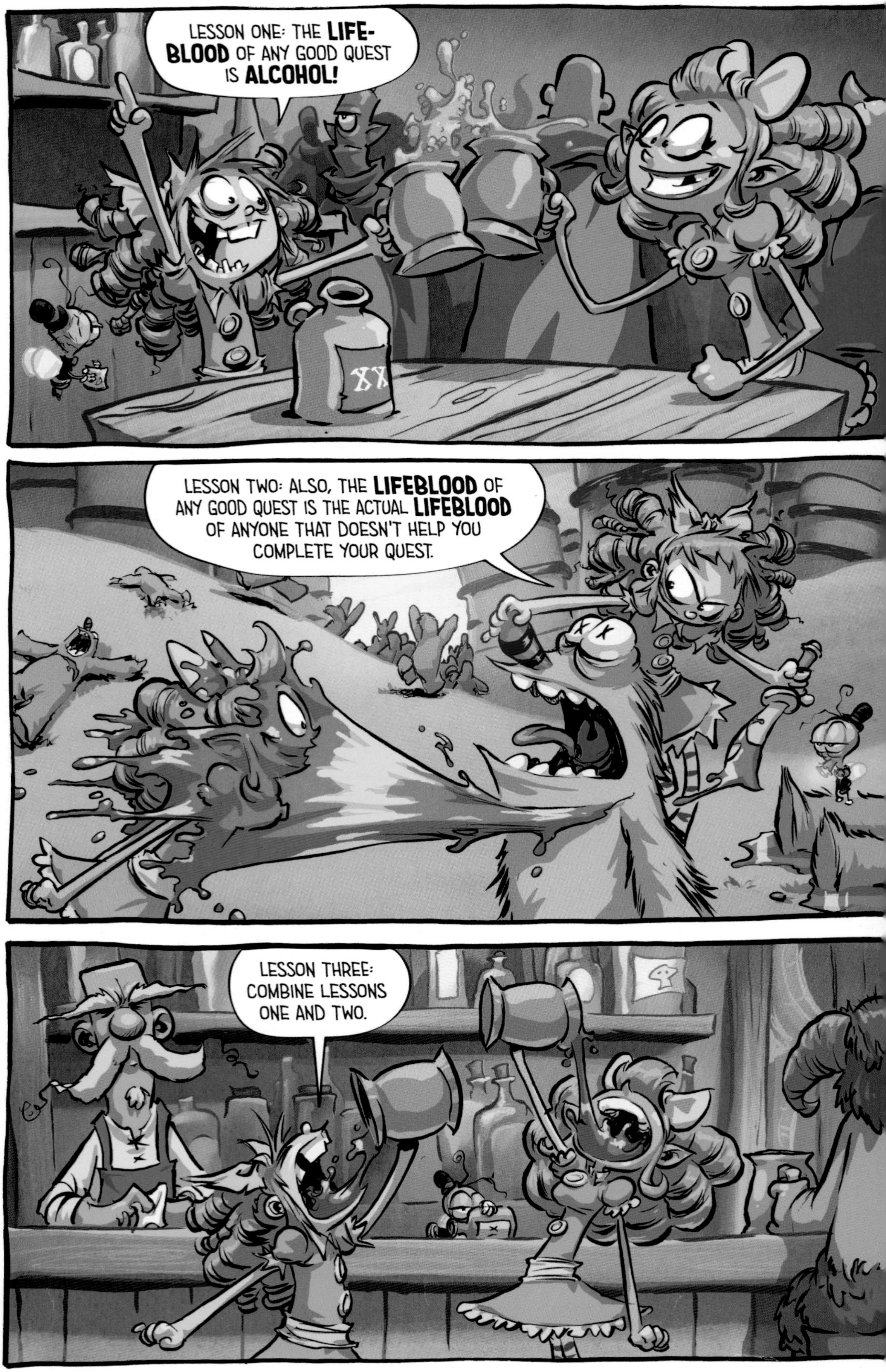
LESSON ONE: THE **LIFE-BLOOD** OF ANY GOOD QUEST IS **ALCOHOL!**
XX
LESSON TWO: ALSO, THE **LIFEBLOOD** OF ANY GOOD QUEST IS THE ACTUAL **LIFEBLOOD** OF ANYONE THAT DOESN'T HELP YOU COMPLETE YOUR QUEST.
LESSON THREE: COMBINE LESSONS ONE AND TWO.

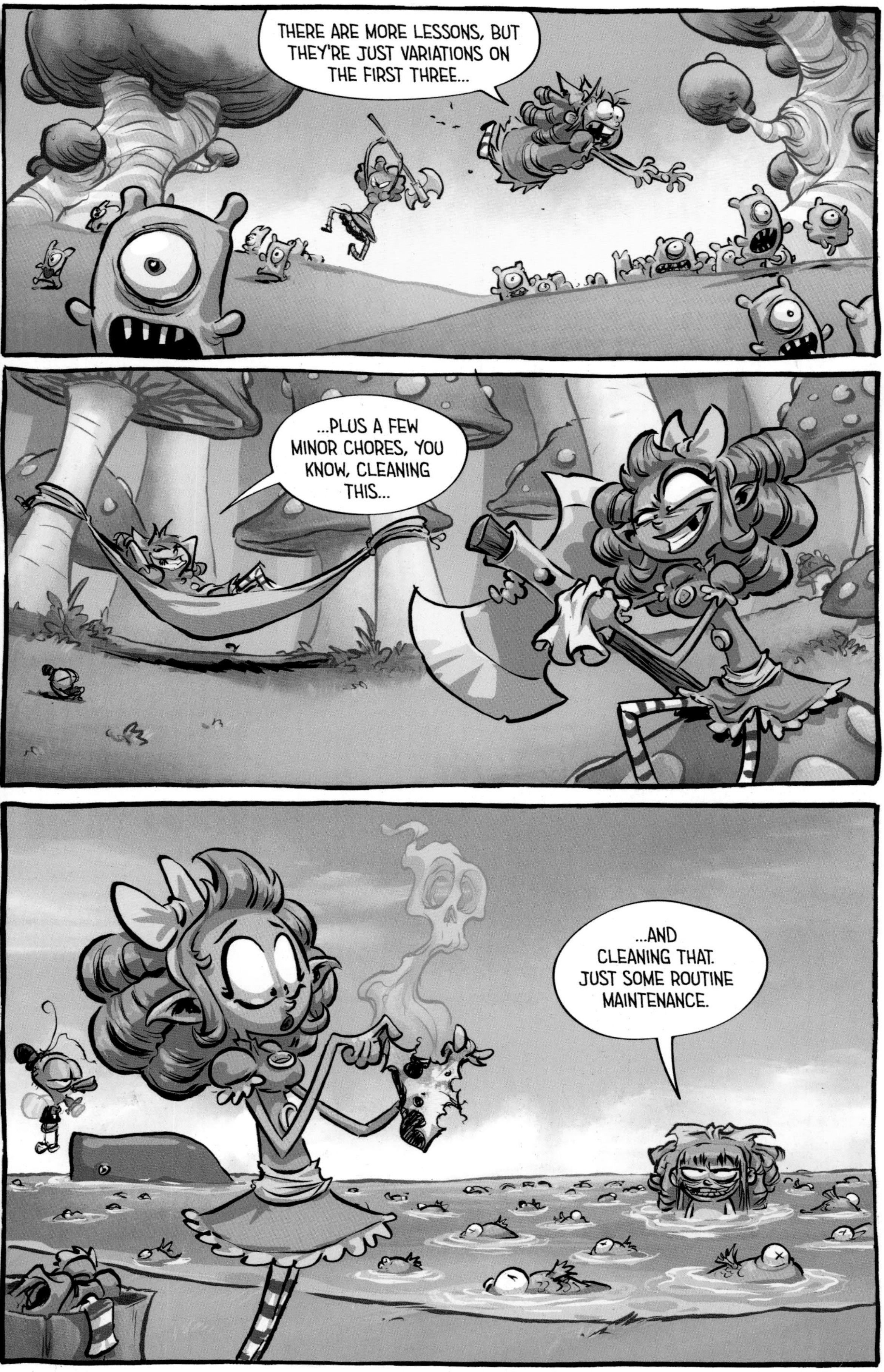
THERE ARE MORE LESSONS, BUT THEY'RE JUST VARIATIONS ON THE FIRST THREE...
...PLUS A FEW MINOR CHORES, YOU KNOW, CLEANING THIS...
...AND CLEANING THAT. JUST SOME ROUTINE MAINTENANCE.

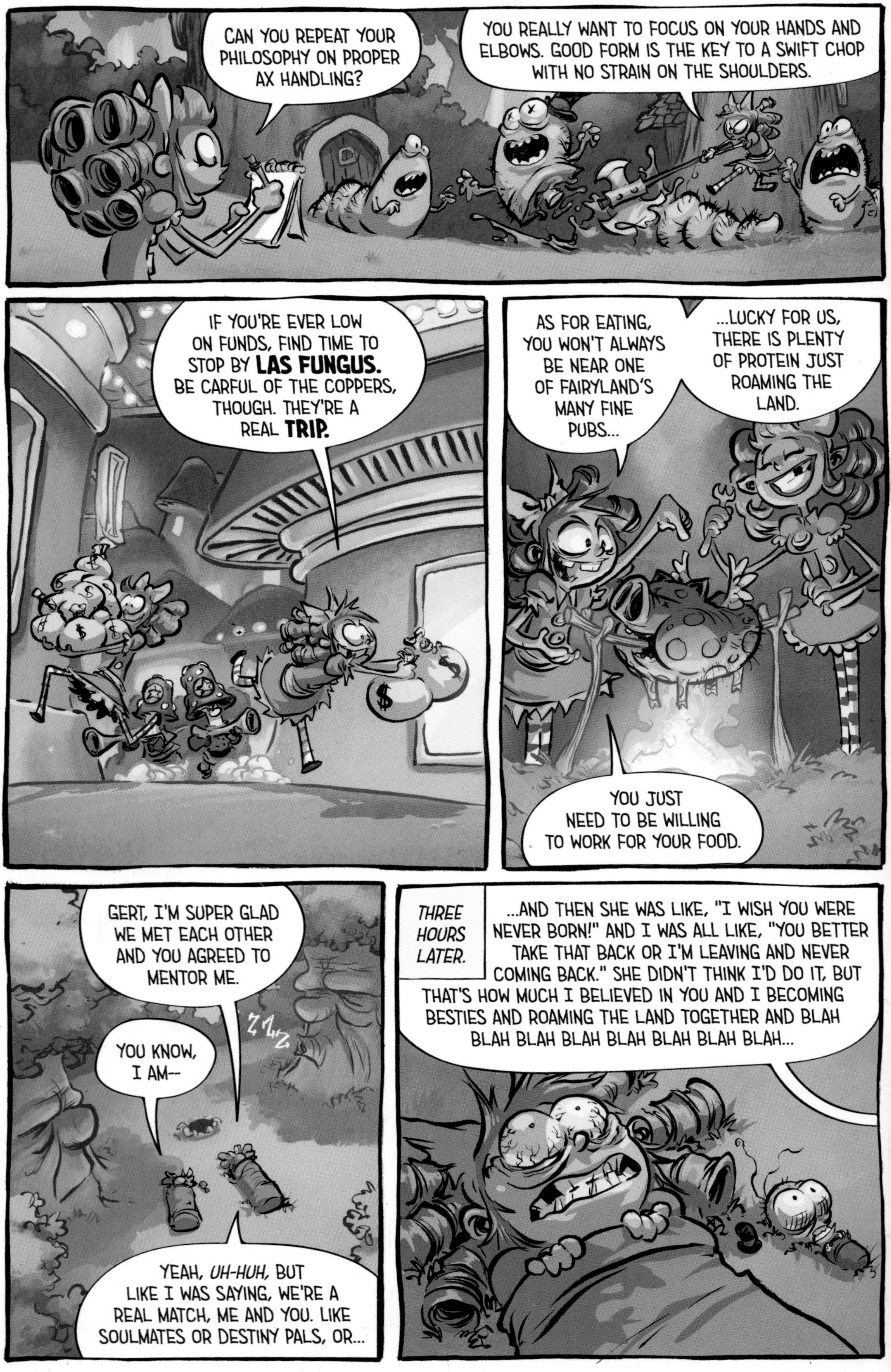

CAN YOU REPEAT YOUR PHILOSOPHY ON PROPER AX HANDLING?
YOU REALLY WANT TO FOCUS ON YOUR HANDS AND ELBOWS. GOOD FORM IS THE KEY TO A SWIFT CHOP WITH NO STRAIN ON THE SHOULDERS.
IF YOU'RE EVER LOW ON FUNDS, FIND TIME TO STOP BY **LAS FUNGUS.** BE CARFUL OF THE COPPERS, THOUGH. THEY'RE A REAL **TRIP.**
AS FOR EATING, YOU WON'T ALWAYS BE NEAR ONE OF FAIRYLAND'S MANY FINE PUBS...
...LUCKY FOR US, THERE IS PLENTY OF PROTEIN JUST ROAMING THE LAND.
YOU JUST NEED TO BE WILLING TO WORK FOR YOUR FOOD.
GERT, I'M SUPER GLAD WE MET EACH OTHER AND YOU AGREED TO MENTOR ME.
YOU KNOW, I AM--
ZZZ
YEAH, *UH-HUH,* BUT LIKE I WAS SAYING, WE'RE A REAL MATCH, ME AND YOU. LIKE SOULMATES OR DESTINY PALS, OR...
THREE HOURS LATER.
...AND THEN SHE WAS LIKE, "I WISH YOU WERE NEVER BORN!" AND I WAS ALL LIKE, "YOU BETTER TAKE THAT BACK OR I'M LEAVING AND NEVER COMING BACK." SHE DIDN'T THINK I'D DO IT, BUT THAT'S HOW MUCH I BELIEVED IN YOU AND I BECOMING BESTIES AND ROAMING THE LAND TOGETHER AND BLAH BLAH BLAH BLAH BLAH BLAH BLAH BLAH...

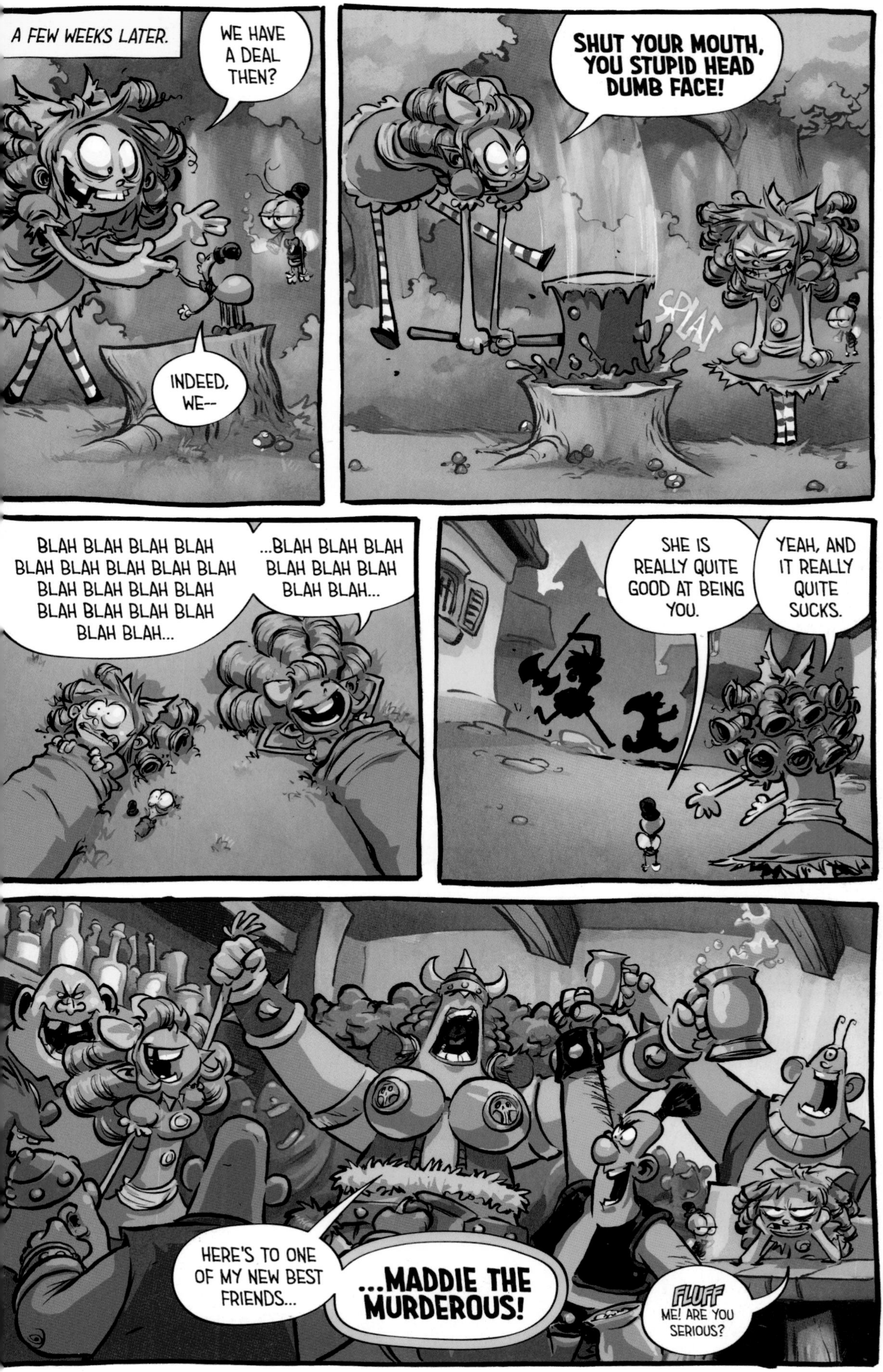
A FEW WEEKS LATER.
WE HAVE A DEAL THEN?
INDEED, WE--
SHUT YOUR MOUTH, YOU STUPID HEAD DUMB FACE!
SPLAT
BLAH BLAH BLAH BLAH BLAH BLAH BLAH BLAH BLAH BLAH BLAH BLAH BLAH BLAH BLAH BLAH BLAH BLAH BLAH...
...BLAH BLAH BLAH BLAH BLAH BLAH BLAH BLAH...
SHE IS REALLY QUITE GOOD AT BEING YOU.
YEAH, AND IT REALLY QUITE SUCKS.
HERE'S TO ONE OF MY NEW BEST FRIENDS...
...MADDIE THE MURDEROUS!
FLUFF
ME! ARE YOU SERIOUS?

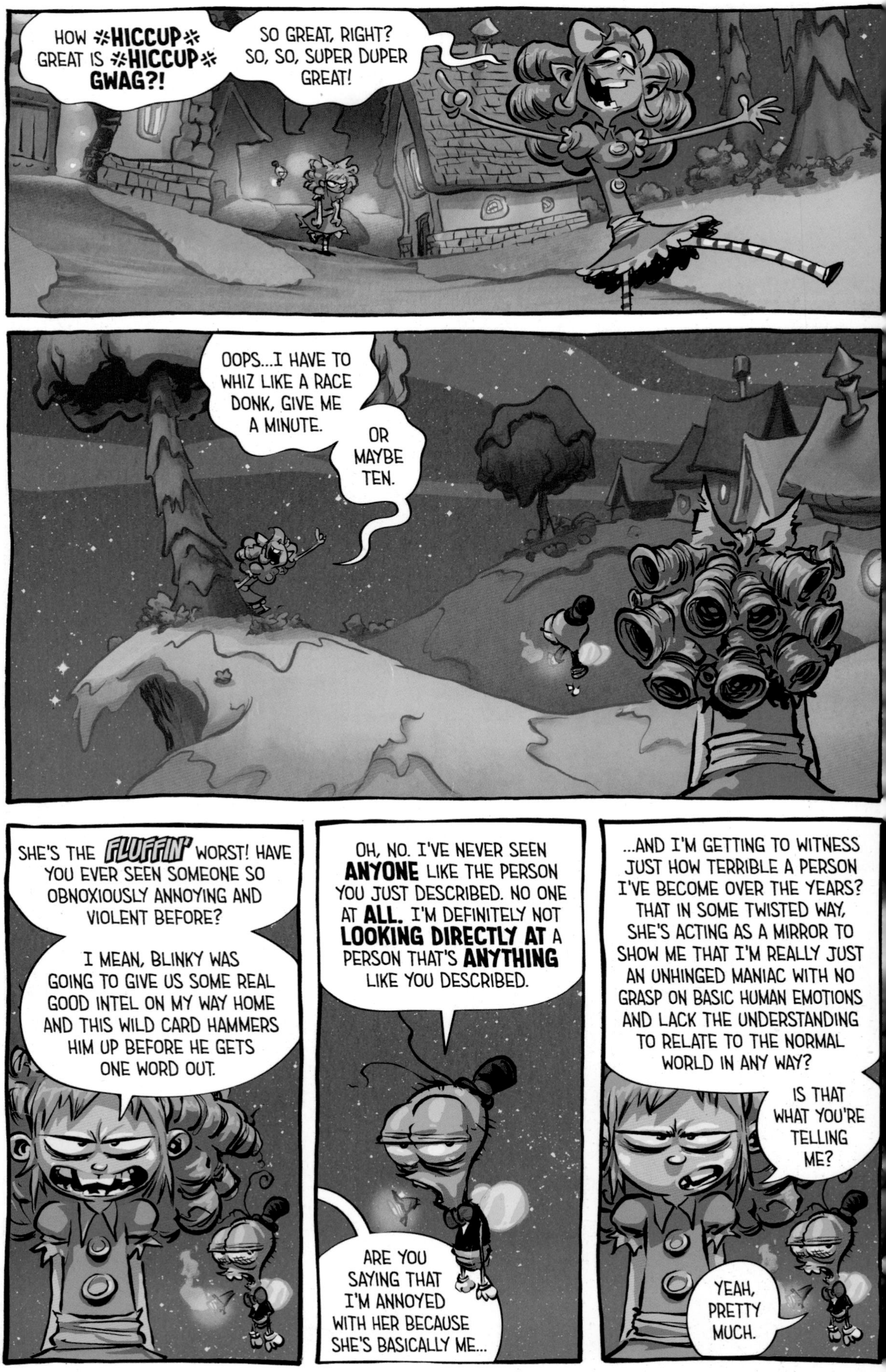
HOW ⁂HICCUP⁂ GREAT IS ⁂HICCUP⁂ GWAG?!
SO GREAT, RIGHT? SO, SO, SUPER DUPER GREAT!
OOPS...I HAVE TO WHIZ LIKE A RACE DONK, GIVE ME A MINUTE.
OR MAYBE TEN.
SHE'S THE FLUFFIN' WORST! HAVE YOU EVER SEEN SOMEONE SO OBNOXIOUSLY ANNOYING AND VIOLENT BEFORE?
I MEAN, BLINKY WAS GOING TO GIVE US SOME REAL GOOD INTEL ON MY WAY HOME AND THIS WILD CARD HAMMERS HIM UP BEFORE HE GETS ONE WORD OUT.
OH, NO. I'VE NEVER SEEN ANYONE LIKE THE PERSON YOU JUST DESCRIBED. NO ONE AT ALL. I'M DEFINITELY NOT LOOKING DIRECTLY AT A PERSON THAT'S ANYTHING LIKE YOU DESCRIBED.
ARE YOU SAYING THAT I'M ANNOYED WITH HER BECAUSE SHE'S BASICALLY ME...
...AND I'M GETTING TO WITNESS JUST HOW TERRIBLE A PERSON I'VE BECOME OVER THE YEARS? THAT IN SOME TWISTED WAY, SHE'S ACTING AS A MIRROR TO SHOW ME THAT I'M REALLY JUST AN UNHINGED MANIAC WITH NO GRASP ON BASIC HUMAN EMOTIONS AND LACK THE UNDERSTANDING TO RELATE TO THE NORMAL WORLD IN ANY WAY?
IS THAT WHAT YOU'RE TELLING ME?
YEAH, PRETTY MUCH.

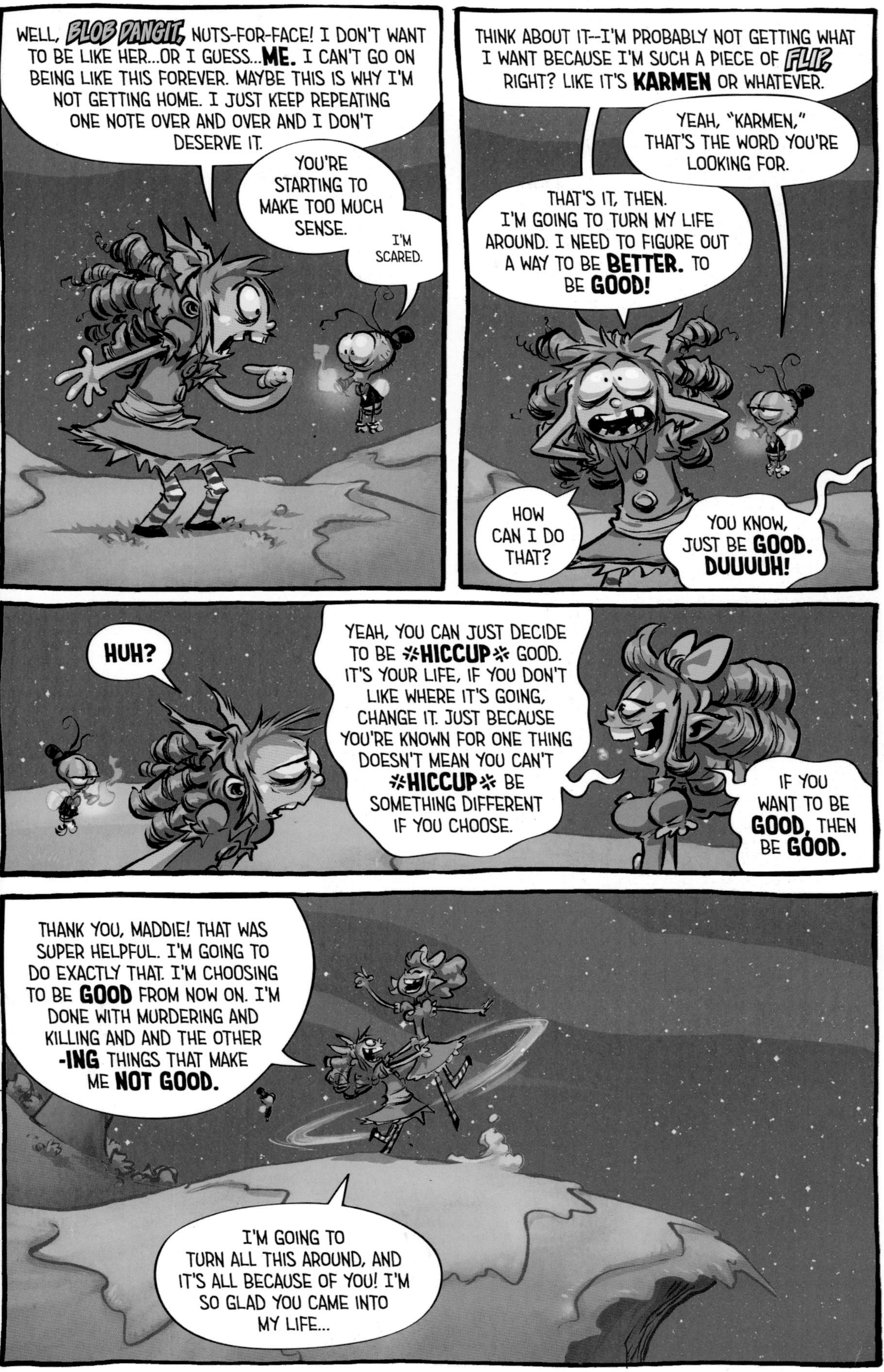

WELL, BLOB DANGIT, NUTS-FOR-FACE! I DON'T WANT TO BE LIKE HER...OR I GUESS...ME. I CAN'T GO ON BEING LIKE THIS FOREVER. MAYBE THIS IS WHY I'M NOT GETTING HOME. I JUST KEEP REPEATING ONE NOTE OVER AND OVER AND I DON'T DESERVE IT.
YOU'RE STARTING TO MAKE TOO MUCH SENSE.
I'M SCARED.
THINK ABOUT IT--I'M PROBABLY NOT GETTING WHAT I WANT BECAUSE I'M SUCH A PIECE OF FLIP, RIGHT? LIKE IT'S KARMEN OR WHATEVER.
YEAH, "KARMEN," THAT'S THE WORD YOU'RE LOOKING FOR.
THAT'S IT, THEN. I'M GOING TO TURN MY LIFE AROUND. I NEED TO FIGURE OUT A WAY TO BE BETTER. TO BE GOOD!
HOW CAN I DO THAT?
YOU KNOW, JUST BE GOOD. DUUUUH!
HUH?
YEAH, YOU CAN JUST DECIDE TO BE *HICCUP* GOOD. IT'S YOUR LIFE, IF YOU DON'T LIKE WHERE IT'S GOING, CHANGE IT. JUST BECAUSE YOU'RE KNOWN FOR ONE THING DOESN'T MEAN YOU CAN'T *HICCUP* BE SOMETHING DIFFERENT IF YOU CHOOSE.
IF YOU WANT TO BE GOOD, THEN BE GOOD.
THANK YOU, MADDIE! THAT WAS SUPER HELPFUL. I'M GOING TO DO EXACTLY THAT. I'M CHOOSING TO BE GOOD FROM NOW ON. I'M DONE WITH MURDERING AND KILLING AND AND THE OTHER -ING THINGS THAT MAKE ME NOT GOOD.
I'M GOING TO TURN ALL THIS AROUND, AND IT'S ALL BECAUSE OF YOU! I'M SO GLAD YOU CAME INTO MY LIFE...

...UNFORTUNATELY, NOW I'M GOING TO HAVE TO ASK YOU TO **LEAVE IT.**

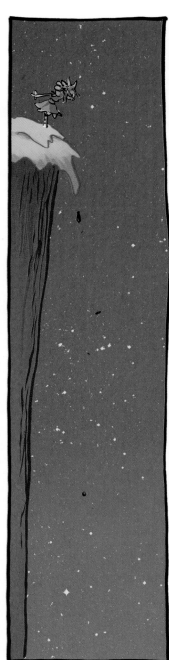

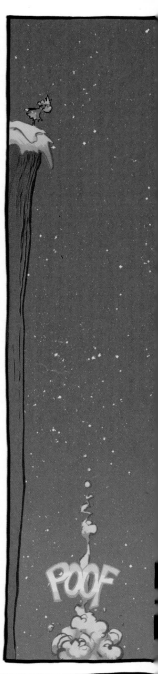

POOF

WHAT ABOUT ALL THAT, "I'M GONNA BE **GOOD** AND TURN THIS ALL AROUND." STUFF YOU JUST SAID?

OH, IT'S STARTING NOW. THAT DIDN'T COUNT.

HOW WAS I SUPPOSED TO LEARN HOW TO BE GOOD WITH THAT ANNOYING *HUGGER PUFFER* RUNNING HER GOBBSTOPPER AT ALL HOURS OF THE NIGHT?

FAIR ENOUGH.

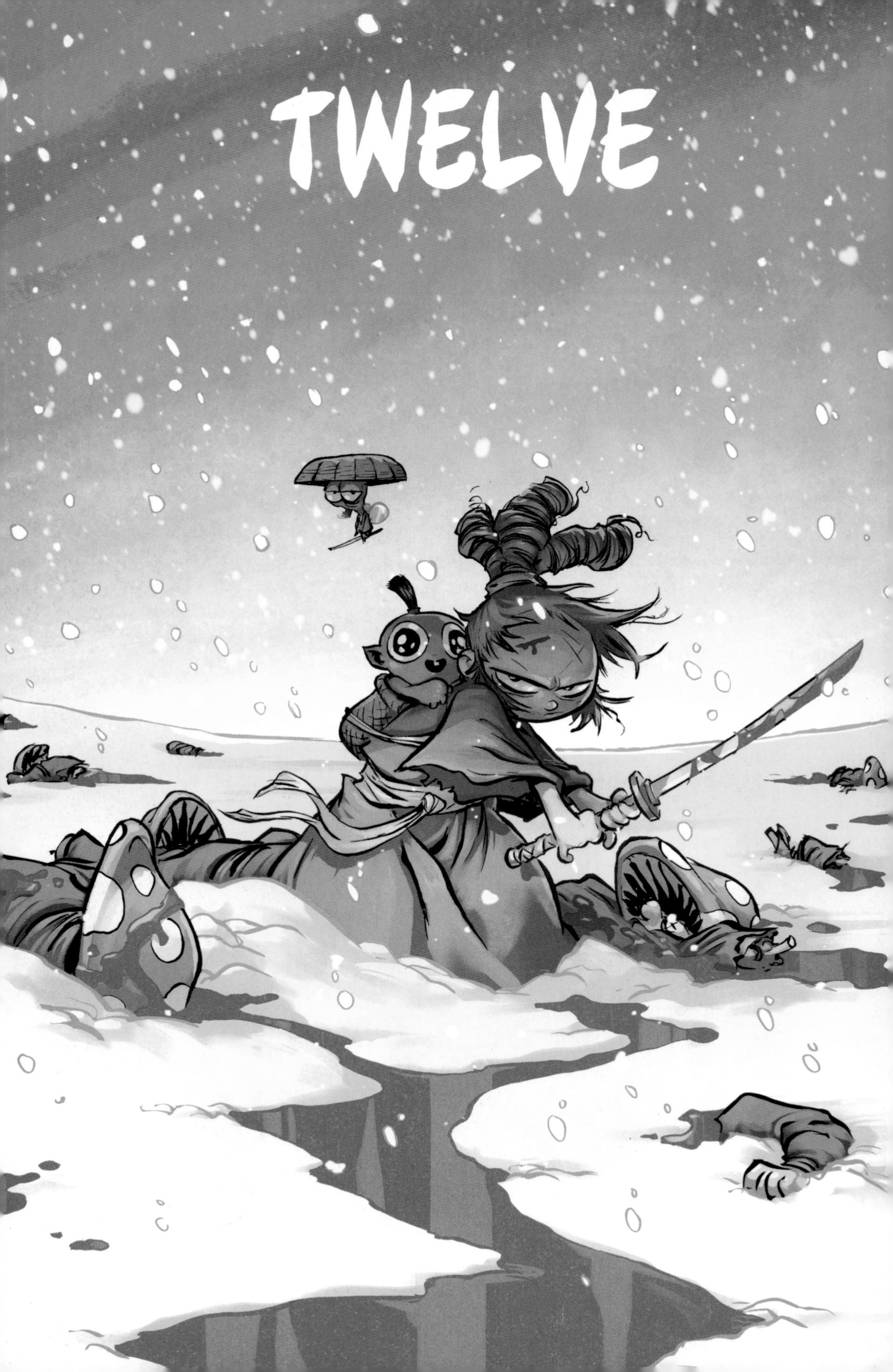
TWELVE

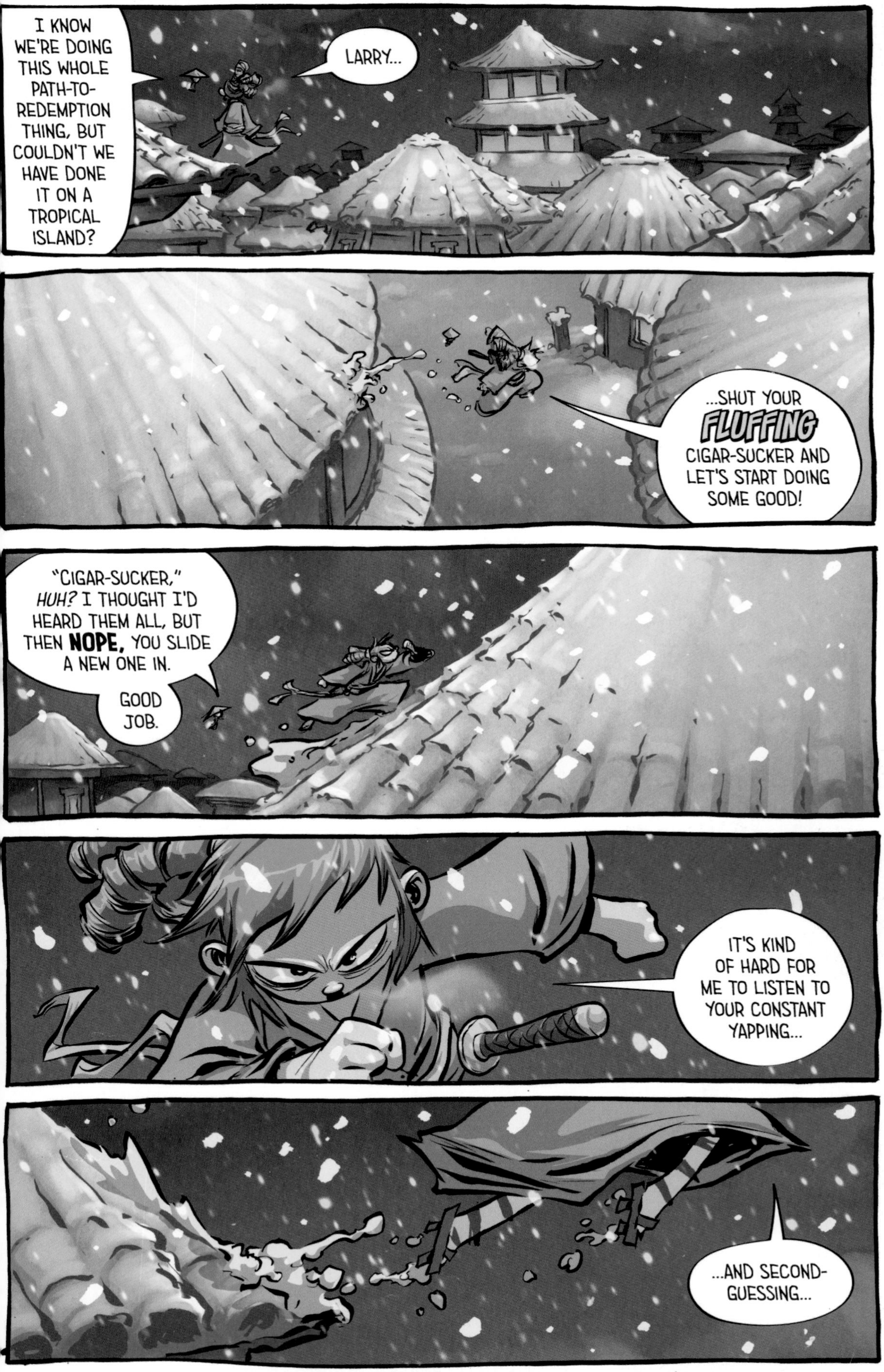
I KNOW WE'RE DOING THIS WHOLE PATH-TO-REDEMPTION THING, BUT COULDN'T WE HAVE DONE IT ON A TROPICAL ISLAND?
LARRY...
...SHUT YOUR FLUFFING CIGAR-SUCKER AND LET'S START DOING SOME GOOD!
"CIGAR-SUCKER," HUH? I THOUGHT I'D HEARD THEM ALL, BUT THEN NOPE, YOU SLIDE A NEW ONE IN.
GOOD JOB.
IT'S KIND OF HARD FOR ME TO LISTEN TO YOUR CONSTANT YAPPING...
...AND SECOND-GUESSING...

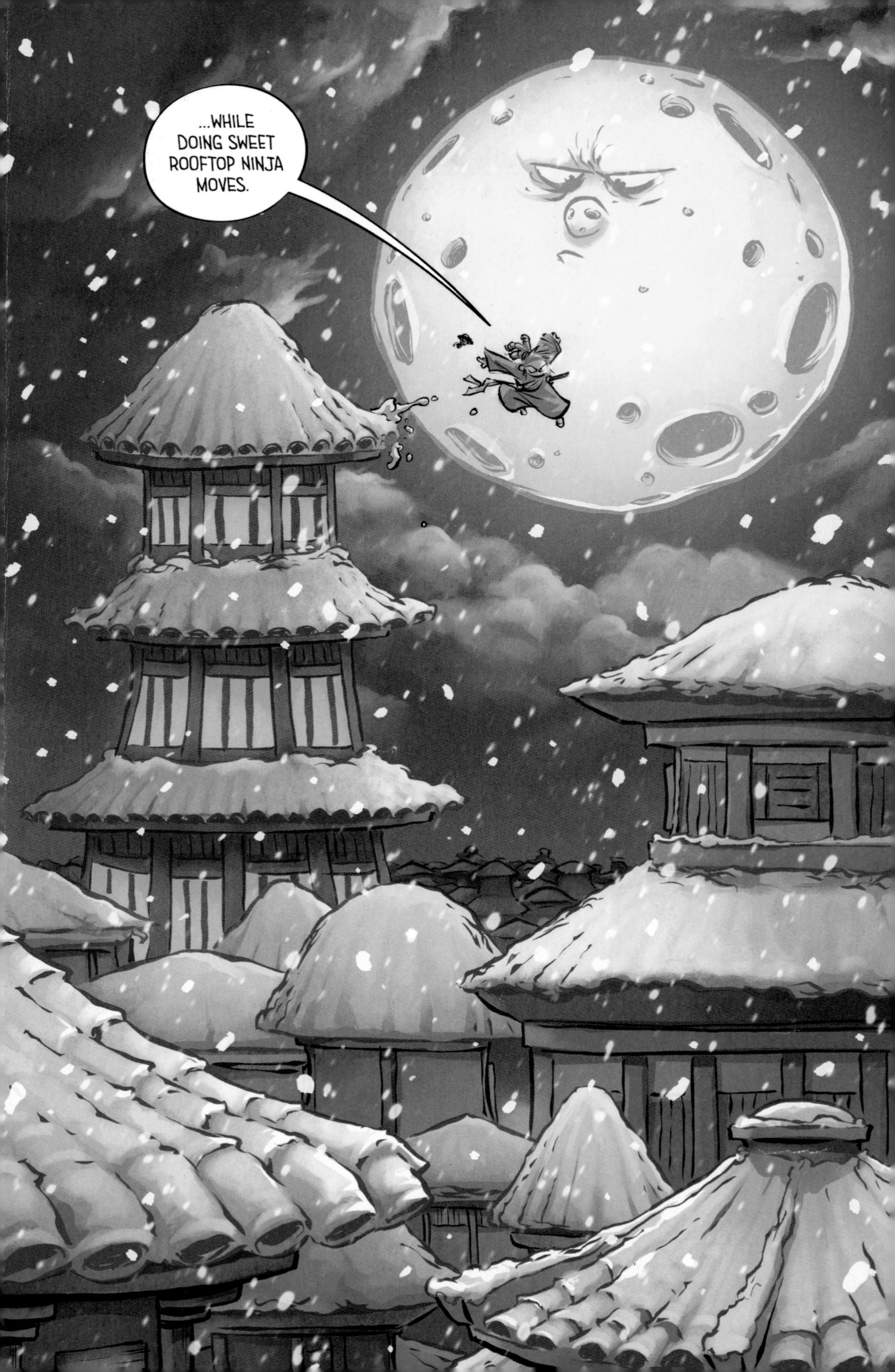
...WHILE DOING SWEET ROOFTOP NINJA MOVES.

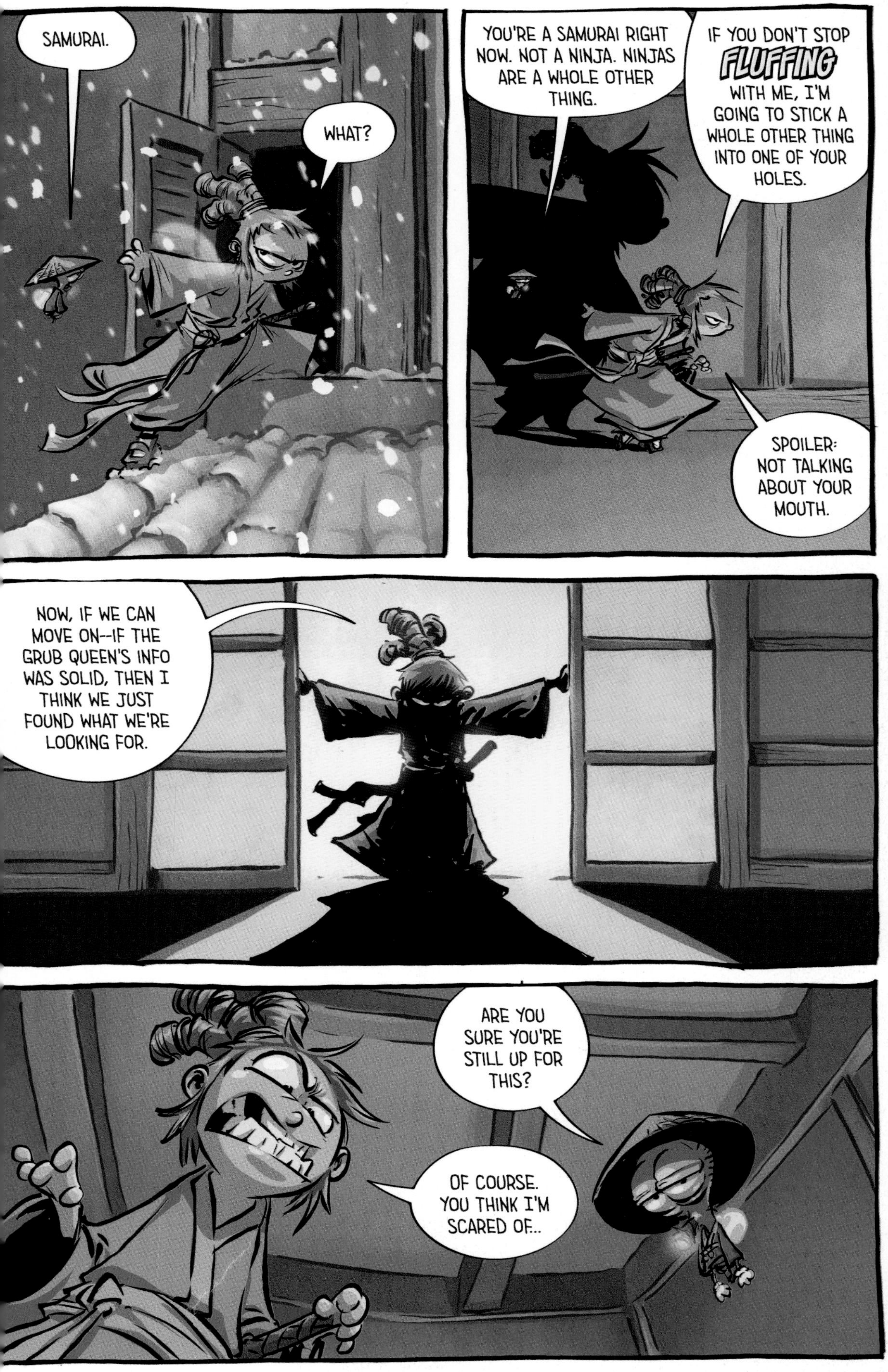
SAMURAI.
WHAT?
YOU'RE A SAMURAI RIGHT NOW. NOT A NINJA. NINJAS ARE A WHOLE OTHER THING.
IF YOU DON'T STOP FLUFFING WITH ME, I'M GOING TO STICK A WHOLE OTHER THING INTO ONE OF YOUR HOLES.
SPOILER: NOT TALKING ABOUT YOUR MOUTH.
NOW, IF WE CAN MOVE ON--IF THE GRUB QUEEN'S INFO WAS SOLID, THEN I THINK WE JUST FOUND WHAT WE'RE LOOKING FOR.
ARE YOU SURE YOU'RE STILL UP FOR THIS?
OF COURSE. YOU THINK I'M SCARED OF...

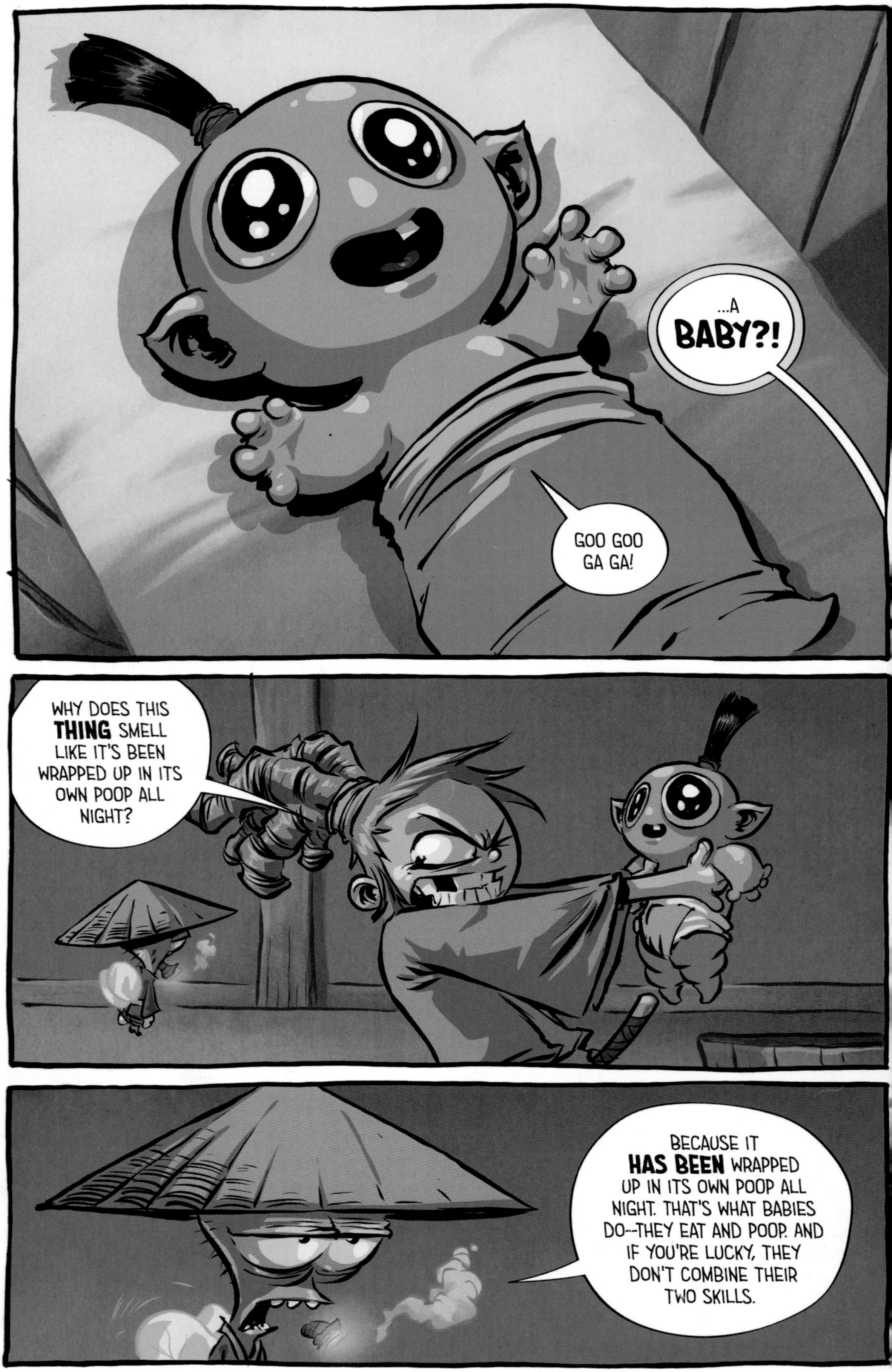
...A BABY?!
GOO GOO GA GA!
WHY DOES THIS THING SMELL LIKE IT'S BEEN WRAPPED UP IN ITS OWN POOP ALL NIGHT?
BECAUSE IT HAS BEEN WRAPPED UP IN ITS OWN POOP ALL NIGHT. THAT'S WHAT BABIES DO--THEY EAT AND POOP. AND IF YOU'RE LUCKY, THEY DON'T COMBINE THEIR TWO SKILLS.

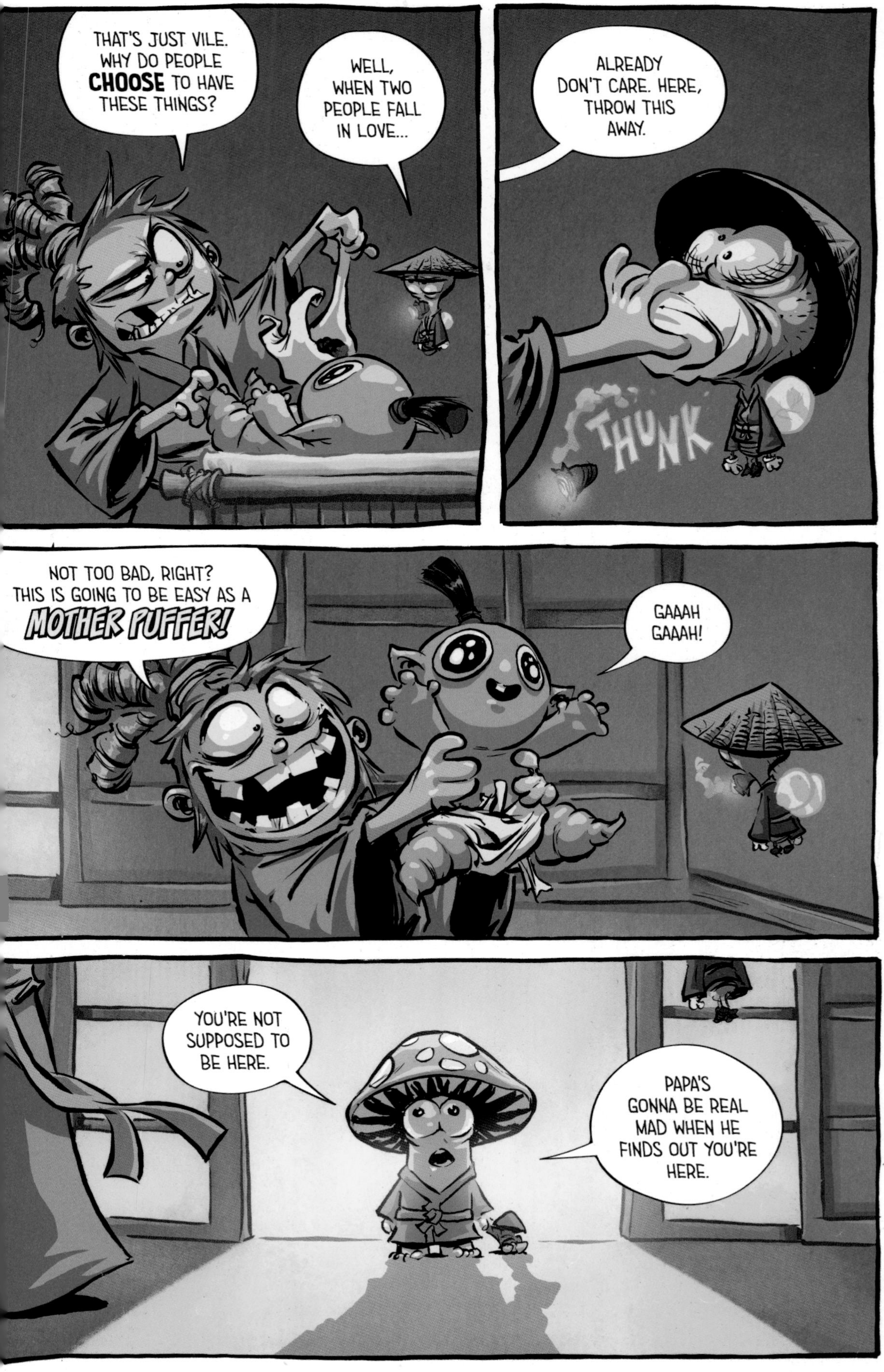
THAT'S JUST VILE. WHY DO PEOPLE **CHOOSE** TO HAVE THESE THINGS?
WELL, WHEN TWO PEOPLE FALL IN LOVE...
ALREADY DON'T CARE. HERE, THROW THIS AWAY.
THUNK
NOT TOO BAD, RIGHT? THIS IS GOING TO BE EASY AS A MOTHER PUFFER!
GAAAH GAAAH!
YOU'RE NOT SUPPOSED TO BE HERE.
PAPA'S GONNA BE REAL MAD WHEN HE FINDS OUT YOU'RE HERE.

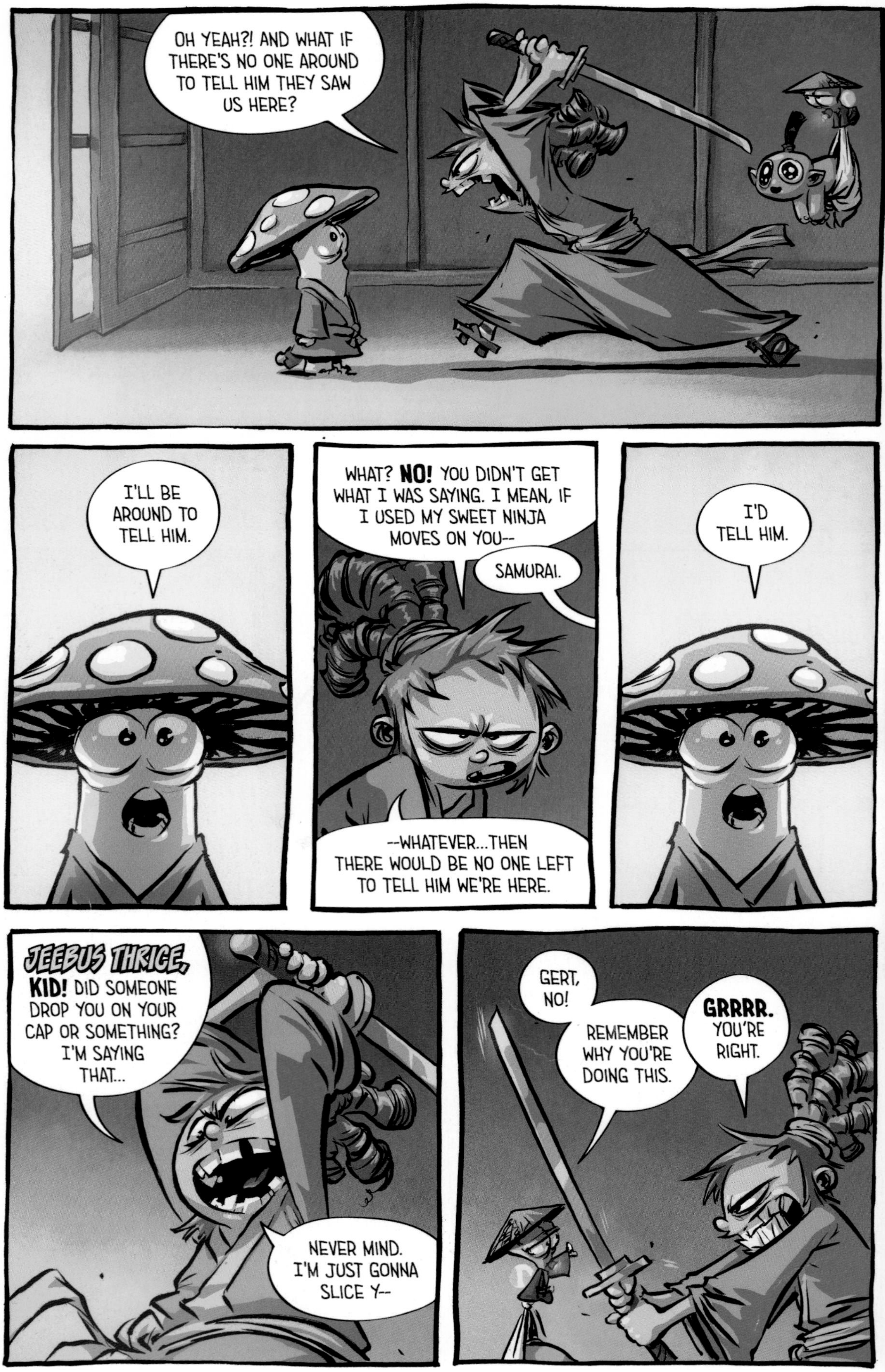
OH YEAH?! AND WHAT IF THERE'S NO ONE AROUND TO TELL HIM THEY SAW US HERE?
I'LL BE AROUND TO TELL HIM.
WHAT? **NO!** YOU DIDN'T GET WHAT I WAS SAYING. I MEAN, IF I USED MY SWEET NINJA MOVES ON YOU--
SAMURAI.
--WHATEVER...THEN THERE WOULD BE NO ONE LEFT TO TELL HIM WE'RE HERE.
I'D TELL HIM.
JEEBUS THRICE, KID! DID SOMEONE DROP YOU ON YOUR CAP OR SOMETHING? I'M SAYING THAT...
NEVER MIND. I'M JUST GONNA SLICE Y--
GERT, NO!
REMEMBER WHY YOU'RE DOING THIS.
GRRRR. YOU'RE RIGHT.

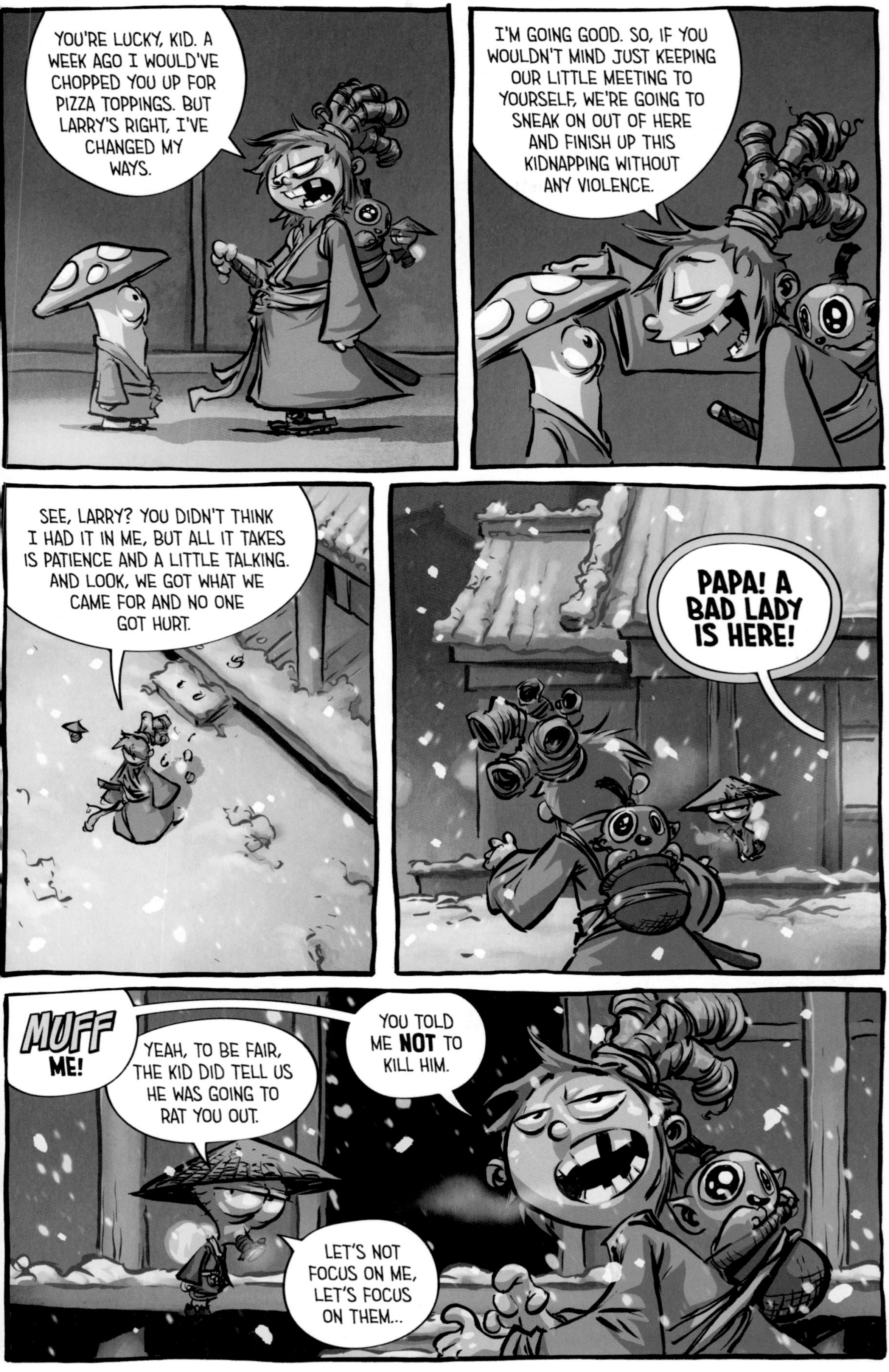
YOU'RE LUCKY, KID. A WEEK AGO I WOULD'VE CHOPPED YOU UP FOR PIZZA TOPPINGS. BUT LARRY'S RIGHT, I'VE CHANGED MY WAYS.
I'M GOING GOOD. SO, IF YOU WOULDN'T MIND JUST KEEPING OUR LITTLE MEETING TO YOURSELF, WE'RE GOING TO SNEAK ON OUT OF HERE AND FINISH UP THIS KIDNAPPING WITHOUT ANY VIOLENCE.
SEE, LARRY? YOU DIDN'T THINK I HAD IT IN ME, BUT ALL IT TAKES IS PATIENCE AND A LITTLE TALKING. AND LOOK, WE GOT WHAT WE CAME FOR AND NO ONE GOT HURT.
PAPA! A BAD LADY IS HERE!
MUFF ME!
YEAH, TO BE FAIR, THE KID DID TELL US HE WAS GOING TO RAT YOU OUT.
YOU TOLD ME NOT TO KILL HIM.
LET'S NOT FOCUS ON ME, LET'S FOCUS ON THEM...

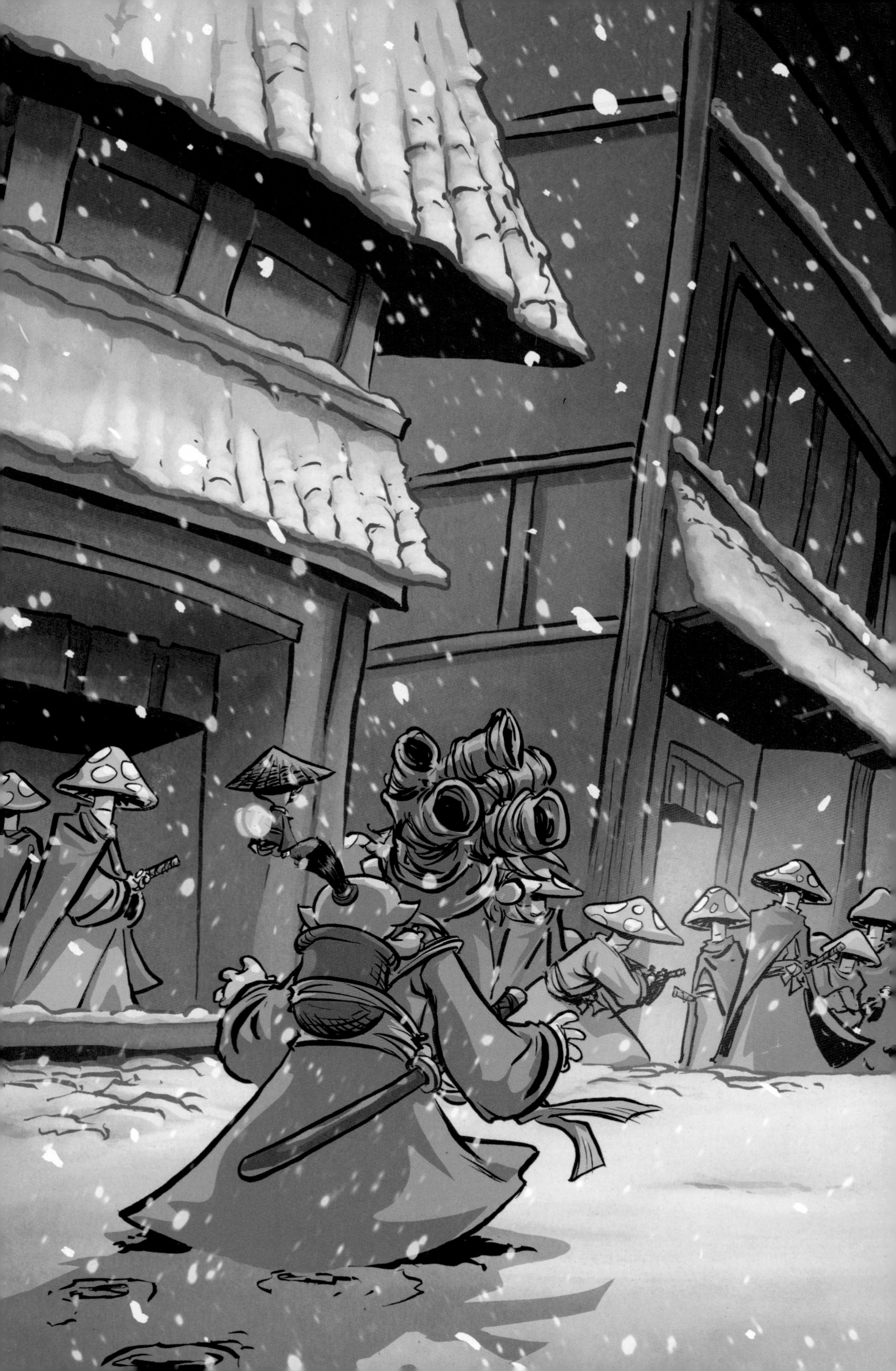

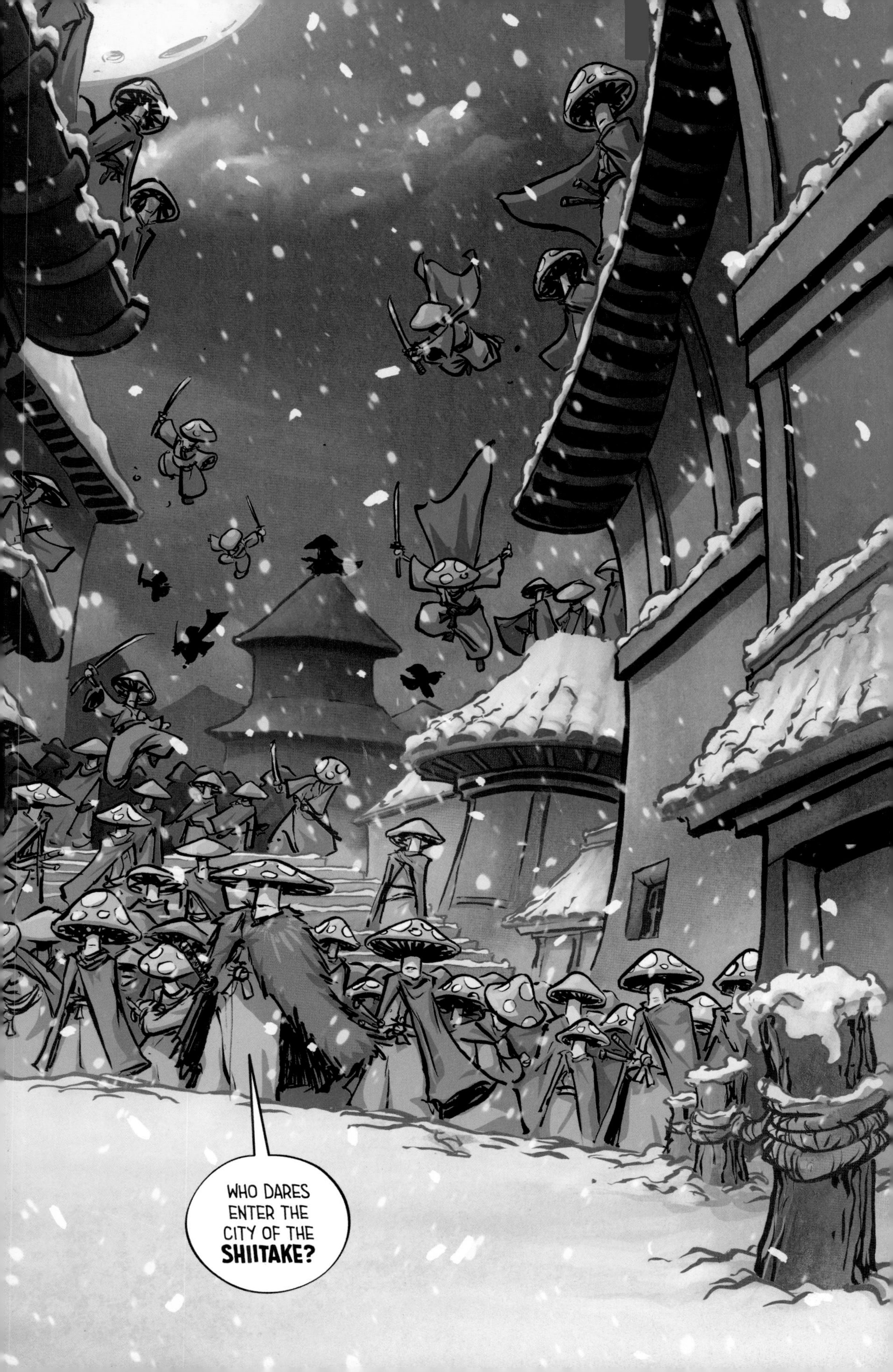
WHO DARES ENTER THE CITY OF THE SHIITAKE?

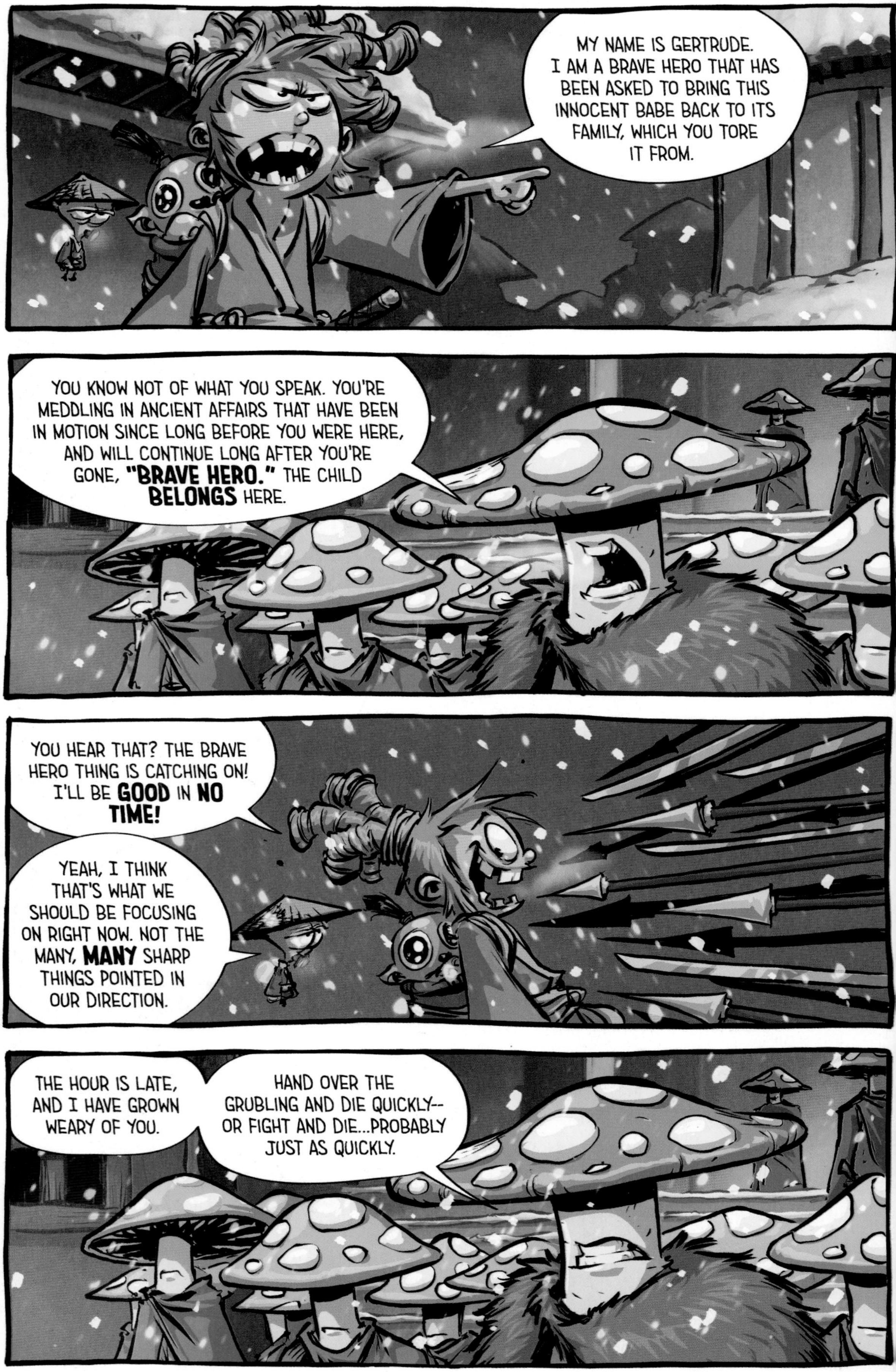
MY NAME IS GERTRUDE. I AM A BRAVE HERO THAT HAS BEEN ASKED TO BRING THIS INNOCENT BABE BACK TO ITS FAMILY, WHICH YOU TORE IT FROM.
YOU KNOW NOT OF WHAT YOU SPEAK. YOU'RE MEDDLING IN ANCIENT AFFAIRS THAT HAVE BEEN IN MOTION SINCE LONG BEFORE YOU WERE HERE, AND WILL CONTINUE LONG AFTER YOU'RE GONE, **"BRAVE HERO."** THE CHILD **BELONGS** HERE.
YOU HEAR THAT? THE BRAVE HERO THING IS CATCHING ON! I'LL BE **GOOD** IN **NO TIME!**
YEAH, I THINK THAT'S WHAT WE SHOULD BE FOCUSING ON RIGHT NOW. NOT THE MANY, **MANY** SHARP THINGS POINTED IN OUR DIRECTION.
THE HOUR IS LATE, AND I HAVE GROWN WEARY OF YOU.
HAND OVER THE GRUBLING AND DIE QUICKLY-- OR FIGHT AND DIE...PROBABLY JUST AS QUICKLY.

I HAVE MADE A VOW TO LIVE MY LIFE WITH HONOR AND PURITY, SO I CANNOT DO HARM TO OTHERS UNLESS THEY FIRST DO HARM UNTO ME.

VERY WELL.

SHIITAKE! DO HARM UNTO HER AND GET THAT **GRUB!**

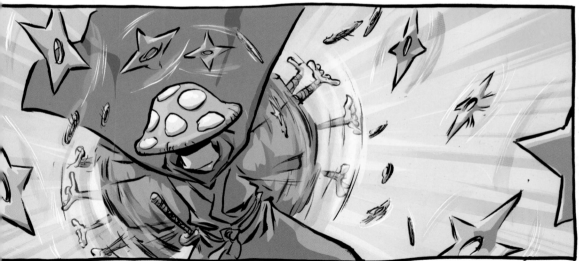

THWIP
THWIP
THIWP
THWIP
THWIP
THWIP
THWIP
THWIP
THWIP

SON OF A **LICH!**

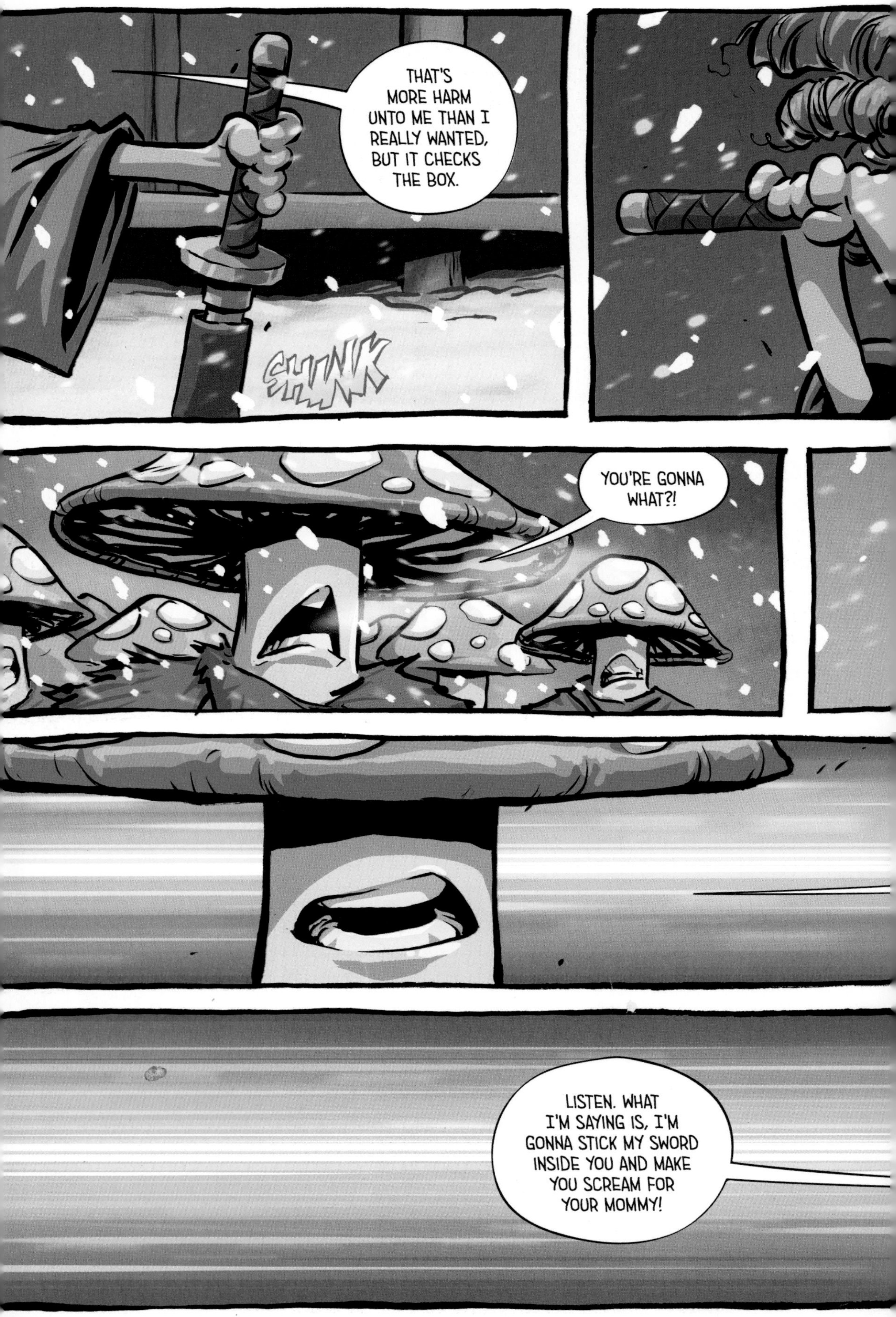
THAT'S MORE HARM UNTO ME THAN I REALLY WANTED, BUT IT CHECKS THE BOX.
SHINK
YOU'RE GONNA WHAT?!
LISTEN. WHAT I'M SAYING IS, I'M GONNA STICK MY SWORD INSIDE YOU AND MAKE YOU SCREAM FOR YOUR MOMMY!

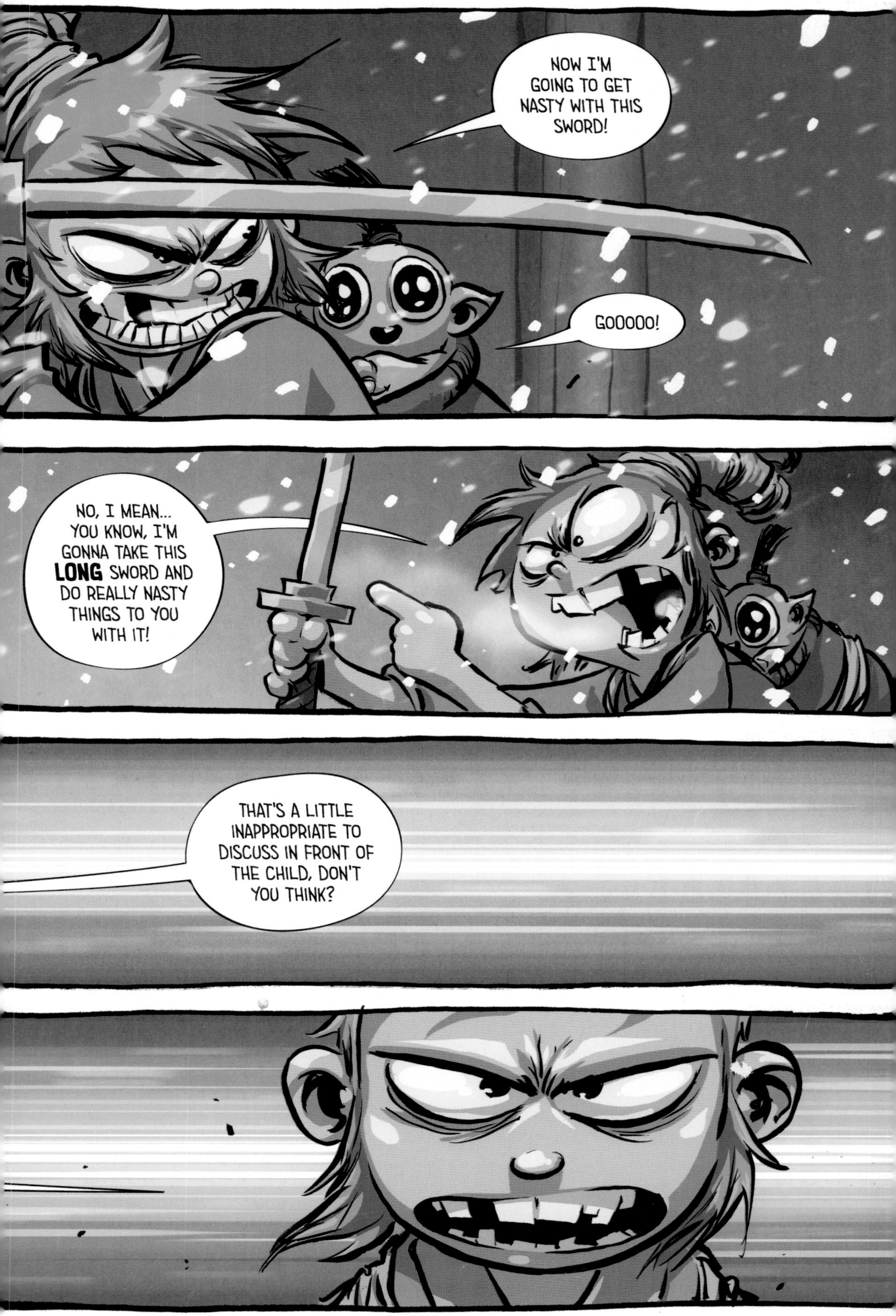
NOW I'M GOING TO GET NASTY WITH THIS SWORD!
GOOOOO!
NO, I MEAN... YOU KNOW, I'M GONNA TAKE THIS **LONG** SWORD AND DO REALLY NASTY THINGS TO YOU WITH IT!
THAT'S A LITTLE INAPPROPRIATE TO DISCUSS IN FRONT OF THE CHILD, DON'T YOU THINK?

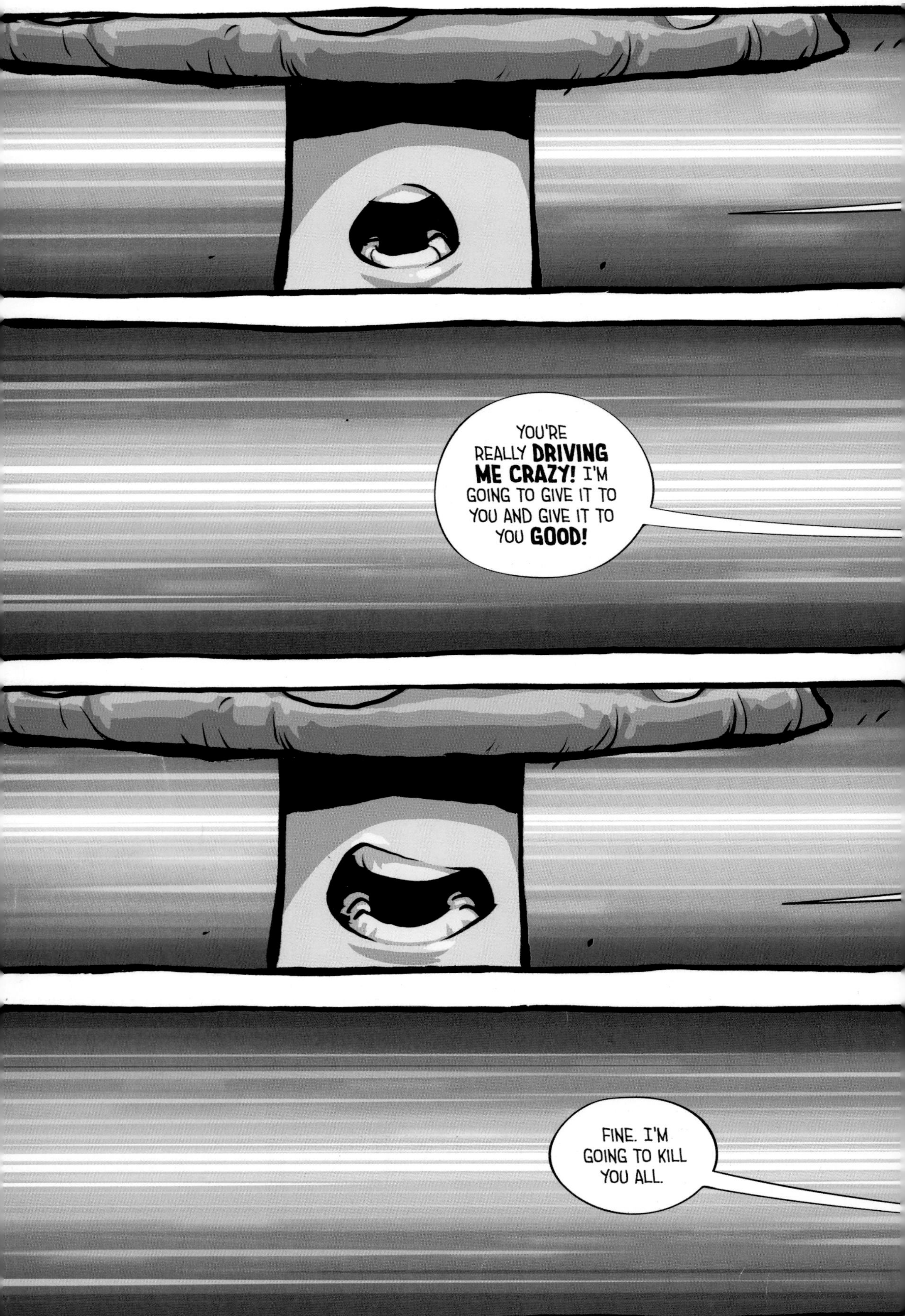
YOU'RE REALLY **DRIVING ME CRAZY!** I'M GOING TO GIVE IT TO YOU AND GIVE IT TO YOU **GOOD!**
FINE. I'M GOING TO KILL YOU ALL.

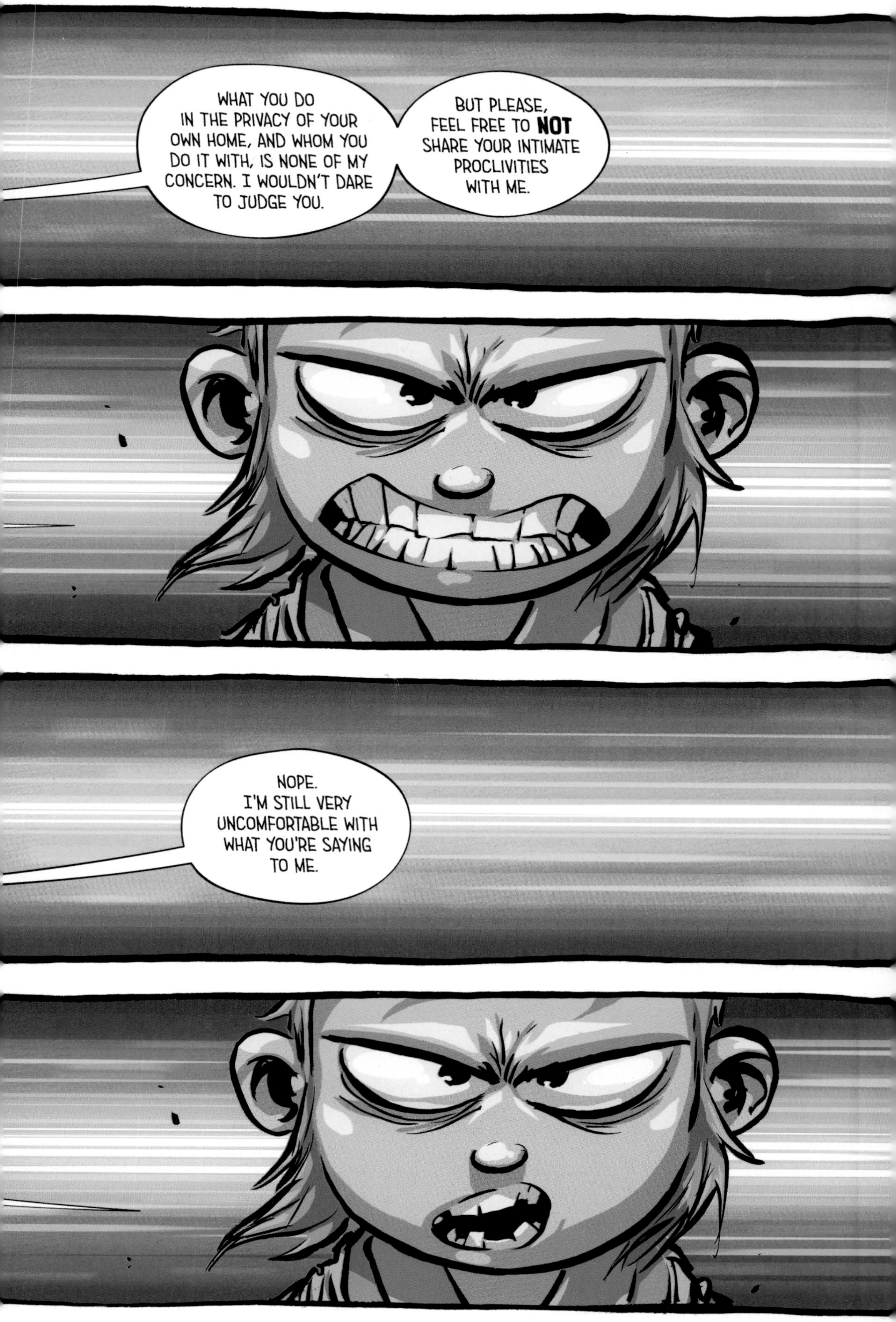
WHAT YOU DO IN THE PRIVACY OF YOUR OWN HOME, AND WHOM YOU DO IT WITH, IS NONE OF MY CONCERN. I WOULDN'T DARE TO JUDGE YOU.
BUT PLEASE, FEEL FREE TO **NOT** SHARE YOUR INTIMATE PROCLIVITIES WITH ME.
NOPE. I'M STILL VERY UNCOMFORTABLE WITH WHAT YOU'RE SAYING TO ME.

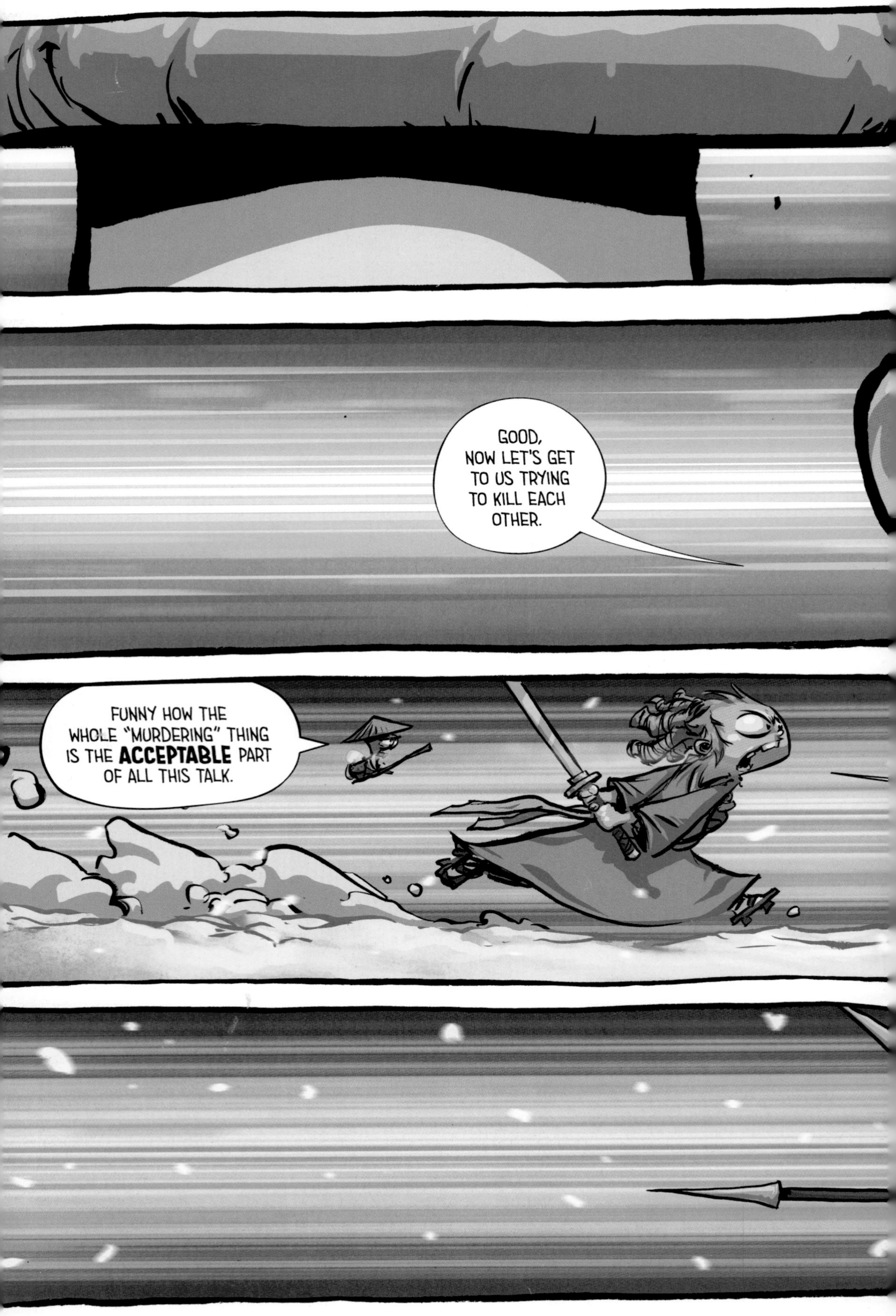
GOOD, NOW LET'S GET TO US TRYING TO KILL EACH OTHER.
FUNNY HOW THE WHOLE "MURDERING" THING IS THE **ACCEPTABLE** PART OF ALL THIS TALK.

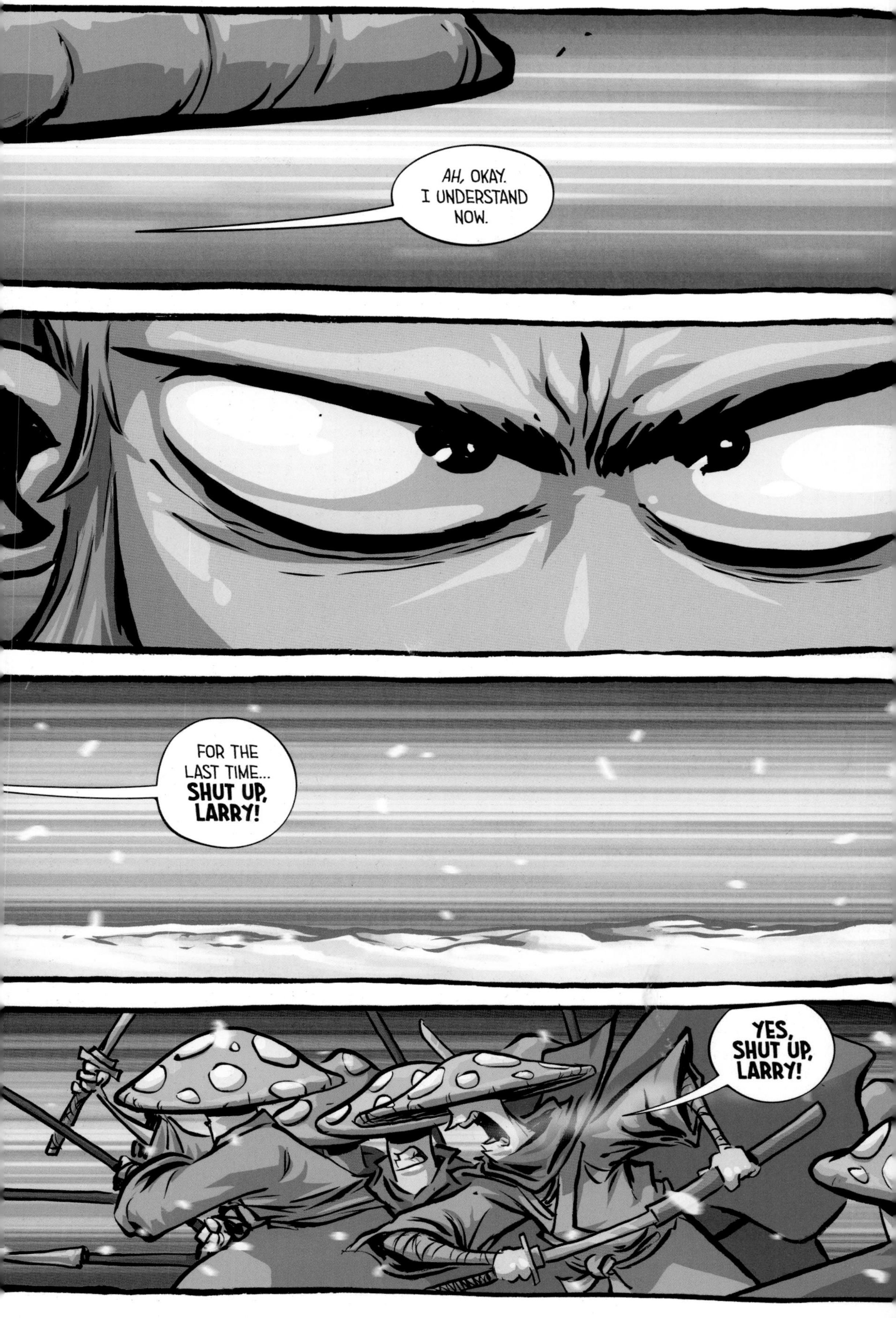
AH, OKAY. I UNDERSTAND NOW.
FOR THE LAST TIME... **SHUT UP, LARRY!**
YES, SHUT UP, LARRY!

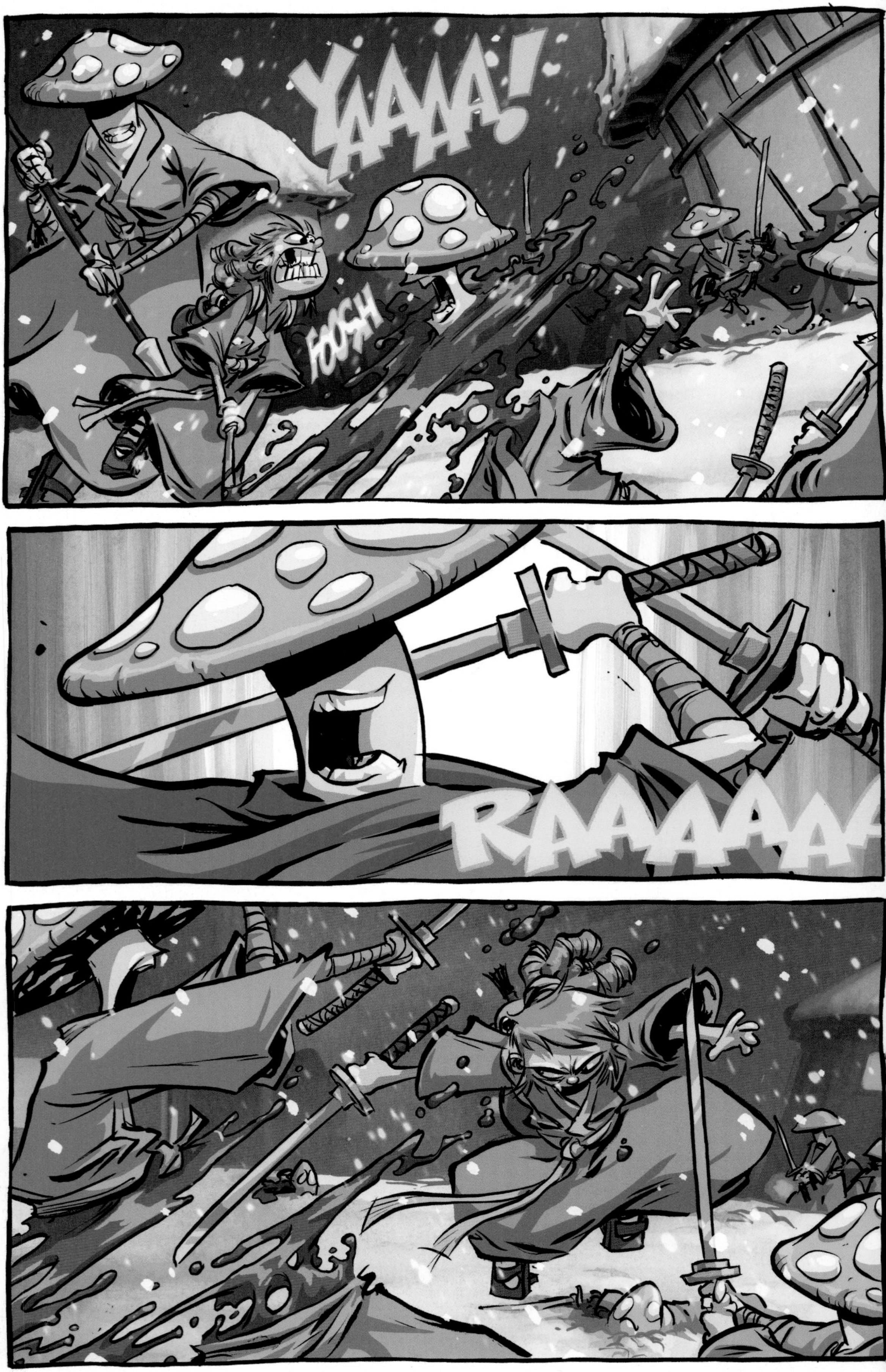
YAAAA!
FOOSH
RAAAAA

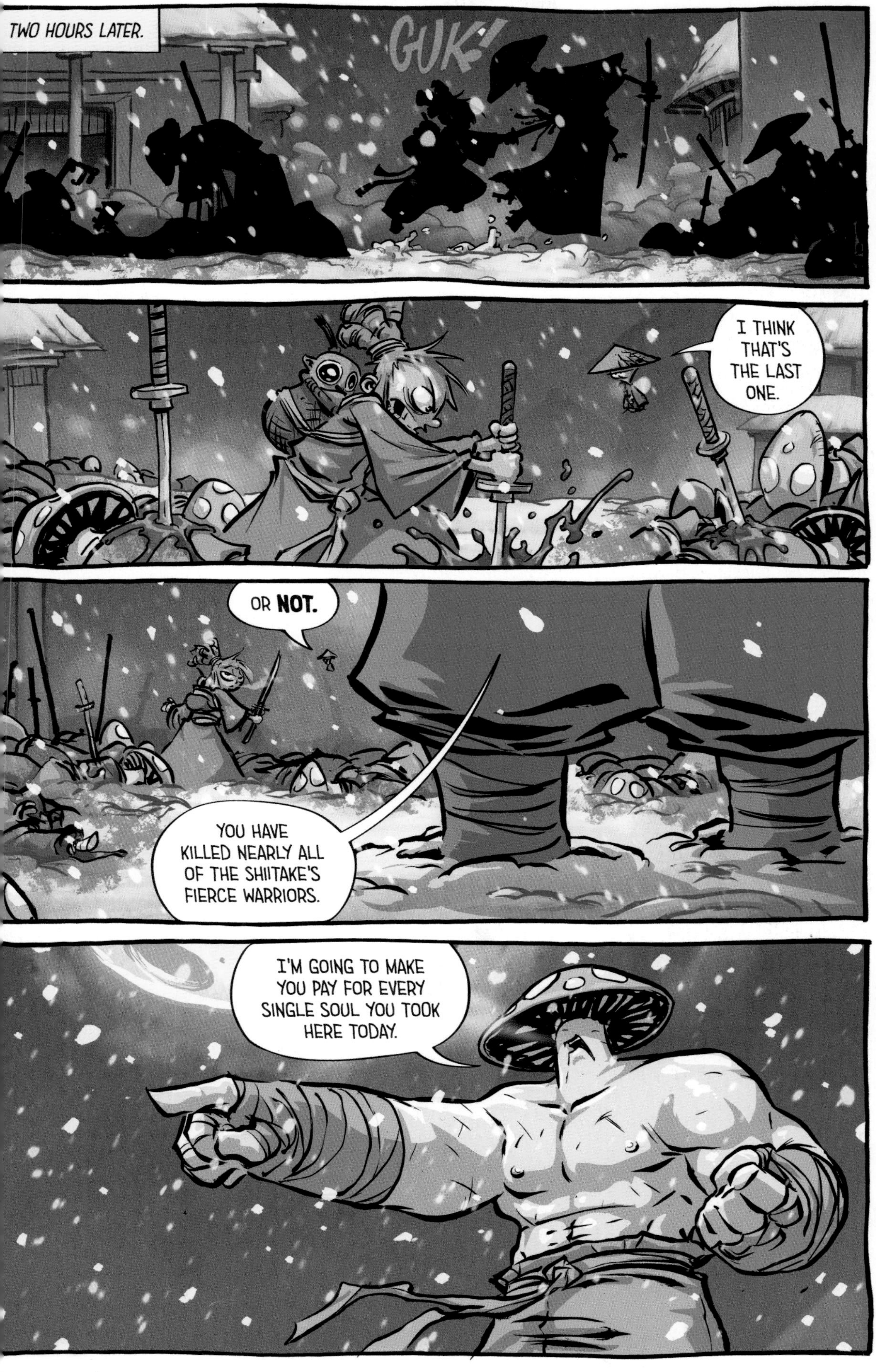
TWO HOURS LATER.
GUK!
I THINK THAT'S THE LAST ONE.
OR NOT.
YOU HAVE KILLED NEARLY ALL OF THE SHIITAKE'S FIERCE WARRIORS.
I'M GOING TO MAKE YOU PAY FOR EVERY SINGLE SOUL YOU TOOK HERE TODAY.

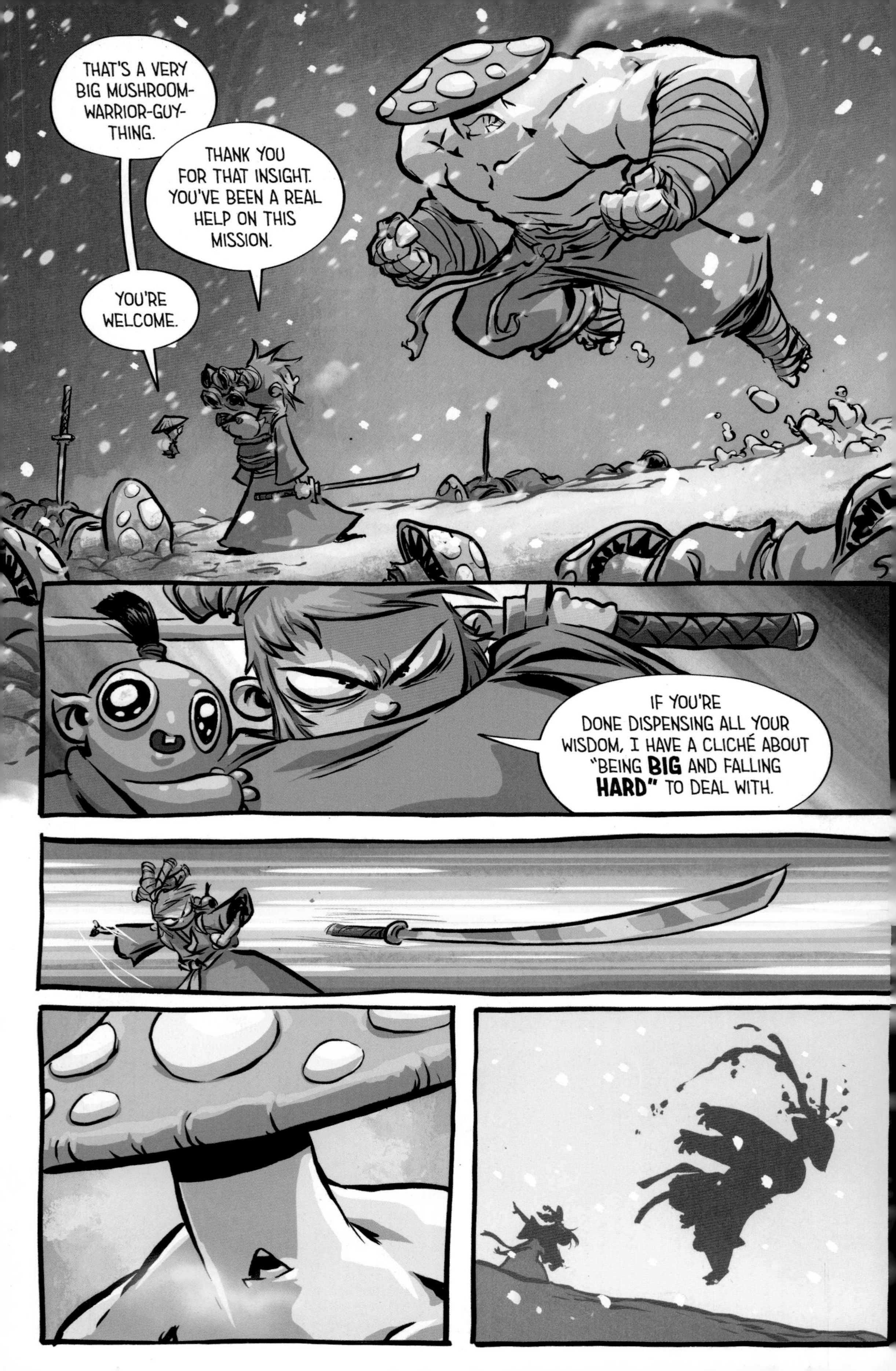

THAT'S A VERY BIG MUSHROOM-WARRIOR-GUY-THING.
THANK YOU FOR THAT INSIGHT. YOU'VE BEEN A REAL HELP ON THIS MISSION.
YOU'RE WELCOME.
IF YOU'RE DONE DISPENSING ALL YOUR WISDOM, I HAVE A CLICHÉ ABOUT "BEING **BIG** AND FALLING **HARD**" TO DEAL WITH.

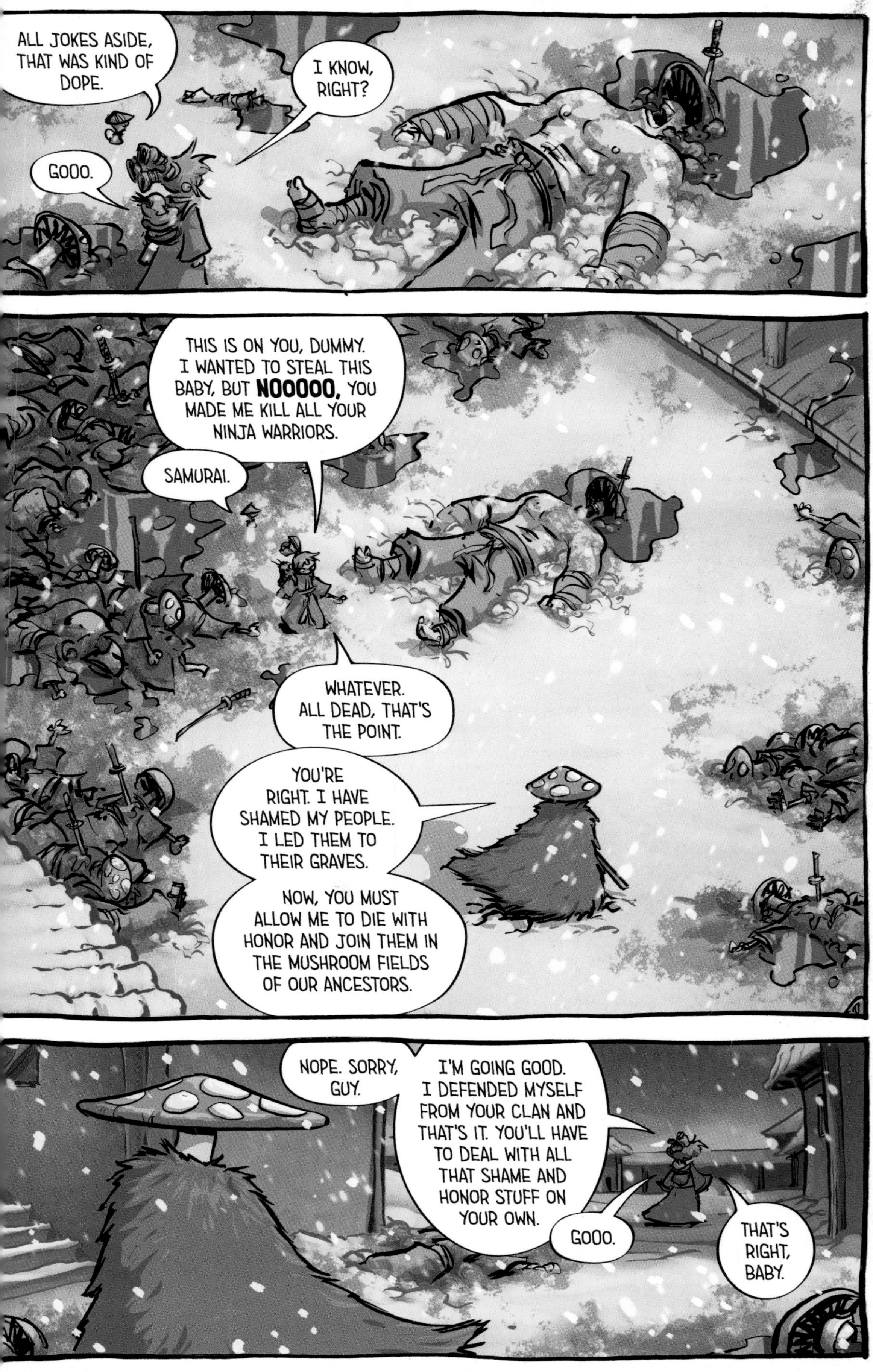

ALL JOKES ASIDE, THAT WAS KIND OF DOPE.
I KNOW, RIGHT?
GOOO.
THIS IS ON YOU, DUMMY. I WANTED TO STEAL THIS BABY, BUT **NOOOOO,** YOU MADE ME KILL ALL YOUR NINJA WARRIORS.
SAMURAI.
WHATEVER. ALL DEAD, THAT'S THE POINT.
YOU'RE RIGHT. I HAVE SHAMED MY PEOPLE. I LED THEM TO THEIR GRAVES.
NOW, YOU MUST ALLOW ME TO DIE WITH HONOR AND JOIN THEM IN THE MUSHROOM FIELDS OF OUR ANCESTORS.
NOPE. SORRY, GUY.
I'M GOING GOOD. I DEFENDED MYSELF FROM YOUR CLAN AND THAT'S IT. YOU'LL HAVE TO DEAL WITH ALL THAT SHAME AND HONOR STUFF ON YOUR OWN.
GOOO.
THAT'S RIGHT, BABY.

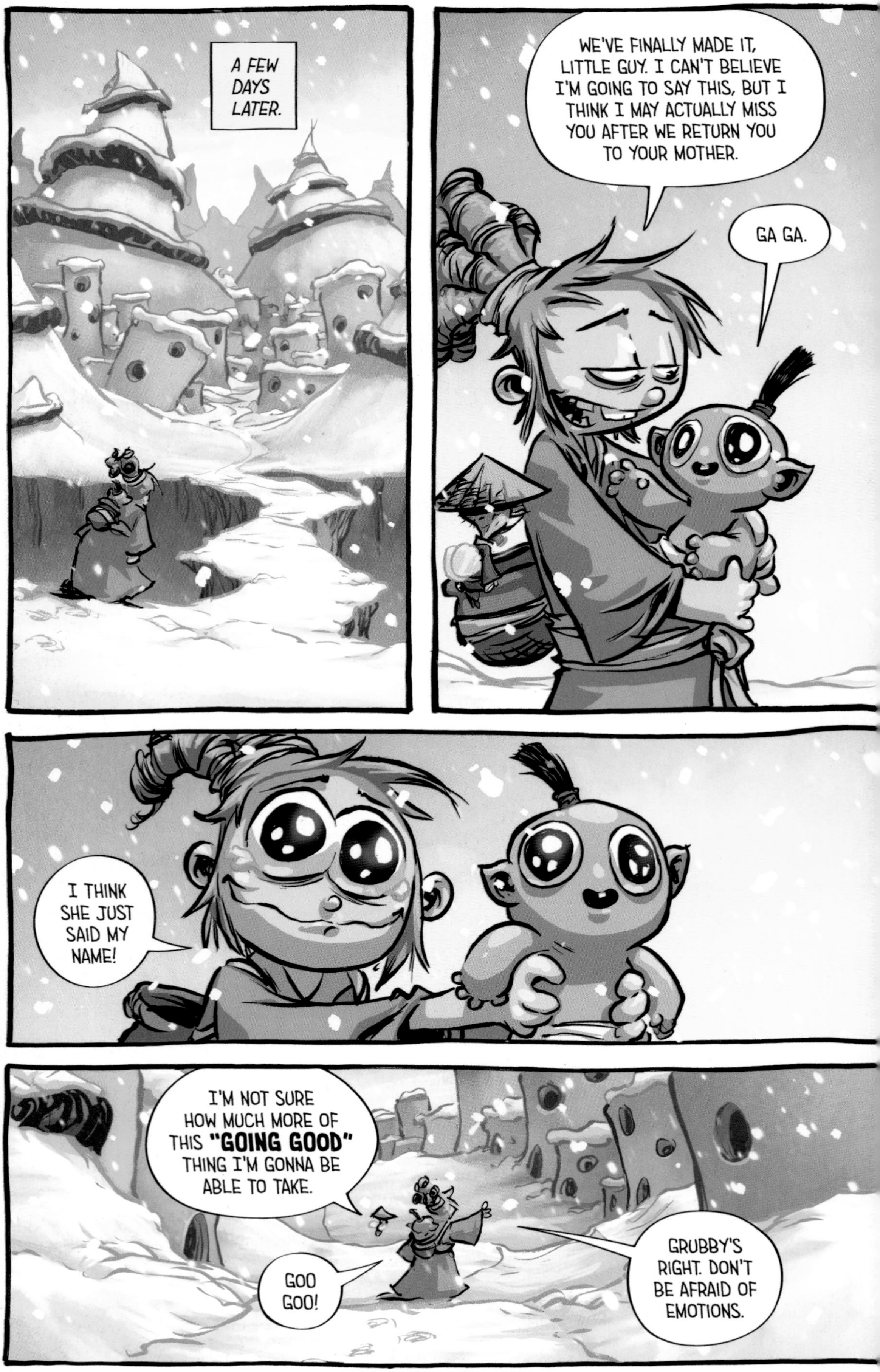
A FEW DAYS LATER.
WE'VE FINALLY MADE IT, LITTLE GUY. I CAN'T BELIEVE I'M GOING TO SAY THIS, BUT I THINK I MAY ACTUALLY MISS YOU AFTER WE RETURN YOU TO YOUR MOTHER.
GA GA.
I THINK SHE JUST SAID MY NAME!
I'M NOT SURE HOW MUCH MORE OF THIS **"GOING GOOD"** THING I'M GONNA BE ABLE TO TAKE.
GOO GOO!
GRUBBY'S RIGHT. DON'T BE AFRAID OF EMOTIONS.

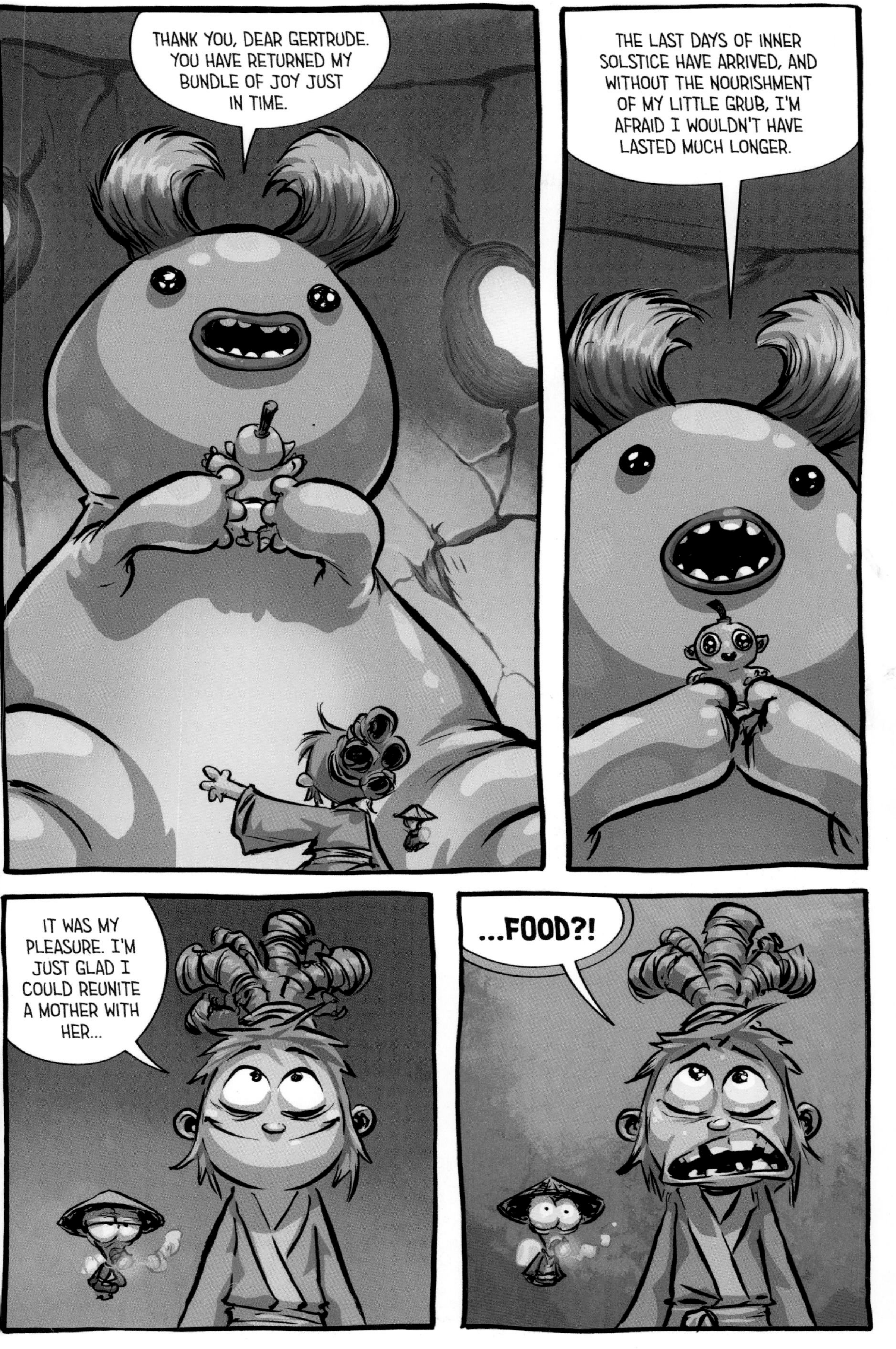
THANK YOU, DEAR GERTRUDE. YOU HAVE RETURNED MY BUNDLE OF JOY JUST IN TIME.
THE LAST DAYS OF INNER SOLSTICE HAVE ARRIVED, AND WITHOUT THE NOURISHMENT OF MY LITTLE GRUB, I'M AFRAID I WOULDN'T HAVE LASTED MUCH LONGER.
IT WAS MY PLEASURE. I'M JUST GLAD I COULD REUNITE A MOTHER WITH HER...
...FOOD?!

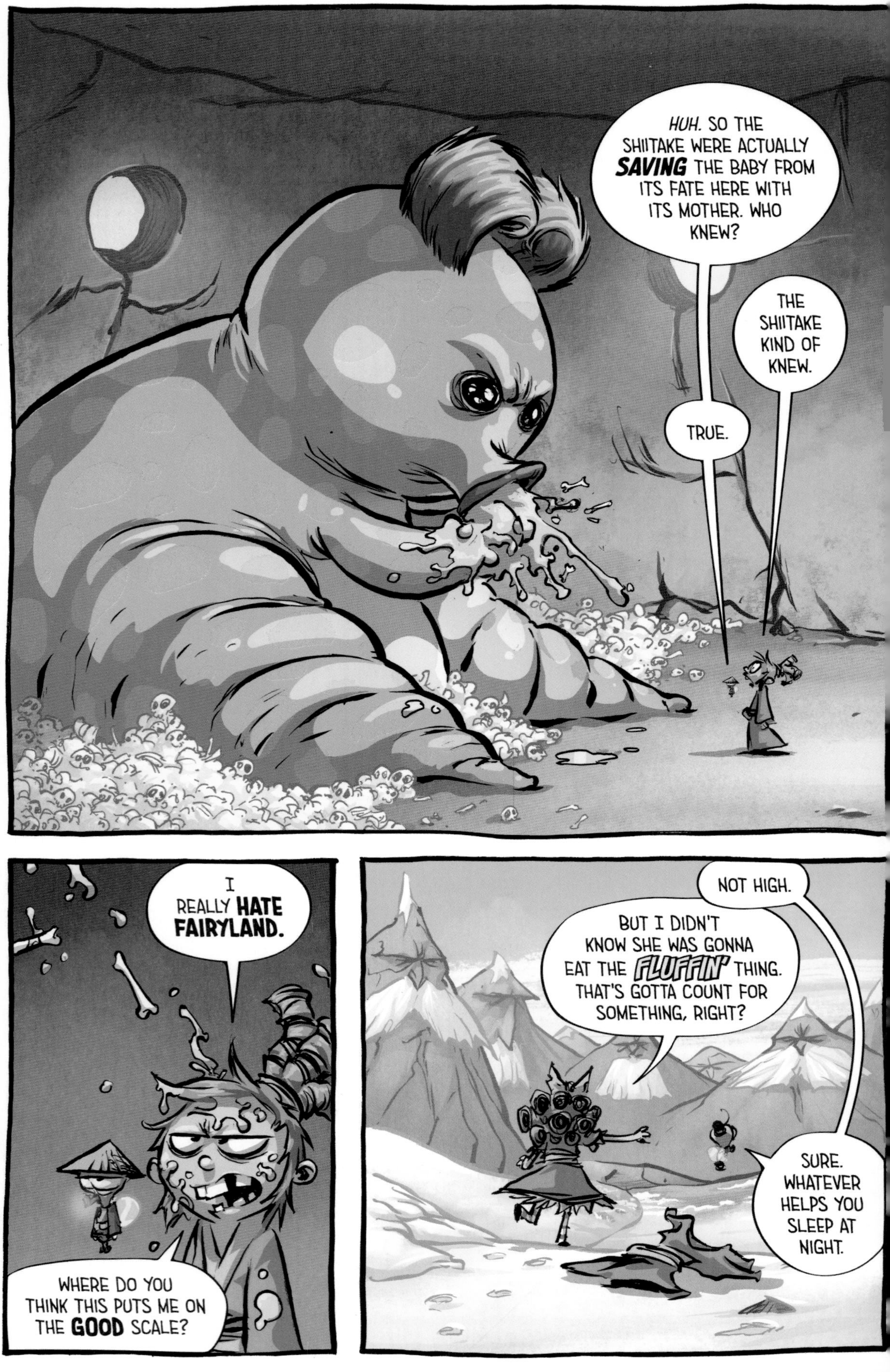
HUH. SO THE SHIITAKE WERE ACTUALLY SAVING THE BABY FROM ITS FATE HERE WITH ITS MOTHER. WHO KNEW?
THE SHIITAKE KIND OF KNEW.
TRUE.
I REALLY HATE FAIRYLAND.
WHERE DO YOU THINK THIS PUTS ME ON THE GOOD SCALE?
NOT HIGH.
BUT I DIDN'T KNOW SHE WAS GONNA EAT THE FLUFFIN' THING. THAT'S GOTTA COUNT FOR SOMETHING, RIGHT?
SURE. WHATEVER HELPS YOU SLEEP AT NIGHT.

THIRTEEN

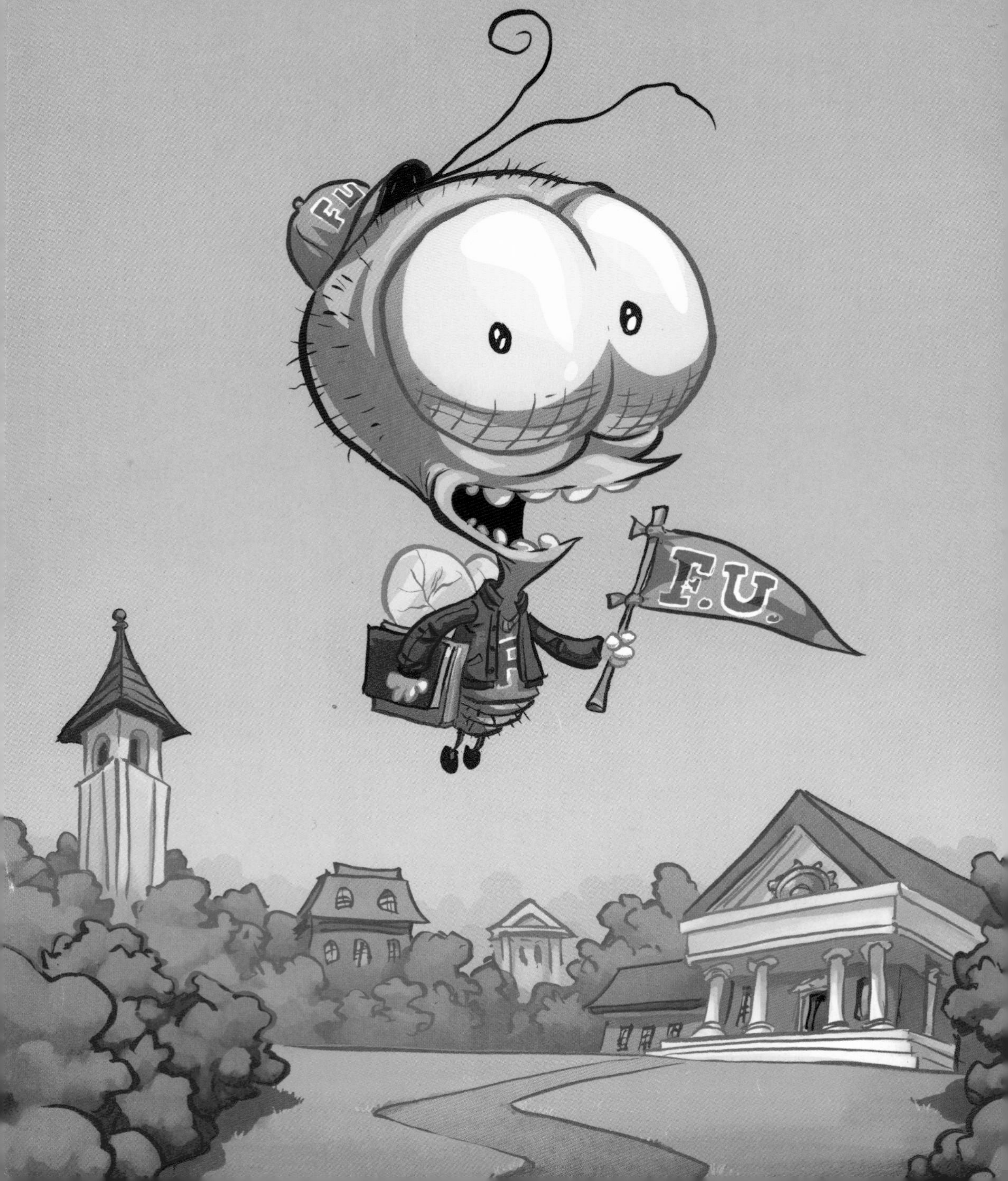
F.U.

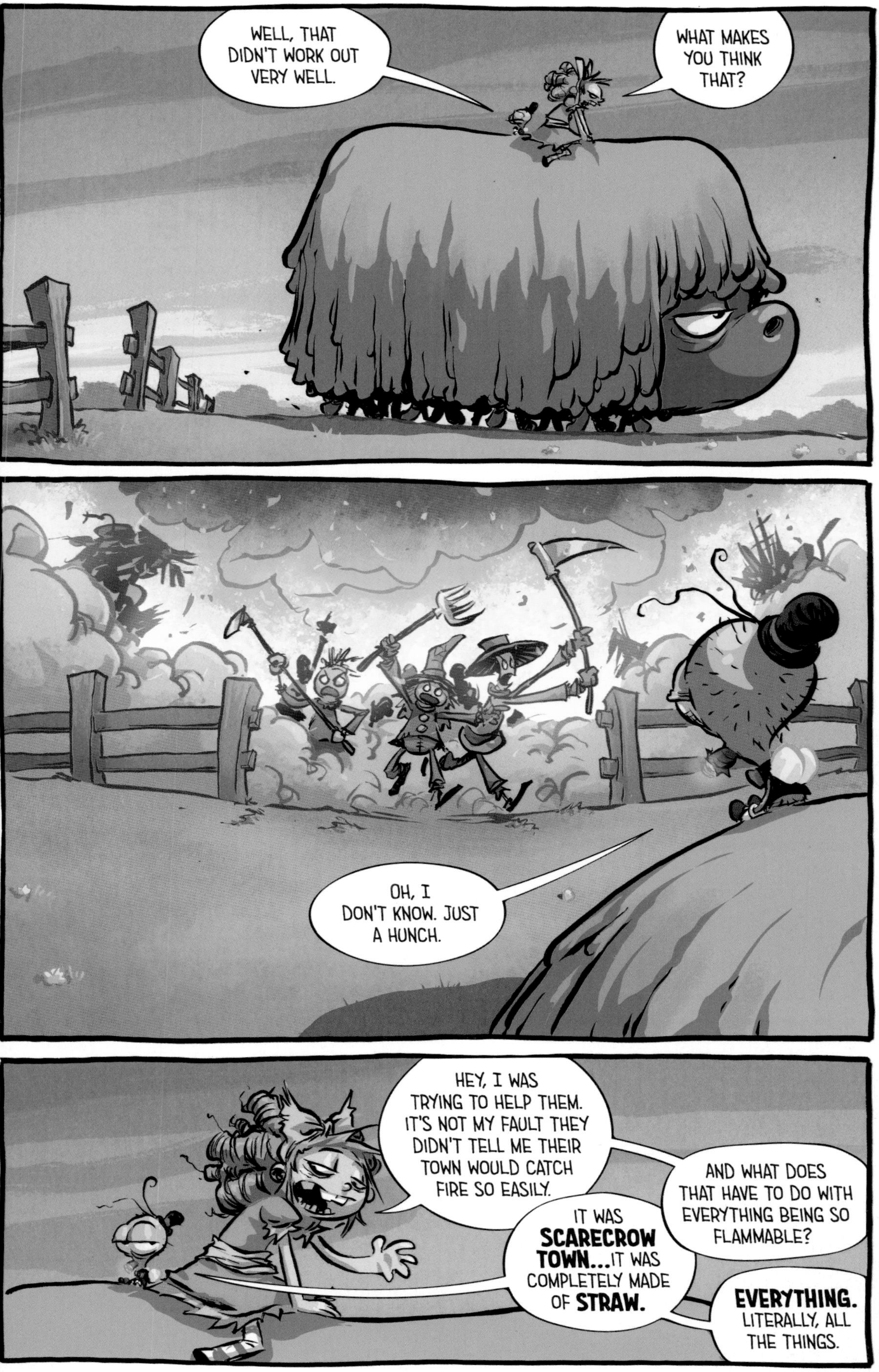
WELL, THAT DIDN'T WORK OUT VERY WELL.
WHAT MAKES YOU THINK THAT?
OH, I DON'T KNOW. JUST A HUNCH.
HEY, I WAS TRYING TO HELP THEM. IT'S NOT MY FAULT THEY DIDN'T TELL ME THEIR TOWN WOULD CATCH FIRE SO EASILY.
AND WHAT DOES THAT HAVE TO DO WITH EVERYTHING BEING SO FLAMMABLE?
IT WAS **SCARECROW TOWN...** IT WAS COMPLETELY MADE OF **STRAW.**
EVERYTHING. LITERALLY, ALL THE THINGS.

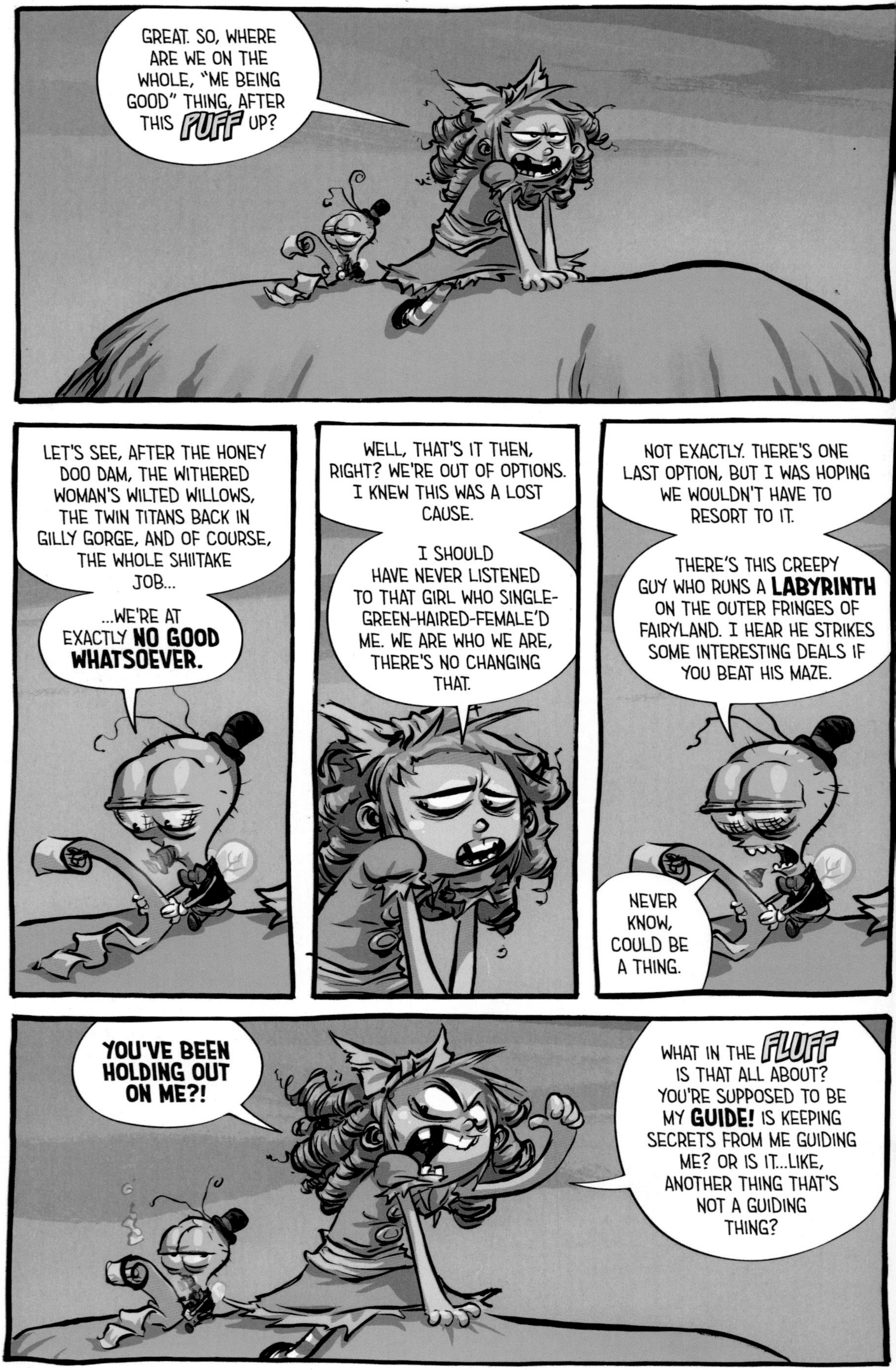
GREAT. SO, WHERE ARE WE ON THE WHOLE, "ME BEING GOOD" THING, AFTER THIS PUFF UP?
LET'S SEE, AFTER THE HONEY DOO DAM, THE WITHERED WOMAN'S WILTED WILLOWS, THE TWIN TITANS BACK IN GILLY GORGE, AND OF COURSE, THE WHOLE SHIITAKE JOB...
...WE'RE AT EXACTLY **NO GOOD WHATSOEVER.**
WELL, THAT'S IT THEN, RIGHT? WE'RE OUT OF OPTIONS. I KNEW THIS WAS A LOST CAUSE.
I SHOULD HAVE NEVER LISTENED TO THAT GIRL WHO SINGLE-GREEN-HAIRED-FEMALE'D ME. WE ARE WHO WE ARE, THERE'S NO CHANGING THAT.
NOT EXACTLY. THERE'S ONE LAST OPTION, BUT I WAS HOPING WE WOULDN'T HAVE TO RESORT TO IT.
THERE'S THIS CREEPY GUY WHO RUNS A **LABYRINTH** ON THE OUTER FRINGES OF FAIRYLAND. I HEAR HE STRIKES SOME INTERESTING DEALS IF YOU BEAT HIS MAZE.
NEVER KNOW, COULD BE A THING.
YOU'VE BEEN HOLDING OUT ON ME?!
WHAT IN THE FLUFF IS THAT ALL ABOUT? YOU'RE SUPPOSED TO BE MY **GUIDE!** IS KEEPING SECRETS FROM ME GUIDING ME? OR IS IT...LIKE, ANOTHER THING THAT'S NOT A GUIDING THING?

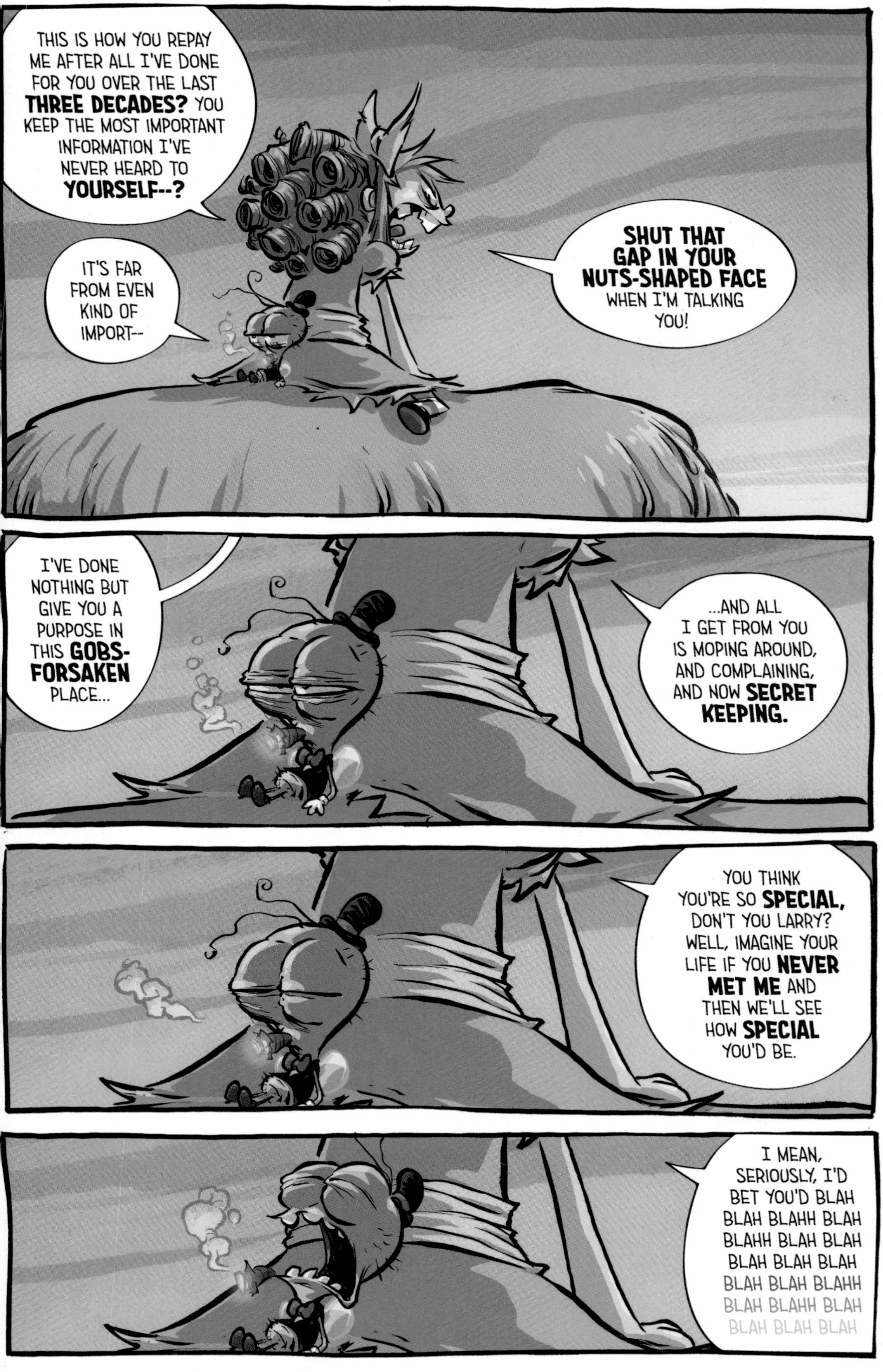
THIS IS HOW YOU REPAY ME AFTER ALL I'VE DONE FOR YOU OVER THE LAST **THREE DECADES?** YOU KEEP THE MOST IMPORTANT INFORMATION I'VE NEVER HEARD TO **YOURSELF--?**
IT'S FAR FROM EVEN KIND OF IMPORT--
SHUT THAT GAP IN YOUR NUTS-SHAPED FACE WHEN I'M TALKING YOU!
I'VE DONE NOTHING BUT GIVE YOU A PURPOSE IN THIS **GOBS-FORSAKEN** PLACE...
...AND ALL I GET FROM YOU IS MOPING AROUND, AND COMPLAINING, AND NOW **SECRET KEEPING.**
YOU THINK YOU'RE SO **SPECIAL,** DON'T YOU LARRY? WELL, IMAGINE YOUR LIFE IF YOU **NEVER MET ME** AND THEN WE'LL SEE HOW **SPECIAL** YOU'D BE.
I MEAN, SERIOUSLY, I'D BET YOU'D BLAH BLAH BLAHH BLAH BLAHH BLAH BLAH BLAH BLAH BLAH BLAH BLAH BLAHH BLAH BLAHH BLAH BLAH BLAH BLAH

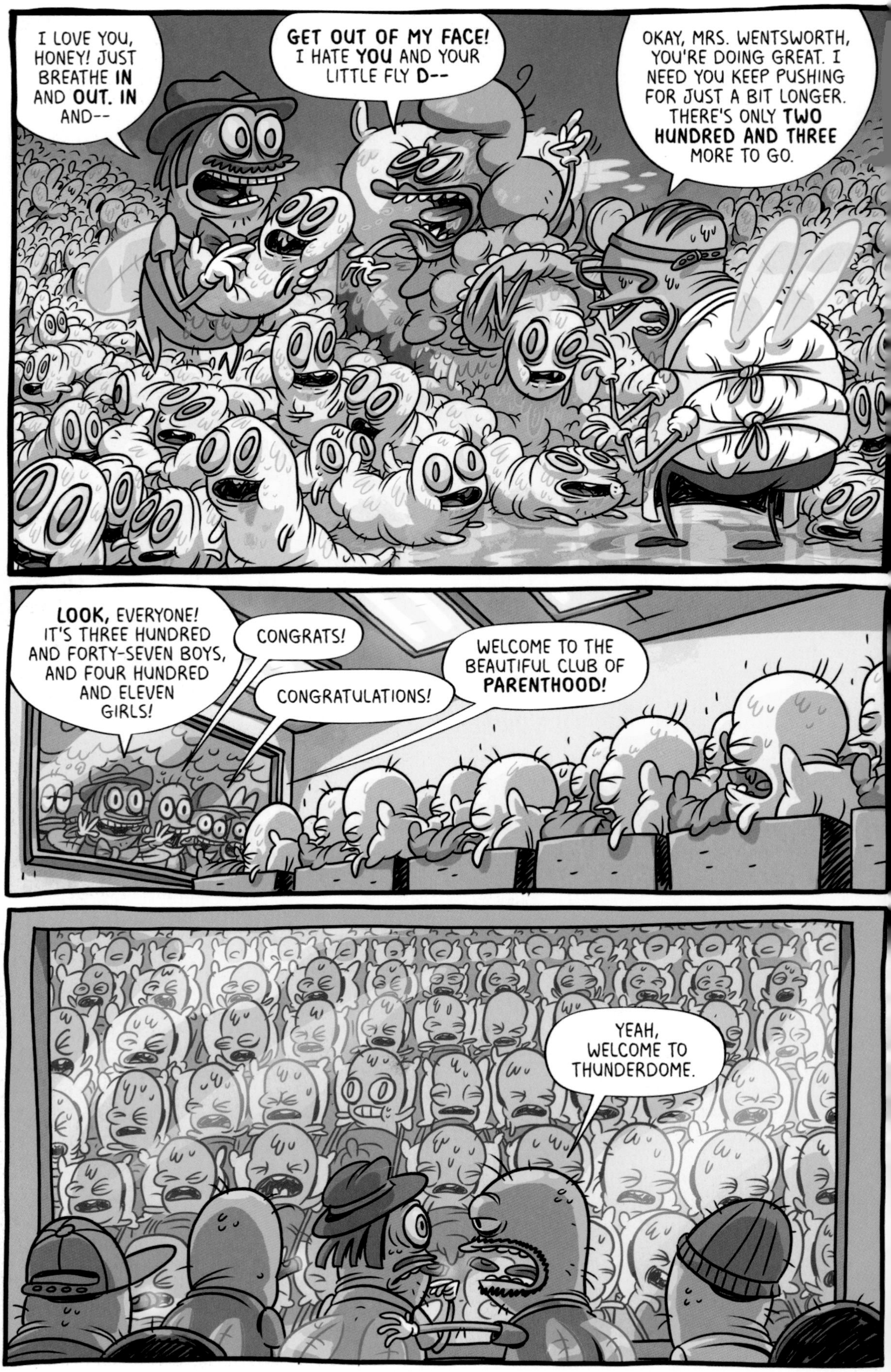

I LOVE YOU, HONEY! JUST BREATHE IN AND OUT. IN AND--
GET OUT OF MY FACE! I HATE YOU AND YOUR LITTLE FLY D--
OKAY, MRS. WENTSWORTH, YOU'RE DOING GREAT. I NEED YOU KEEP PUSHING FOR JUST A BIT LONGER. THERE'S ONLY TWO HUNDRED AND THREE MORE TO GO.
LOOK, EVERYONE! IT'S THREE HUNDRED AND FORTY-SEVEN BOYS, AND FOUR HUNDRED AND ELEVEN GIRLS!
CONGRATS!
CONGRATULATIONS!
WELCOME TO THE BEAUTIFUL CLUB OF PARENTHOOD!
YEAH, WELCOME TO THUNDERDOME.

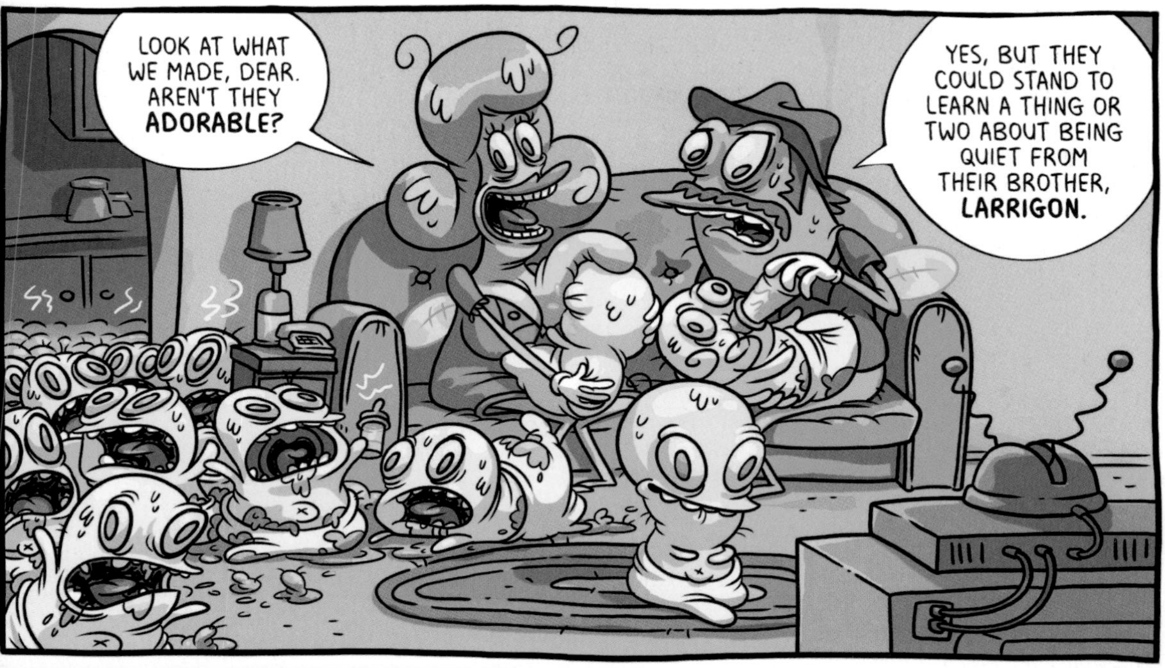
LOOK AT WHAT WE MADE, DEAR. AREN'T THEY **ADORABLE?**
YES, BUT THEY COULD STAND TO LEARN A THING OR TWO ABOUT BEING QUIET FROM THEIR BROTHER, **LARRIGON.**

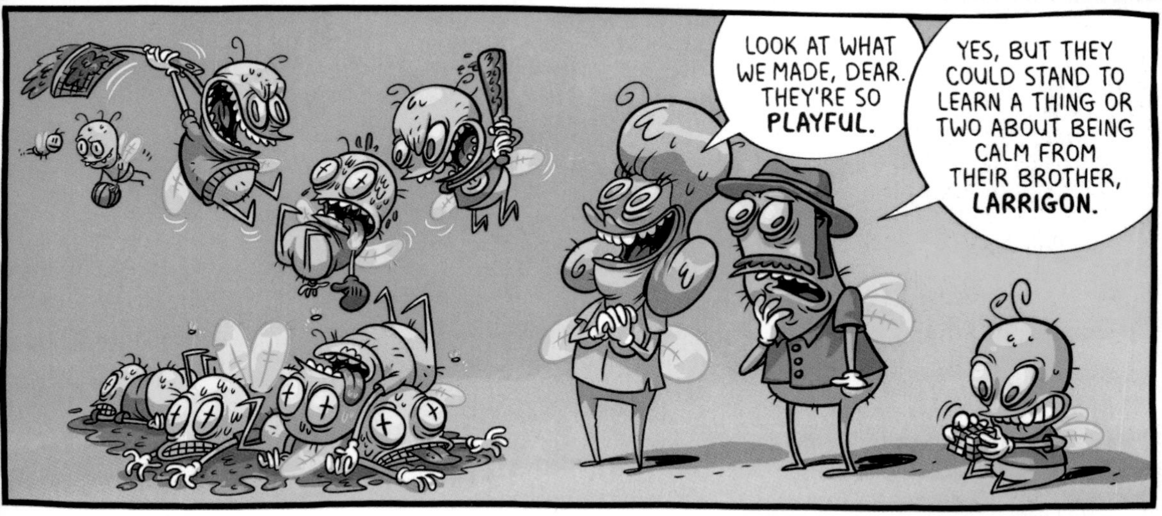
LOOK AT WHAT WE MADE, DEAR. THEY'RE SO **PLAYFUL.**
YES, BUT THEY COULD STAND TO LEARN A THING OR TWO ABOUT BEING CALM FROM THEIR BROTHER, **LARRIGON.**

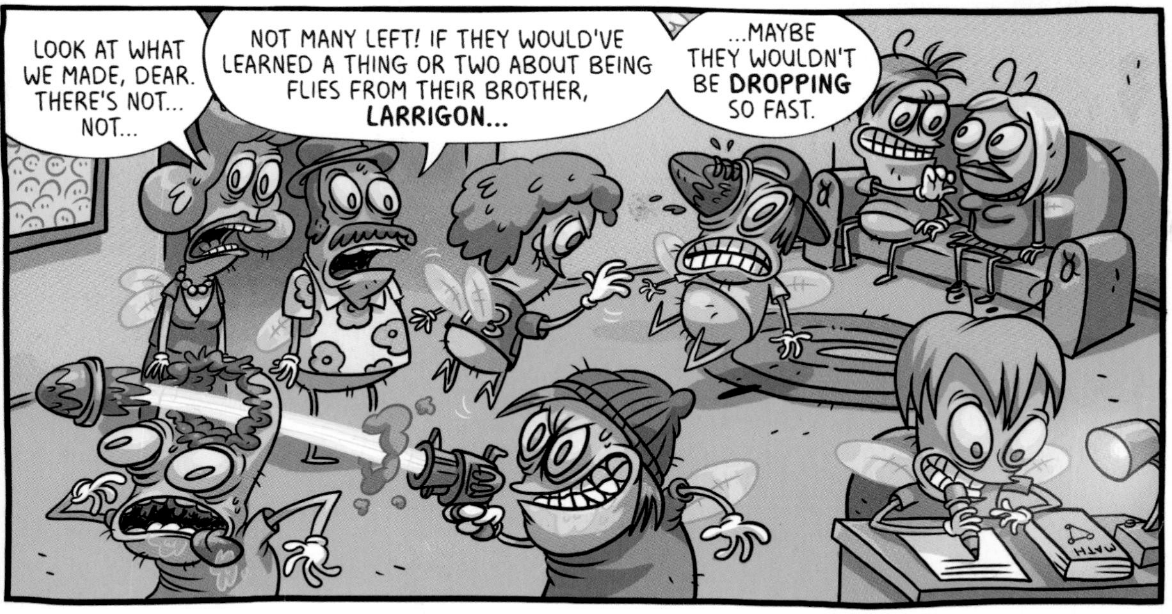
LOOK AT WHAT WE MADE, DEAR. THERE'S NOT... NOT...
NOT MANY LEFT! IF THEY WOULD'VE LEARNED A THING OR TWO ABOUT BEING FLIES FROM THEIR BROTHER, **LARRIGON...**
...MAYBE THEY WOULDN'T BE **DROPPING** SO FAST.
MATH

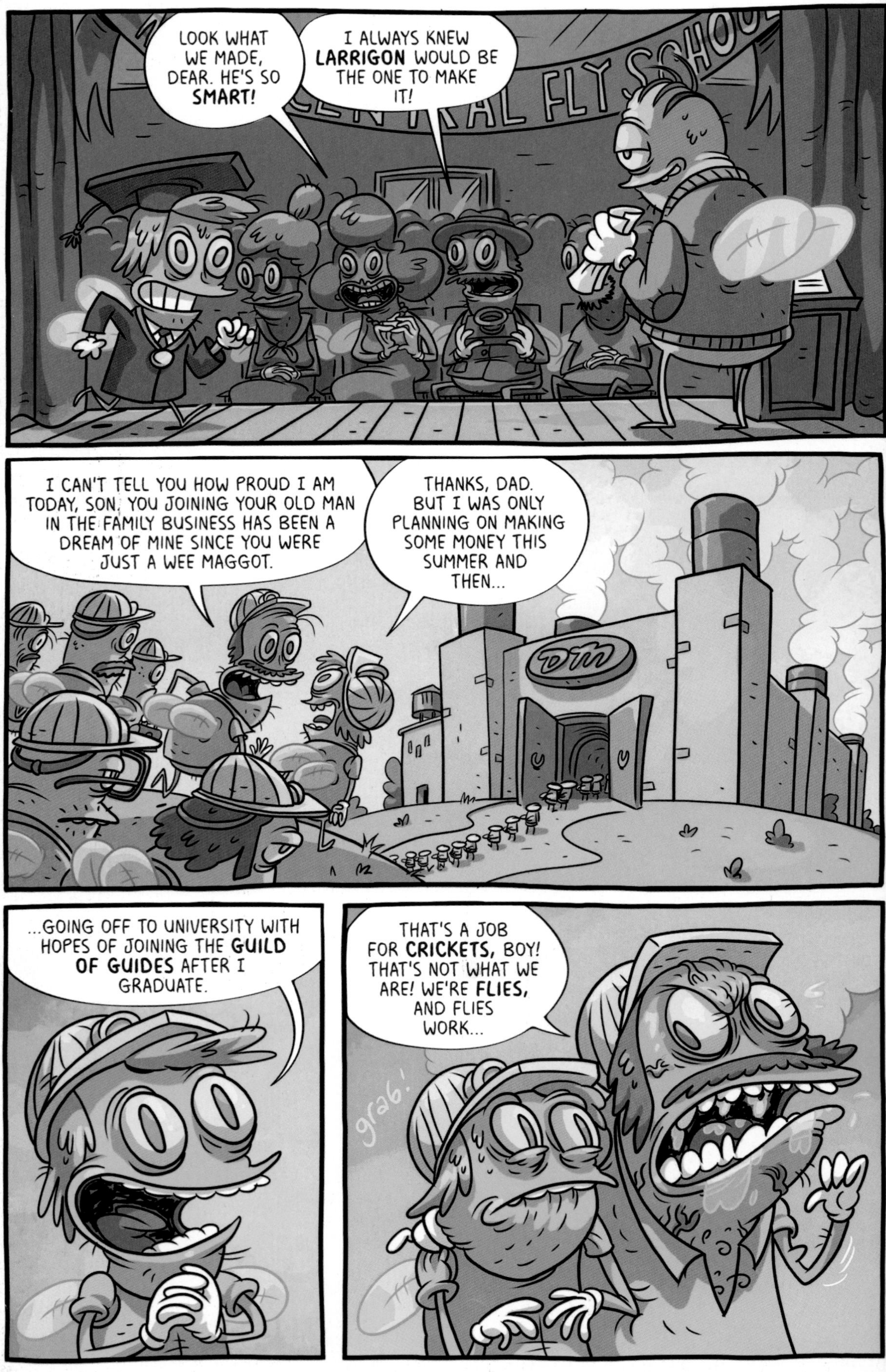
CENTRAL FLY SCHOOL
LOOK WHAT WE MADE, DEAR. HE'S SO **SMART!**
I ALWAYS KNEW **LARRIGON** WOULD BE THE ONE TO MAKE IT!
I CAN'T TELL YOU HOW PROUD I AM TODAY, SON. YOU JOINING YOUR OLD MAN IN THE FAMILY BUSINESS HAS BEEN A DREAM OF MINE SINCE YOU WERE JUST A WEE MAGGOT.
THANKS, DAD. BUT I WAS ONLY PLANNING ON MAKING SOME MONEY THIS SUMMER AND THEN...
DM
...GOING OFF TO UNIVERSITY WITH HOPES OF JOINING THE **GUILD OF GUIDES** AFTER I GRADUATE.
THAT'S A JOB FOR **CRICKETS,** BOY! THAT'S NOT WHAT WE ARE! WE'RE **FLIES,** AND FLIES WORK...
grab!

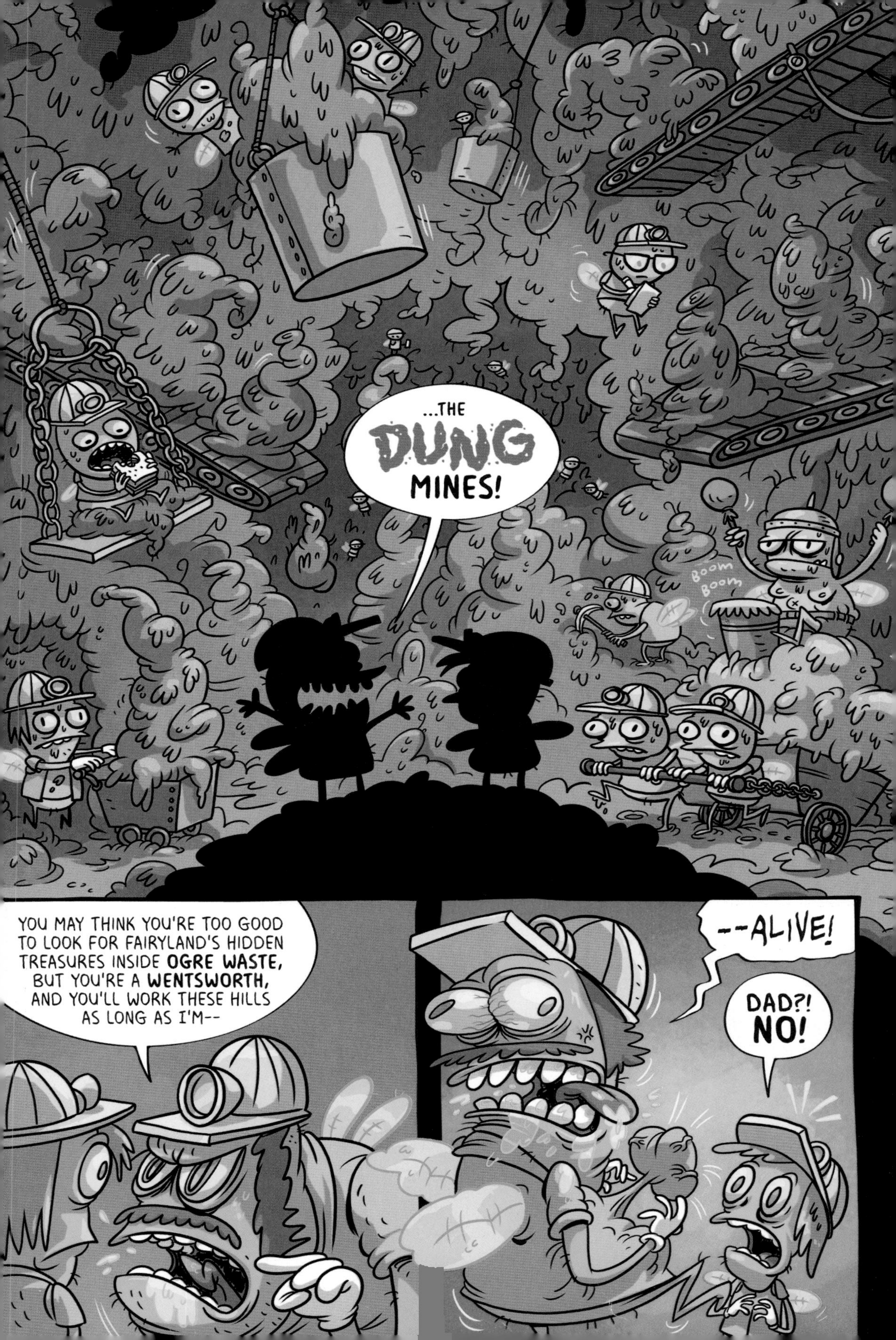
...THE DUNG MINES!
Boom Boom
YOU MAY THINK YOU'RE TOO GOOD TO LOOK FOR FAIRYLAND'S HIDDEN TREASURES INSIDE OGRE WASTE, BUT YOU'RE A WENTSWORTH, AND YOU'LL WORK THESE HILLS AS LONG AS I'M--
--ALIVE!
DAD?! NO!

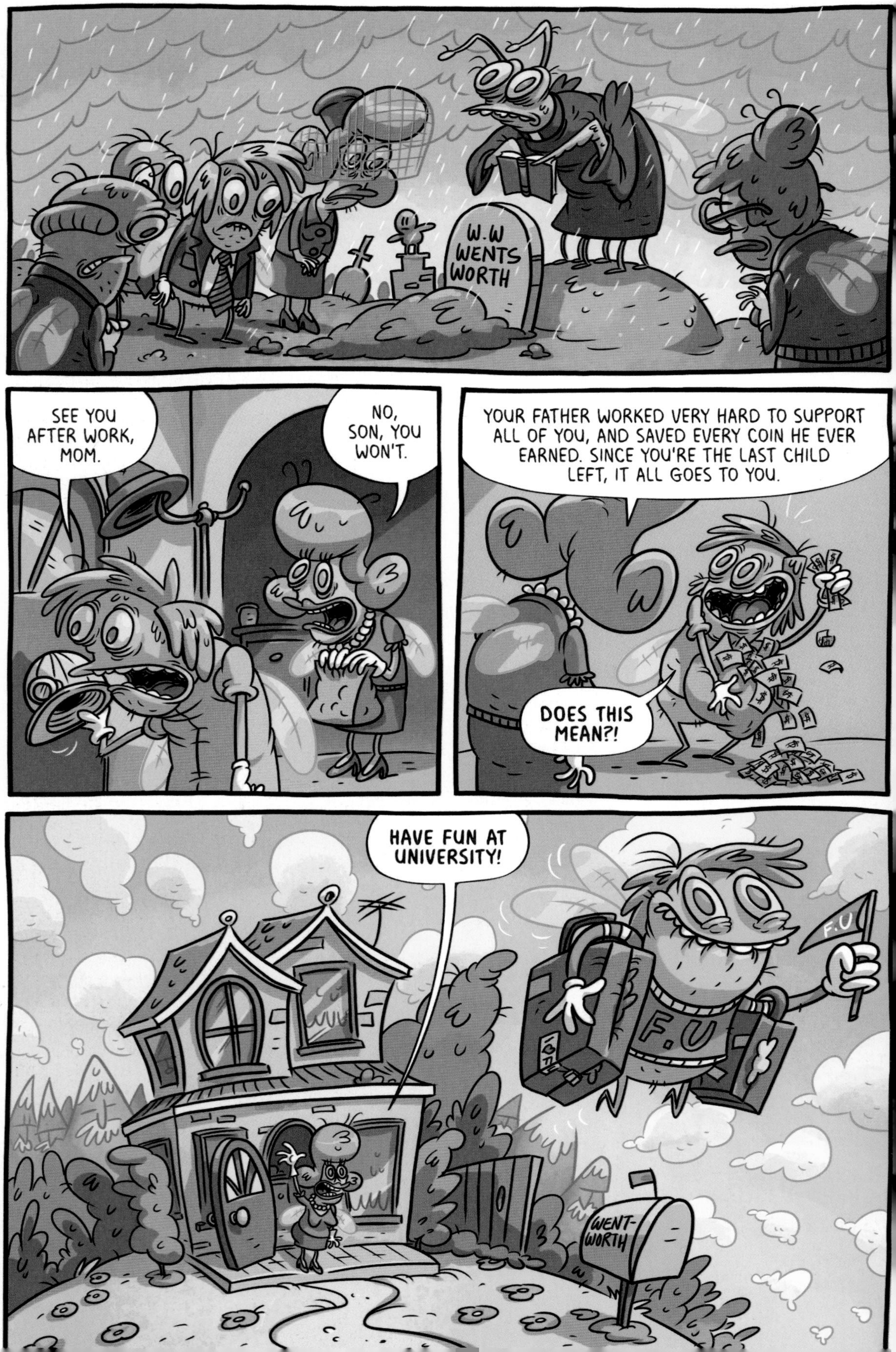
W.W WENTS WORTH
SEE YOU AFTER WORK, MOM.
NO, SON, YOU WON'T.
YOUR FATHER WORKED VERY HARD TO SUPPORT ALL OF YOU, AND SAVED EVERY COIN HE EVER EARNED. SINCE YOU'RE THE LAST CHILD LEFT, IT ALL GOES TO YOU.
DOES THIS MEAN?!
HAVE FUN AT UNIVERSITY!
F.U
F.U
WENT-WORTH

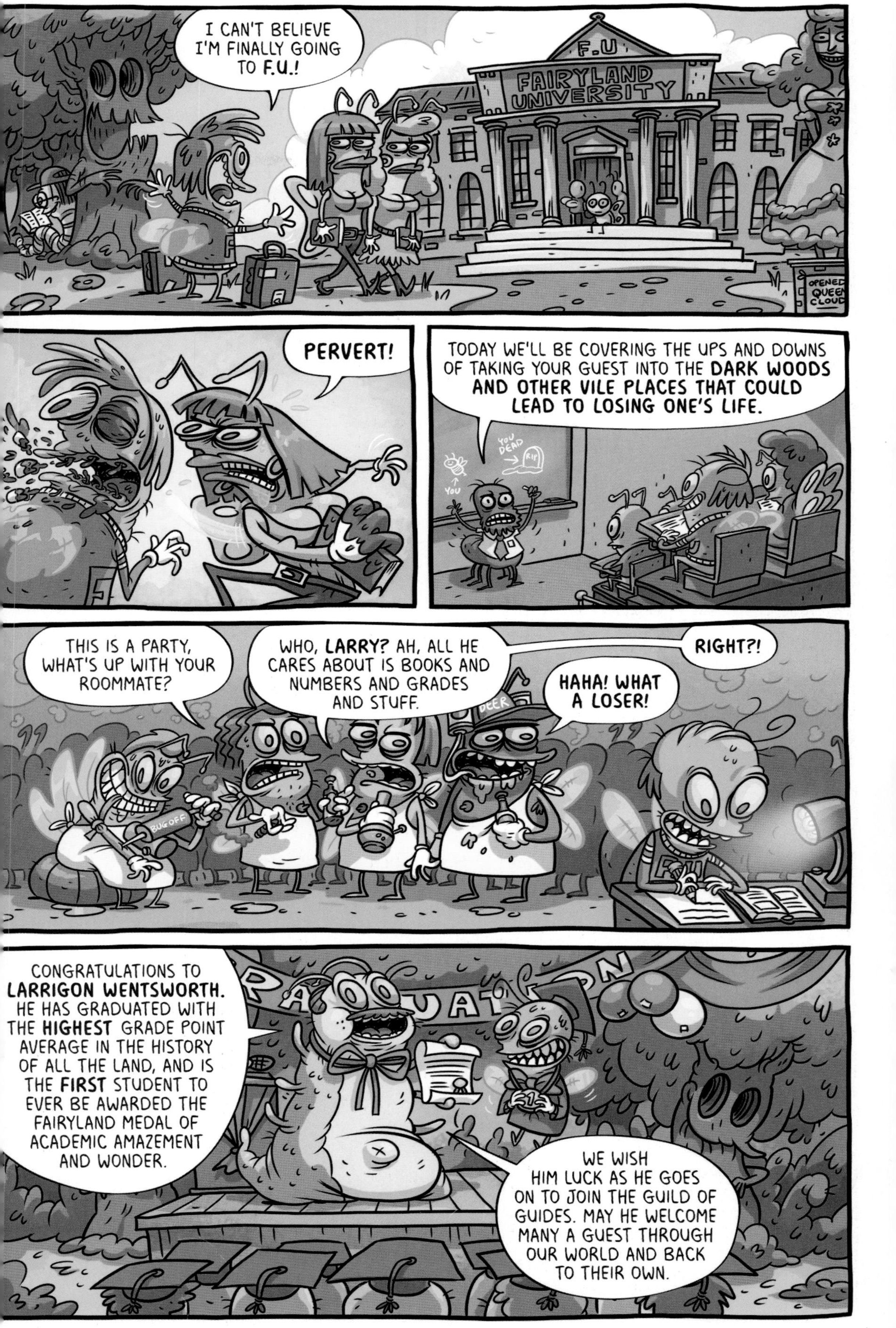

F.U
FAIRYLAND UNIVERSITY
I CAN'T BELIEVE I'M FINALLY GOING TO F.U.!
PERVERT!
TODAY WE'LL BE COVERING THE UPS AND DOWNS OF TAKING YOUR GUEST INTO THE DARK WOODS AND OTHER VILE PLACES THAT COULD LEAD TO LOSING ONE'S LIFE.
YOU DEAD
RIP
YOU
THIS IS A PARTY, WHAT'S UP WITH YOUR ROOMMATE?
WHO, LARRY? AH, ALL HE CARES ABOUT IS BOOKS AND NUMBERS AND GRADES AND STUFF.
RIGHT?!
HAHA! WHAT A LOSER!
BUG OFF
DEER
CONGRATULATIONS TO LARRIGON WENTSWORTH. HE HAS GRADUATED WITH THE HIGHEST GRADE POINT AVERAGE IN THE HISTORY OF ALL THE LAND, AND IS THE FIRST STUDENT TO EVER BE AWARDED THE FAIRYLAND MEDAL OF ACADEMIC AMAZEMENT AND WONDER.
WE WISH HIM LUCK AS HE GOES ON TO JOIN THE GUILD OF GUIDES. MAY HE WELCOME MANY A GUEST THROUGH OUR WORLD AND BACK TO THEIR OWN.

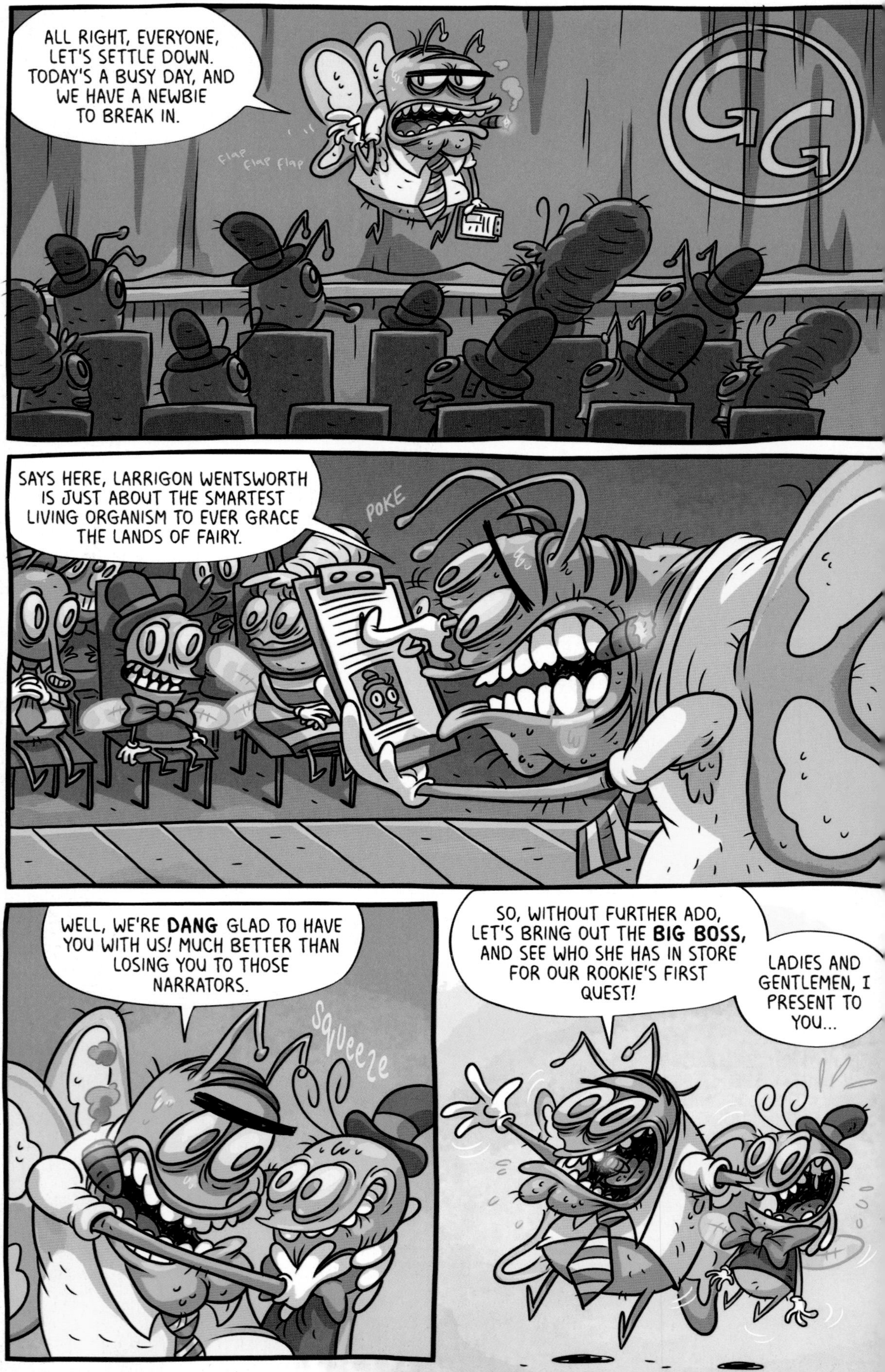
ALL RIGHT, EVERYONE, LET'S SETTLE DOWN. TODAY'S A BUSY DAY, AND WE HAVE A NEWBIE TO BREAK IN.
flap flap flap
SAYS HERE, LARRIGON WENTSWORTH IS JUST ABOUT THE SMARTEST LIVING ORGANISM TO EVER GRACE THE LANDS OF FAIRY.
POKE
WELL, WE'RE **DANG** GLAD TO HAVE YOU WITH US! MUCH BETTER THAN LOSING YOU TO THOSE NARRATORS.
squeeze
SO, WITHOUT FURTHER ADO, LET'S BRING OUT THE **BIG BOSS**, AND SEE WHO SHE HAS IN STORE FOR OUR ROOKIE'S FIRST QUEST!
LADIES AND GENTLEMEN, I PRESENT TO YOU...

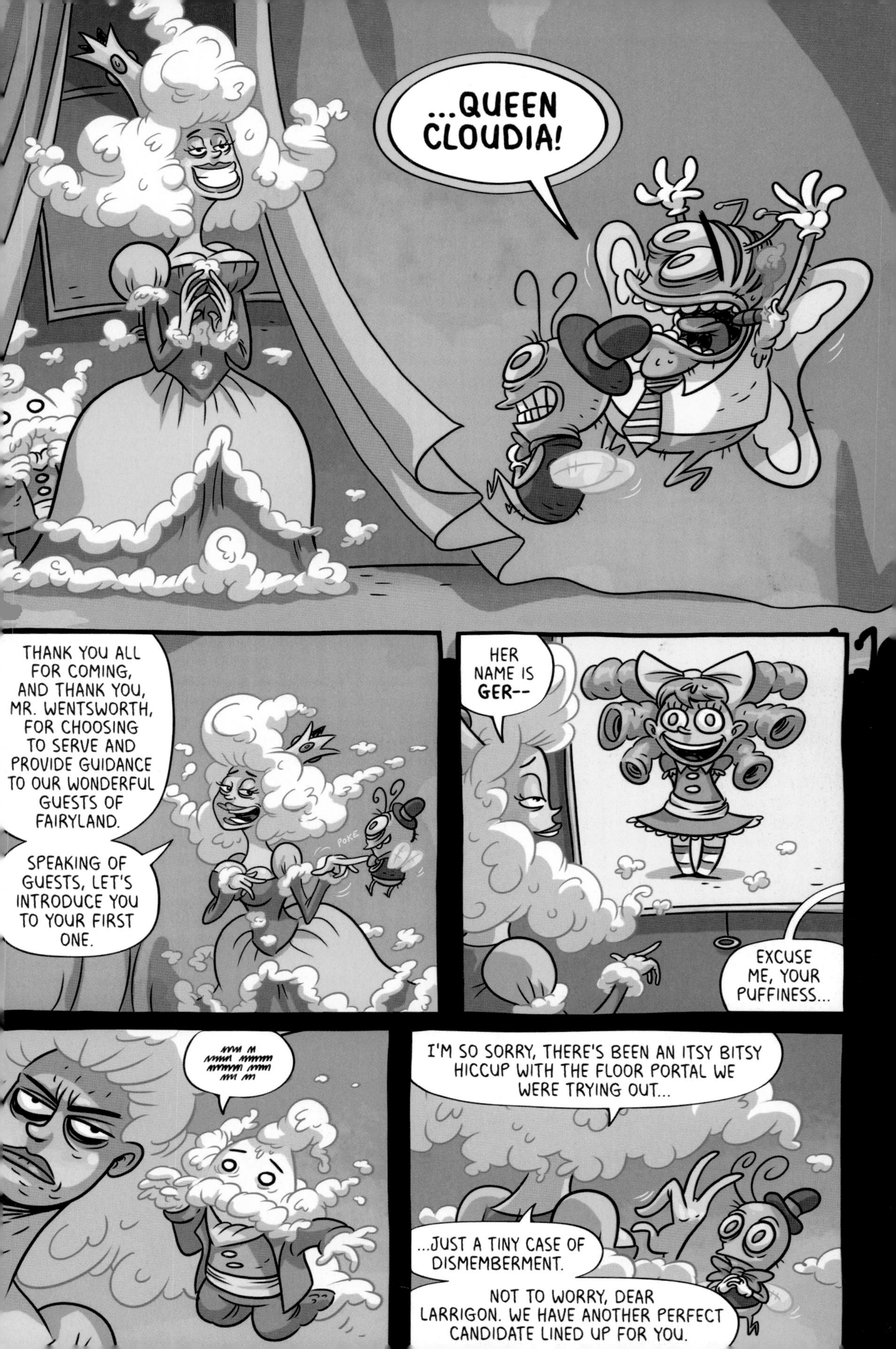
...QUEEN CLOUDIA!
THANK YOU ALL FOR COMING, AND THANK YOU, MR. WENTSWORTH, FOR CHOOSING TO SERVE AND PROVIDE GUIDANCE TO OUR WONDERFUL GUESTS OF FAIRYLAND.
SPEAKING OF GUESTS, LET'S INTRODUCE YOU TO YOUR FIRST ONE.
POKE
HER NAME IS GER--
EXCUSE ME, YOUR PUFFINESS...
I'M SO SORRY, THERE'S BEEN AN ITSY BITSY HICCUP WITH THE FLOOR PORTAL WE WERE TRYING OUT...
...JUST A TINY CASE OF DISMEMBERMENT.
NOT TO WORRY, DEAR LARRIGON. WE HAVE ANOTHER PERFECT CANDIDATE LINED UP FOR YOU.

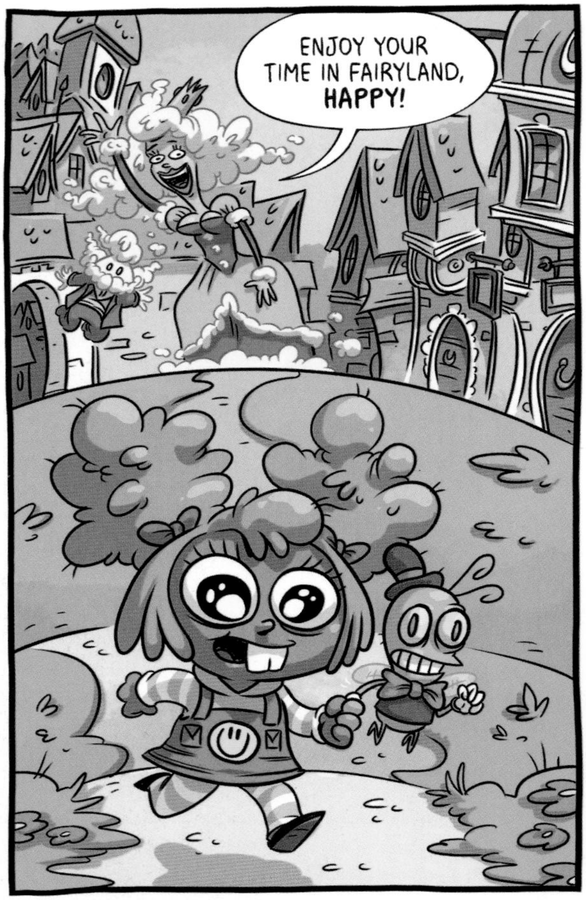
ENJOY YOUR TIME IN FAIRYLAND, **HAPPY!**

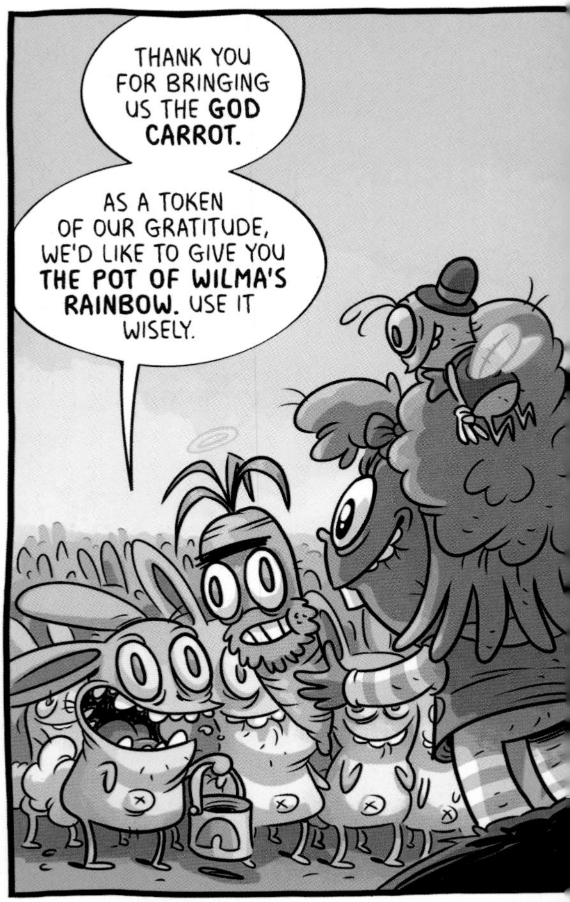
THANK YOU FOR BRINGING US THE **GOD CARROT.**
AS A TOKEN OF OUR GRATITUDE, WE'D LIKE TO GIVE YOU **THE POT OF WILMA'S RAINBOW.** USE IT WISELY.

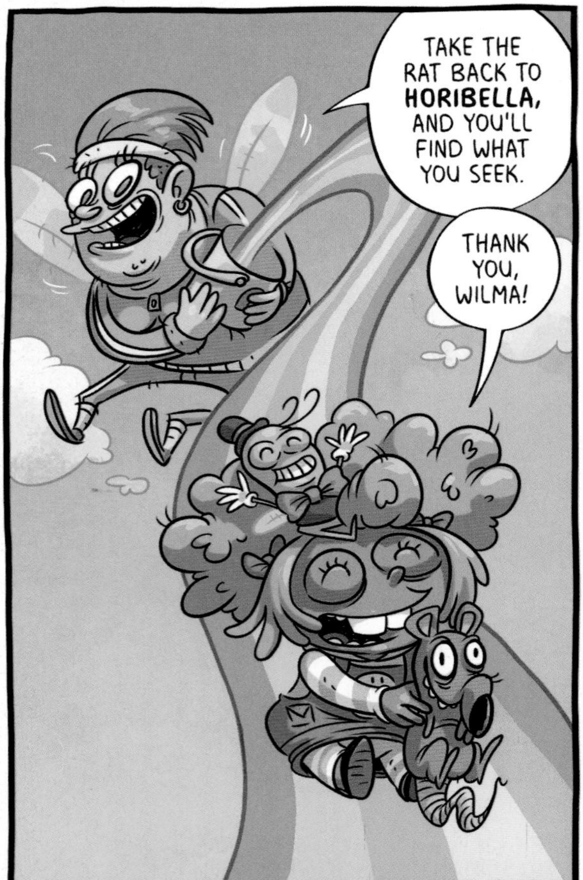
TAKE THE RAT BACK TO **HORIBELLA,** AND YOU'LL FIND WHAT YOU SEEK.
THANK YOU, WILMA!

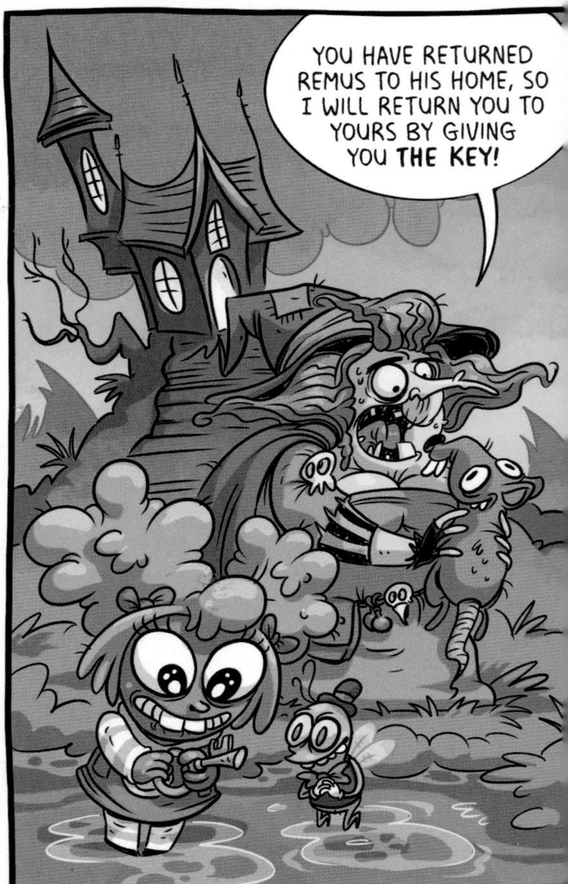
YOU HAVE RETURNED REMUS TO HIS HOME, SO I WILL RETURN YOU TO YOURS BY GIVING YOU **THE KEY!**

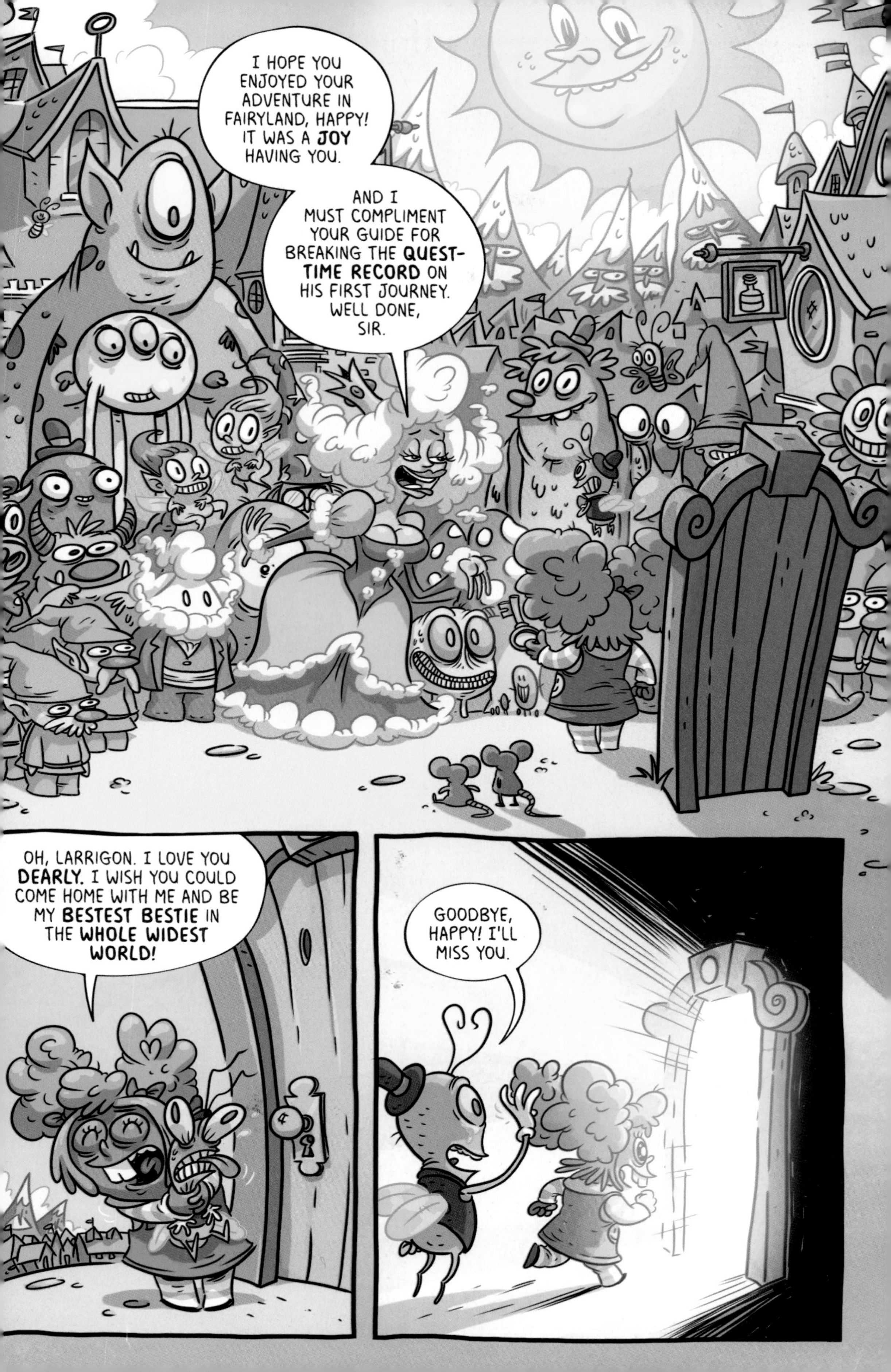

I HOPE YOU ENJOYED YOUR ADVENTURE IN FAIRYLAND, HAPPY! IT WAS A **JOY** HAVING YOU.
AND I MUST COMPLIMENT YOUR GUIDE FOR BREAKING THE **QUEST-TIME RECORD** ON HIS FIRST JOURNEY. WELL DONE, SIR.
OH, LARRIGON. I LOVE YOU **DEARLY.** I WISH YOU COULD COME HOME WITH ME AND BE MY **BESTEST BESTIE** IN THE **WHOLE WIDEST WORLD!**
GOODBYE, HAPPY! I'LL MISS YOU.

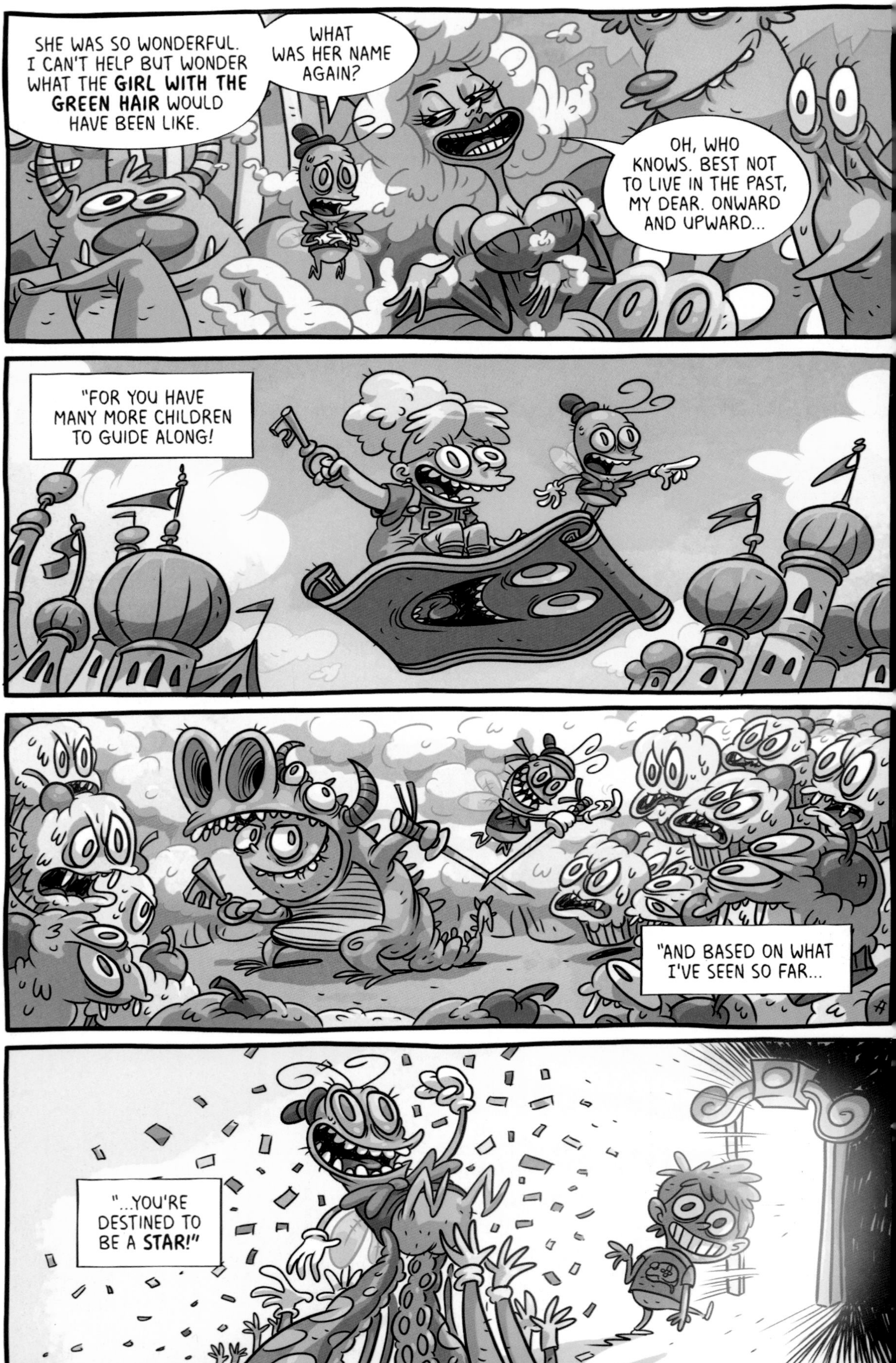
SHE WAS SO WONDERFUL. I CAN'T HELP BUT WONDER WHAT THE **GIRL WITH THE GREEN HAIR** WOULD HAVE BEEN LIKE.
WHAT WAS HER NAME AGAIN?
OH, WHO KNOWS. BEST NOT TO LIVE IN THE PAST, MY DEAR. ONWARD AND UPWARD...
"FOR YOU HAVE MANY MORE CHILDREN TO GUIDE ALONG!
"AND BASED ON WHAT I'VE SEEN SO FAR...
"...YOU'RE DESTINED TO BE A **STAR!**"

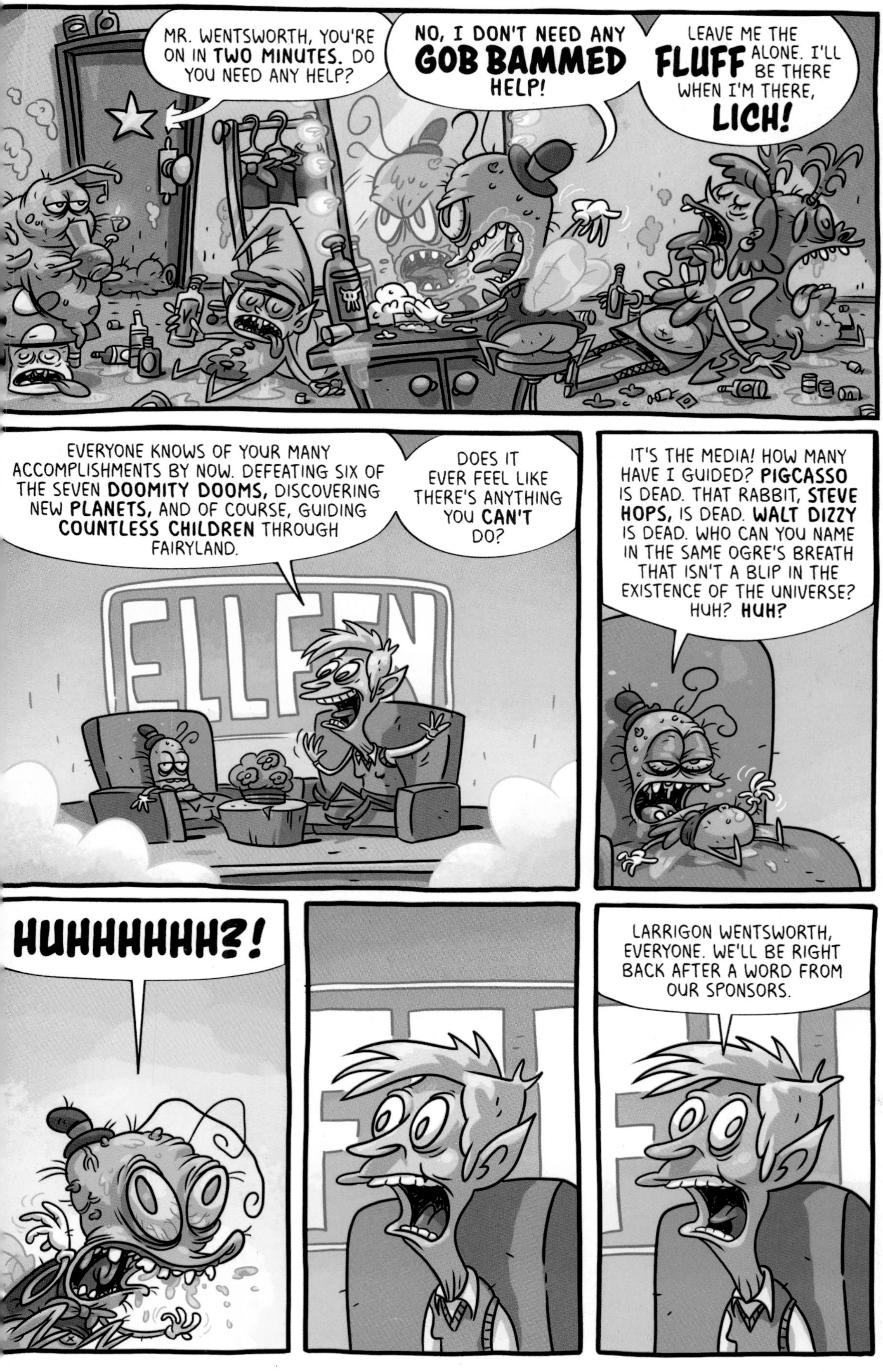
MR. WENTSWORTH, YOU'RE ON IN TWO MINUTES. DO YOU NEED ANY HELP?
NO, I DON'T NEED ANY GOB BAMMED HELP!
LEAVE ME THE FLUFF ALONE. I'LL BE THERE WHEN I'M THERE, LICH!
EVERYONE KNOWS OF YOUR MANY ACCOMPLISHMENTS BY NOW. DEFEATING SIX OF THE SEVEN DOOMITY DOOMS, DISCOVERING NEW PLANETS, AND OF COURSE, GUIDING COUNTLESS CHILDREN THROUGH FAIRYLAND.
DOES IT EVER FEEL LIKE THERE'S ANYTHING YOU CAN'T DO?
ELLEN
IT'S THE MEDIA! HOW MANY HAVE I GUIDED? PIGCASSO IS DEAD. THAT RABBIT, STEVE HOPS, IS DEAD. WALT DIZZY IS DEAD. WHO CAN YOU NAME IN THE SAME OGRE'S BREATH THAT ISN'T A BLIP IN THE EXISTENCE OF THE UNIVERSE? HUH? HUH?
HUHHHHHH?!
LARRIGON WENTSWORTH, EVERYONE. WE'LL BE RIGHT BACK AFTER A WORD FROM OUR SPONSORS.

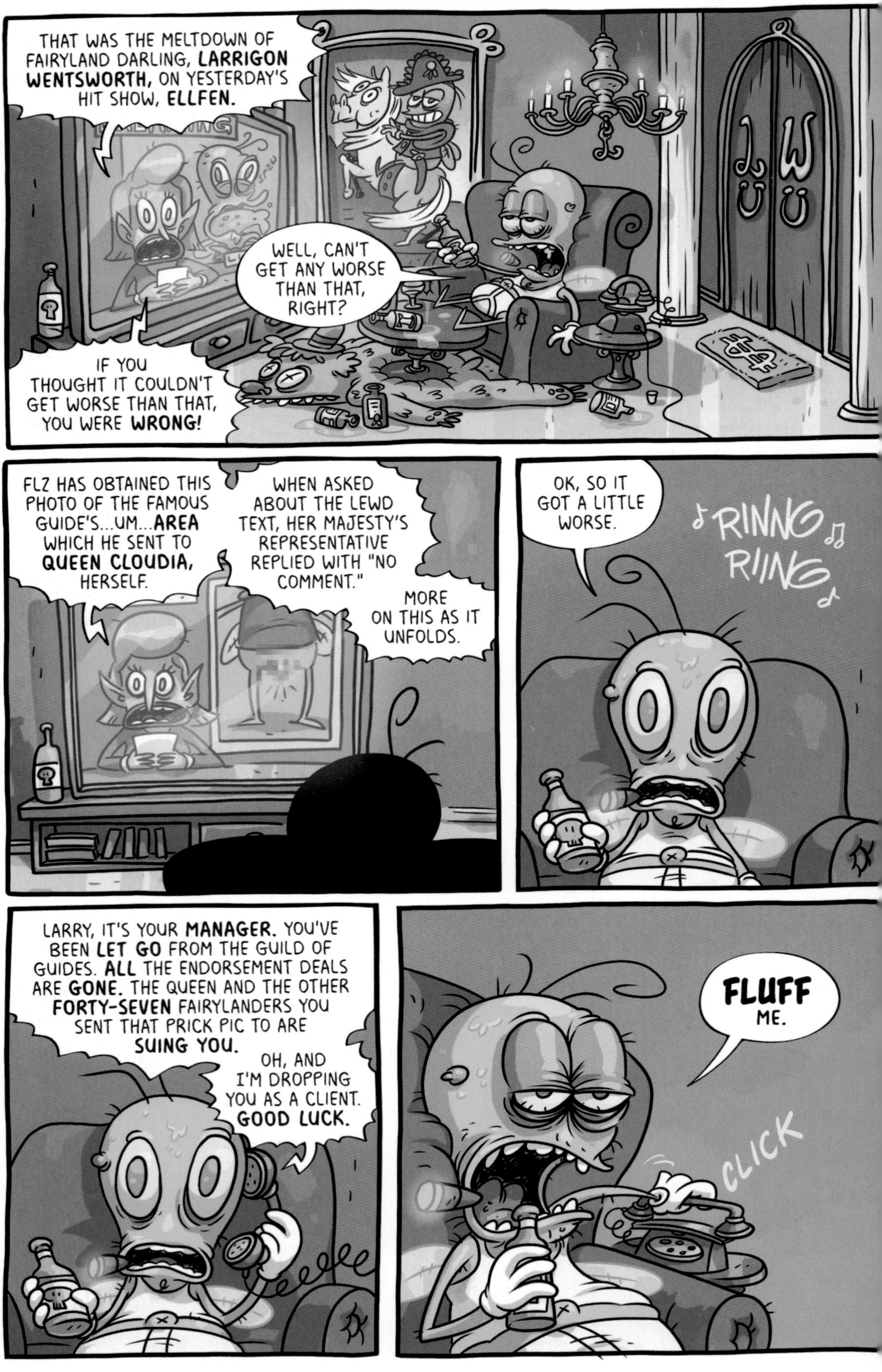
THAT WAS THE MELTDOWN OF FAIRYLAND DARLING, **LARRIGON WENTSWORTH,** ON YESTERDAY'S HIT SHOW, **ELLFEN.**
WELL, CAN'T GET ANY WORSE THAN THAT, RIGHT?
IF YOU THOUGHT IT COULDN'T GET WORSE THAN THAT, YOU WERE **WRONG!**
FLZ HAS OBTAINED THIS PHOTO OF THE FAMOUS GUIDE'S...UM...**AREA** WHICH HE SENT TO **QUEEN CLOUDIA,** HERSELF.
WHEN ASKED ABOUT THE LEWD TEXT, HER MAJESTY'S REPRESENTATIVE REPLIED WITH "NO COMMENT."
MORE ON THIS AS IT UNFOLDS.
OK, SO IT GOT A LITTLE WORSE.
RINNG RIING
LARRY, IT'S YOUR **MANAGER.** YOU'VE BEEN **LET GO** FROM THE GUILD OF GUIDES. **ALL** THE ENDORSEMENT DEALS ARE **GONE.** THE QUEEN AND THE OTHER **FORTY-SEVEN** FAIRYLANDERS YOU SENT THAT PRICK PIC TO ARE **SUING YOU.**
OH, AND I'M DROPPING YOU AS A CLIENT. **GOOD LUCK.**
FLUFF ME.
CLICK

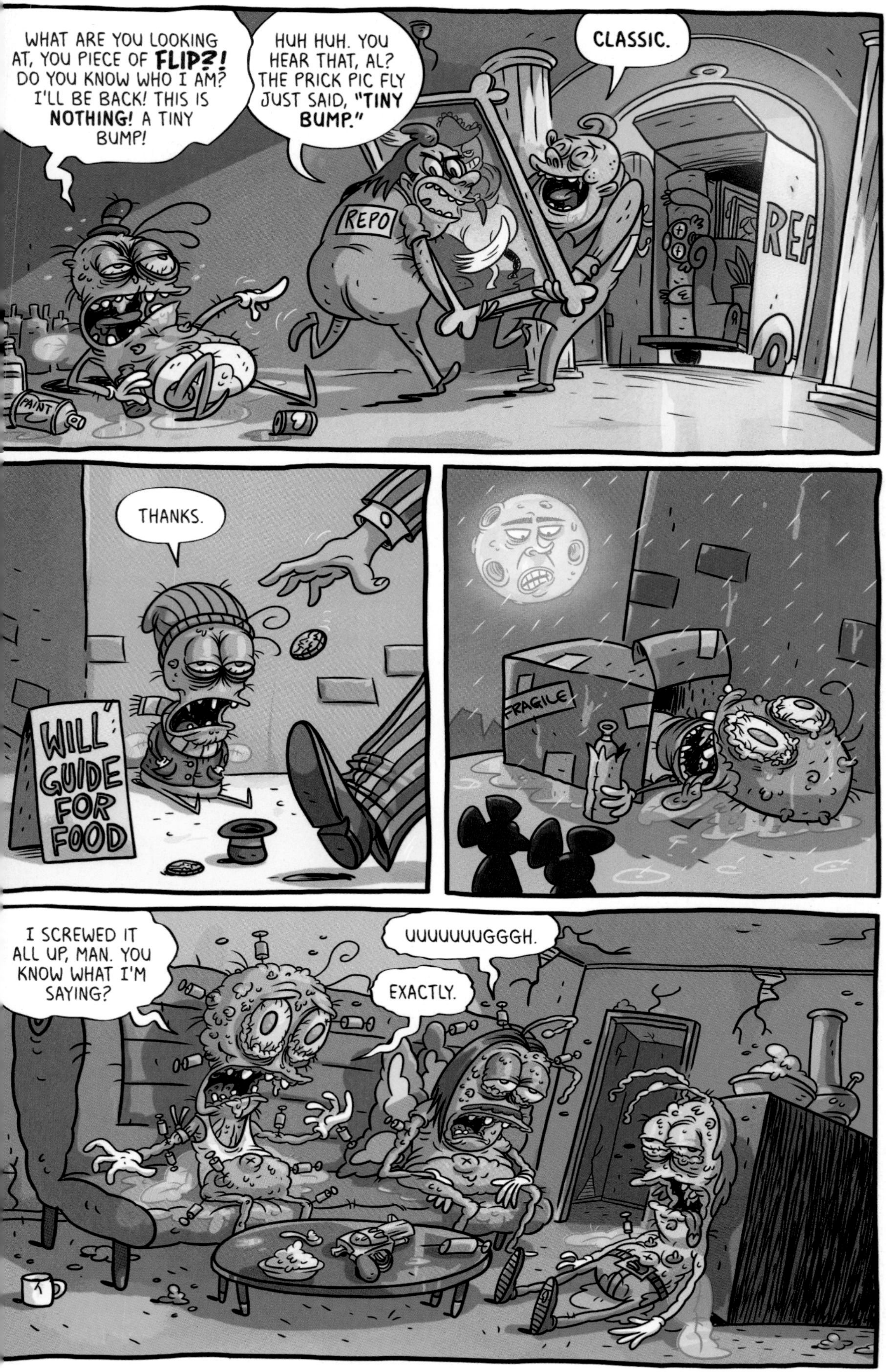
WHAT ARE YOU LOOKING AT, YOU PIECE OF **FLIP?!** DO YOU KNOW WHO I AM? I'LL BE BACK! THIS IS **NOTHING!** A TINY BUMP!
HUH HUH. YOU HEAR THAT, AL? THE PRICK PIC FLY JUST SAID, **"TINY BUMP."**
CLASSIC.
REPO
REP
PAINT
THANKS.
WILL GUIDE FOR FOOD
FRAGILE
I SCREWED IT ALL UP, MAN. YOU KNOW WHAT I'M SAYING?
UUUUUUUGGGH.
EXACTLY.

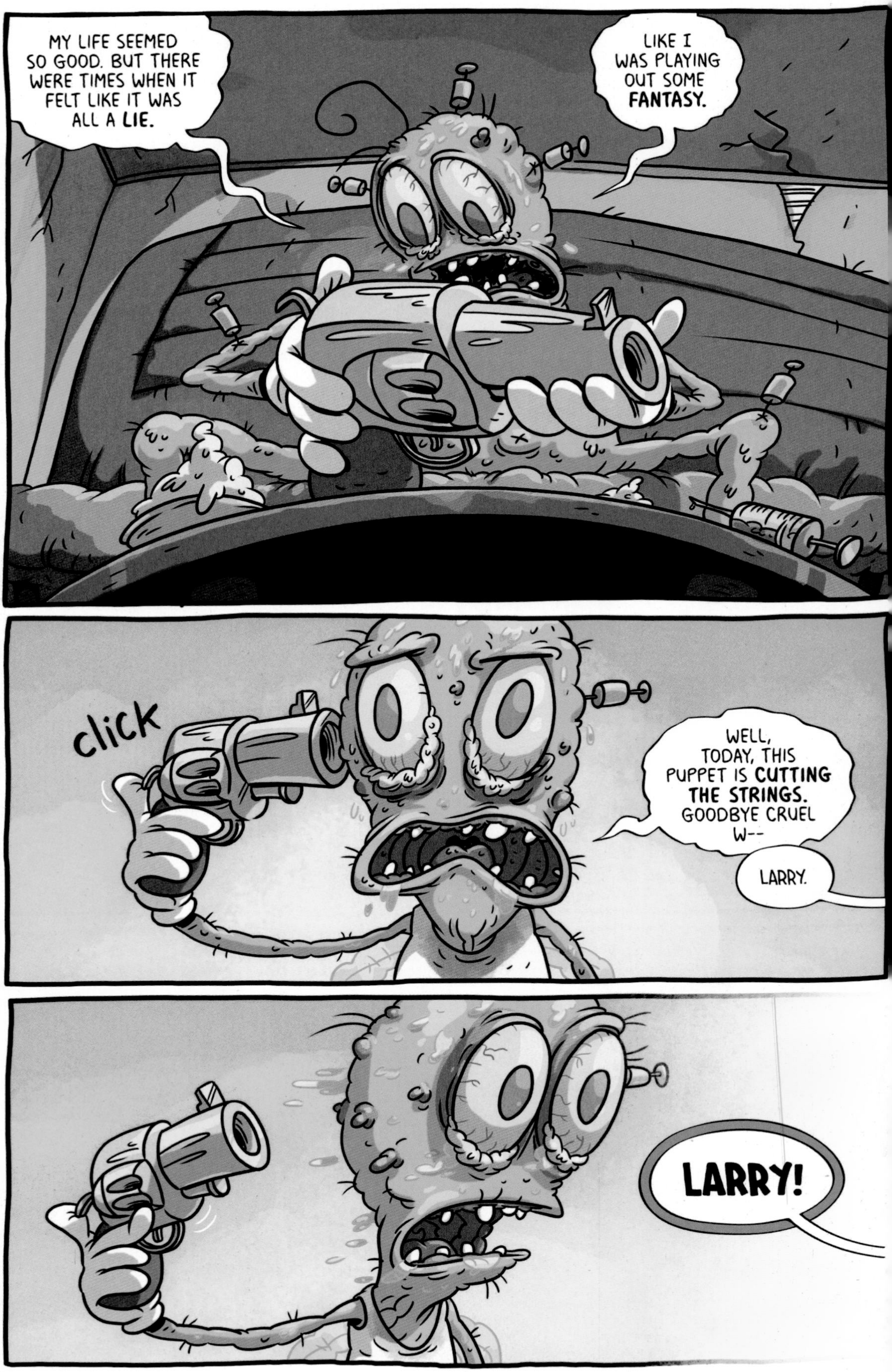
MY LIFE SEEMED SO GOOD. BUT THERE WERE TIMES WHEN IT FELT LIKE IT WAS ALL A **LIE.**
LIKE I WAS PLAYING OUT SOME **FANTASY.**
click
WELL, TODAY, THIS PUPPET IS **CUTTING THE STRINGS.** GOODBYE CRUEL W--
LARRY.
LARRY!

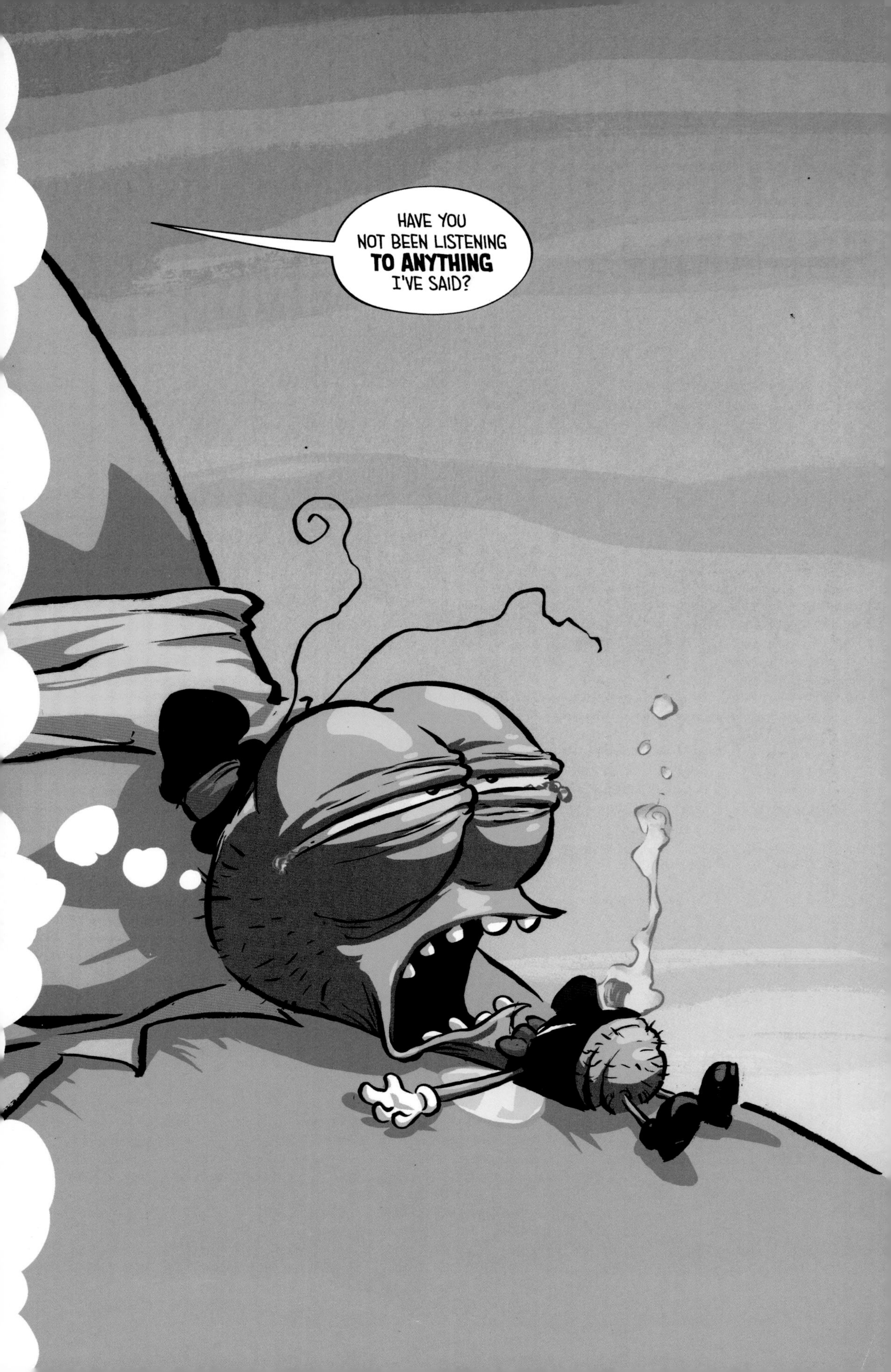
HAVE YOU NOT BEEN LISTENING **TO ANYTHING** I'VE SAID?

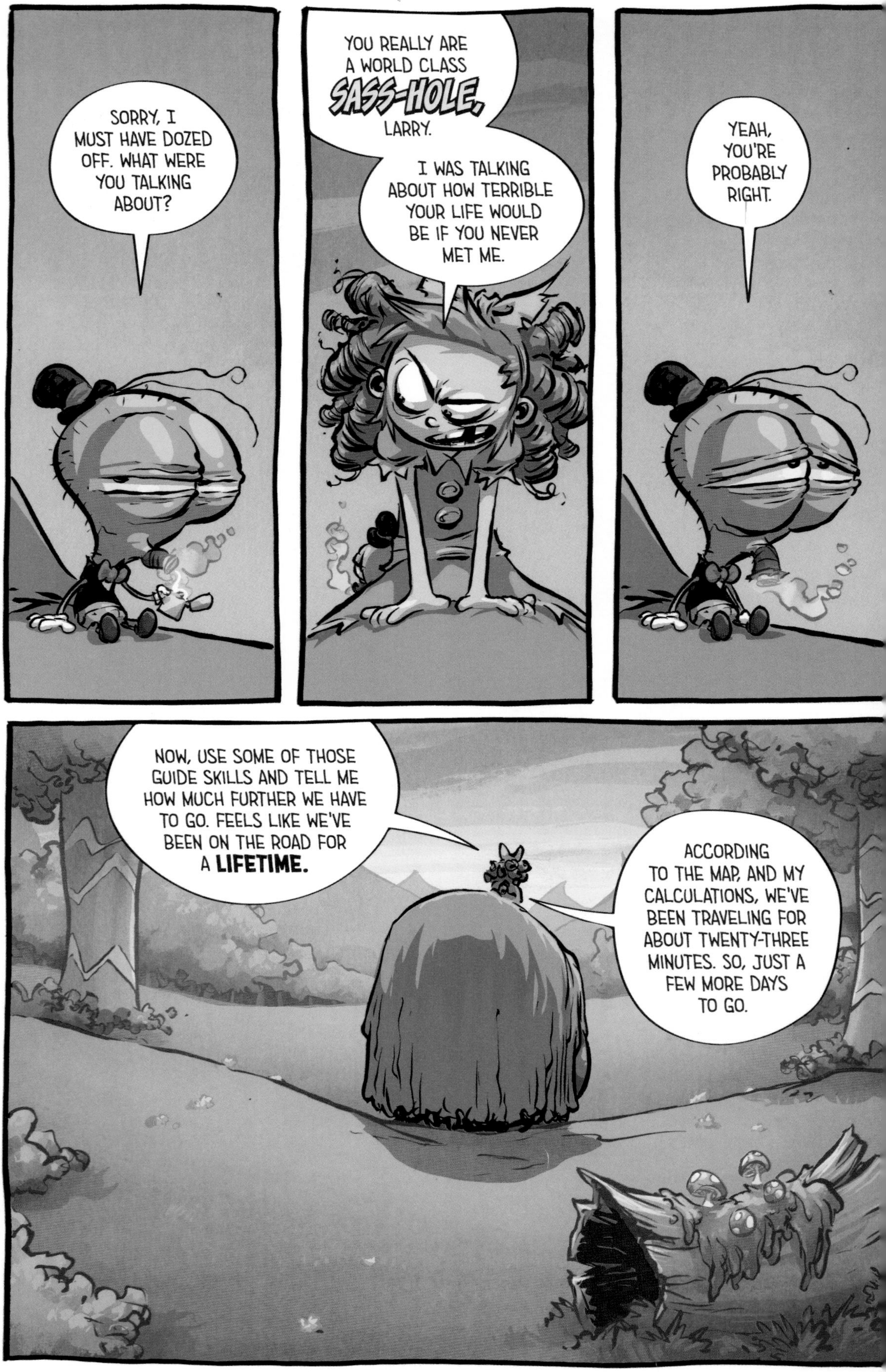
SORRY, I MUST HAVE DOZED OFF. WHAT WERE YOU TALKING ABOUT?
YOU REALLY ARE A WORLD CLASS SASS-HOLE, LARRY.
I WAS TALKING ABOUT HOW TERRIBLE YOUR LIFE WOULD BE IF YOU NEVER MET ME.
YEAH, YOU'RE PROBABLY RIGHT.
NOW, USE SOME OF THOSE GUIDE SKILLS AND TELL ME HOW MUCH FURTHER WE HAVE TO GO. FEELS LIKE WE'VE BEEN ON THE ROAD FOR A **LIFETIME.**
ACCORDING TO THE MAP, AND MY CALCULATIONS, WE'VE BEEN TRAVELING FOR ABOUT TWENTY-THREE MINUTES. SO, JUST A FEW MORE DAYS TO GO.

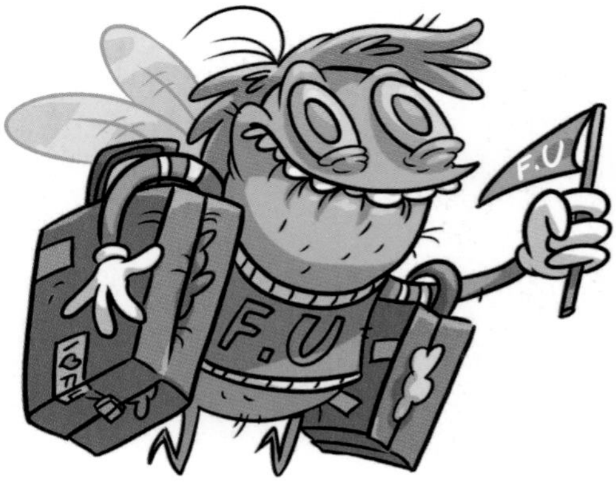
F.U
F.U

FOURTEEN

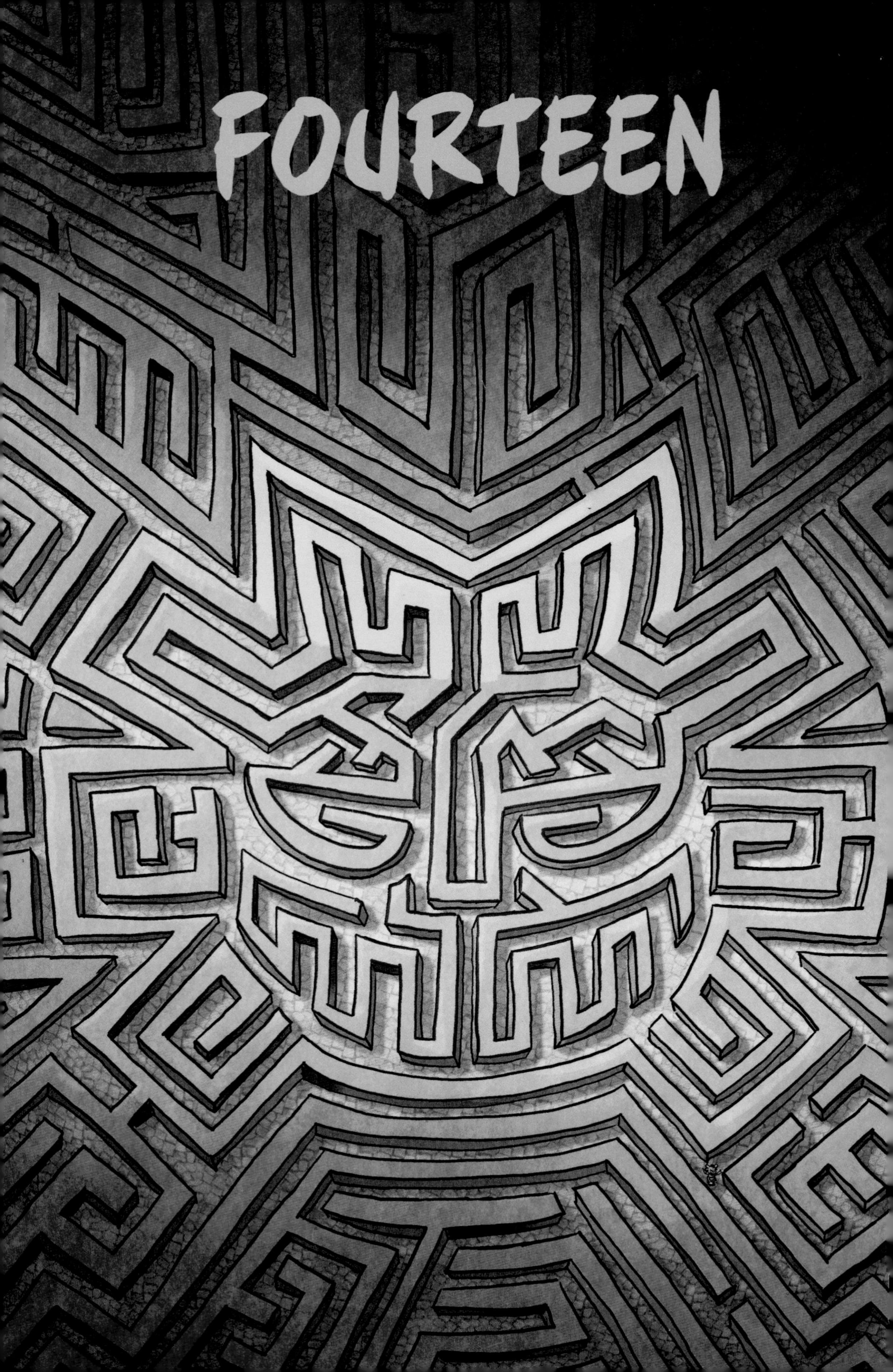

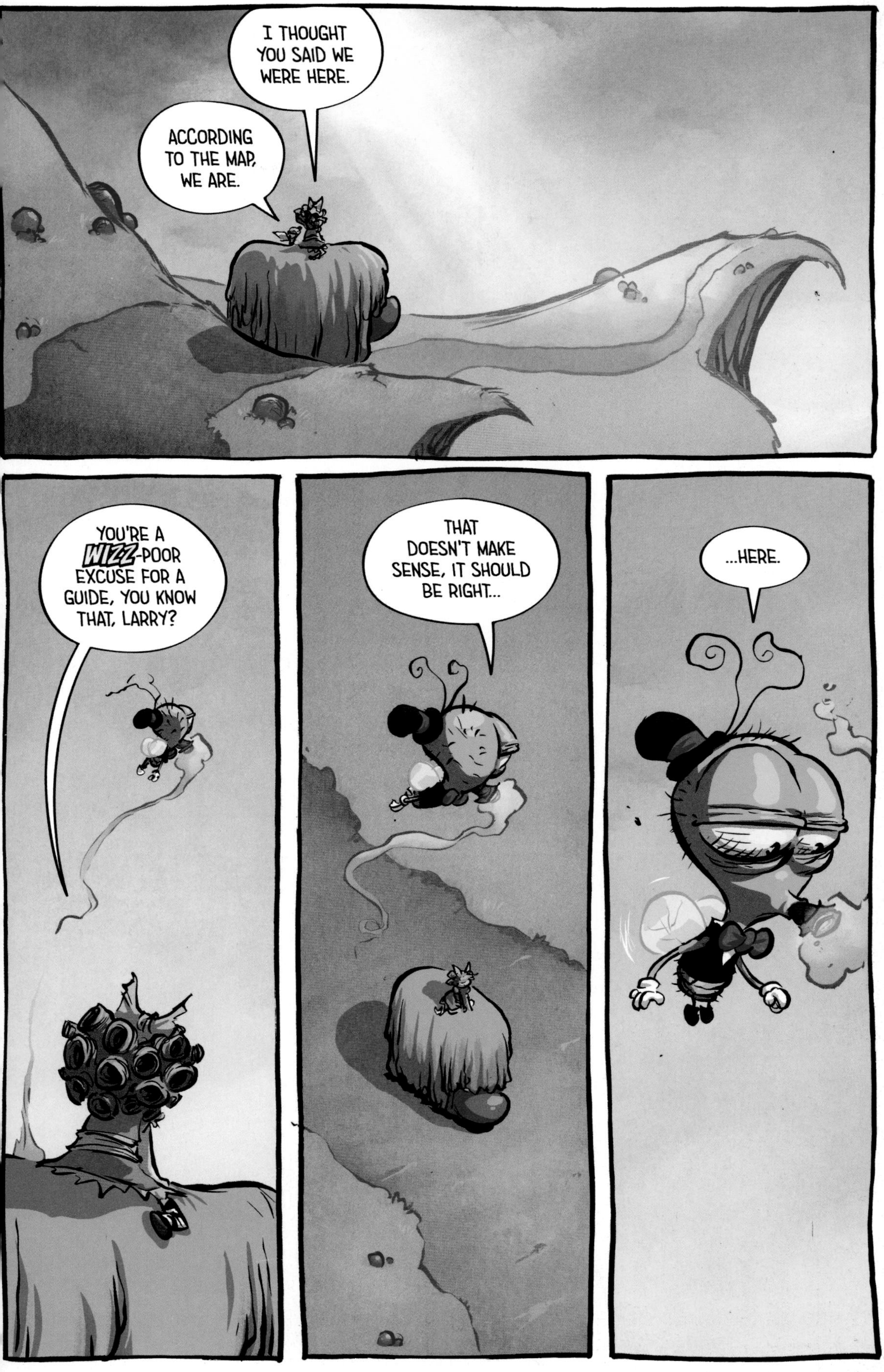
I THOUGHT YOU SAID WE WERE HERE.
ACCORDING TO THE MAP, WE ARE.
YOU'RE A WIZZ-POOR EXCUSE FOR A GUIDE, YOU KNOW THAT, LARRY?
THAT DOESN'T MAKE SENSE, IT SHOULD BE RIGHT...
...HERE.

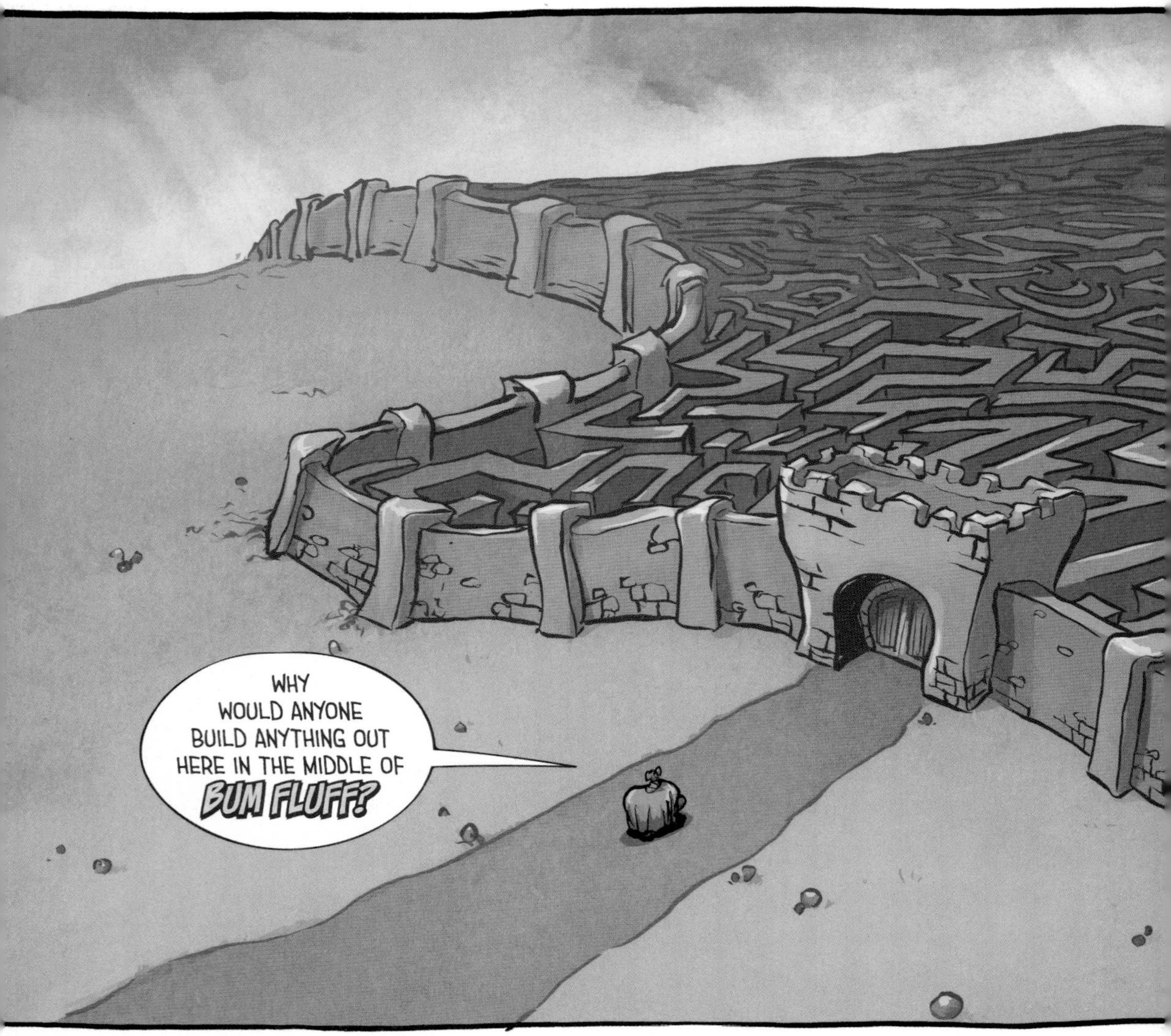
WHY WOULD ANYONE BUILD ANYTHING OUT HERE IN THE MIDDLE OF BUM FLUFF?

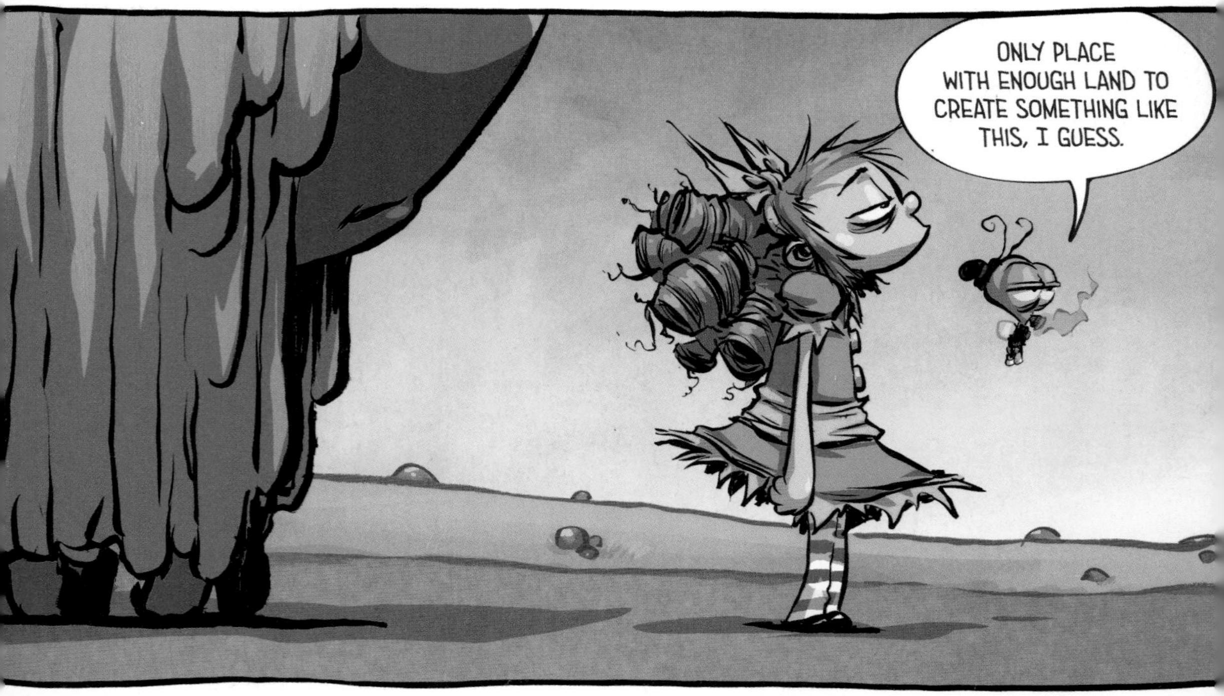
ONLY PLACE WITH ENOUGH LAND TO CREATE SOMETHING LIKE THIS, I GUESS.

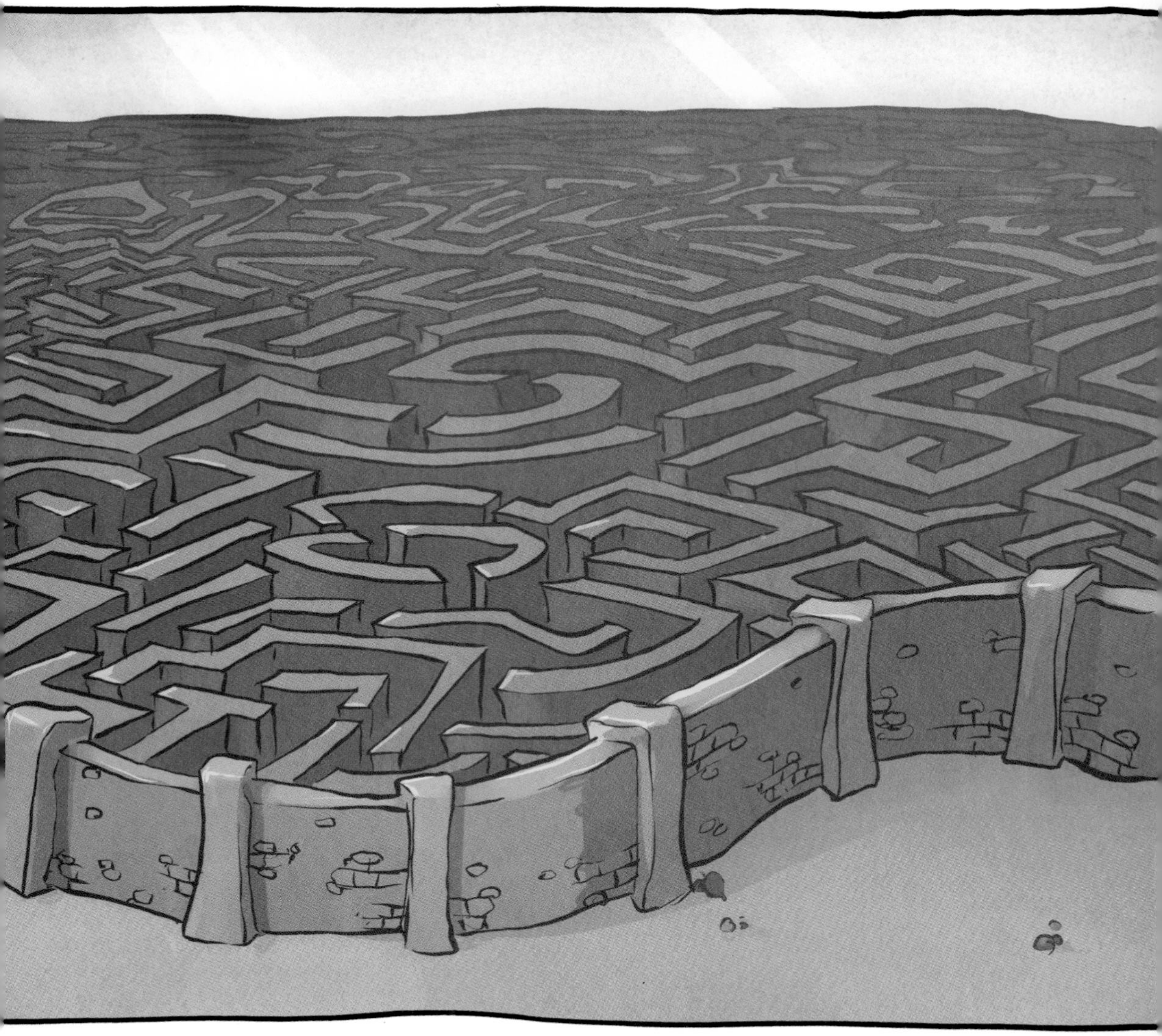

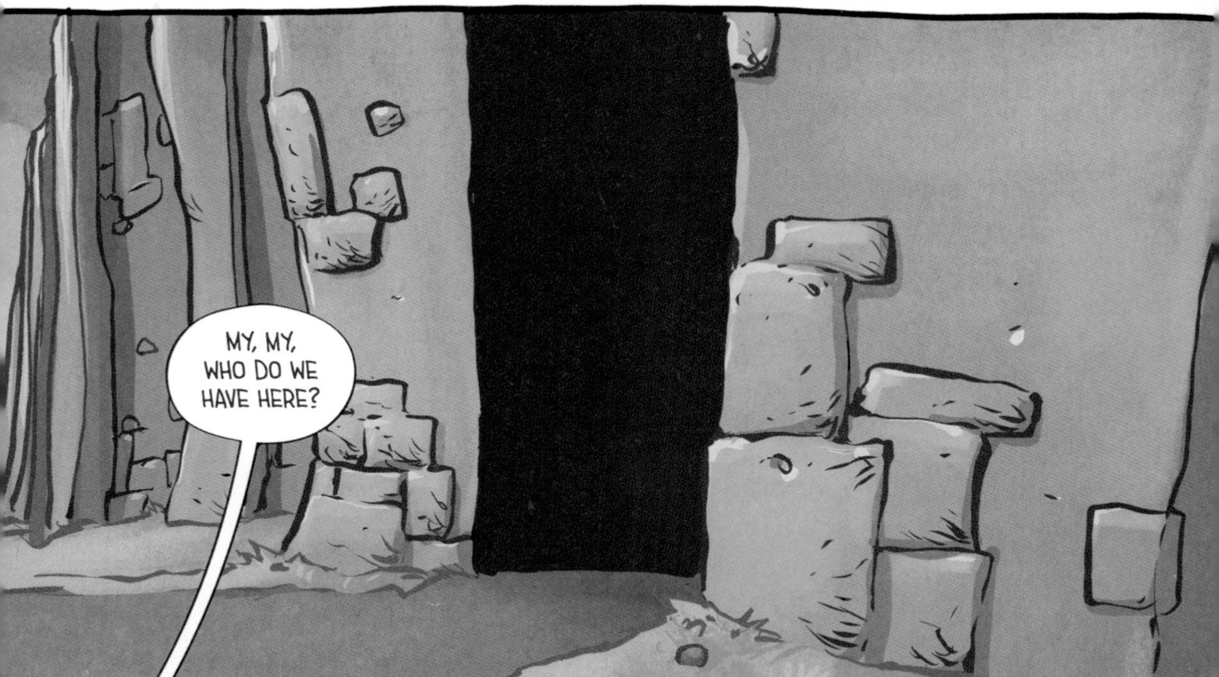
MY, MY, WHO DO WE HAVE HERE?

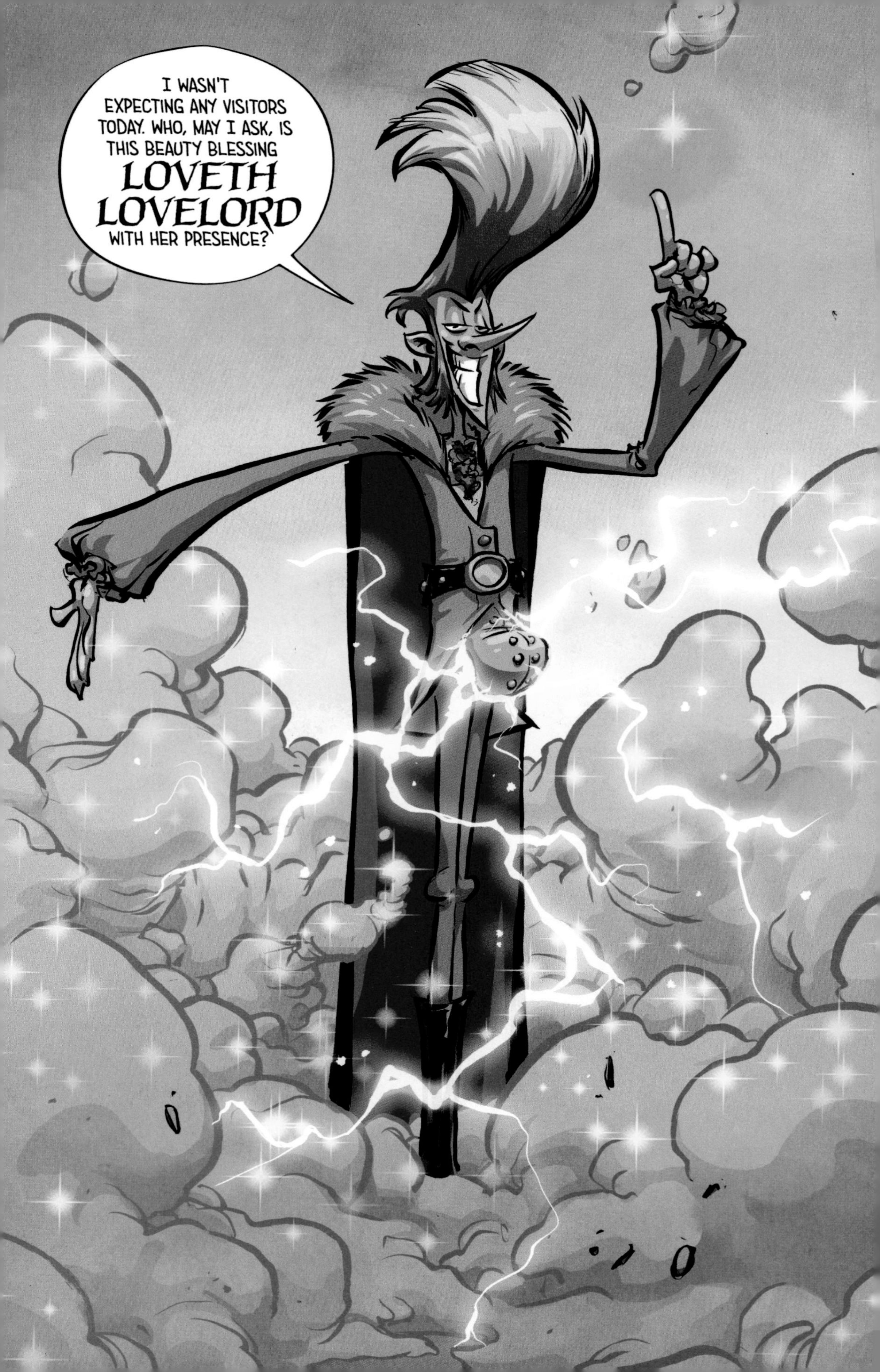
I WASN'T EXPECTING ANY VISITORS TODAY. WHO, MAY I ASK, IS THIS BEAUTY BLESSING LOVETH LOVELORD WITH HER PRESENCE?

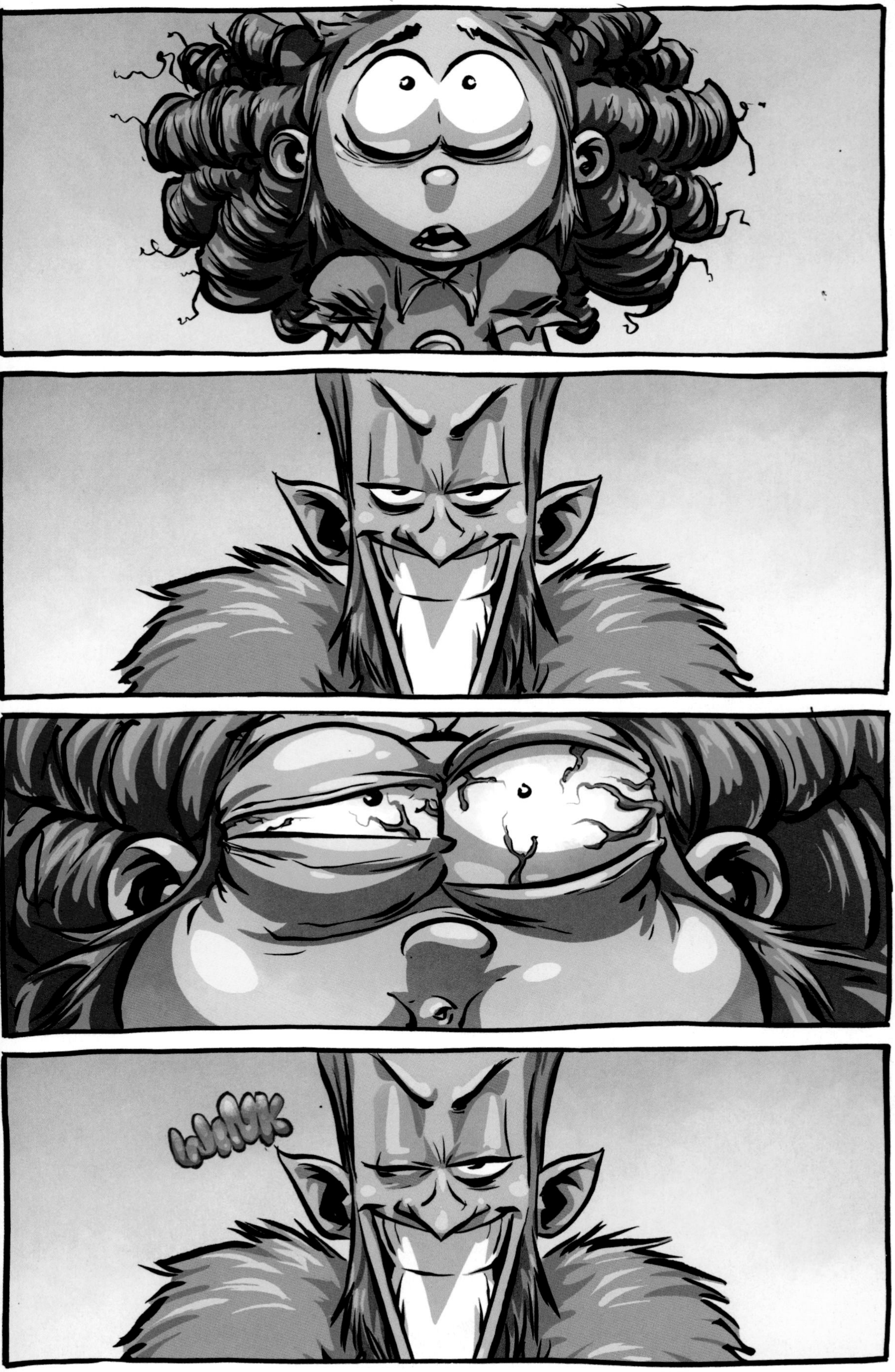
WINK

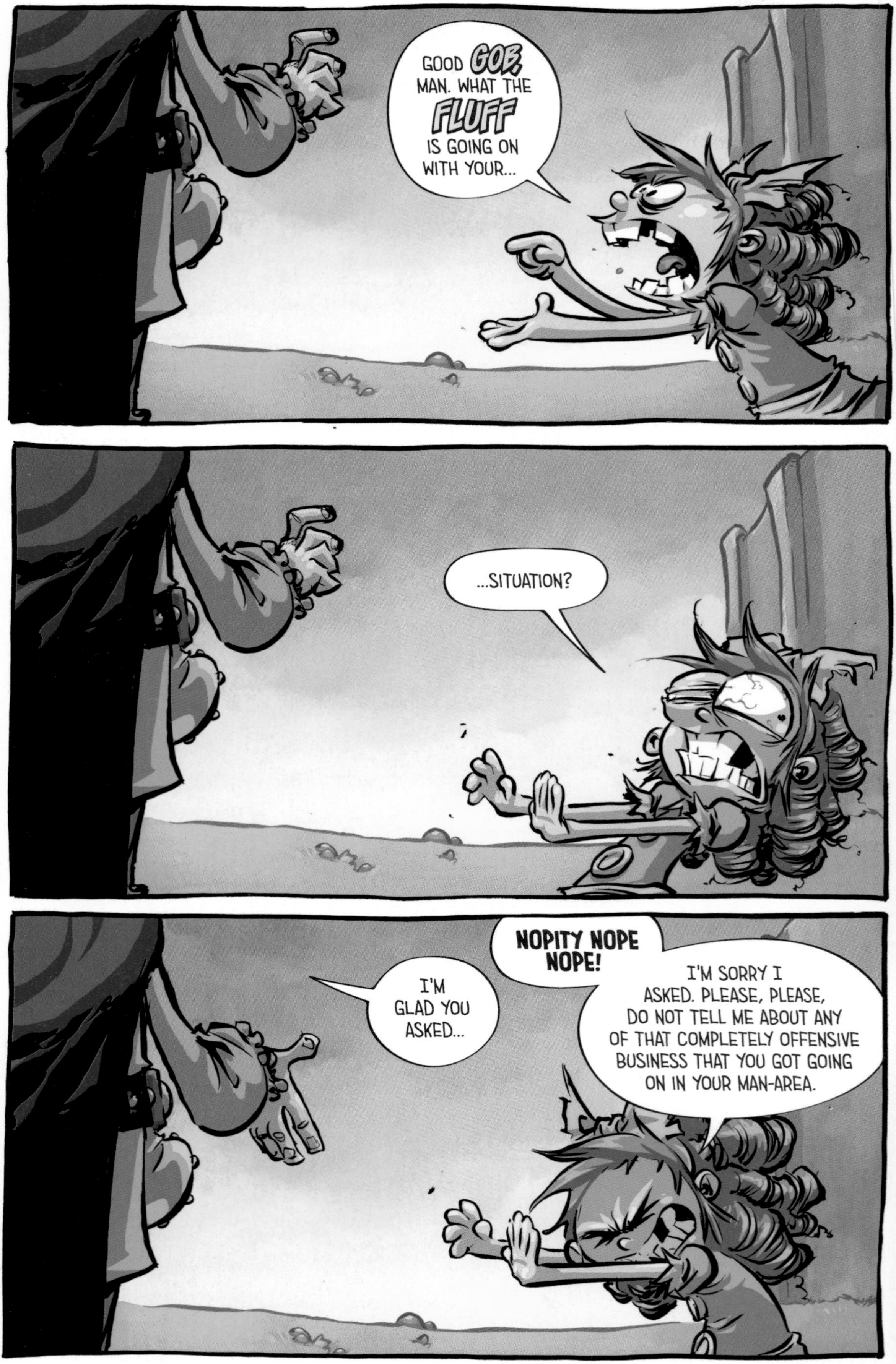
GOOD GOB, MAN. WHAT THE FLUFF IS GOING ON WITH YOUR...
...SITUATION?
I'M GLAD YOU ASKED...
NOPITY NOPE NOPE!
I'M SORRY I ASKED. PLEASE, PLEASE, DO NOT TELL ME ABOUT ANY OF THAT COMPLETELY OFFENSIVE BUSINESS THAT YOU GOT GOING ON IN YOUR MAN-AREA.

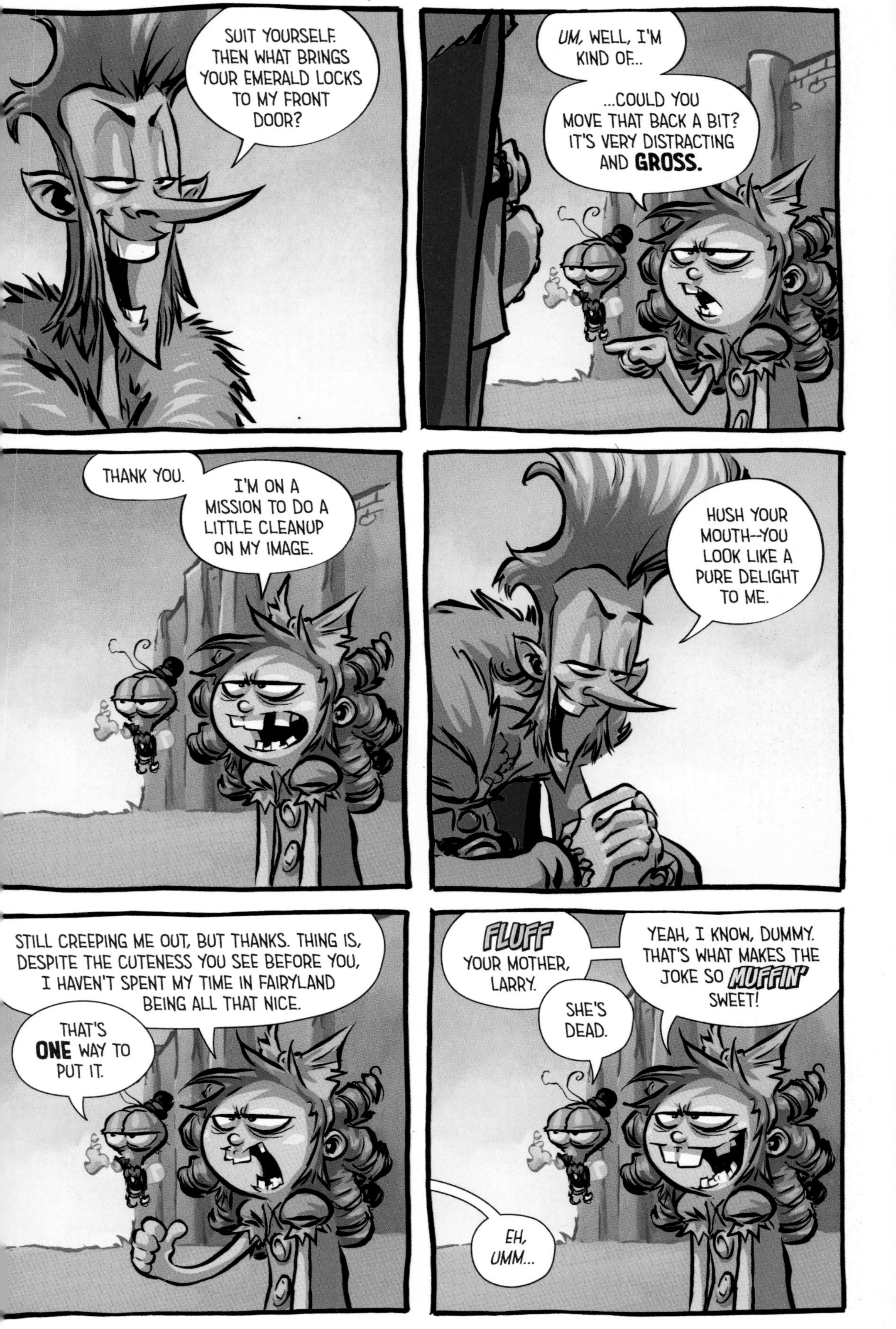
SUIT YOURSELF. THEN WHAT BRINGS YOUR EMERALD LOCKS TO MY FRONT DOOR?
UM, WELL, I'M KIND OF...
...COULD YOU MOVE THAT BACK A BIT? IT'S VERY DISTRACTING AND GROSS.
THANK YOU.
I'M ON A MISSION TO DO A LITTLE CLEANUP ON MY IMAGE.
HUSH YOUR MOUTH--YOU LOOK LIKE A PURE DELIGHT TO ME.
STILL CREEPING ME OUT, BUT THANKS. THING IS, DESPITE THE CUTENESS YOU SEE BEFORE YOU, I HAVEN'T SPENT MY TIME IN FAIRYLAND BEING ALL THAT NICE.
THAT'S ONE WAY TO PUT IT.
FLUFF YOUR MOTHER, LARRY.
SHE'S DEAD.
YEAH, I KNOW, DUMMY. THAT'S WHAT MAKES THE JOKE SO MUFFIN' SWEET!
EH, UMM...

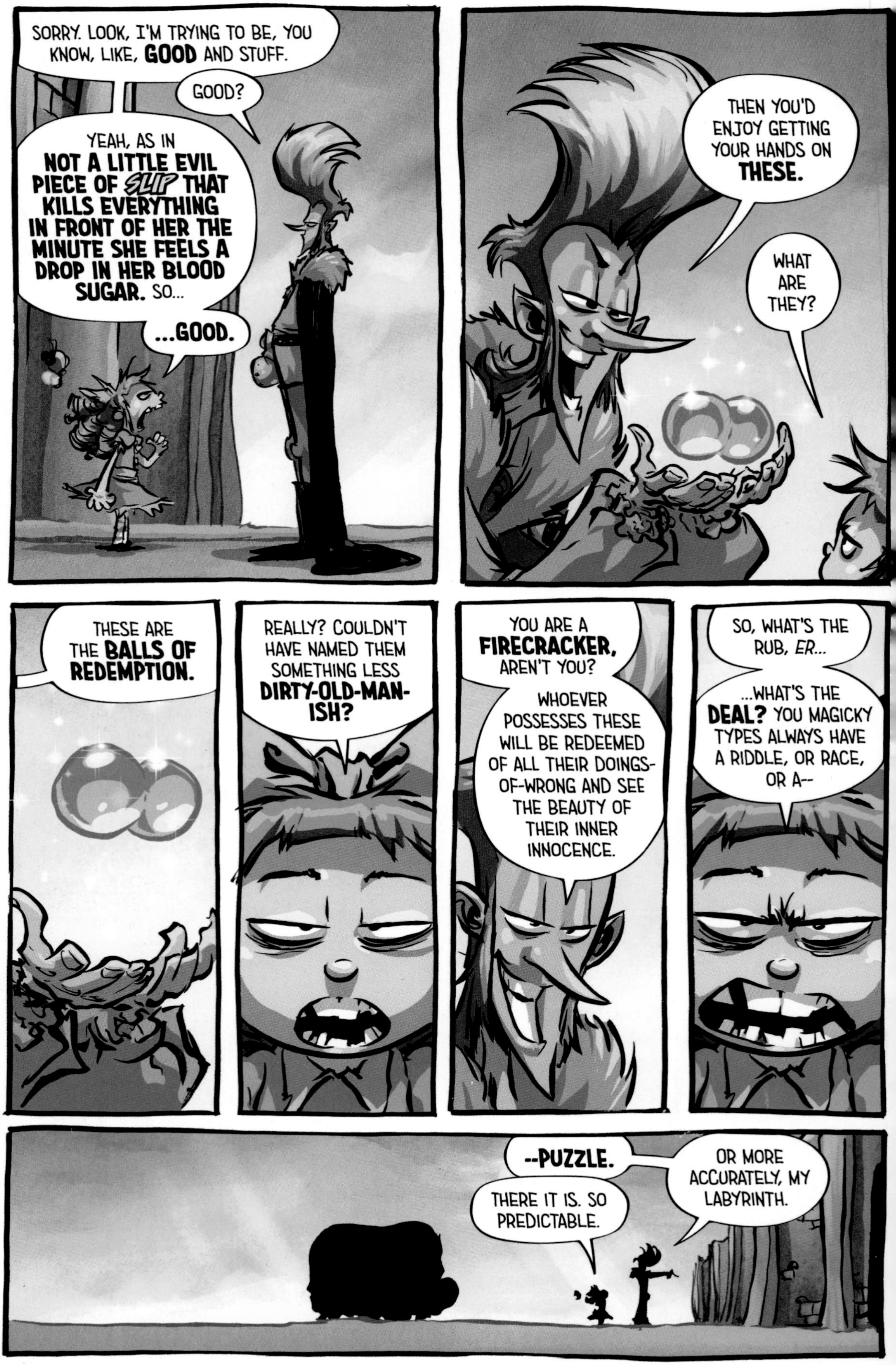
SORRY. LOOK, I'M TRYING TO BE, YOU KNOW, LIKE, GOOD AND STUFF.
GOOD?
YEAH, AS IN NOT A LITTLE EVIL PIECE OF SLIP THAT KILLS EVERYTHING IN FRONT OF HER THE MINUTE SHE FEELS A DROP IN HER BLOOD SUGAR. SO...
...GOOD.
THEN YOU'D ENJOY GETTING YOUR HANDS ON THESE.
WHAT ARE THEY?
THESE ARE THE BALLS OF REDEMPTION.
REALLY? COULDN'T HAVE NAMED THEM SOMETHING LESS DIRTY-OLD-MAN-ISH?
YOU ARE A FIRECRACKER, AREN'T YOU?
WHOEVER POSSESSES THESE WILL BE REDEEMED OF ALL THEIR DOINGS-OF-WRONG AND SEE THE BEAUTY OF THEIR INNER INNOCENCE.
SO, WHAT'S THE RUB, ER...
...WHAT'S THE DEAL? YOU MAGICKY TYPES ALWAYS HAVE A RIDDLE, OR RACE, OR A--
--PUZZLE.
THERE IT IS. SO PREDICTABLE.
OR MORE ACCURATELY, MY LABYRINTH.

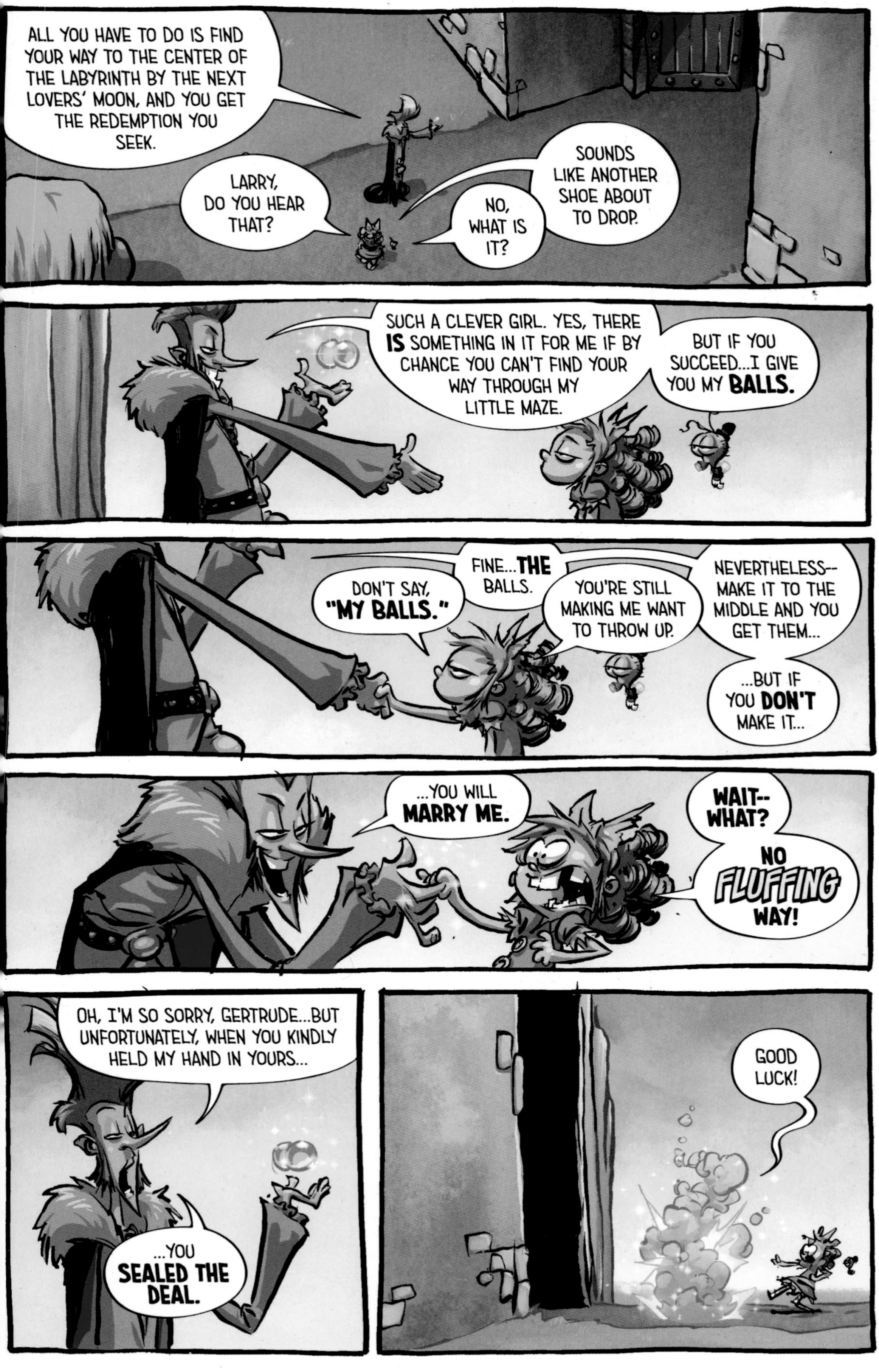
ALL YOU HAVE TO DO IS FIND YOUR WAY TO THE CENTER OF THE LABYRINTH BY THE NEXT LOVERS' MOON, AND YOU GET THE REDEMPTION YOU SEEK.
LARRY, DO YOU HEAR THAT?
NO, WHAT IS IT?
SOUNDS LIKE ANOTHER SHOE ABOUT TO DROP.
SUCH A CLEVER GIRL. YES, THERE IS SOMETHING IN IT FOR ME IF BY CHANCE YOU CAN'T FIND YOUR WAY THROUGH MY LITTLE MAZE.
BUT IF YOU SUCCEED...I GIVE YOU MY BALLS.
DON'T SAY, "MY BALLS."
FINE...THE BALLS.
YOU'RE STILL MAKING ME WANT TO THROW UP.
NEVERTHELESS-- MAKE IT TO THE MIDDLE AND YOU GET THEM...
...BUT IF YOU DON'T MAKE IT...
...YOU WILL MARRY ME.
WAIT-- WHAT?
NO FLUFFING WAY!
OH, I'M SO SORRY, GERTRUDE...BUT UNFORTUNATELY, WHEN YOU KINDLY HELD MY HAND IN YOURS...
...YOU SEALED THE DEAL.
GOOD LUCK!

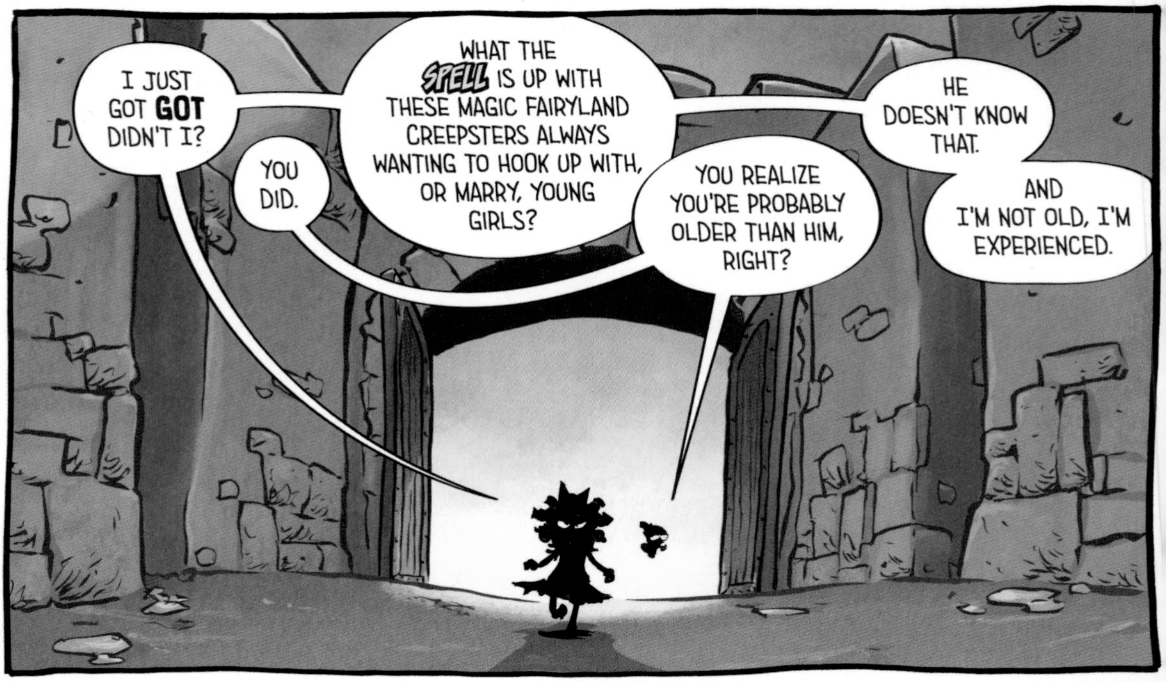
I JUST GOT **GOT** DIDN'T I?
YOU DID.
WHAT THE SPELL IS UP WITH THESE MAGIC FAIRYLAND CREEPSTERS ALWAYS WANTING TO HOOK UP WITH, OR MARRY, YOUNG GIRLS?
YOU REALIZE YOU'RE PROBABLY OLDER THAN HIM, RIGHT?
HE DOESN'T KNOW THAT.
AND I'M NOT OLD, I'M EXPERIENCED.

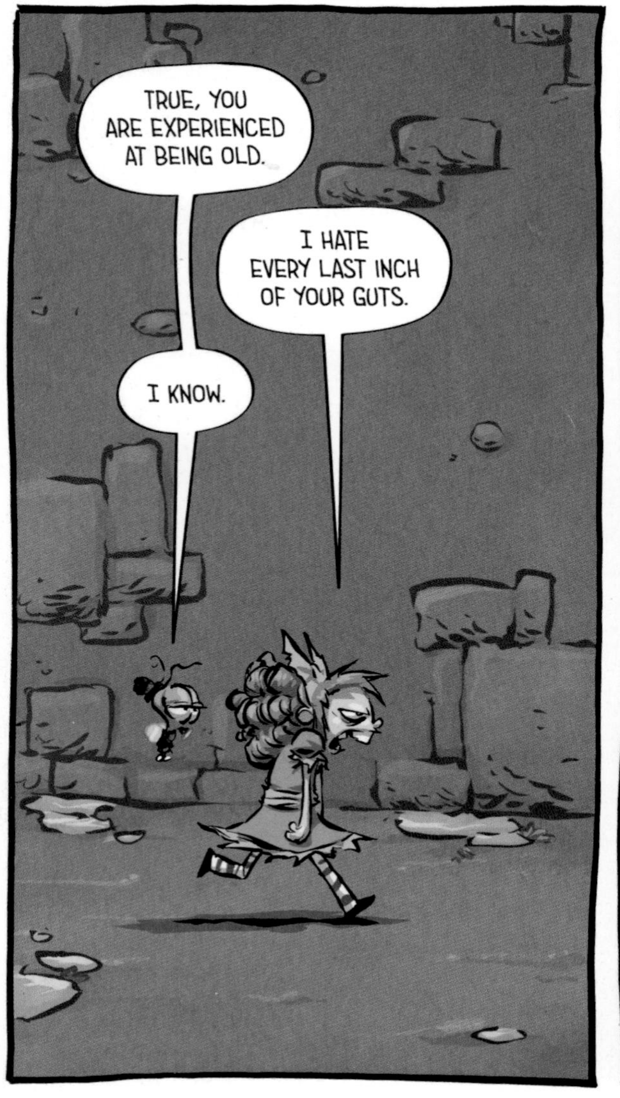
TRUE, YOU ARE EXPERIENCED AT BEING OLD.
I HATE EVERY LAST INCH OF YOUR GUTS.
I KNOW.

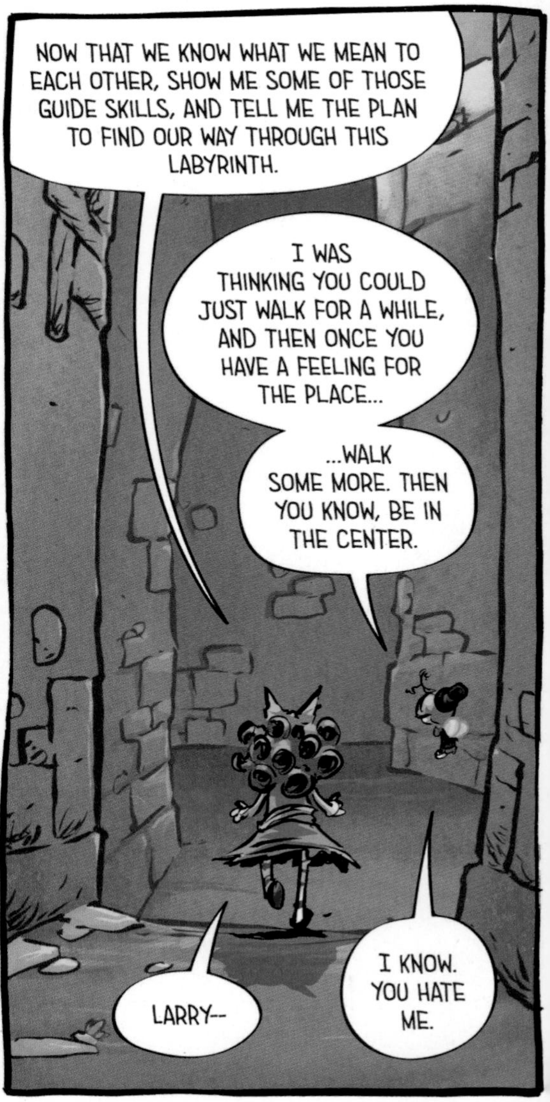
NOW THAT WE KNOW WHAT WE MEAN TO EACH OTHER, SHOW ME SOME OF THOSE GUIDE SKILLS, AND TELL ME THE PLAN TO FIND OUR WAY THROUGH THIS LABYRINTH.
I WAS THINKING YOU COULD JUST WALK FOR A WHILE, AND THEN ONCE YOU HAVE A FEELING FOR THE PLACE...
...WALK SOME MORE. THEN YOU KNOW, BE IN THE CENTER.
LARRY--
I KNOW. YOU HATE ME.

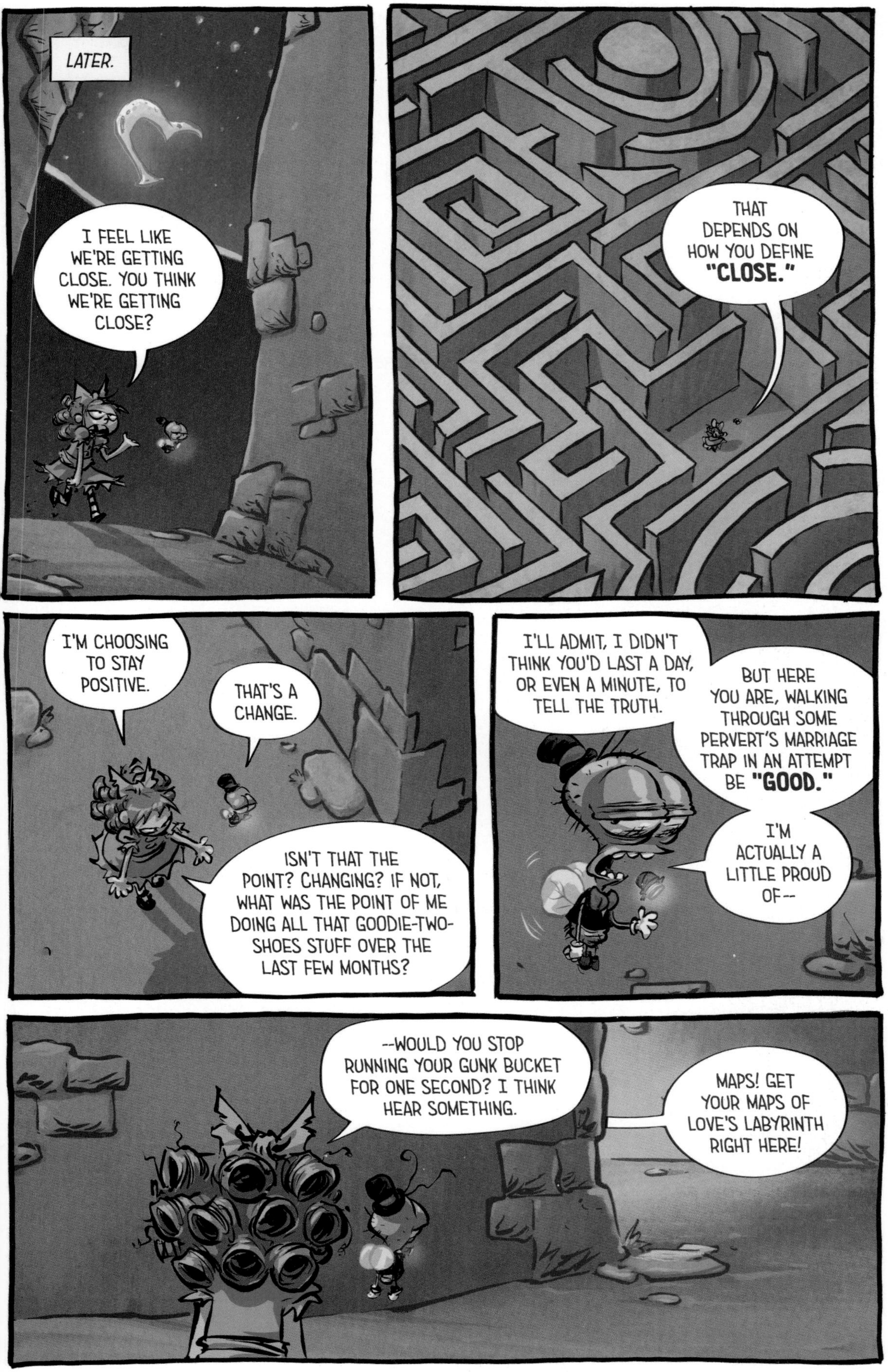
LATER.
I FEEL LIKE WE'RE GETTING CLOSE. YOU THINK WE'RE GETTING CLOSE?
THAT DEPENDS ON HOW YOU DEFINE **"CLOSE."**
I'M CHOOSING TO STAY POSITIVE.
THAT'S A CHANGE.
ISN'T THAT THE POINT? CHANGING? IF NOT, WHAT WAS THE POINT OF ME DOING ALL THAT GOODIE-TWO-SHOES STUFF OVER THE LAST FEW MONTHS?
I'LL ADMIT, I DIDN'T THINK YOU'D LAST A DAY, OR EVEN A MINUTE, TO TELL THE TRUTH.
BUT HERE YOU ARE, WALKING THROUGH SOME PERVERT'S MARRIAGE TRAP IN AN ATTEMPT BE **"GOOD."**
I'M ACTUALLY A LITTLE PROUD OF--
--WOULD YOU STOP RUNNING YOUR GUNK BUCKET FOR ONE SECOND? I THINK HEAR SOMETHING.
MAPS! GET YOUR MAPS OF LOVE'S LABYRINTH RIGHT HERE!

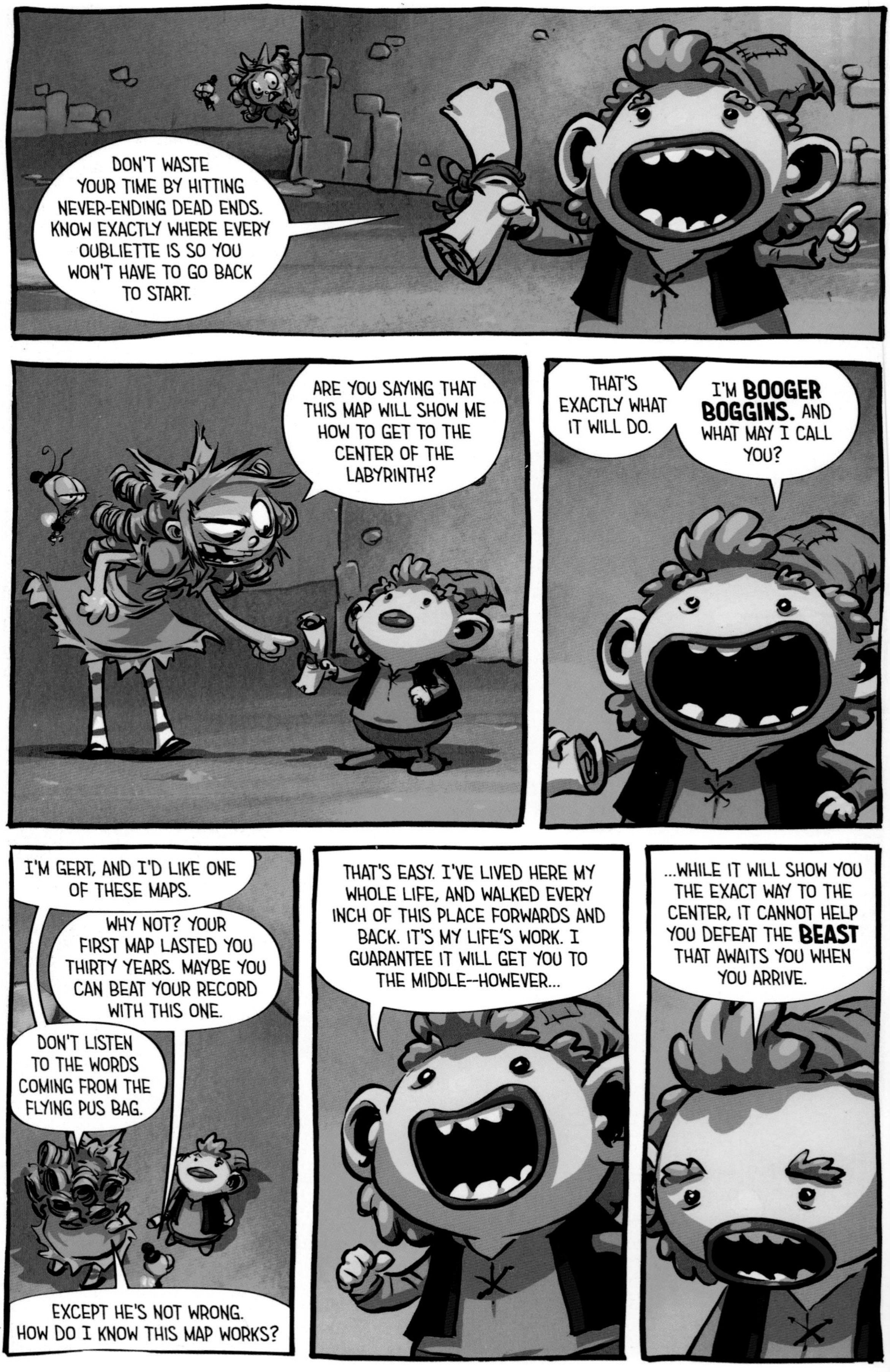
DON'T WASTE YOUR TIME BY HITTING NEVER-ENDING DEAD ENDS. KNOW EXACTLY WHERE EVERY OUBLIETTE IS SO YOU WON'T HAVE TO GO BACK TO START.
ARE YOU SAYING THAT THIS MAP WILL SHOW ME HOW TO GET TO THE CENTER OF THE LABYRINTH?
THAT'S EXACTLY WHAT IT WILL DO.
I'M **BOOGER BOGGINS.** AND WHAT MAY I CALL YOU?
I'M GERT, AND I'D LIKE ONE OF THESE MAPS.
WHY NOT? YOUR FIRST MAP LASTED YOU THIRTY YEARS. MAYBE YOU CAN BEAT YOUR RECORD WITH THIS ONE.
DON'T LISTEN TO THE WORDS COMING FROM THE FLYING PUS BAG.
EXCEPT HE'S NOT WRONG. HOW DO I KNOW THIS MAP WORKS?
THAT'S EASY. I'VE LIVED HERE MY WHOLE LIFE, AND WALKED EVERY INCH OF THIS PLACE FORWARDS AND BACK. IT'S MY LIFE'S WORK. I GUARANTEE IT WILL GET YOU TO THE MIDDLE--HOWEVER...
...WHILE IT WILL SHOW YOU THE EXACT WAY TO THE CENTER, IT CANNOT HELP YOU DEFEAT THE **BEAST** THAT AWAITS YOU WHEN YOU ARRIVE.

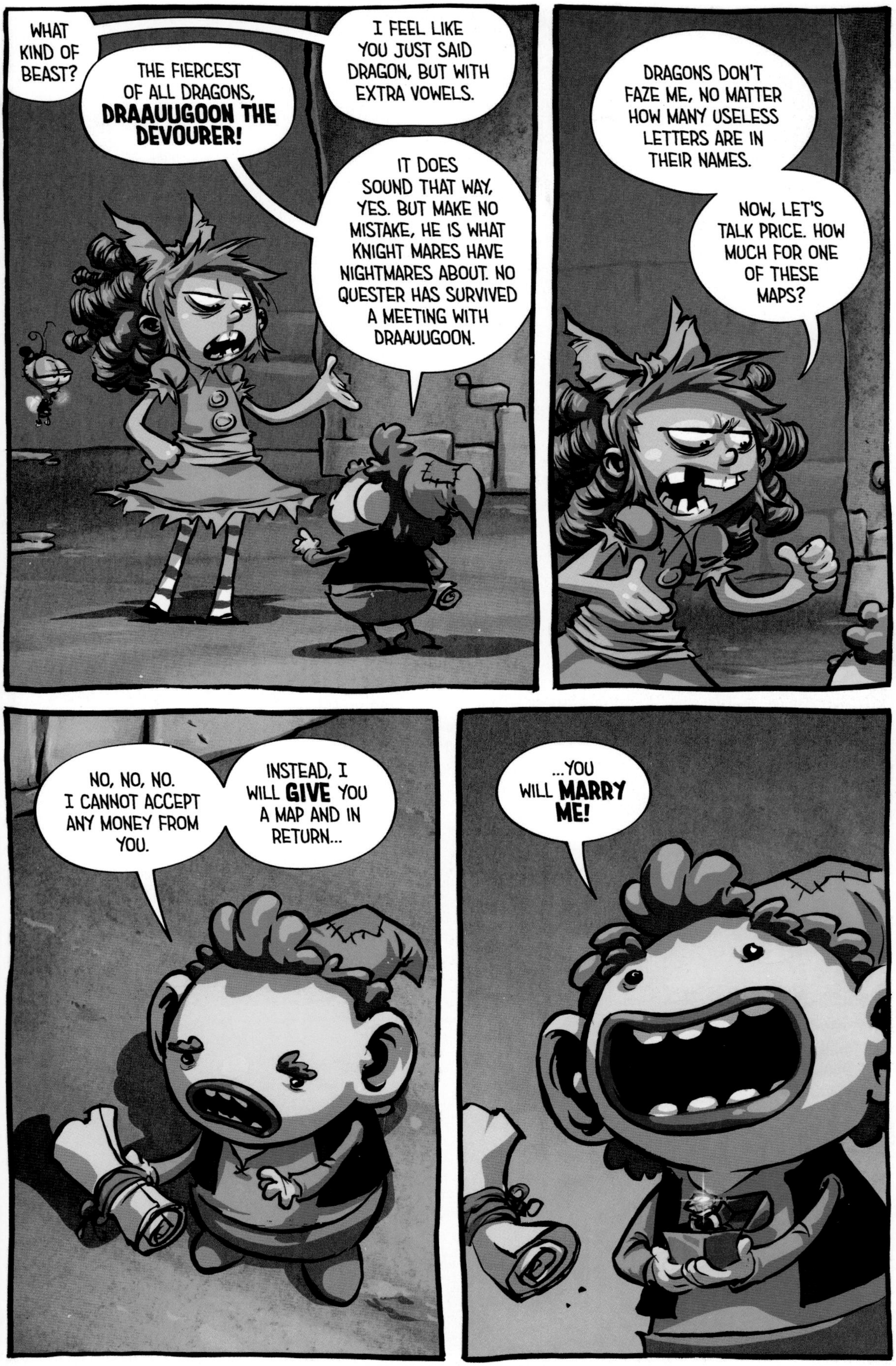
WHAT KIND OF BEAST?
THE FIERCEST OF ALL DRAGONS, **DRAAUUGOON THE DEVOURER!**
I FEEL LIKE YOU JUST SAID DRAGON, BUT WITH EXTRA VOWELS.
IT DOES SOUND THAT WAY, YES. BUT MAKE NO MISTAKE, HE IS WHAT KNIGHT MARES HAVE NIGHTMARES ABOUT. NO QUESTER HAS SURVIVED A MEETING WITH DRAAUUGOON.
DRAGONS DON'T FAZE ME, NO MATTER HOW MANY USELESS LETTERS ARE IN THEIR NAMES.
NOW, LET'S TALK PRICE. HOW MUCH FOR ONE OF THESE MAPS?
NO, NO, NO. I CANNOT ACCEPT ANY MONEY FROM YOU.
INSTEAD, I WILL **GIVE** YOU A MAP AND IN RETURN...
...YOU WILL **MARRY ME!**

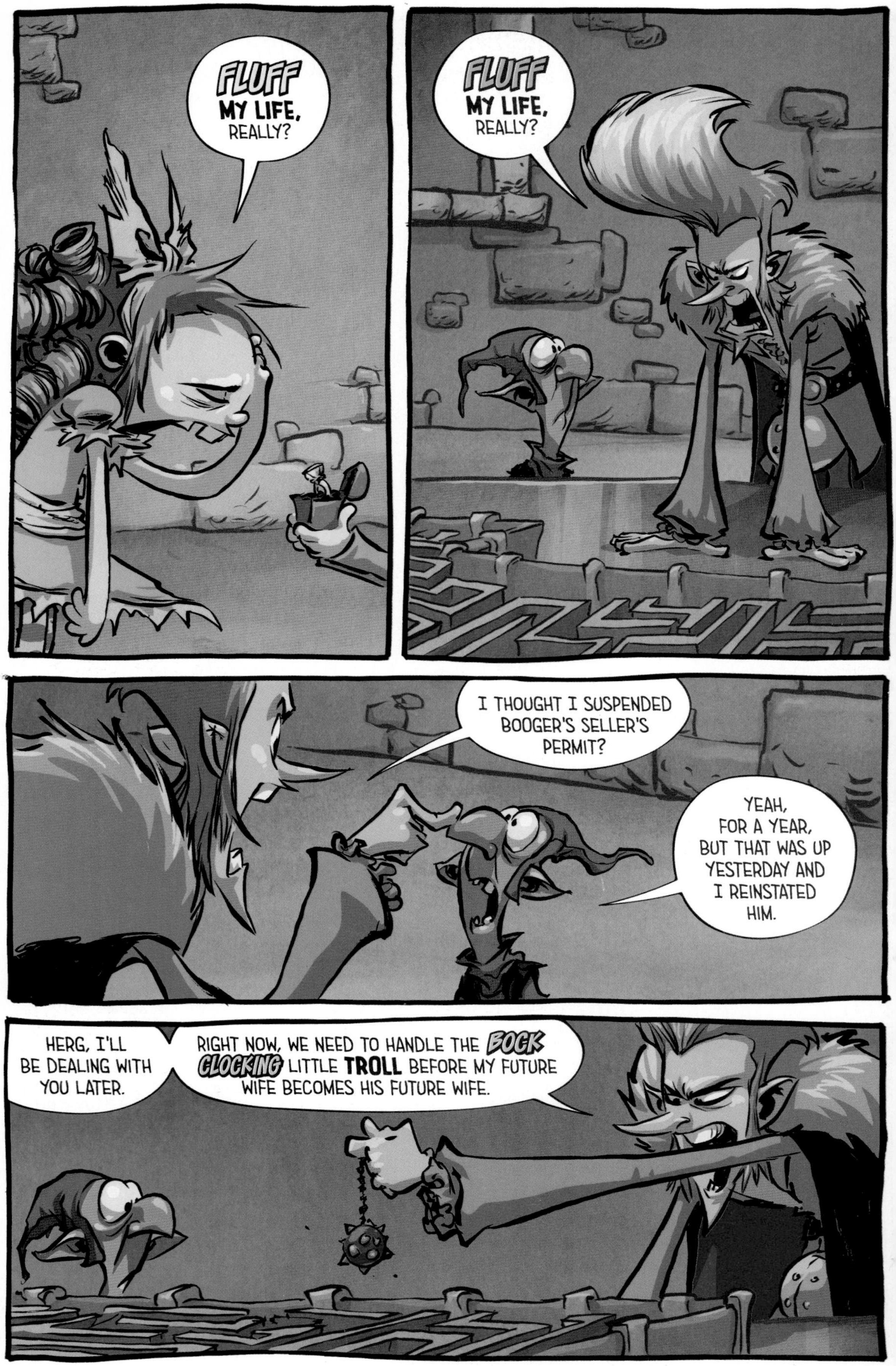
FLUFF MY LIFE, REALLY?
FLUFF MY LIFE, REALLY?
I THOUGHT I SUSPENDED BOOGER'S SELLER'S PERMIT?
YEAH, FOR A YEAR, BUT THAT WAS UP YESTERDAY AND I REINSTATED HIM.
HERG, I'LL BE DEALING WITH YOU LATER.
RIGHT NOW, WE NEED TO HANDLE THE BOCK CLOCKING LITTLE TROLL BEFORE MY FUTURE WIFE BECOMES HIS FUTURE WIFE.

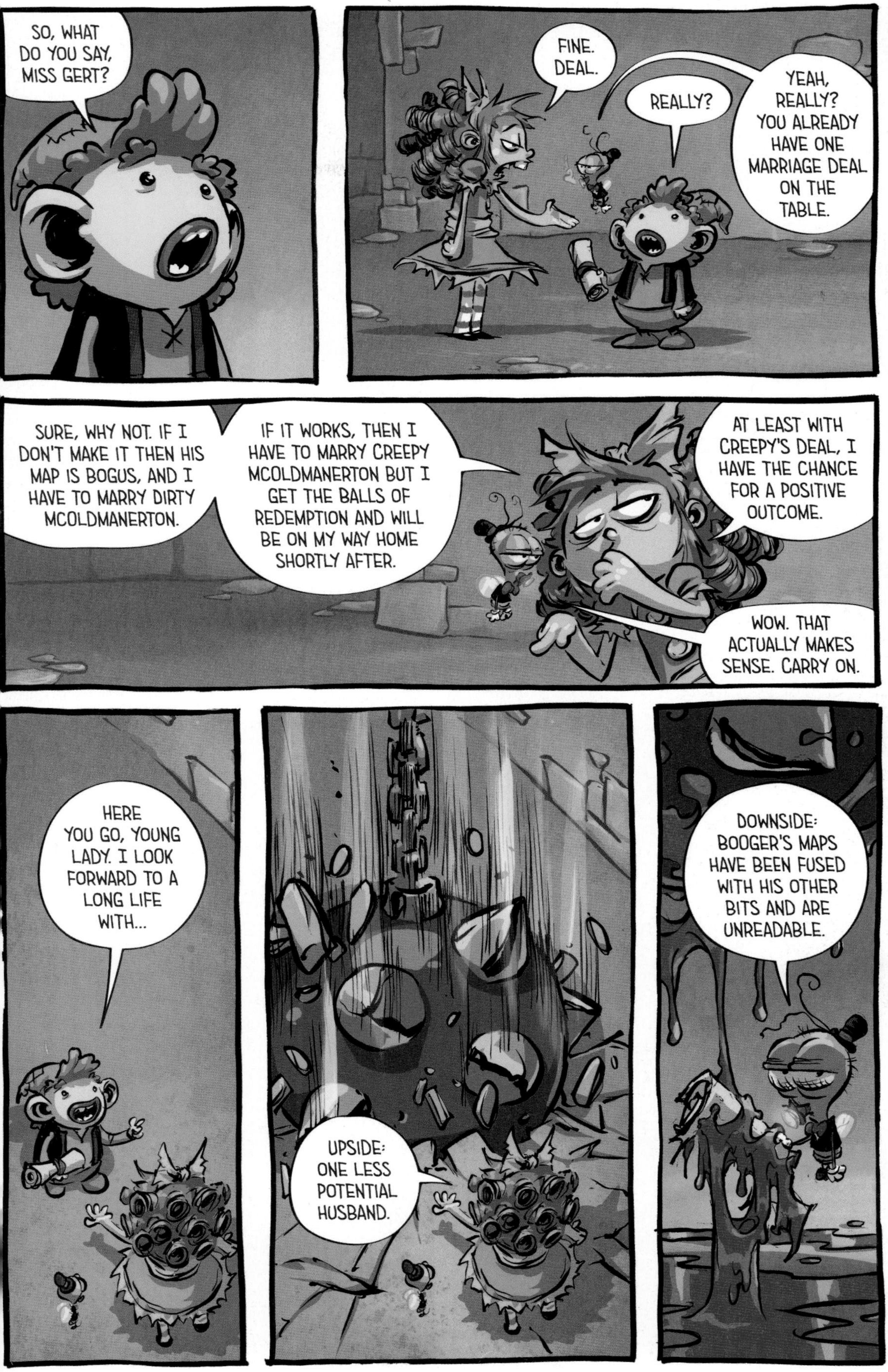
SO, WHAT DO YOU SAY, MISS GERT?
FINE. DEAL.
REALLY?
YEAH, REALLY? YOU ALREADY HAVE ONE MARRIAGE DEAL ON THE TABLE.
SURE, WHY NOT. IF I DON'T MAKE IT THEN HIS MAP IS BOGUS, AND I HAVE TO MARRY DIRTY MCOLDMANERTON.
IF IT WORKS, THEN I HAVE TO MARRY CREEPY MCOLDMANERTON BUT I GET THE BALLS OF REDEMPTION AND WILL BE ON MY WAY HOME SHORTLY AFTER.
AT LEAST WITH CREEPY'S DEAL, I HAVE THE CHANCE FOR A POSITIVE OUTCOME.
WOW. THAT ACTUALLY MAKES SENSE. CARRY ON.
HERE YOU GO, YOUNG LADY. I LOOK FORWARD TO A LONG LIFE WITH...
UPSIDE: ONE LESS POTENTIAL HUSBAND.
DOWNSIDE: BOOGER'S MAPS HAVE BEEN FUSED WITH HIS OTHER BITS AND ARE UNREADABLE.

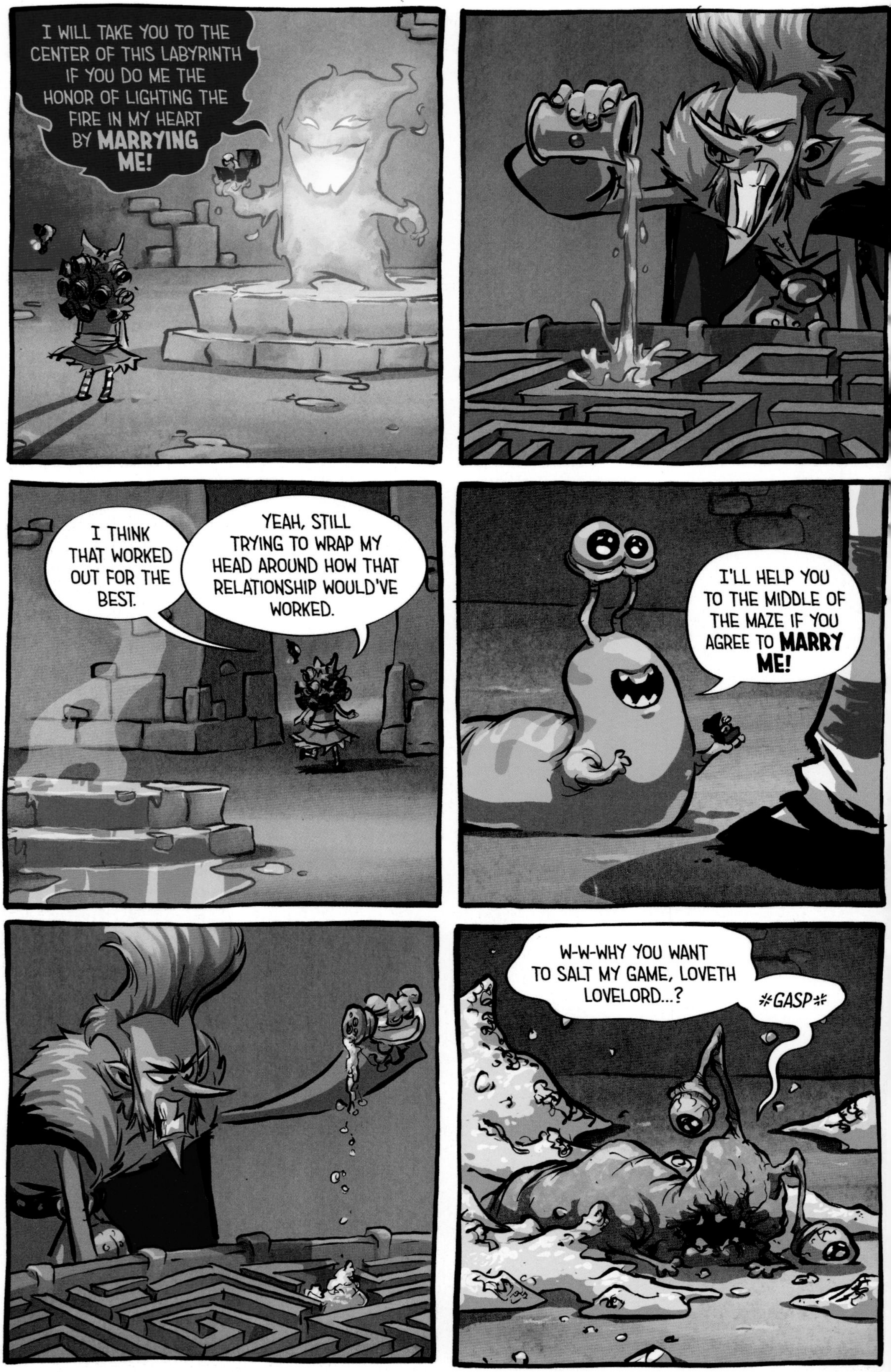
I WILL TAKE YOU TO THE CENTER OF THIS LABYRINTH IF YOU DO ME THE HONOR OF LIGHTING THE FIRE IN MY HEART BY **MARRYING ME!**
I THINK THAT WORKED OUT FOR THE BEST.
YEAH, STILL TRYING TO WRAP MY HEAD AROUND HOW THAT RELATIONSHIP WOULD'VE WORKED.
I'LL HELP YOU TO THE MIDDLE OF THE MAZE IF YOU AGREE TO **MARRY ME!**
W-W-WHY YOU WANT TO SALT MY GAME, LOVETH LOVELORD...?
GASP

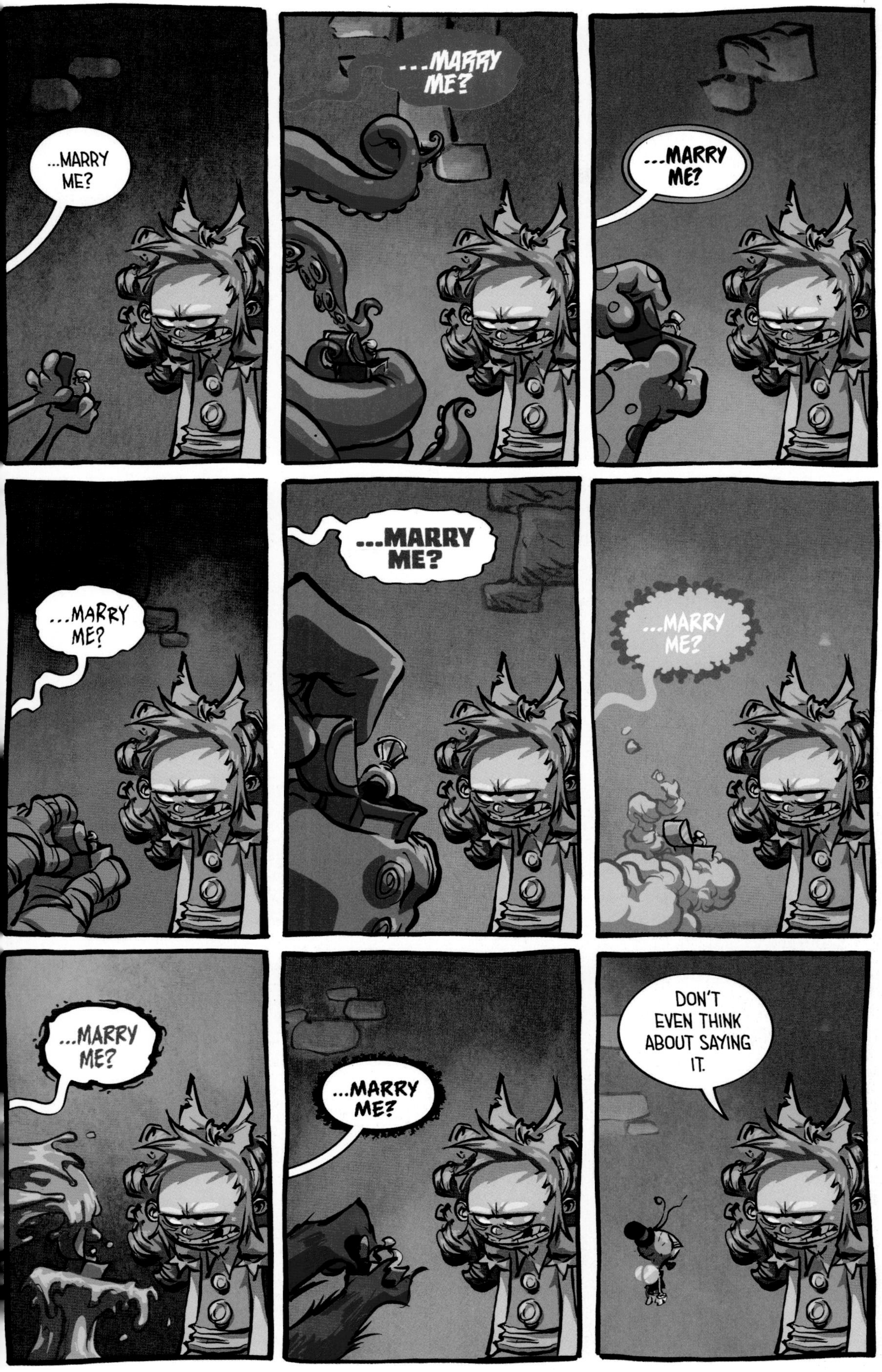
...MARRY ME?
...MARRY ME?
...MARRY ME?
...MARRY ME?
...MARRY ME?
...MARRY ME?
...MARRY ME?
...MARRY ME?
DON'T EVEN THINK ABOUT SAYING IT.

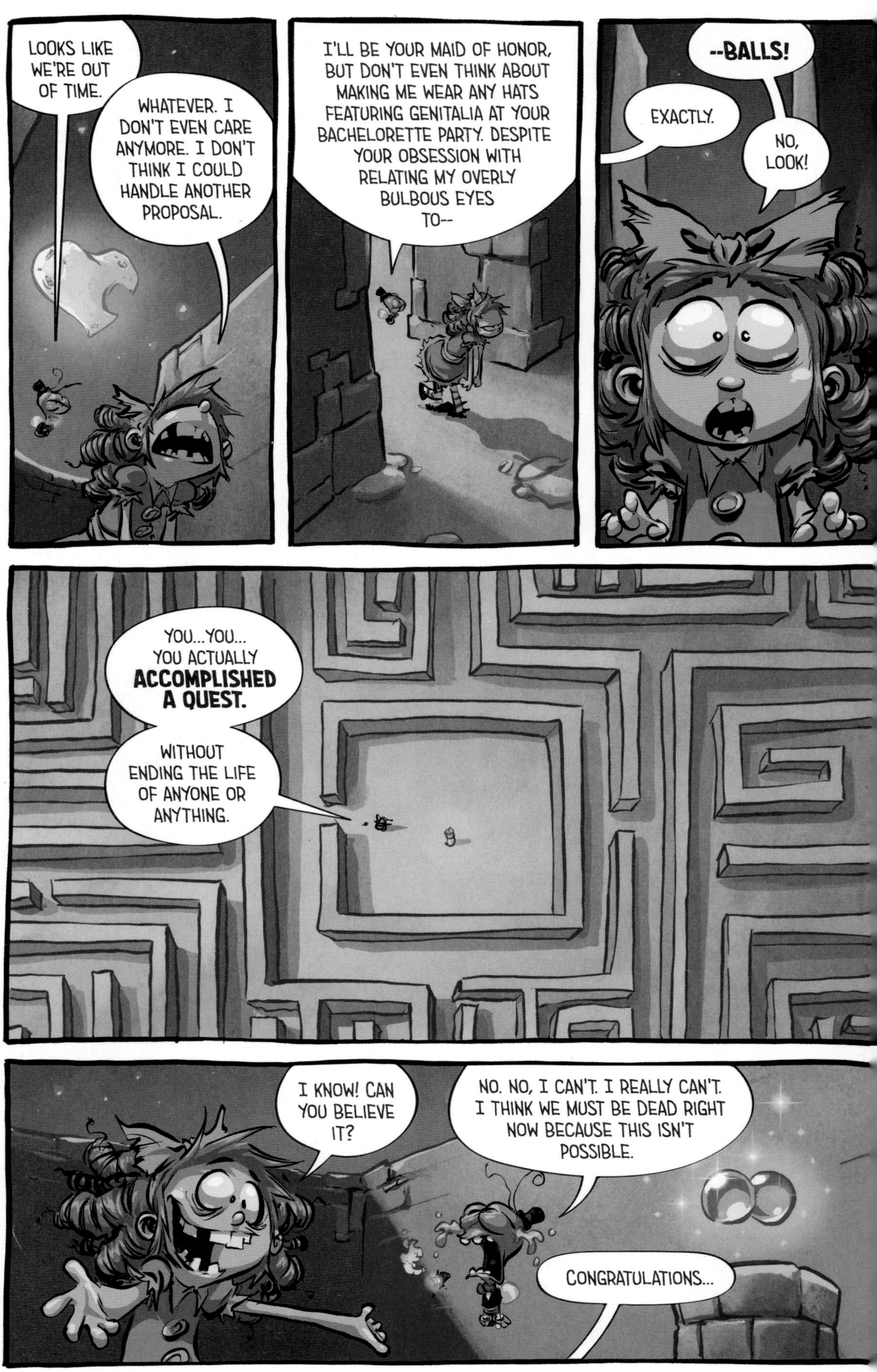
LOOKS LIKE WE'RE OUT OF TIME.
WHATEVER. I DON'T EVEN CARE ANYMORE. I DON'T THINK I COULD HANDLE ANOTHER PROPOSAL.
I'LL BE YOUR MAID OF HONOR, BUT DON'T EVEN THINK ABOUT MAKING ME WEAR ANY HATS FEATURING GENITALIA AT YOUR BACHELORETTE PARTY. DESPITE YOUR OBSESSION WITH RELATING MY OVERLY BULBOUS EYES TO--
--BALLS!
EXACTLY.
NO, LOOK!
YOU...YOU... YOU ACTUALLY **ACCOMPLISHED A QUEST.**
WITHOUT ENDING THE LIFE OF ANYONE OR ANYTHING.
I KNOW! CAN YOU BELIEVE IT?
NO. NO, I CAN'T. I REALLY CAN'T. I THINK WE MUST BE DEAD RIGHT NOW BECAUSE THIS ISN'T POSSIBLE.
CONGRATULATIONS...

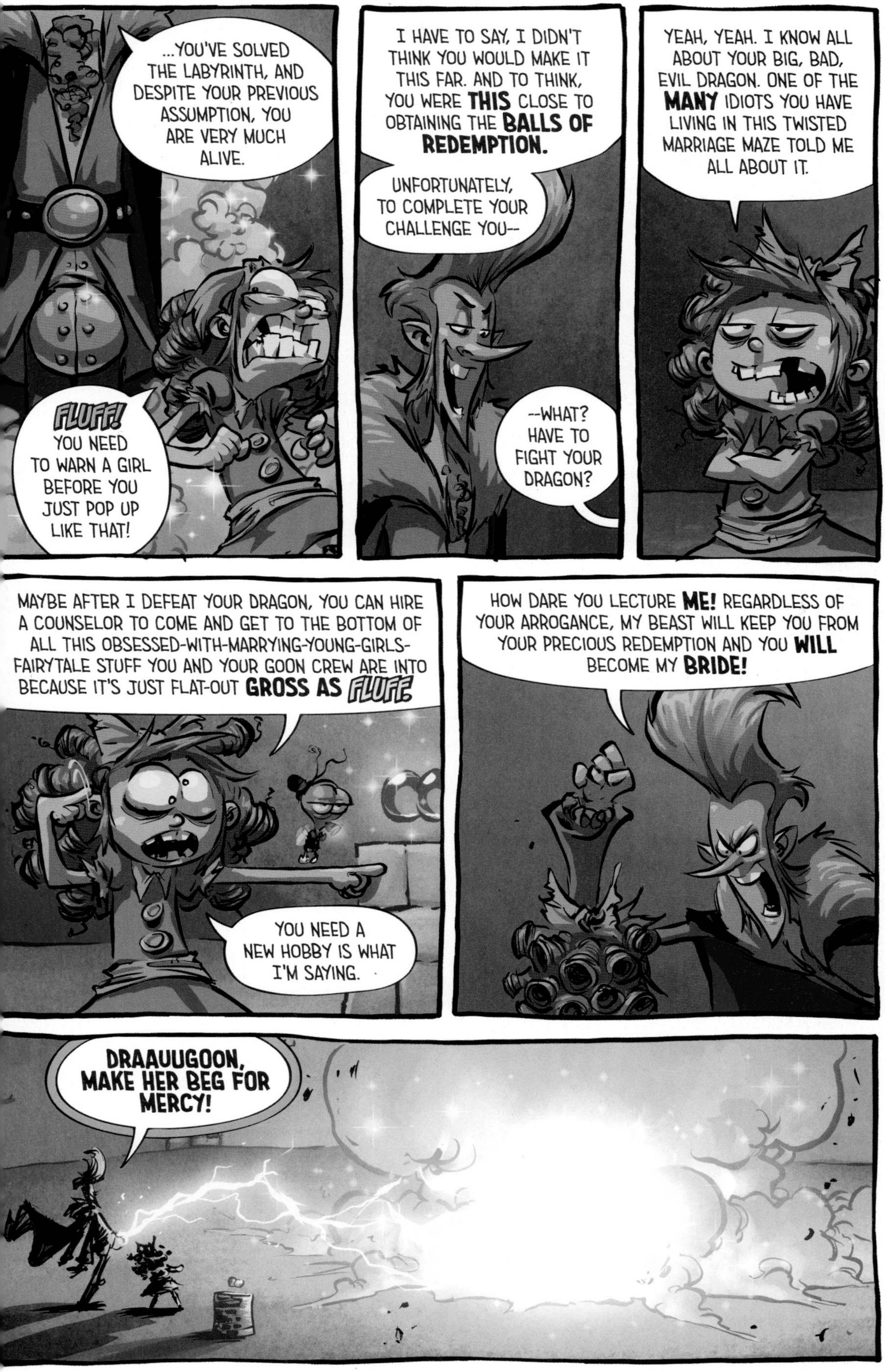
...YOU'VE SOLVED THE LABYRINTH, AND DESPITE YOUR PREVIOUS ASSUMPTION, YOU ARE VERY MUCH ALIVE.
FLUFF! YOU NEED TO WARN A GIRL BEFORE YOU JUST POP UP LIKE THAT!
I HAVE TO SAY, I DIDN'T THINK YOU WOULD MAKE IT THIS FAR. AND TO THINK, YOU WERE THIS CLOSE TO OBTAINING THE BALLS OF REDEMPTION.
UNFORTUNATELY, TO COMPLETE YOUR CHALLENGE YOU--
--WHAT? HAVE TO FIGHT YOUR DRAGON?
YEAH, YEAH. I KNOW ALL ABOUT YOUR BIG, BAD, EVIL DRAGON. ONE OF THE MANY IDIOTS YOU HAVE LIVING IN THIS TWISTED MARRIAGE MAZE TOLD ME ALL ABOUT IT.
MAYBE AFTER I DEFEAT YOUR DRAGON, YOU CAN HIRE A COUNSELOR TO COME AND GET TO THE BOTTOM OF ALL THIS OBSESSED-WITH-MARRYING-YOUNG-GIRLS-FAIRYTALE STUFF YOU AND YOUR GOON CREW ARE INTO BECAUSE IT'S JUST FLAT-OUT GROSS AS FLUFF.
YOU NEED A NEW HOBBY IS WHAT I'M SAYING.
HOW DARE YOU LECTURE ME! REGARDLESS OF YOUR ARROGANCE, MY BEAST WILL KEEP YOU FROM YOUR PRECIOUS REDEMPTION AND YOU WILL BECOME MY BRIDE!
DRAAUUGOON, MAKE HER BEG FOR MERCY!

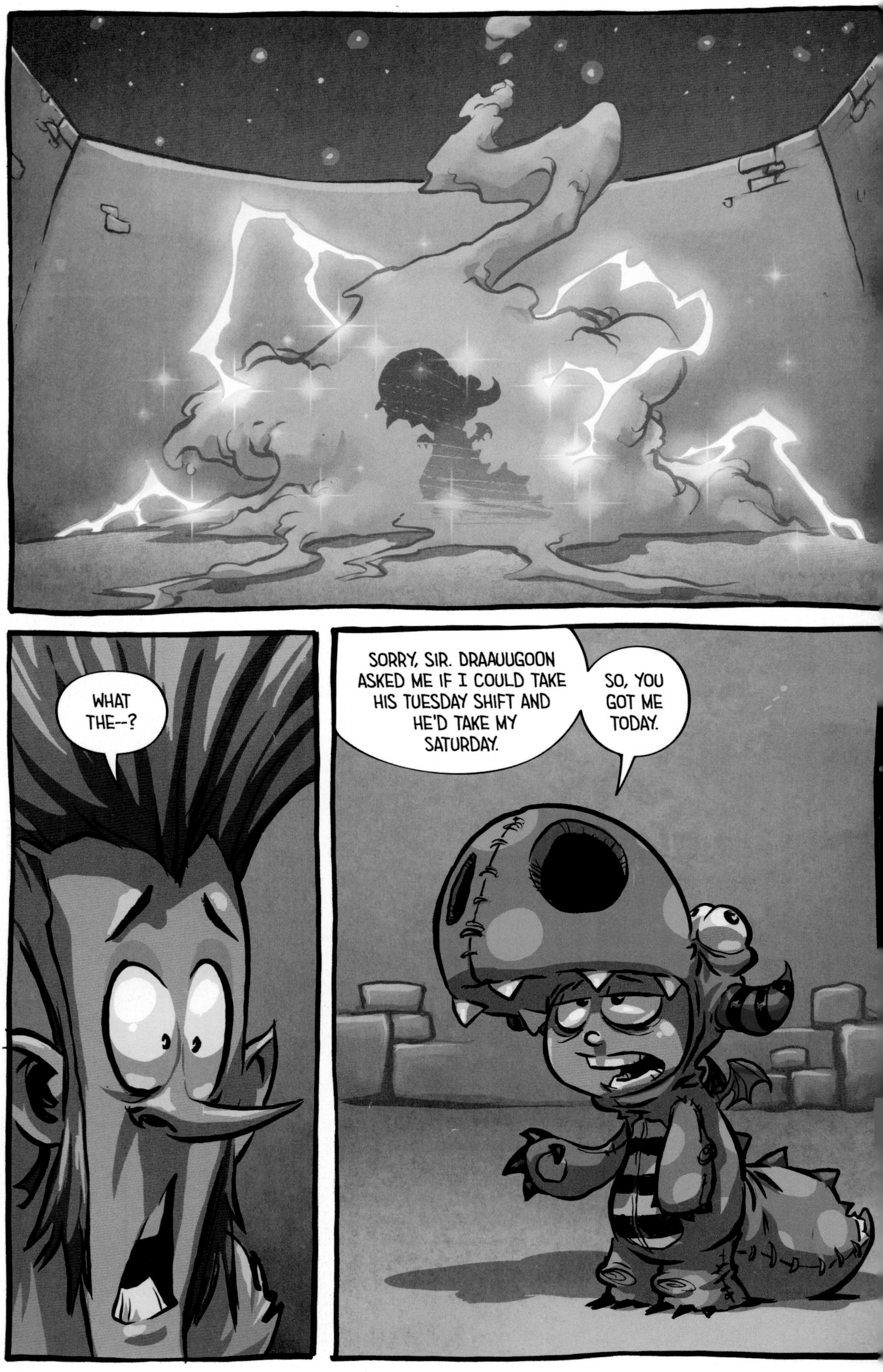
WHAT THE--?
SORRY, SIR. DRAAUUGOON ASKED ME IF I COULD TAKE HIS TUESDAY SHIFT AND HE'D TAKE MY SATURDAY.
SO, YOU GOT ME TODAY.

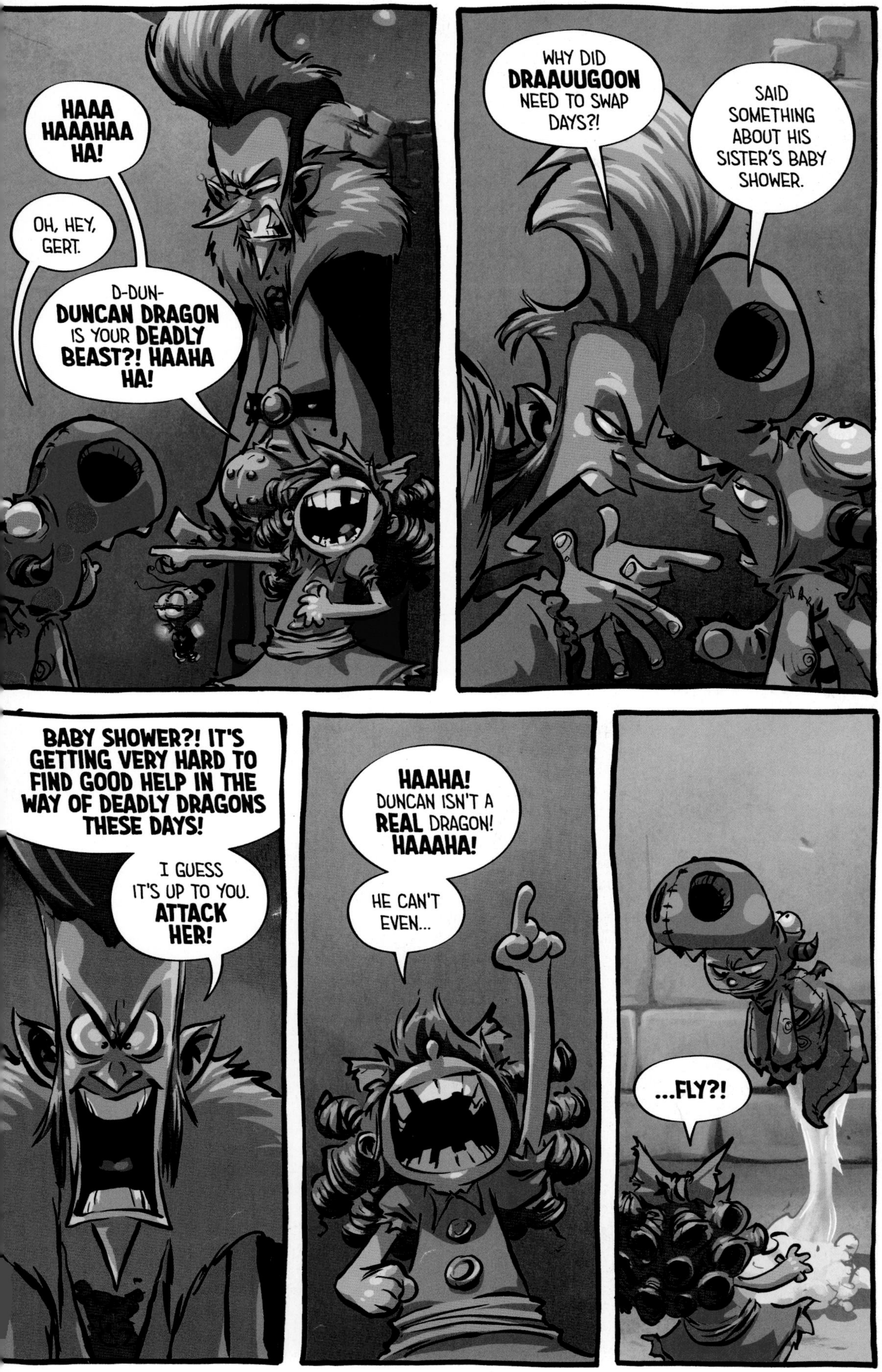
HAAA HAAAHAA HA!
OH, HEY, GERT.
D-DUN- DUNCAN DRAGON IS YOUR DEADLY BEAST?! HAAHA HA!
WHY DID DRAAUUGOON NEED TO SWAP DAYS?!
SAID SOMETHING ABOUT HIS SISTER'S BABY SHOWER.
BABY SHOWER?! IT'S GETTING VERY HARD TO FIND GOOD HELP IN THE WAY OF DEADLY DRAGONS THESE DAYS!
I GUESS IT'S UP TO YOU. ATTACK HER!
HAAHA! DUNCAN ISN'T A REAL DRAGON! HAAAHA!
HE CAN'T EVEN...
...FLY?!

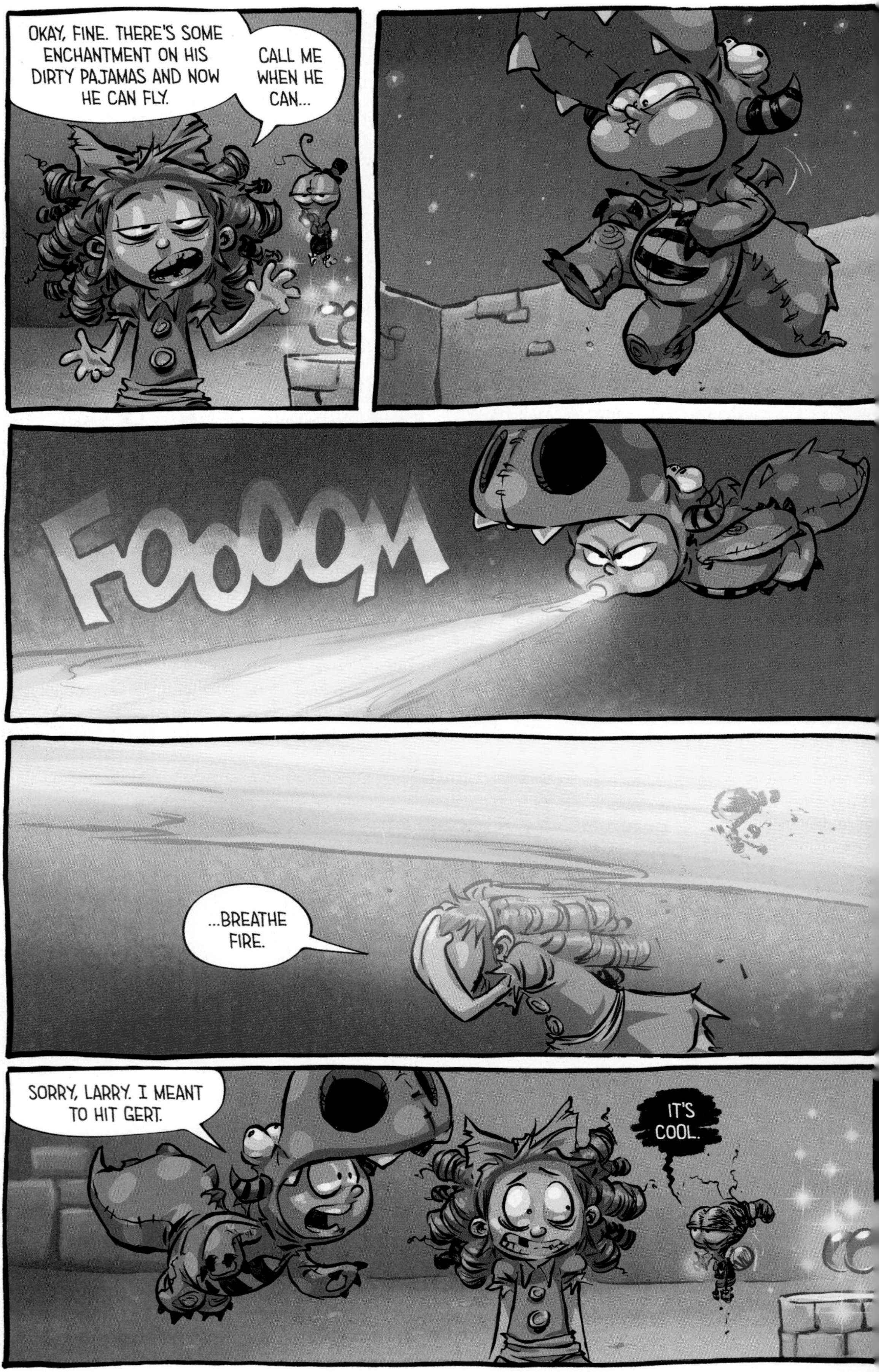
OKAY, FINE. THERE'S SOME ENCHANTMENT ON HIS DIRTY PAJAMAS AND NOW HE CAN FLY.
CALL ME WHEN HE CAN...
FOOOOM
...BREATHE FIRE.
SORRY, LARRY. I MEANT TO HIT GERT.
IT'S COOL.

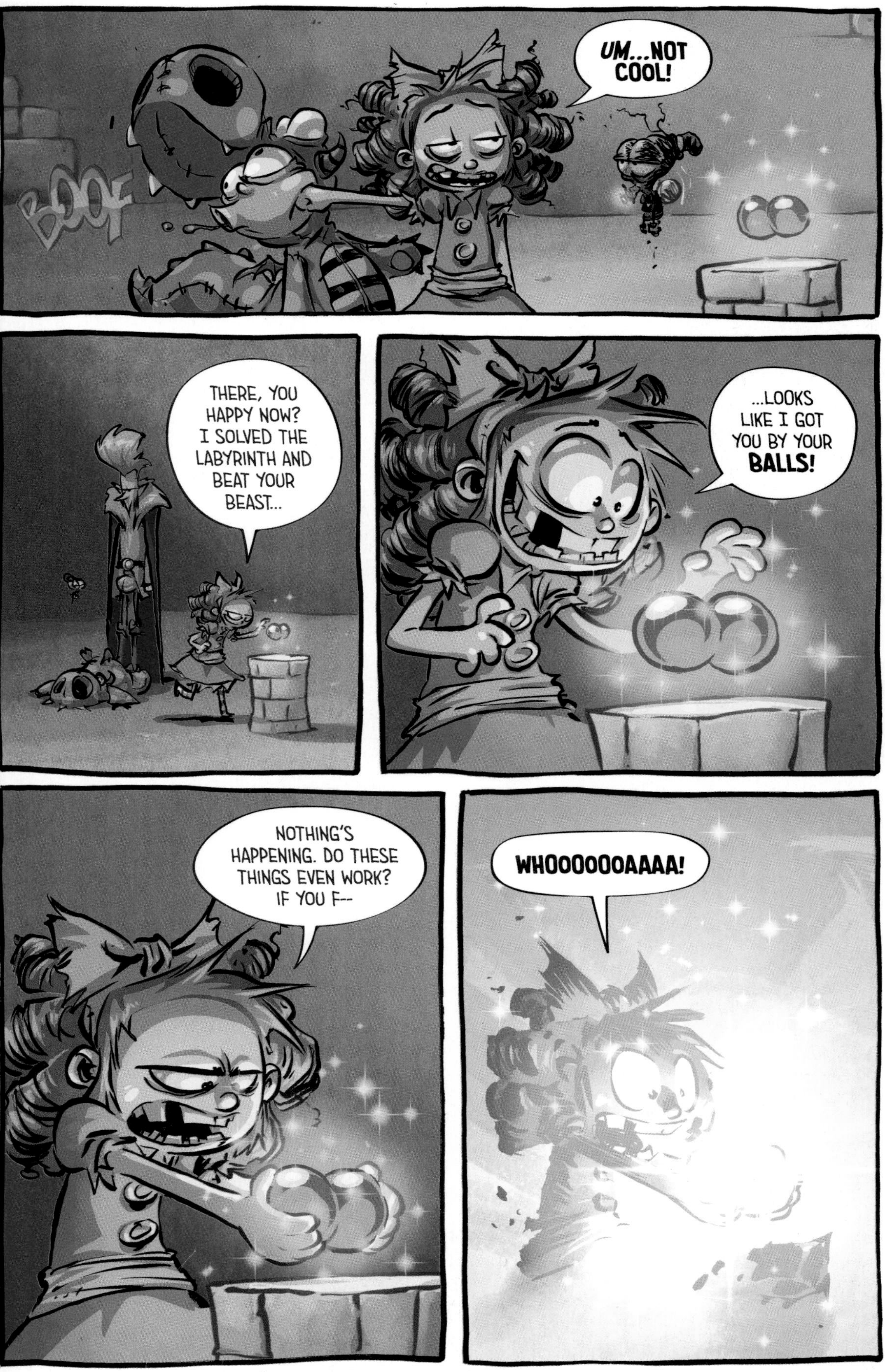
BOOF
UM...NOT COOL!
THERE, YOU HAPPY NOW? I SOLVED THE LABYRINTH AND BEAT YOUR BEAST...
...LOOKS LIKE I GOT YOU BY YOUR BALLS!
NOTHING'S HAPPENING. DO THESE THINGS EVEN WORK? IF YOU F--
WHOOOOOOAAAA!

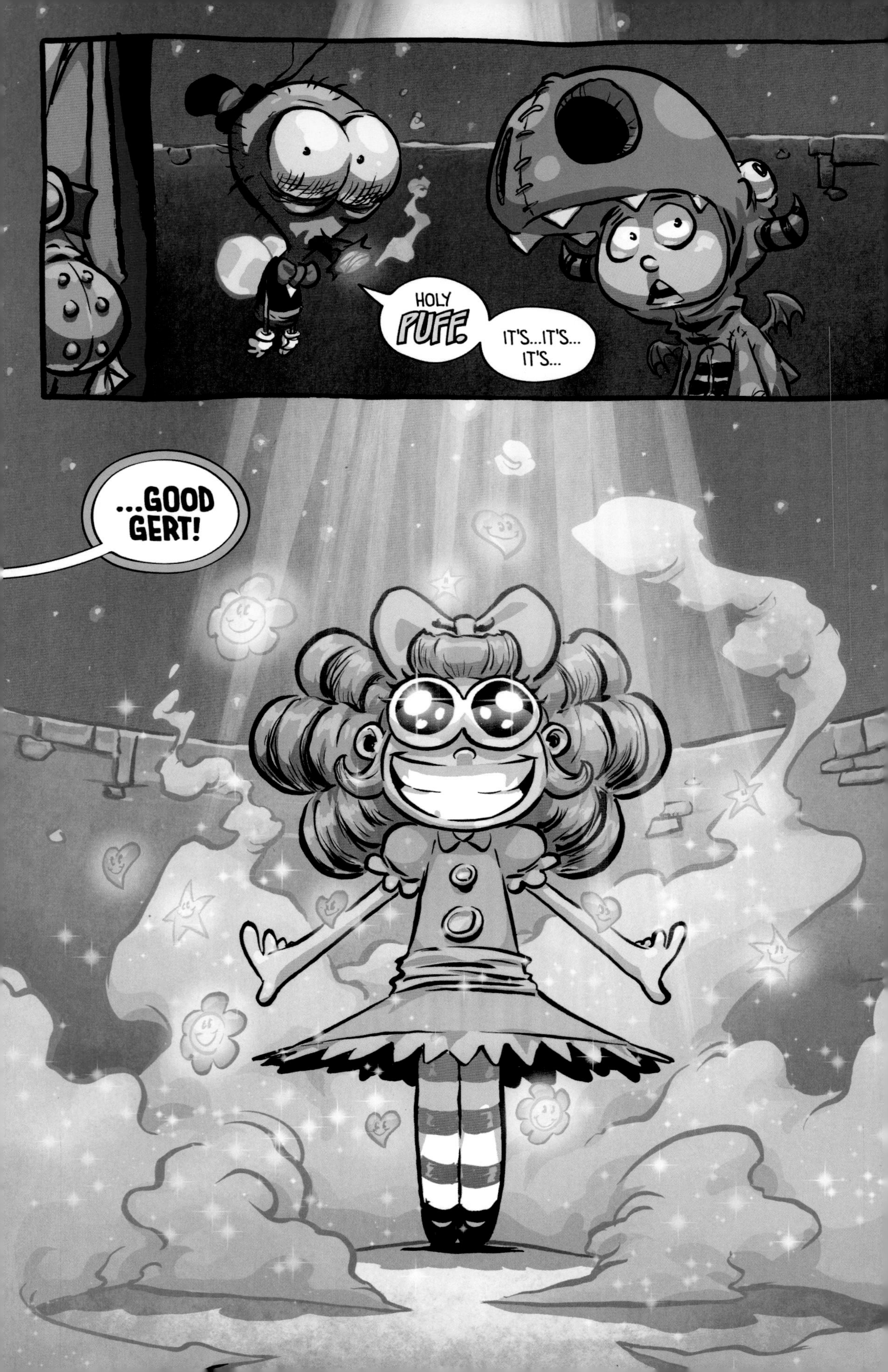

HOLY PUFF.
IT'S...IT'S... IT'S...
...GOOD GERT!

FIFTEEN

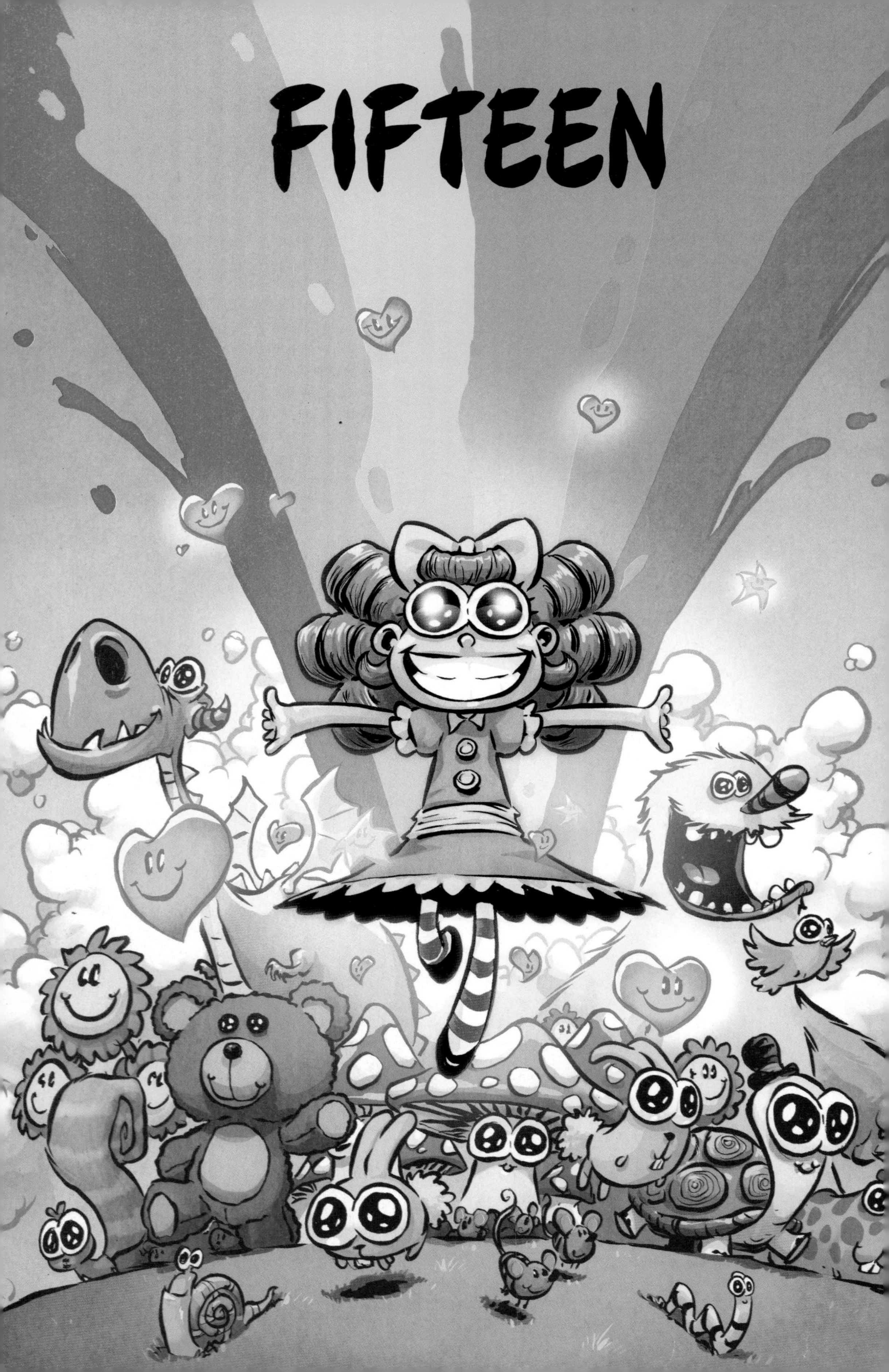

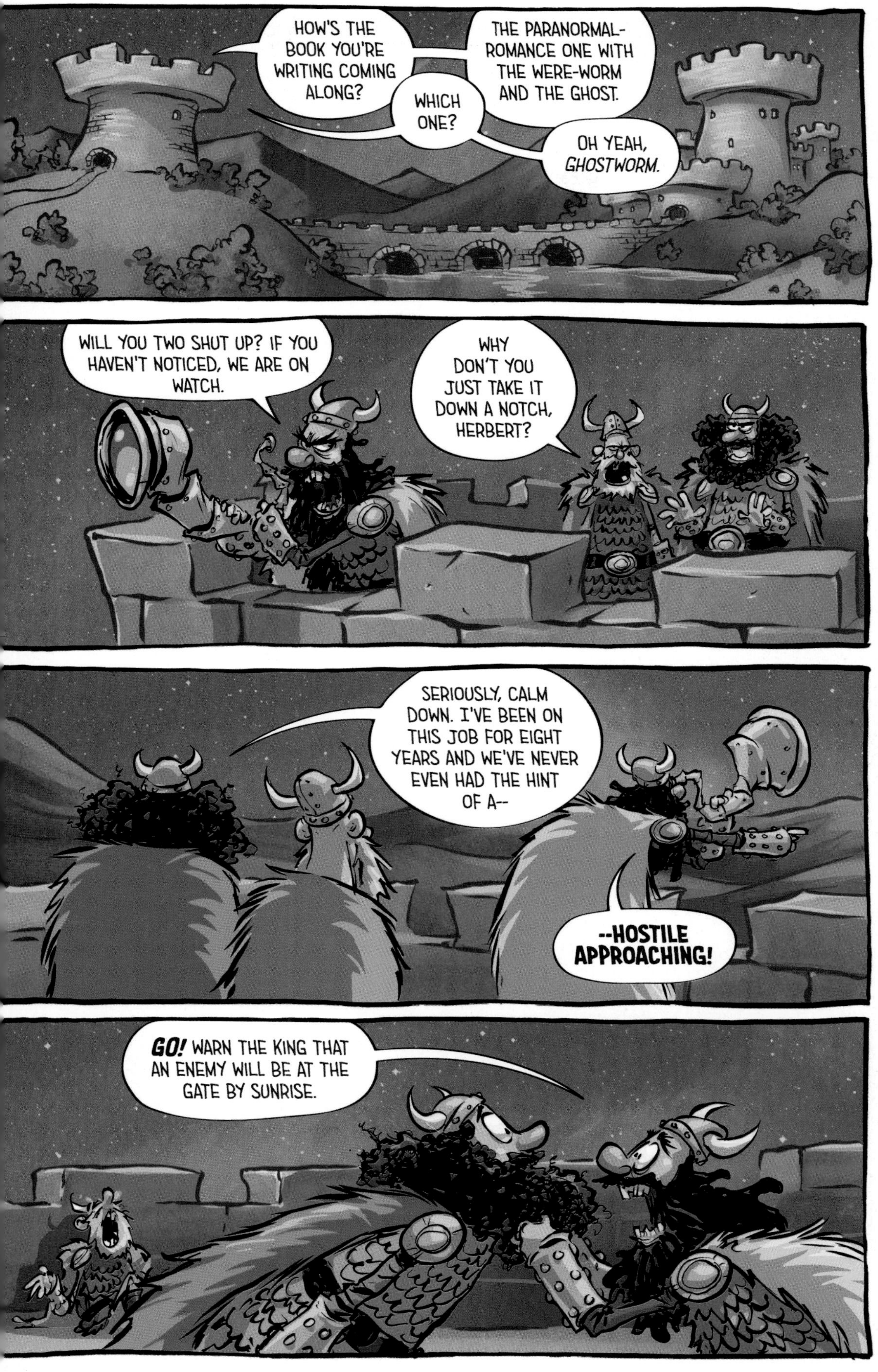
HOW'S THE BOOK YOU'RE WRITING COMING ALONG?
WHICH ONE?
THE PARANORMAL-ROMANCE ONE WITH THE WERE-WORM AND THE GHOST.
OH YEAH, *GHOSTWORM.*
WILL YOU TWO SHUT UP? IF YOU HAVEN'T NOTICED, WE ARE ON WATCH.
WHY DON'T YOU JUST TAKE IT DOWN A NOTCH, HERBERT?
SERIOUSLY, CALM DOWN. I'VE BEEN ON THIS JOB FOR EIGHT YEARS AND WE'VE NEVER EVEN HAD THE HINT OF A--
--HOSTILE APPROACHING!
GO! WARN THE KING THAT AN ENEMY WILL BE AT THE GATE BY SUNRISE.

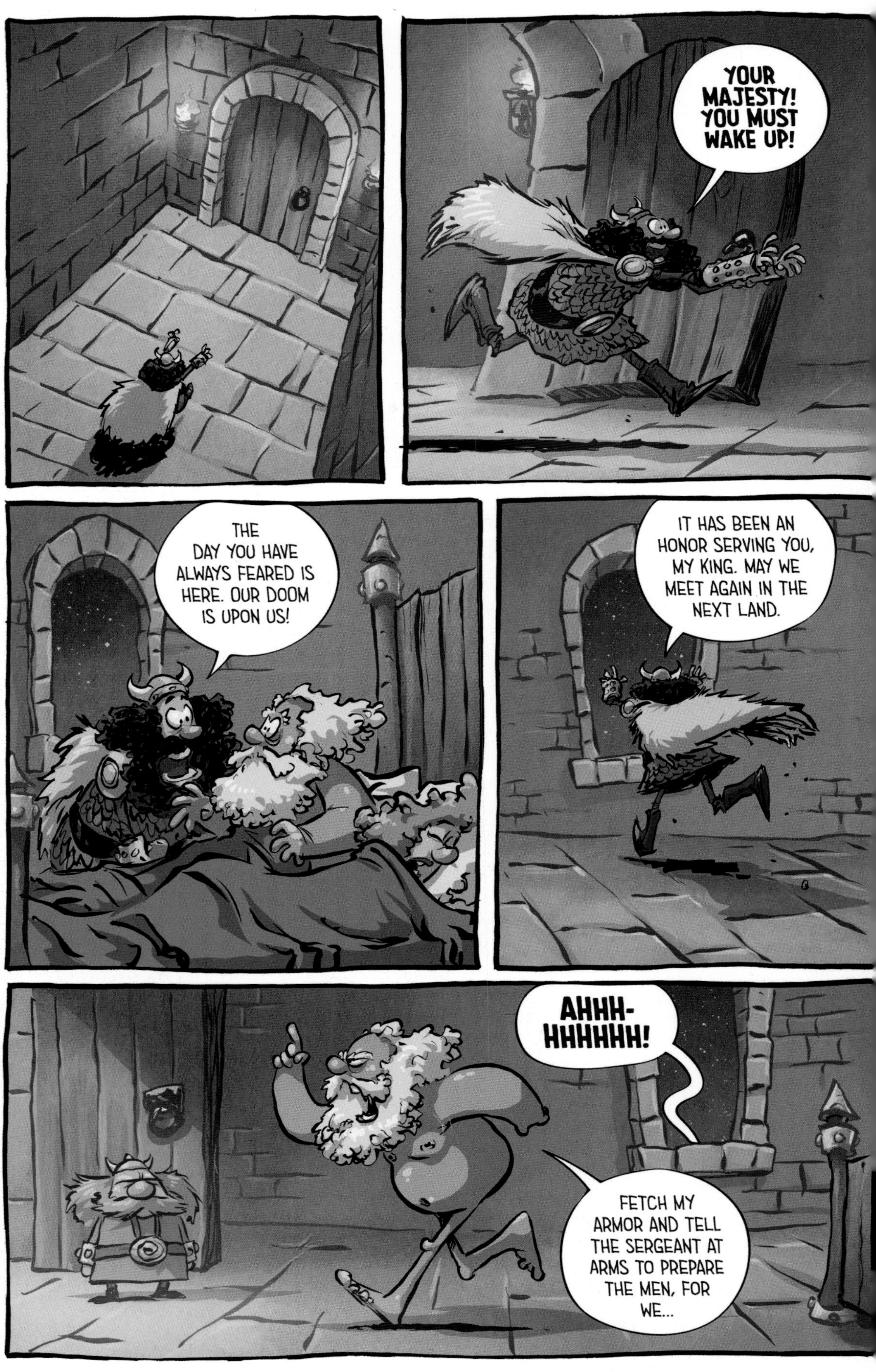
YOUR MAJESTY! YOU MUST WAKE UP!
THE DAY YOU HAVE ALWAYS FEARED IS HERE. OUR DOOM IS UPON US!
IT HAS BEEN AN HONOR SERVING YOU, MY KING. MAY WE MEET AGAIN IN THE NEXT LAND.
AHHH-HHHHHH!
FETCH MY ARMOR AND TELL THE SERGEANT AT ARMS TO PREPARE THE MEN, FOR WE...

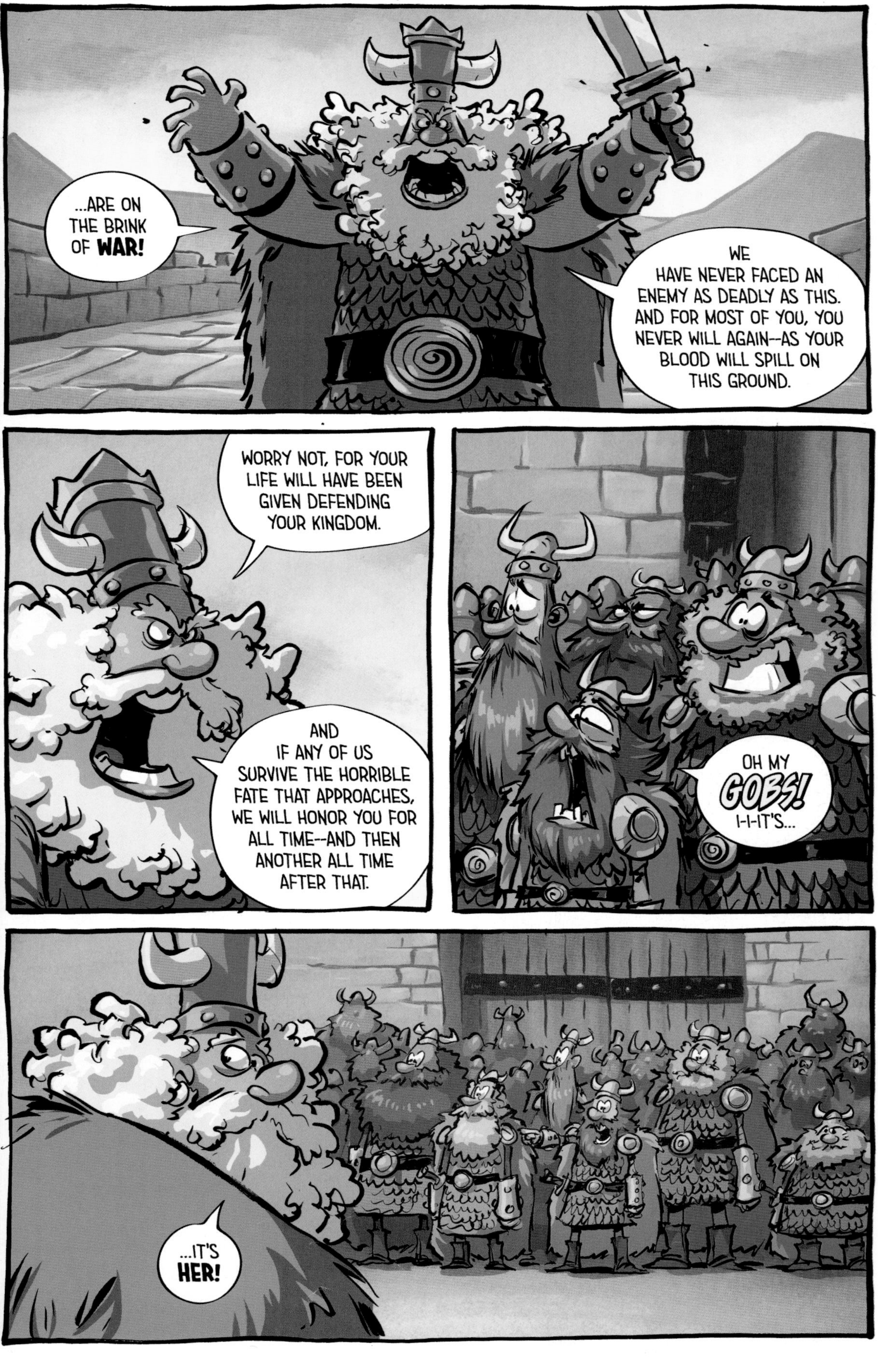
...ARE ON THE BRINK OF **WAR!**
WE HAVE NEVER FACED AN ENEMY AS DEADLY AS THIS. AND FOR MOST OF YOU, YOU NEVER WILL AGAIN--AS YOUR BLOOD WILL SPILL ON THIS GROUND.
WORRY NOT, FOR YOUR LIFE WILL HAVE BEEN GIVEN DEFENDING YOUR KINGDOM.
AND IF ANY OF US SURVIVE THE HORRIBLE FATE THAT APPROACHES, WE WILL HONOR YOU FOR ALL TIME--AND THEN ANOTHER ALL TIME AFTER THAT.
OH MY GOBS! I-I-IT'S...
...IT'S **HER!**

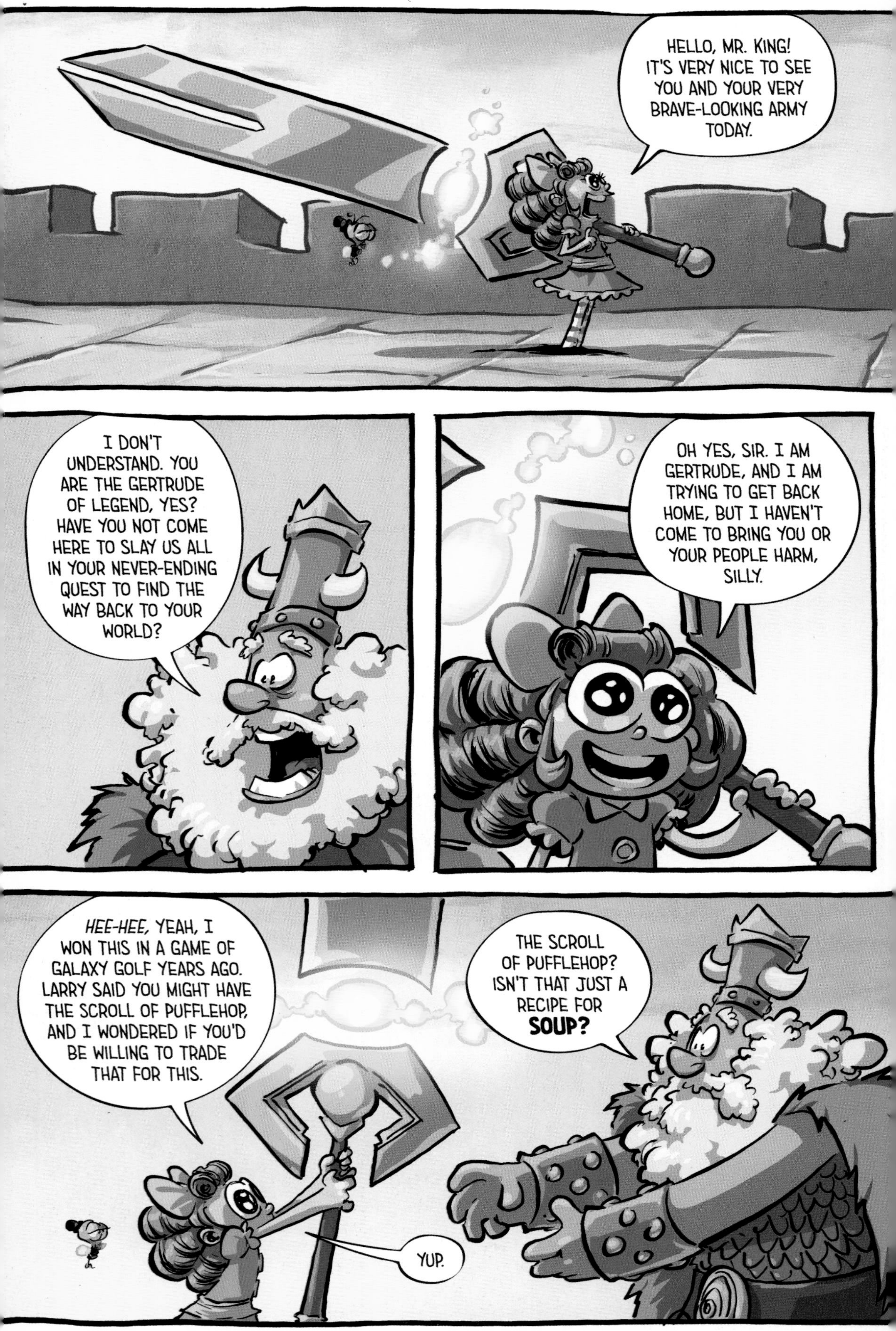
HELLO, MR. KING! IT'S VERY NICE TO SEE YOU AND YOUR VERY BRAVE-LOOKING ARMY TODAY.
I DON'T UNDERSTAND. YOU ARE THE GERTRUDE OF LEGEND, YES? HAVE YOU NOT COME HERE TO SLAY US ALL IN YOUR NEVER-ENDING QUEST TO FIND THE WAY BACK TO YOUR WORLD?
OH YES, SIR. I AM GERTRUDE, AND I AM TRYING TO GET BACK HOME, BUT I HAVEN'T COME TO BRING YOU OR YOUR PEOPLE HARM, SILLY.
HEE-HEE, YEAH, I WON THIS IN A GAME OF GALAXY GOLF YEARS AGO. LARRY SAID YOU MIGHT HAVE THE SCROLL OF PUFFLEHOP, AND I WONDERED IF YOU'D BE WILLING TO TRADE THAT FOR THIS.
YUP.
THE SCROLL OF PUFFLEHOP? ISN'T THAT JUST A RECIPE FOR **SOUP?**

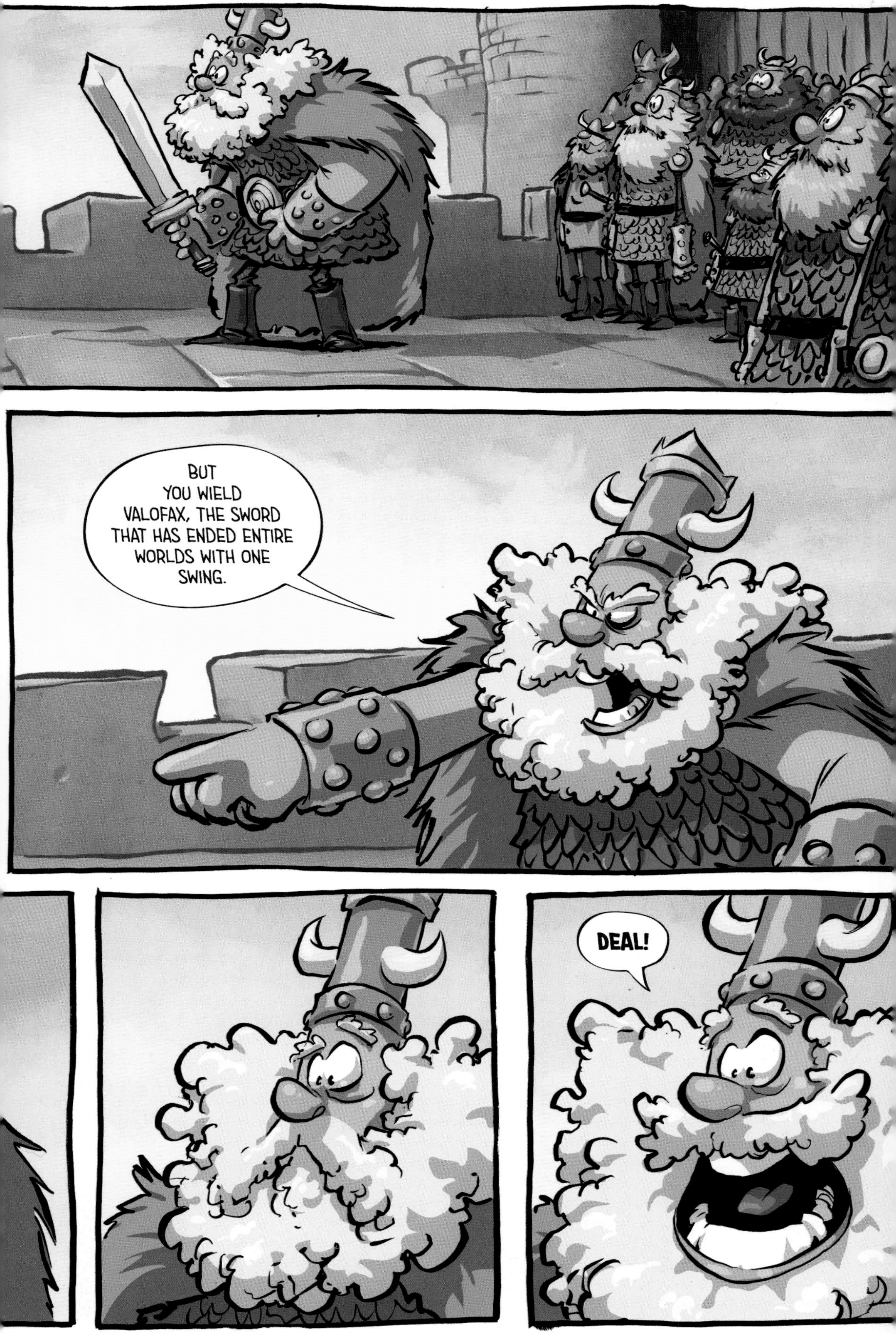
BUT YOU WIELD VALOFAX, THE SWORD THAT HAS ENDED ENTIRE WORLDS WITH ONE SWING.
DEAL!

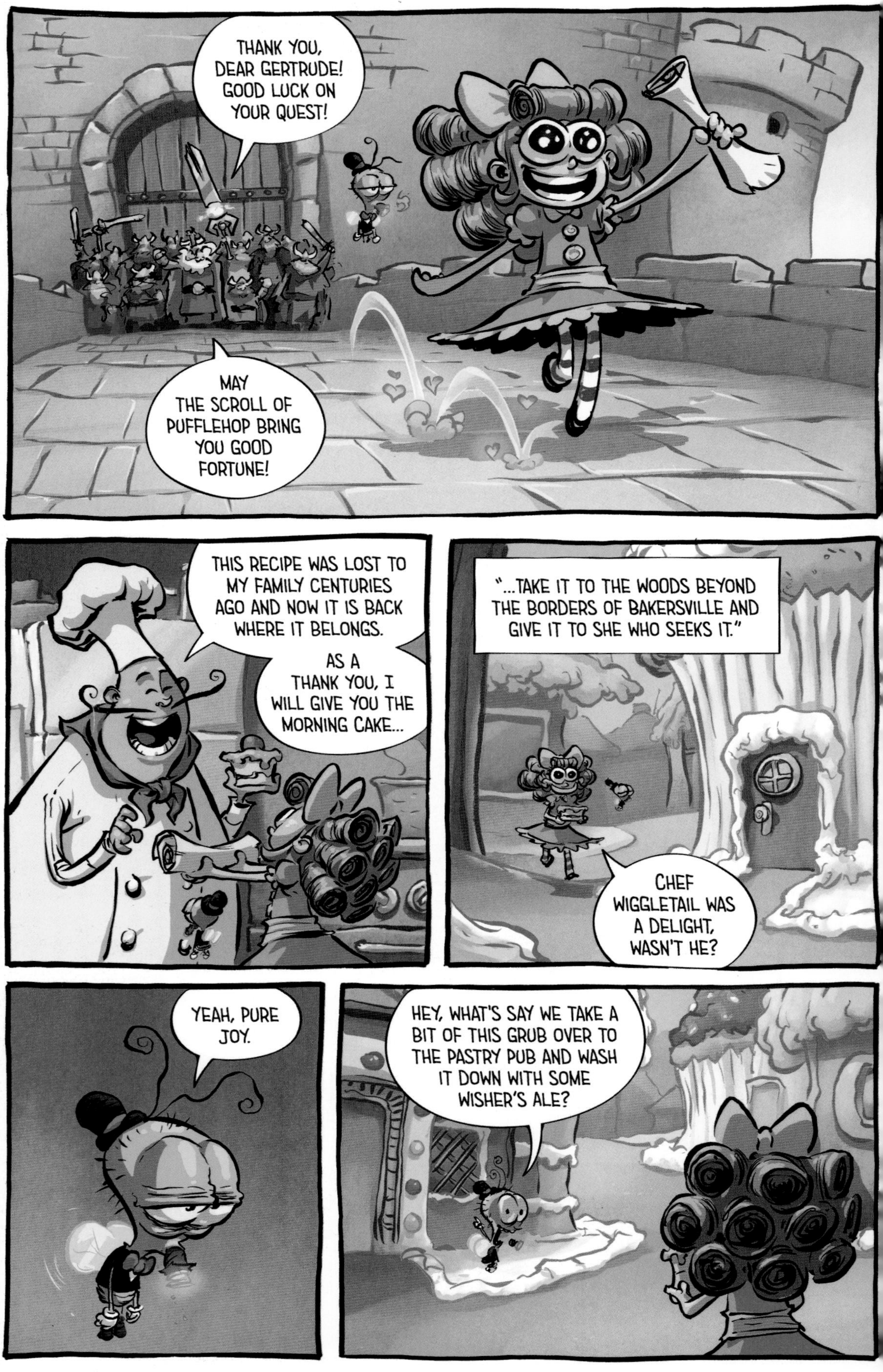
THANK YOU, DEAR GERTRUDE! GOOD LUCK ON YOUR QUEST!
MAY THE SCROLL OF PUFFLEHOP BRING YOU GOOD FORTUNE!
THIS RECIPE WAS LOST TO MY FAMILY CENTURIES AGO AND NOW IT IS BACK WHERE IT BELONGS.
AS A THANK YOU, I WILL GIVE YOU THE MORNING CAKE...
"...TAKE IT TO THE WOODS BEYOND THE BORDERS OF BAKERSVILLE AND GIVE IT TO SHE WHO SEEKS IT."
CHEF WIGGLETAIL WAS A DELIGHT, WASN'T HE?
YEAH, PURE JOY.
HEY, WHAT'S SAY WE TAKE A BIT OF THIS GRUB OVER TO THE PASTRY PUB AND WASH IT DOWN WITH SOME WISHER'S ALE?

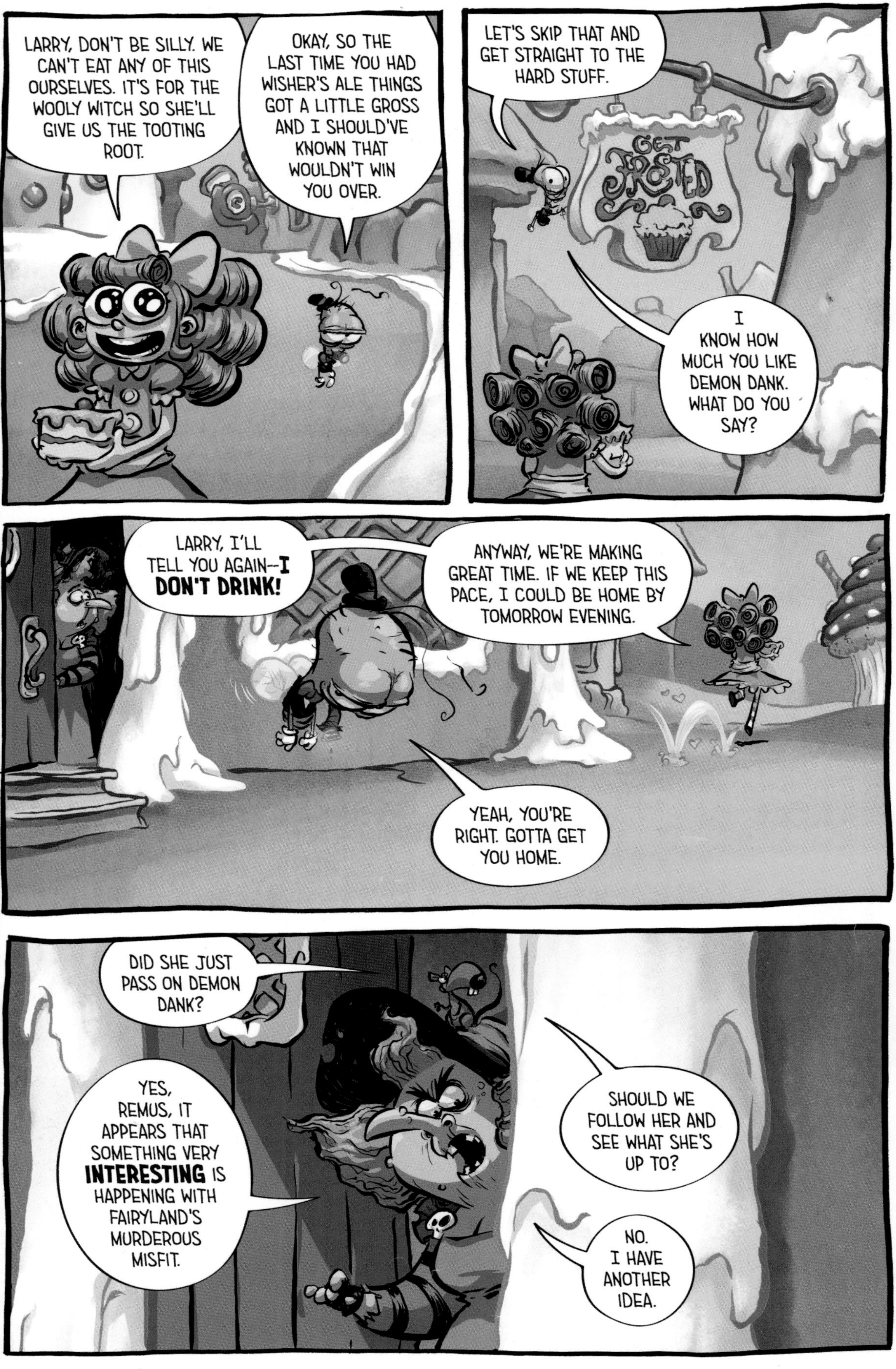
LARRY, DON'T BE SILLY. WE CAN'T EAT ANY OF THIS OURSELVES. IT'S FOR THE WOOLY WITCH SO SHE'LL GIVE US THE TOOTING ROOT.
OKAY, SO THE LAST TIME YOU HAD WISHER'S ALE THINGS GOT A LITTLE GROSS AND I SHOULD'VE KNOWN THAT WOULDN'T WIN YOU OVER.
LET'S SKIP THAT AND GET STRAIGHT TO THE HARD STUFF.
GET FROSTED
I KNOW HOW MUCH YOU LIKE DEMON DANK. WHAT DO YOU SAY?
LARRY, I'LL TELL YOU AGAIN--**I DON'T DRINK!**
ANYWAY, WE'RE MAKING GREAT TIME. IF WE KEEP THIS PACE, I COULD BE HOME BY TOMORROW EVENING.
YEAH, YOU'RE RIGHT. GOTTA GET YOU HOME.
DID SHE JUST PASS ON DEMON DANK?
YES, REMUS, IT APPEARS THAT SOMETHING VERY **INTERESTING** IS HAPPENING WITH FAIRYLAND'S MURDEROUS MISFIT.
SHOULD WE FOLLOW HER AND SEE WHAT SHE'S UP TO?
NO. I HAVE ANOTHER IDEA.

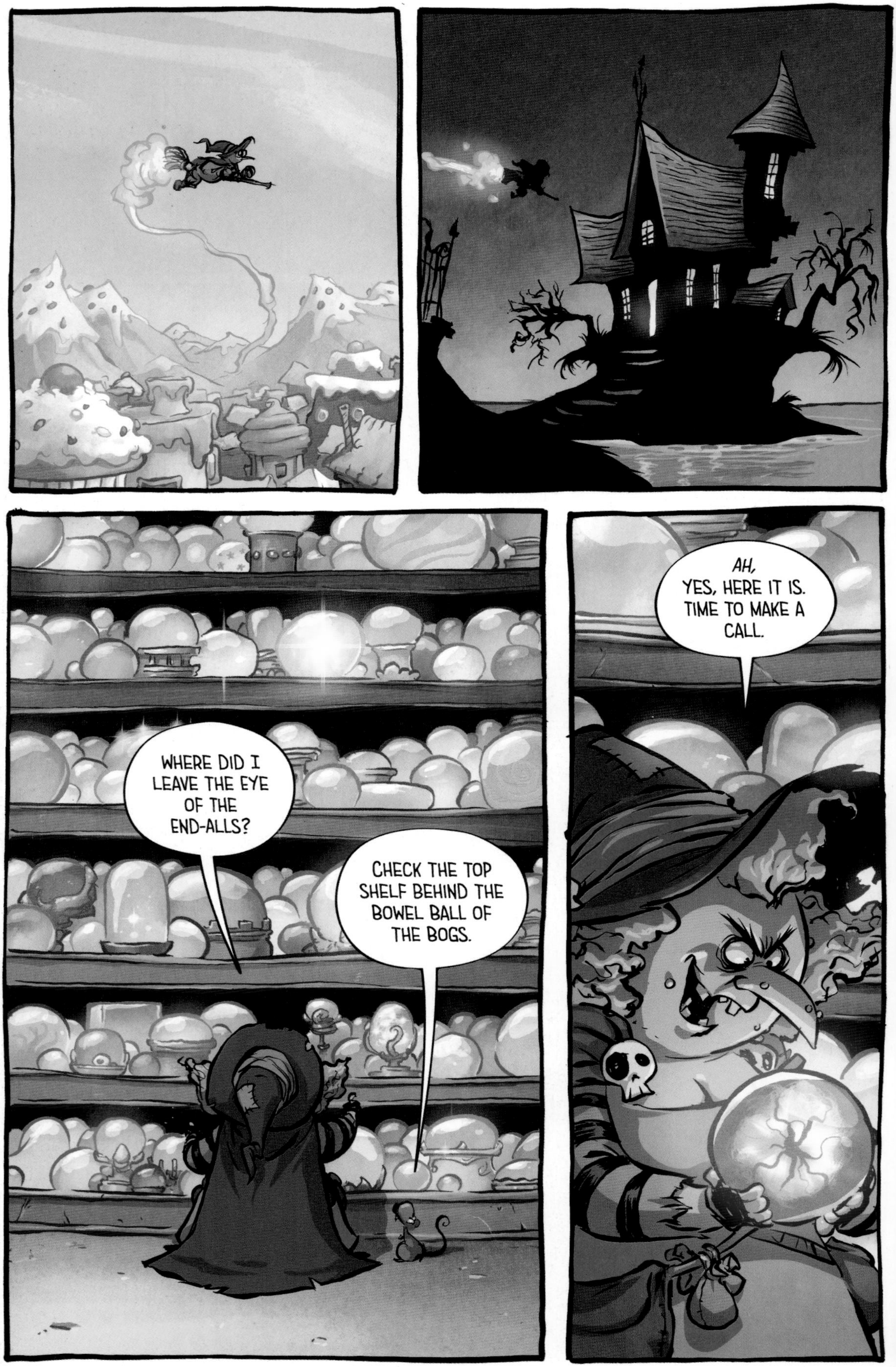
WHERE DID I LEAVE THE EYE OF THE END-ALLS?
CHECK THE TOP SHELF BEHIND THE BOWEL BALL OF THE BOGS.
AH, YES, HERE IT IS. TIME TO MAKE A CALL.

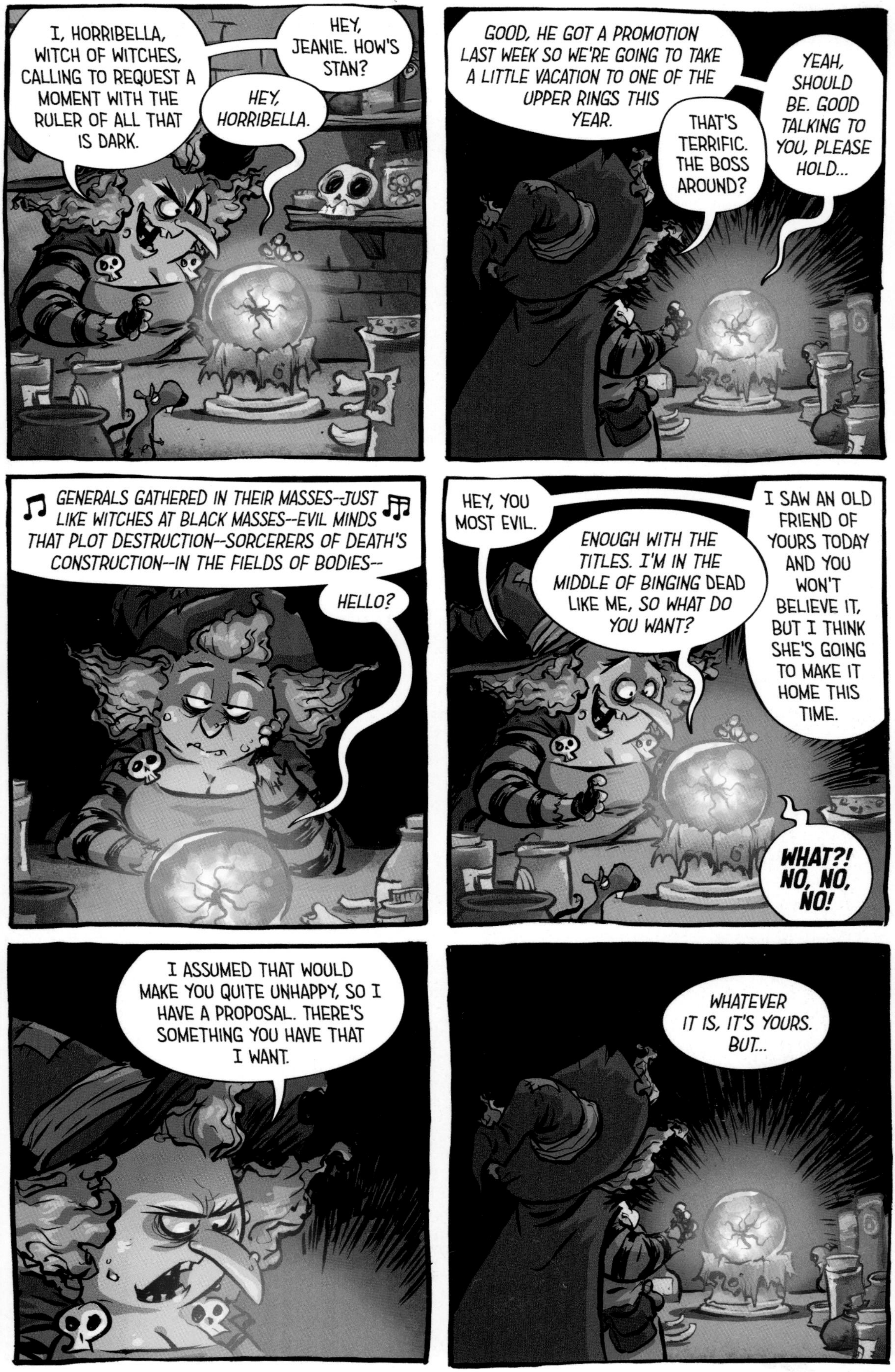
I, HORRIBELLA, WITCH OF WITCHES, CALLING TO REQUEST A MOMENT WITH THE RULER OF ALL THAT IS DARK.
HEY, HORRIBELLA.
HEY, JEANIE. HOW'S STAN?
GOOD, HE GOT A PROMOTION LAST WEEK SO WE'RE GOING TO TAKE A LITTLE VACATION TO ONE OF THE UPPER RINGS THIS YEAR.
THAT'S TERRIFIC. THE BOSS AROUND?
YEAH, SHOULD BE. GOOD TALKING TO YOU, PLEASE HOLD...
♫ GENERALS GATHERED IN THEIR MASSES--JUST LIKE WITCHES AT BLACK MASSES--EVIL MINDS THAT PLOT DESTRUCTION--SORCERERS OF DEATH'S CONSTRUCTION--IN THE FIELDS OF BODIES-- ♬
HELLO?
HEY, YOU MOST EVIL.
ENOUGH WITH THE TITLES. I'M IN THE MIDDLE OF BINGING DEAD LIKE ME, SO WHAT DO YOU WANT?
I SAW AN OLD FRIEND OF YOURS TODAY AND YOU WON'T BELIEVE IT, BUT I THINK SHE'S GOING TO MAKE IT HOME THIS TIME.
WHAT?! NO, NO, NO!
I ASSUMED THAT WOULD MAKE YOU QUITE UNHAPPY, SO I HAVE A PROPOSAL. THERE'S SOMETHING YOU HAVE THAT I WANT.
WHATEVER IT IS, IT'S YOURS. BUT...

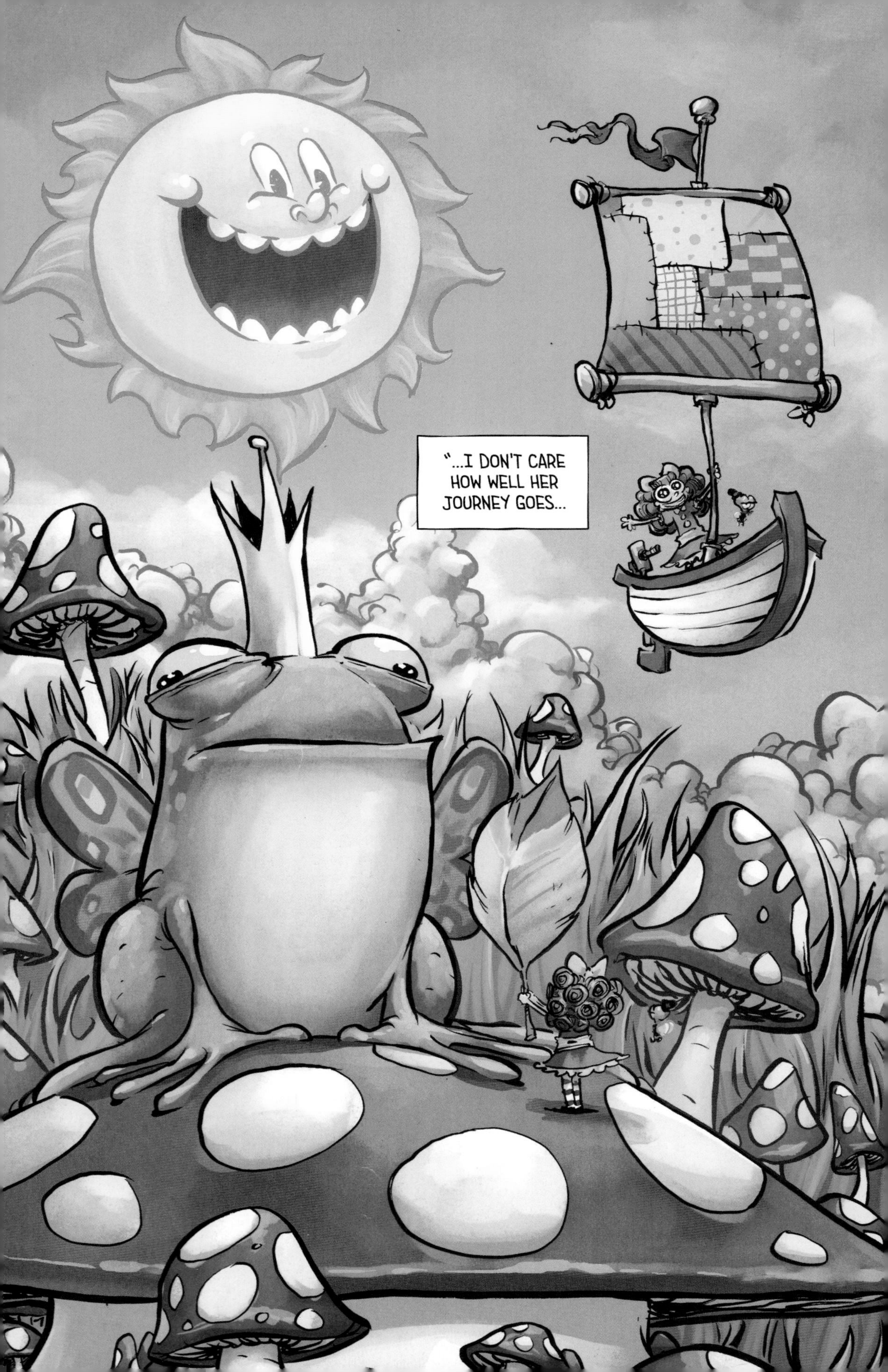
"...I DON'T CARE HOW WELL HER JOURNEY GOES...

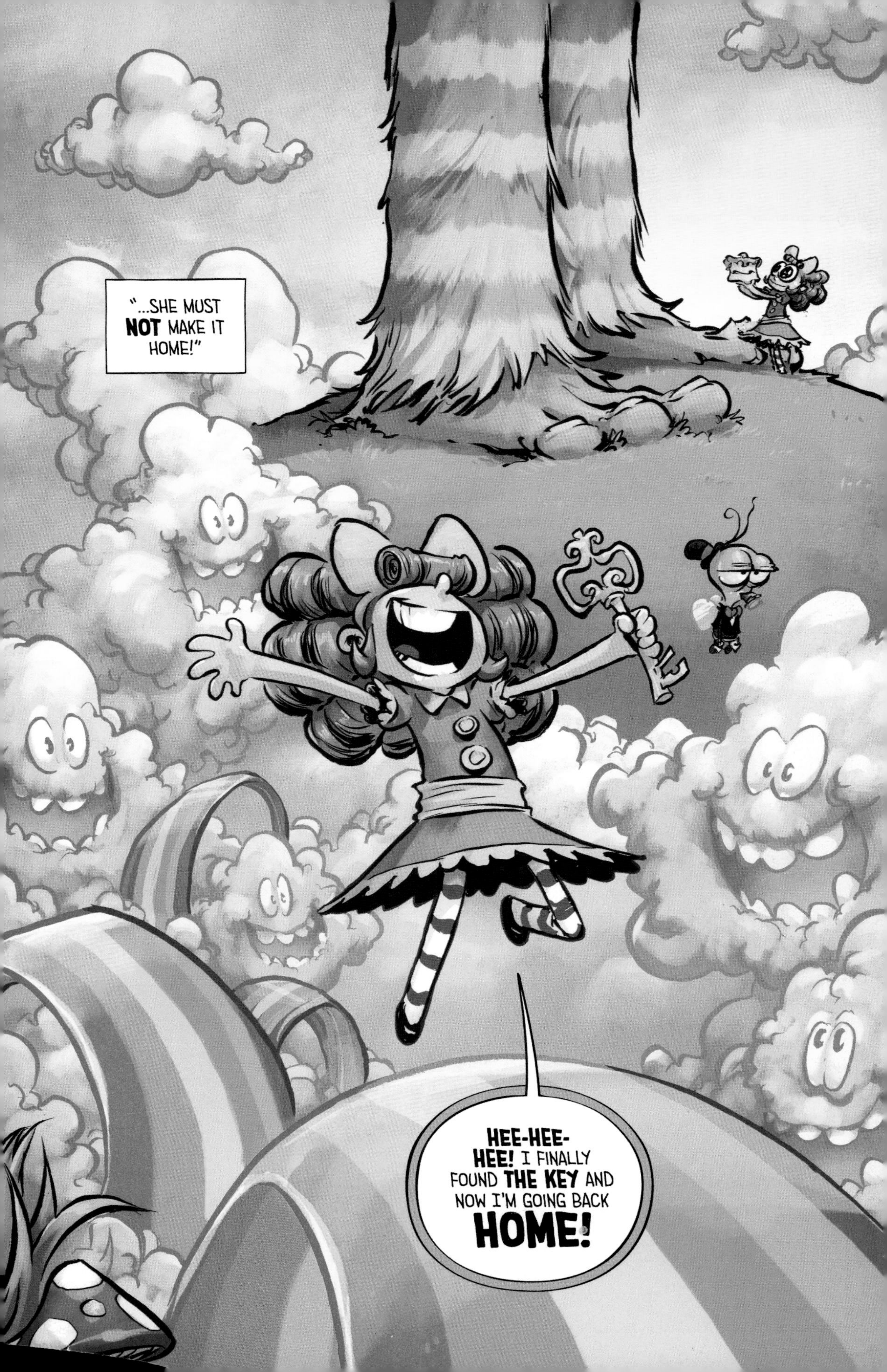
"...SHE MUST NOT MAKE IT HOME!"
HEE-HEE-HEE! I FINALLY FOUND THE KEY AND NOW I'M GOING BACK HOME!

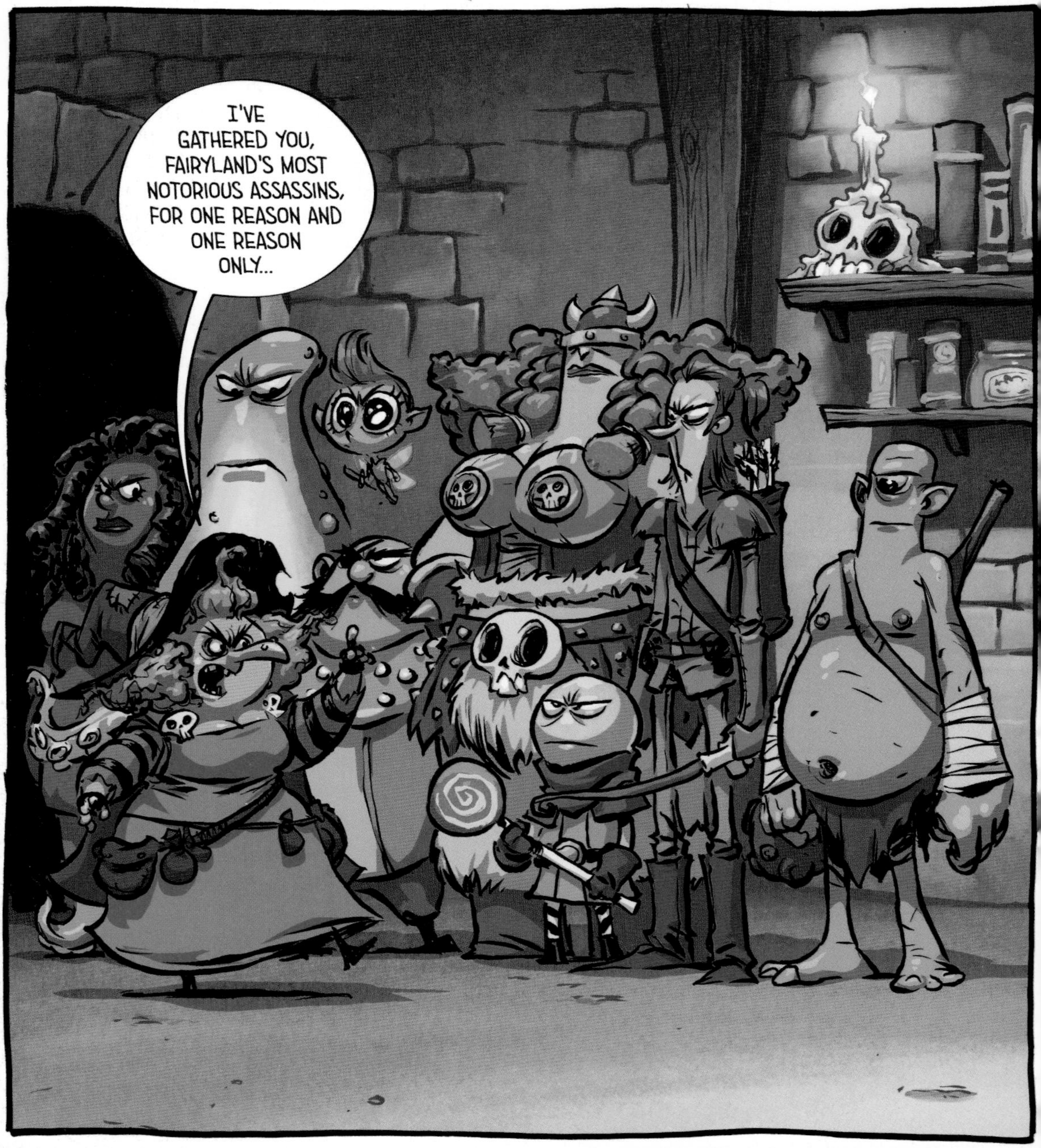
I'VE GATHERED YOU, FAIRYLAND'S MOST NOTORIOUS ASSASSINS, FOR ONE REASON AND ONE REASON ONLY...

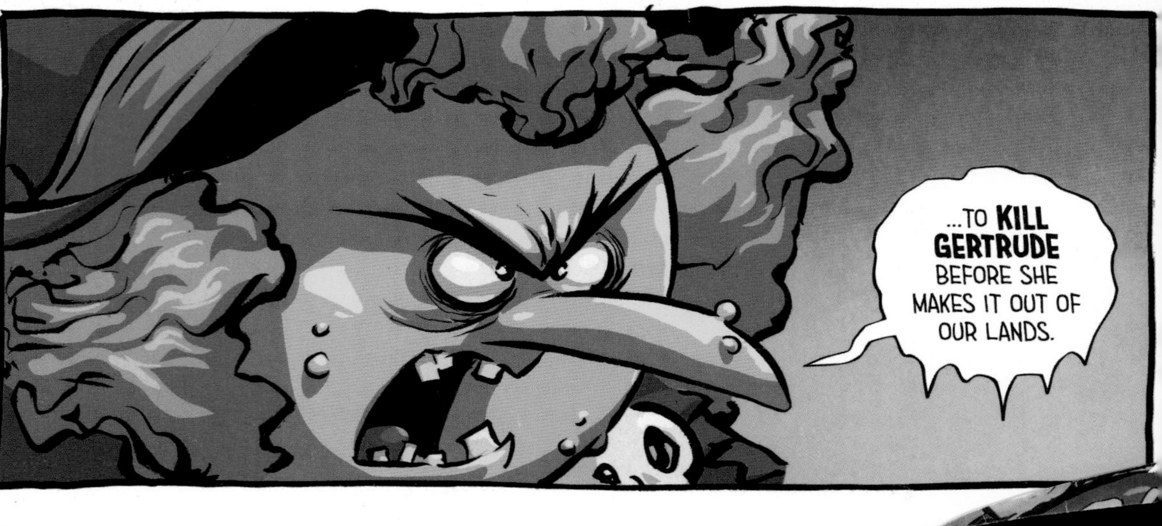
...TO **KILL GERTRUDE** BEFORE SHE MAKES IT OUT OF OUR LANDS.

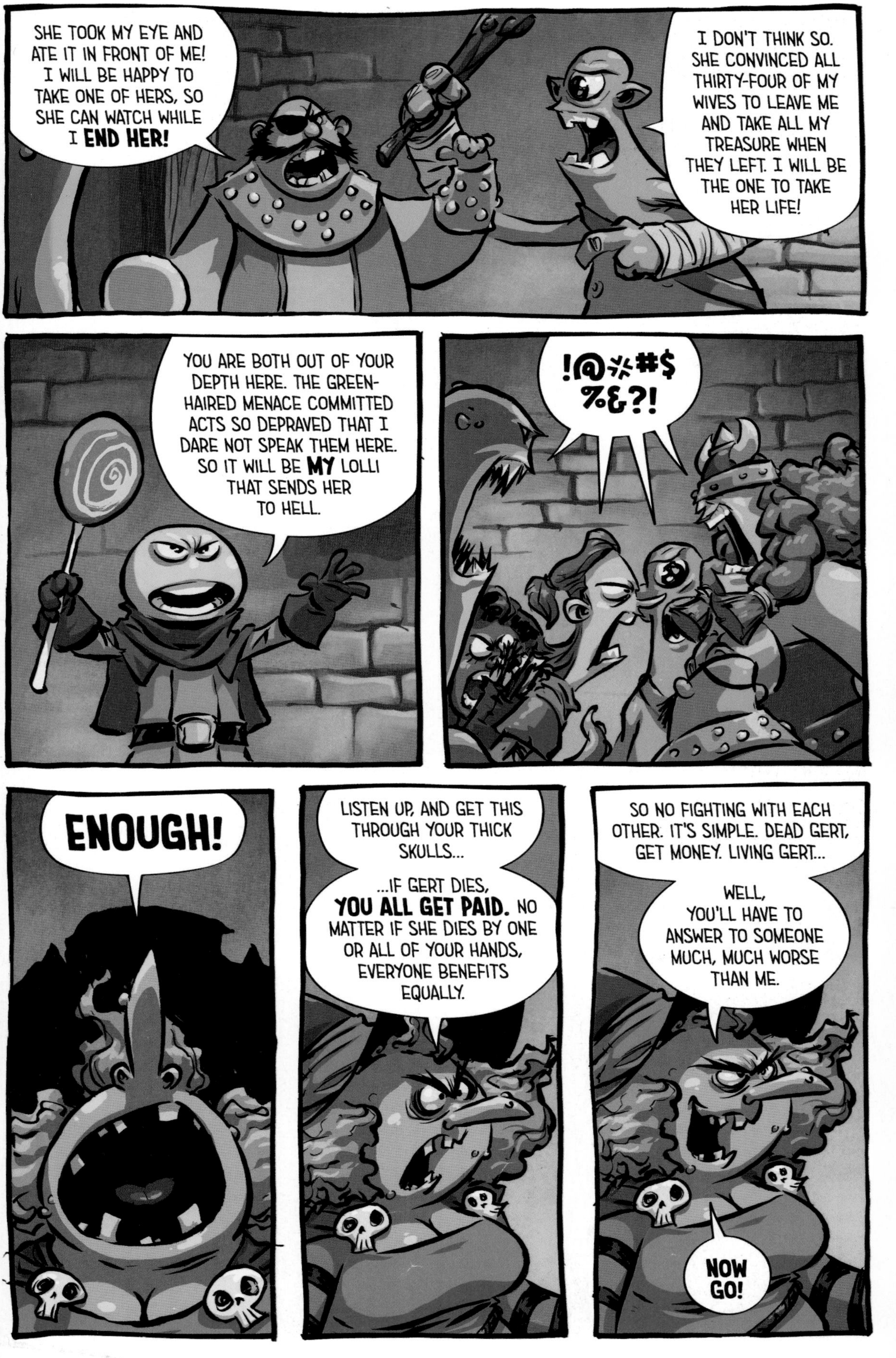
SHE TOOK MY EYE AND ATE IT IN FRONT OF ME! I WILL BE HAPPY TO TAKE ONE OF HERS, SO SHE CAN WATCH WHILE I END HER!
I DON'T THINK SO. SHE CONVINCED ALL THIRTY-FOUR OF MY WIVES TO LEAVE ME AND TAKE ALL MY TREASURE WHEN THEY LEFT. I WILL BE THE ONE TO TAKE HER LIFE!
YOU ARE BOTH OUT OF YOUR DEPTH HERE. THE GREEN-HAIRED MENACE COMMITTED ACTS SO DEPRAVED THAT I DARE NOT SPEAK THEM HERE. SO IT WILL BE MY LOLLI THAT SENDS HER TO HELL.
!@*#$ %&?!
ENOUGH!
LISTEN UP, AND GET THIS THROUGH YOUR THICK SKULLS...
...IF GERT DIES, YOU ALL GET PAID. NO MATTER IF SHE DIES BY ONE OR ALL OF YOUR HANDS, EVERYONE BENEFITS EQUALLY.
SO NO FIGHTING WITH EACH OTHER. IT'S SIMPLE. DEAD GERT, GET MONEY. LIVING GERT...
WELL, YOU'LL HAVE TO ANSWER TO SOMEONE MUCH, MUCH WORSE THAN ME.
NOW GO!

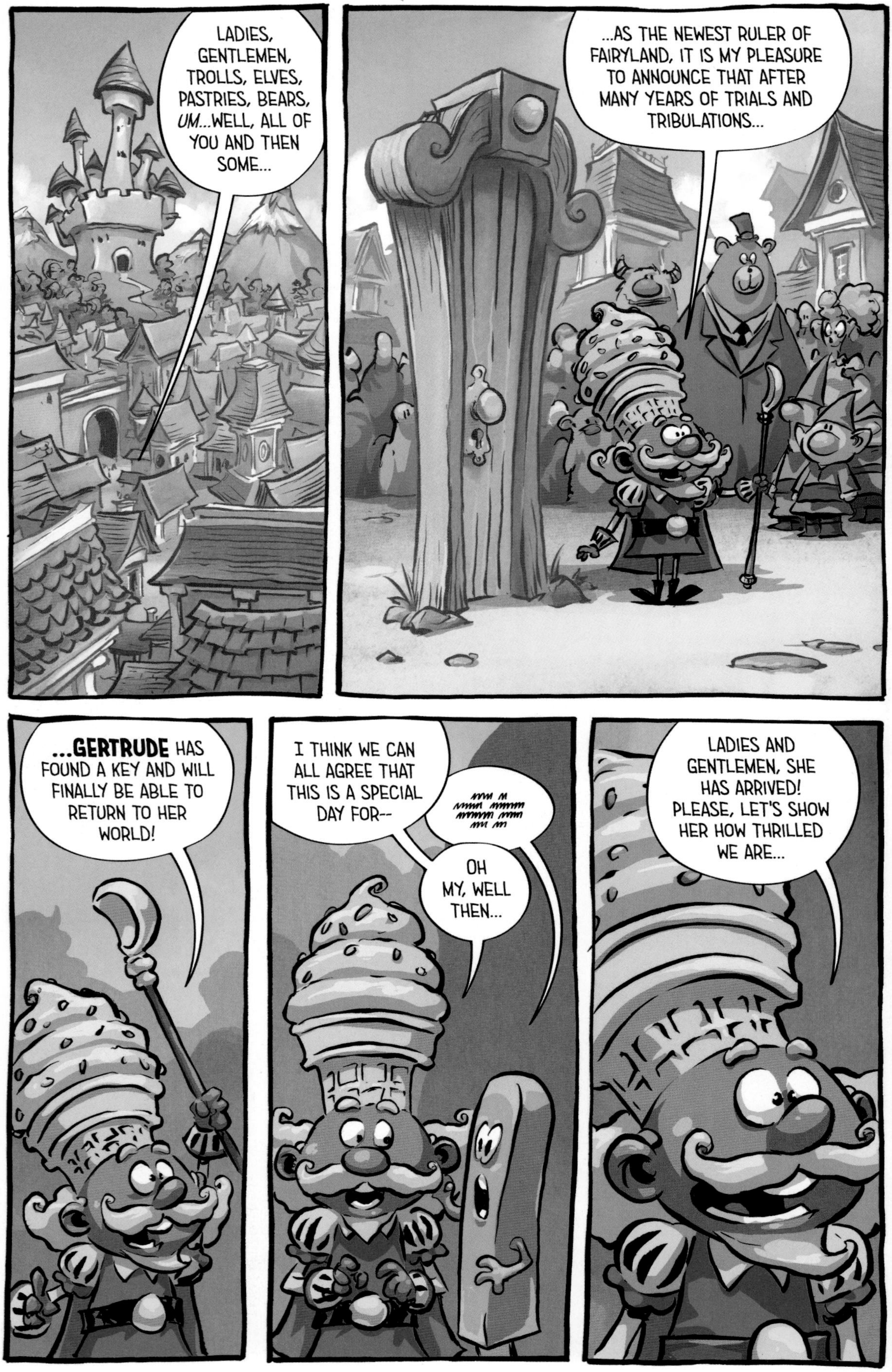
LADIES, GENTLEMEN, TROLLS, ELVES, PASTRIES, BEARS, *UM*...WELL, ALL OF YOU AND THEN SOME...
...AS THE NEWEST RULER OF FAIRYLAND, IT IS MY PLEASURE TO ANNOUNCE THAT AFTER MANY YEARS OF TRIALS AND TRIBULATIONS...
...**GERTRUDE** HAS FOUND A KEY AND WILL FINALLY BE ABLE TO RETURN TO HER WORLD!
I THINK WE CAN ALL AGREE THAT THIS IS A SPECIAL DAY FOR--
OH MY, WELL THEN...
LADIES AND GENTLEMEN, SHE HAS ARRIVED! PLEASE, LET'S SHOW HER HOW THRILLED WE ARE...

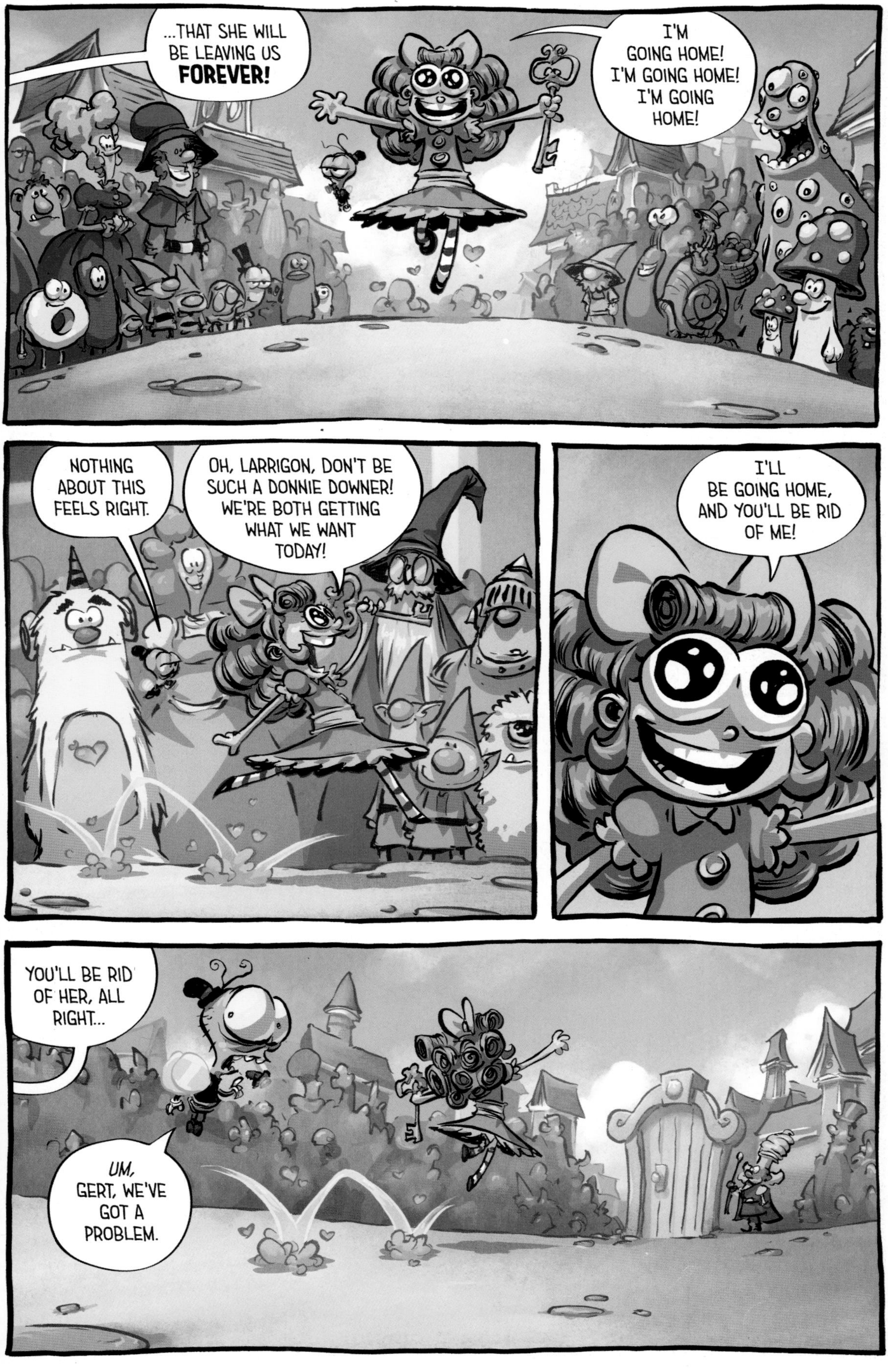
...THAT SHE WILL BE LEAVING US **FOREVER!**
I'M GOING HOME! I'M GOING HOME! I'M GOING HOME!
NOTHING ABOUT THIS FEELS RIGHT.
OH, LARRIGON, DON'T BE SUCH A DONNIE DOWNER! WE'RE BOTH GETTING WHAT WE WANT TODAY!
I'LL BE GOING HOME, AND YOU'LL BE RID OF ME!
YOU'LL BE RID OF HER, ALL RIGHT...
UM, GERT, WE'VE GOT A PROBLEM.

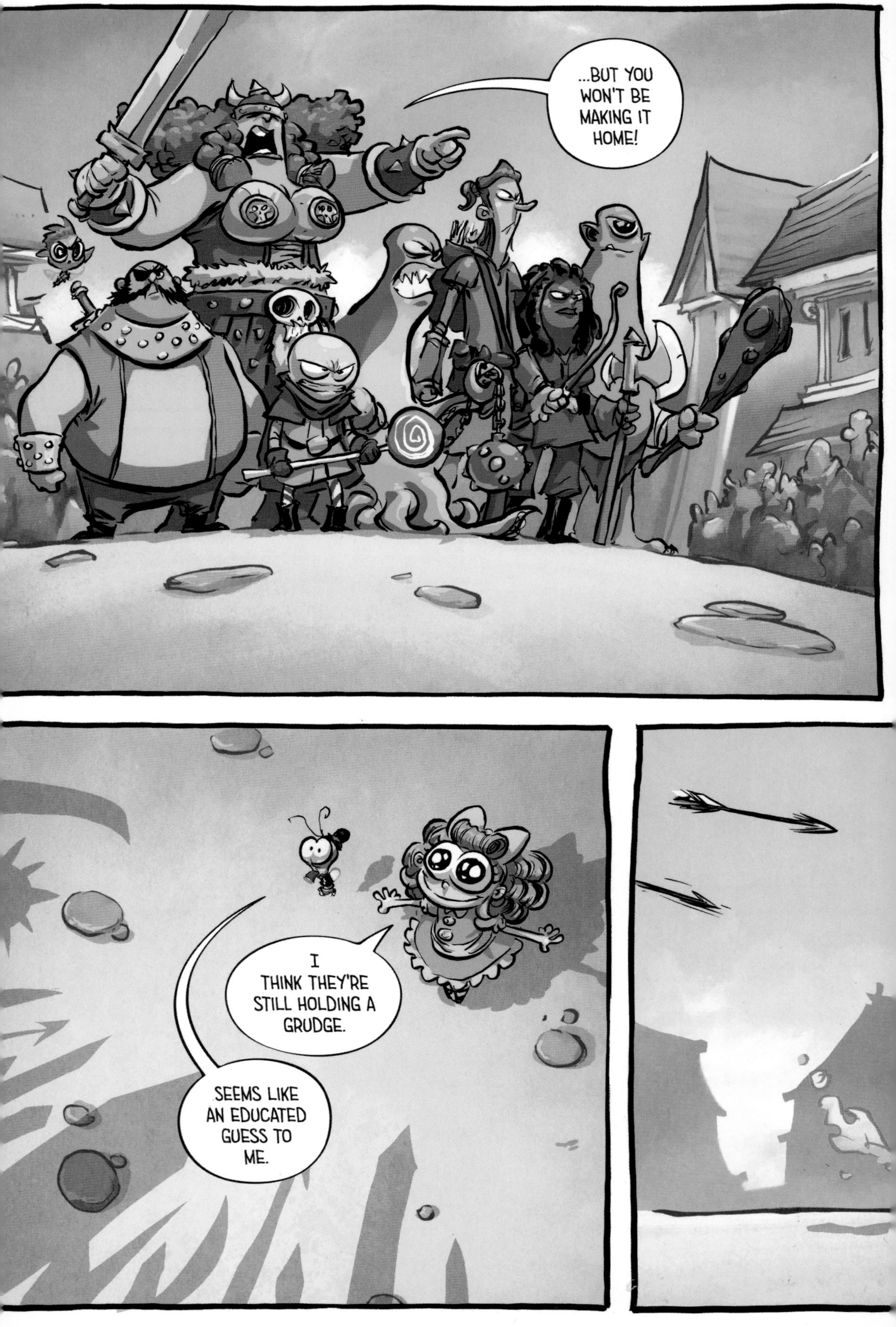
...BUT YOU WON'T BE MAKING IT HOME!
I THINK THEY'RE STILL HOLDING A GRUDGE.
SEEMS LIKE AN EDUCATED GUESS TO ME.

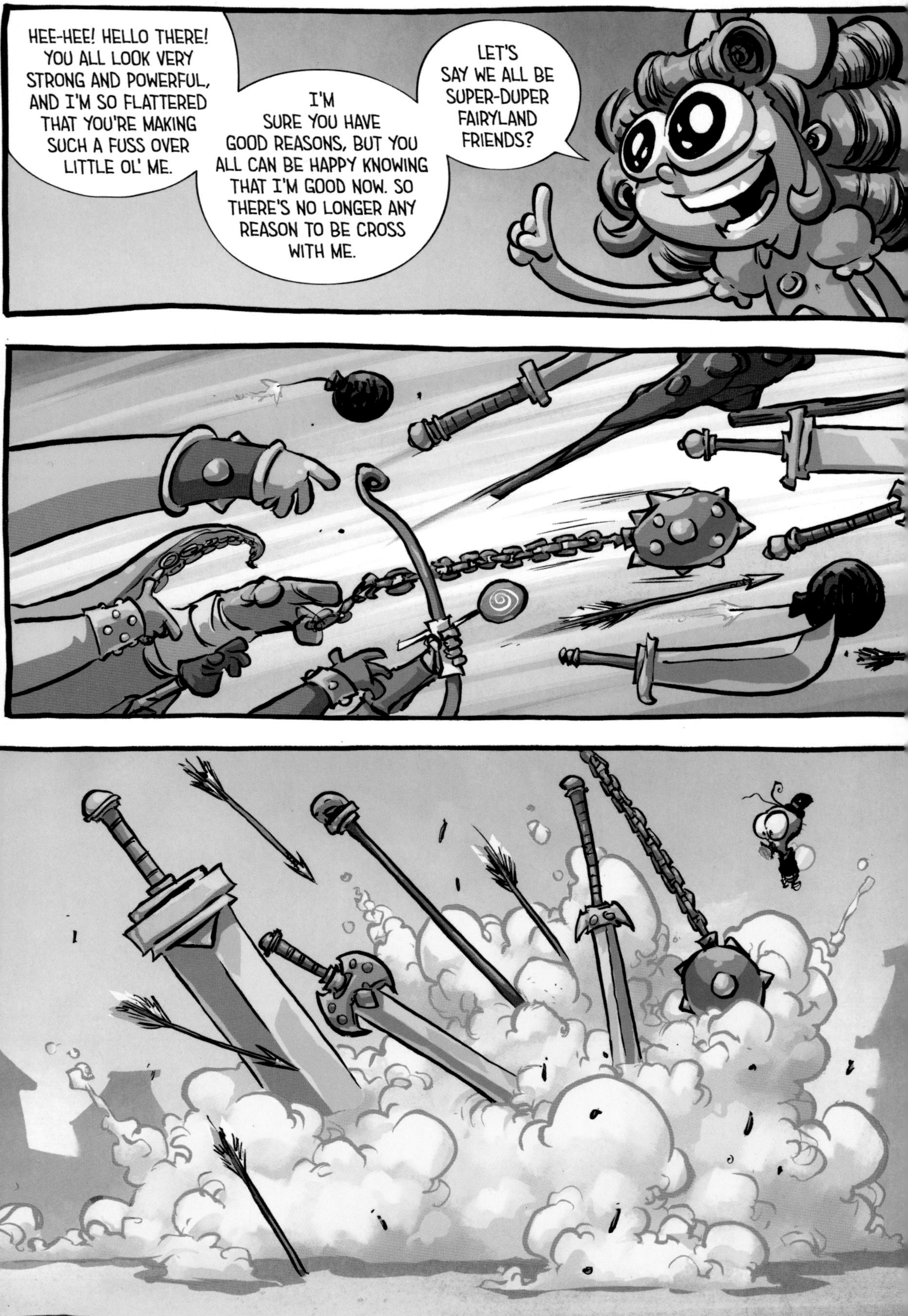
HEE-HEE! HELLO THERE! YOU ALL LOOK VERY STRONG AND POWERFUL, AND I'M SO FLATTERED THAT YOU'RE MAKING SUCH A FUSS OVER LITTLE OL' ME.
I'M SURE YOU HAVE GOOD REASONS, BUT YOU ALL CAN BE HAPPY KNOWING THAT I'M GOOD NOW. SO THERE'S NO LONGER ANY REASON TO BE CROSS WITH ME.
LET'S SAY WE ALL BE SUPER-DUPER FAIRYLAND FRIENDS?

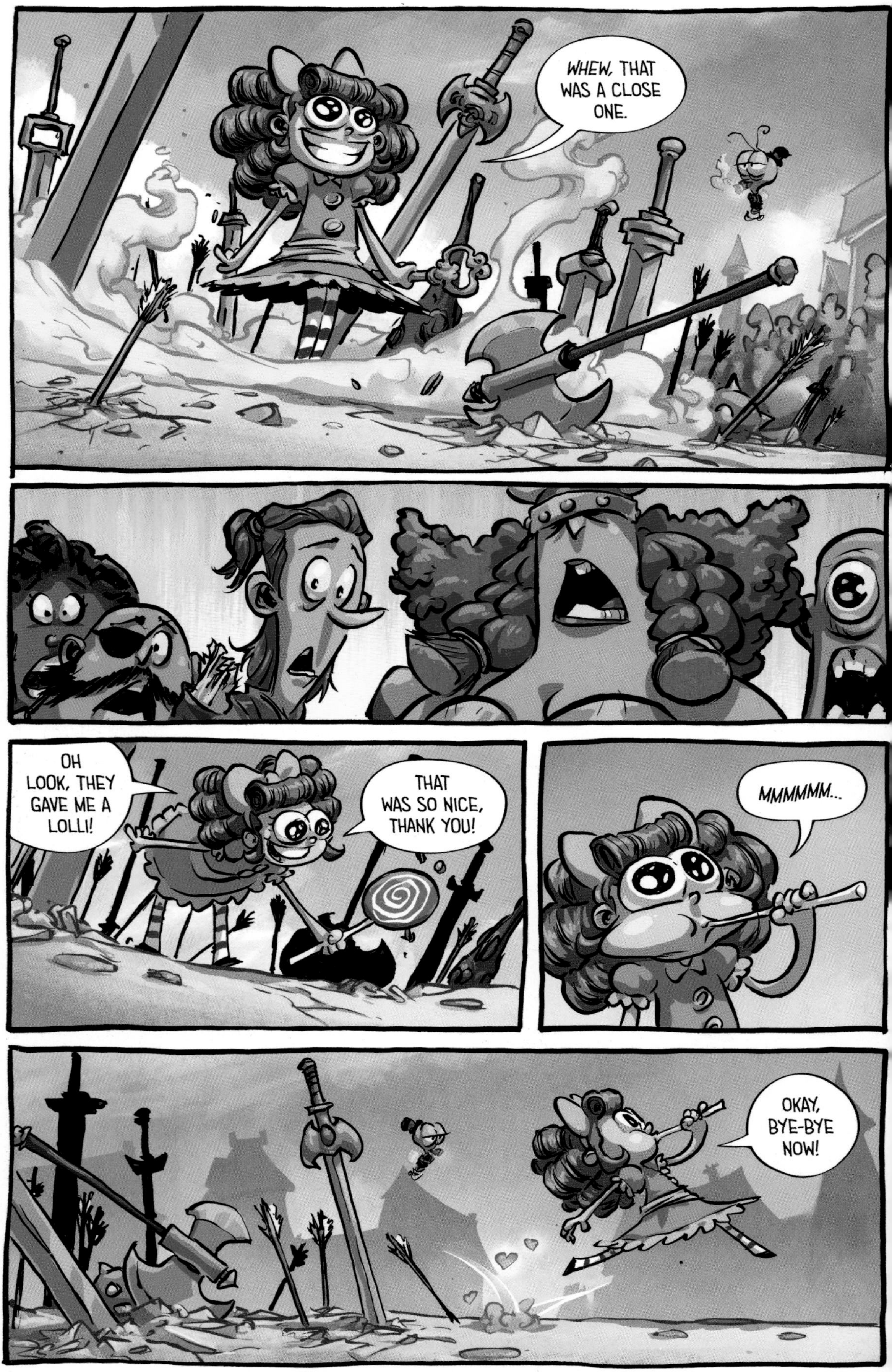
WHEW, THAT WAS A CLOSE ONE.
OH LOOK, THEY GAVE ME A LOLLI!
THAT WAS SO NICE, THANK YOU!
MMMMMM...
OKAY, BYE-BYE NOW!

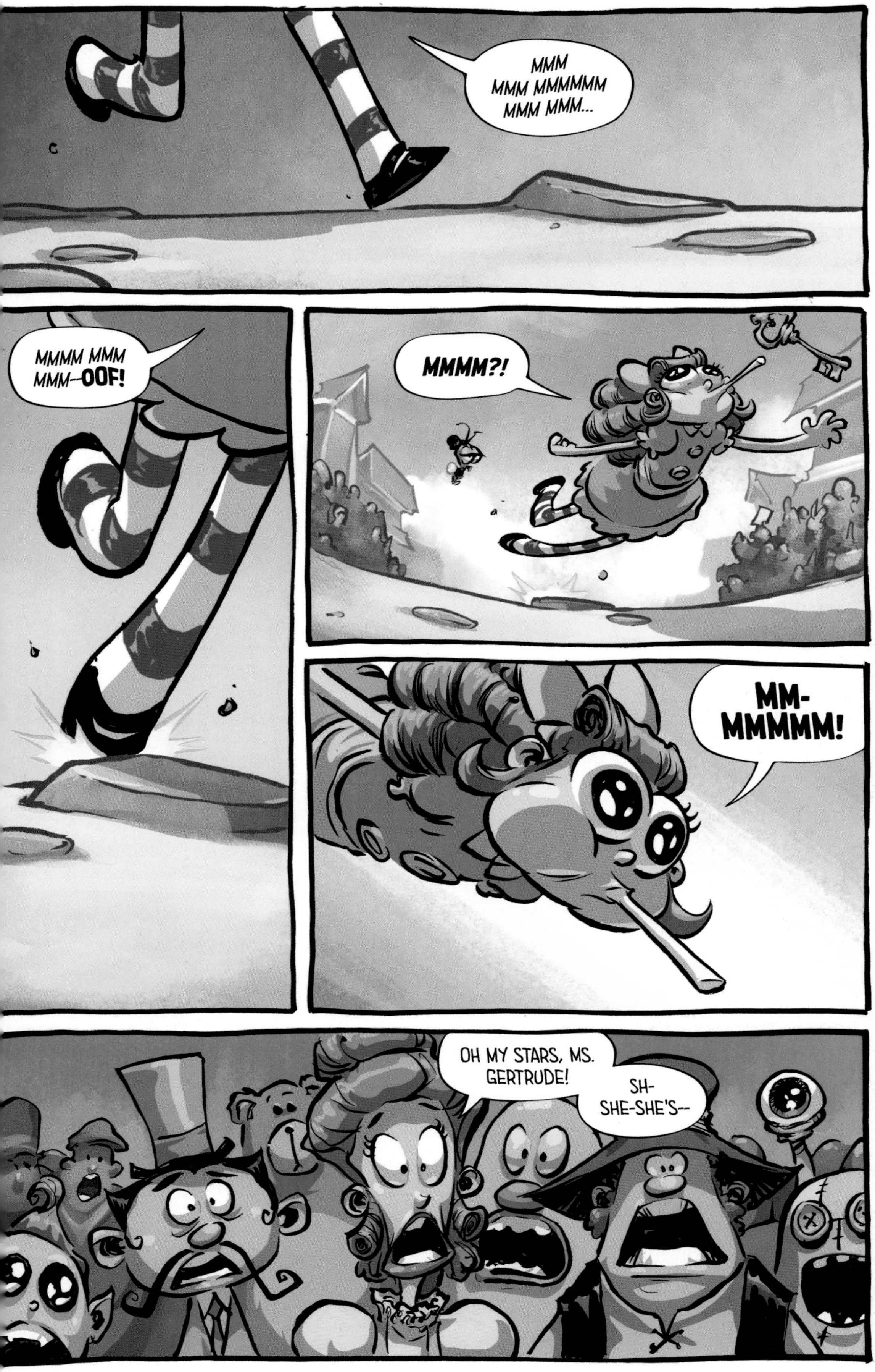
MMM
MMM MMMMMM
MMM MMM...
MMMM MMM
MMM--OOF!
MMMM?!
MM-
MMMMM!
OH MY STARS, MS.
GERTRUDE!
SH-
SHE-SHE'S--

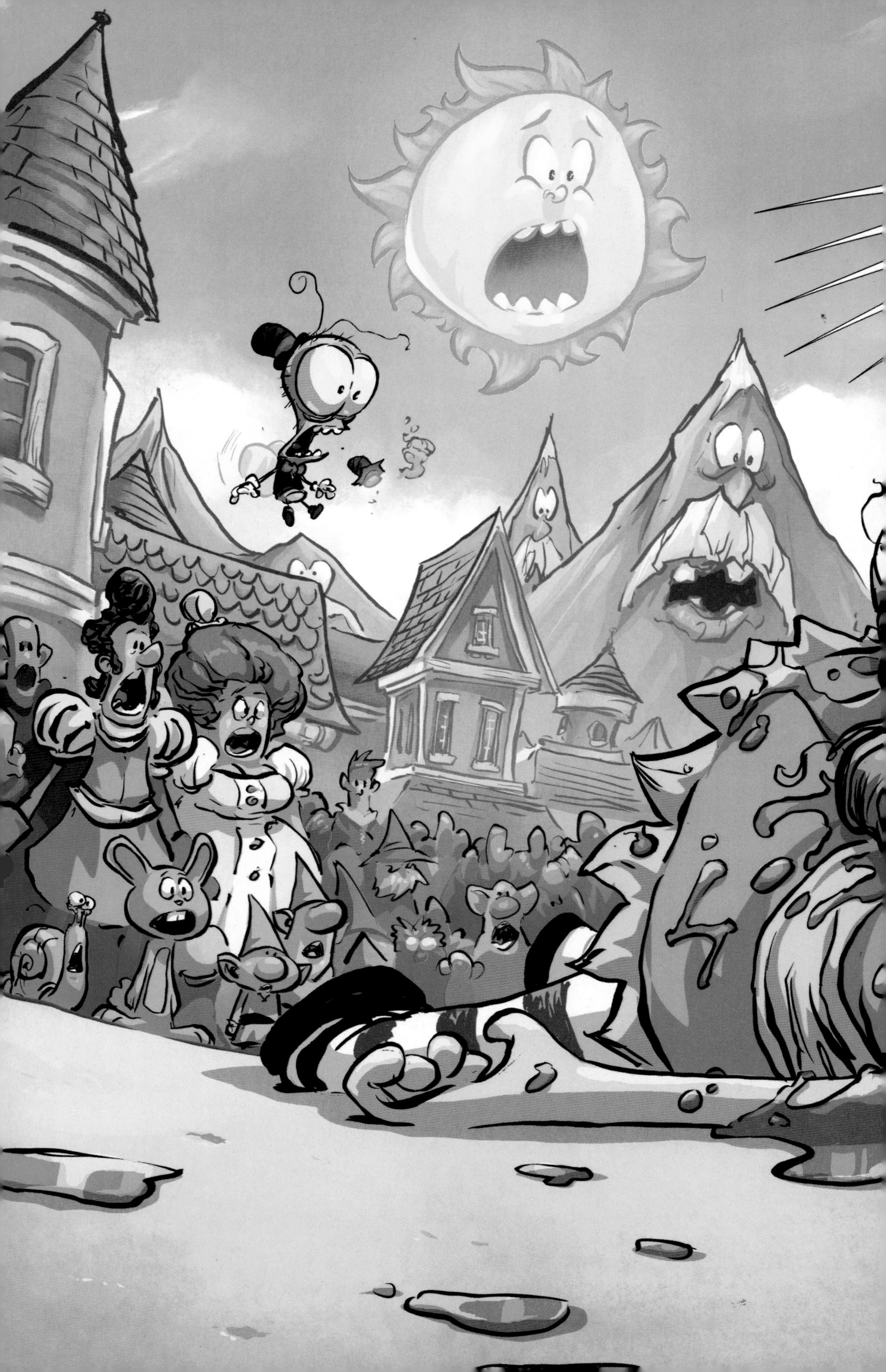

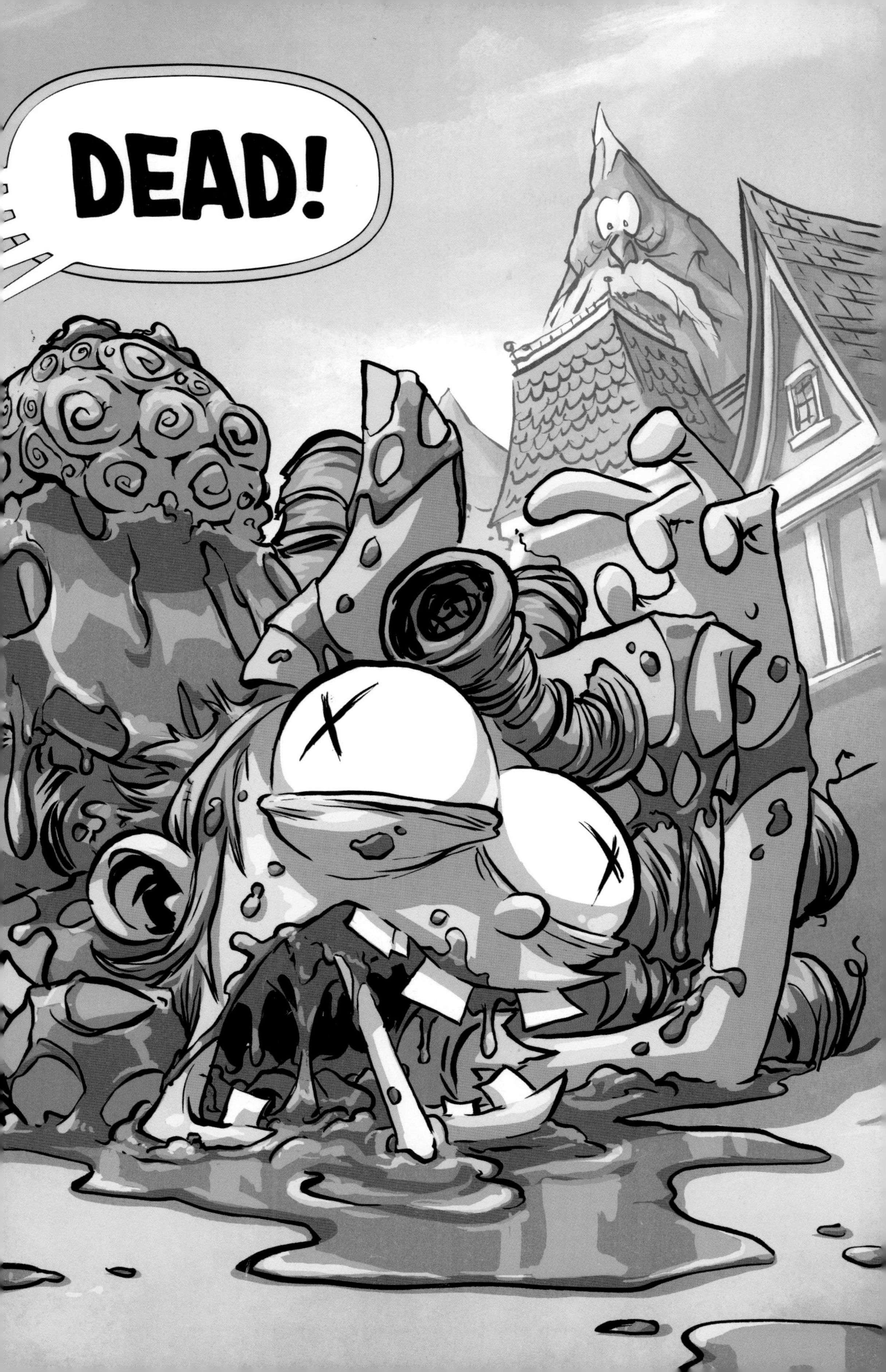
DEAD!

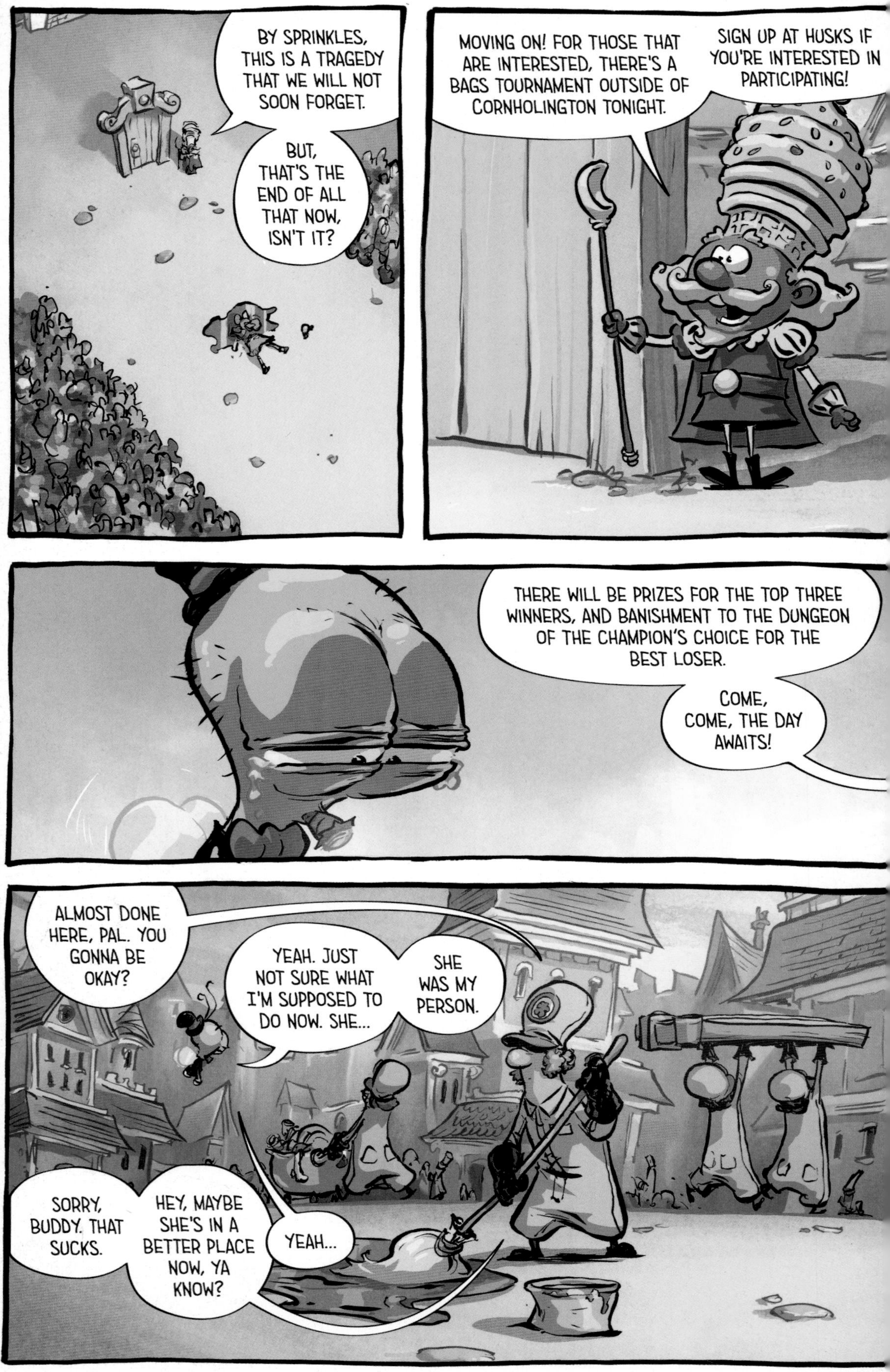
BY SPRINKLES, THIS IS A TRAGEDY THAT WE WILL NOT SOON FORGET.
BUT, THAT'S THE END OF ALL THAT NOW, ISN'T IT?
MOVING ON! FOR THOSE THAT ARE INTERESTED, THERE'S A BAGS TOURNAMENT OUTSIDE OF CORNHOLINGTON TONIGHT.
SIGN UP AT HUSKS IF YOU'RE INTERESTED IN PARTICIPATING!
THERE WILL BE PRIZES FOR THE TOP THREE WINNERS, AND BANISHMENT TO THE DUNGEON OF THE CHAMPION'S CHOICE FOR THE BEST LOSER.
COME, COME, THE DAY AWAITS!
ALMOST DONE HERE, PAL. YOU GONNA BE OKAY?
YEAH. JUST NOT SURE WHAT I'M SUPPOSED TO DO NOW. SHE...
SHE WAS MY PERSON.
SORRY, BUDDY. THAT SUCKS.
HEY, MAYBE SHE'S IN A BETTER PLACE NOW, YA KNOW?
YEAH...

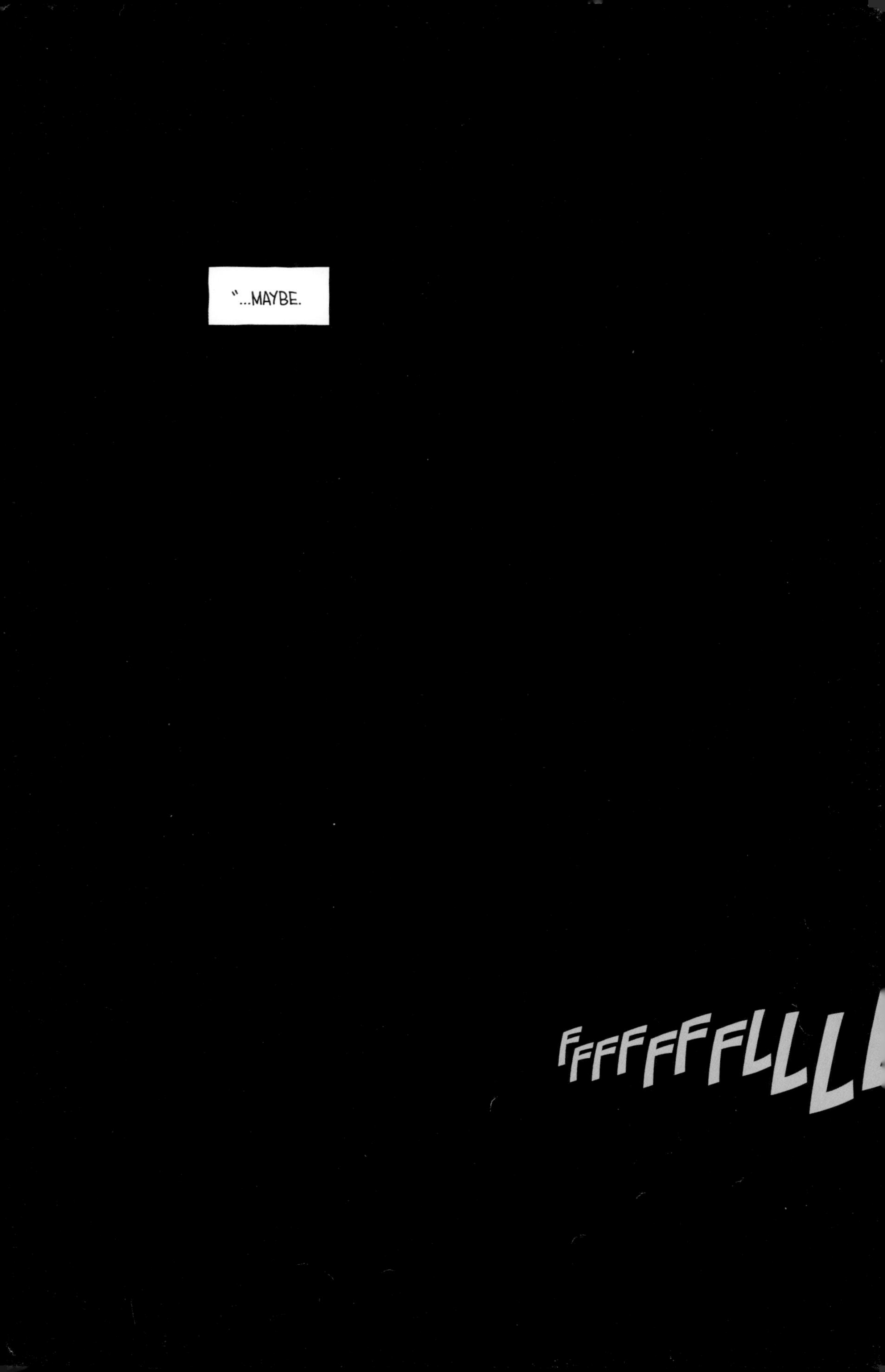
"...MAYBE.
FFFFFFFLLL

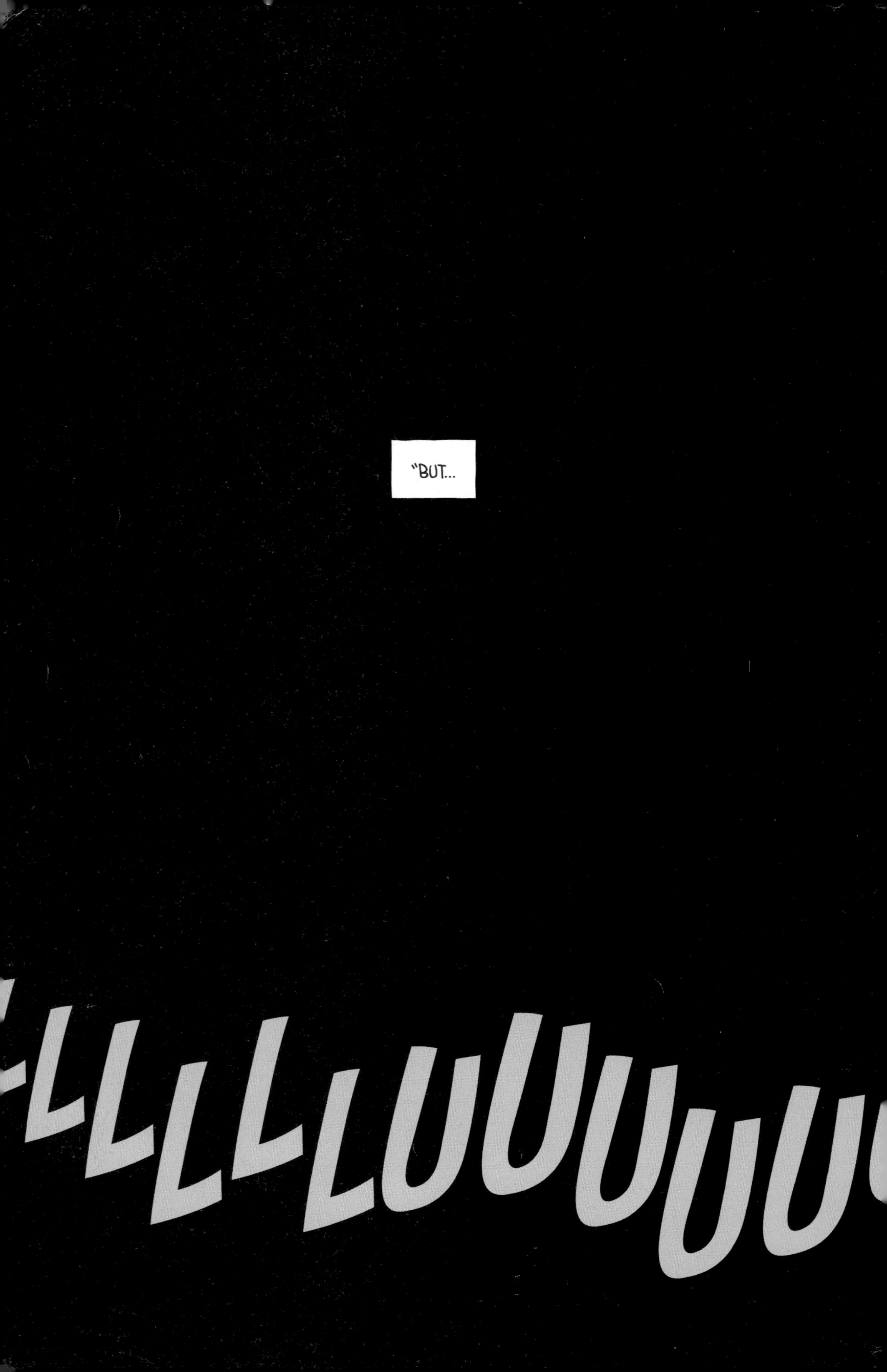
"BUT...
LLLLLUUUUUU

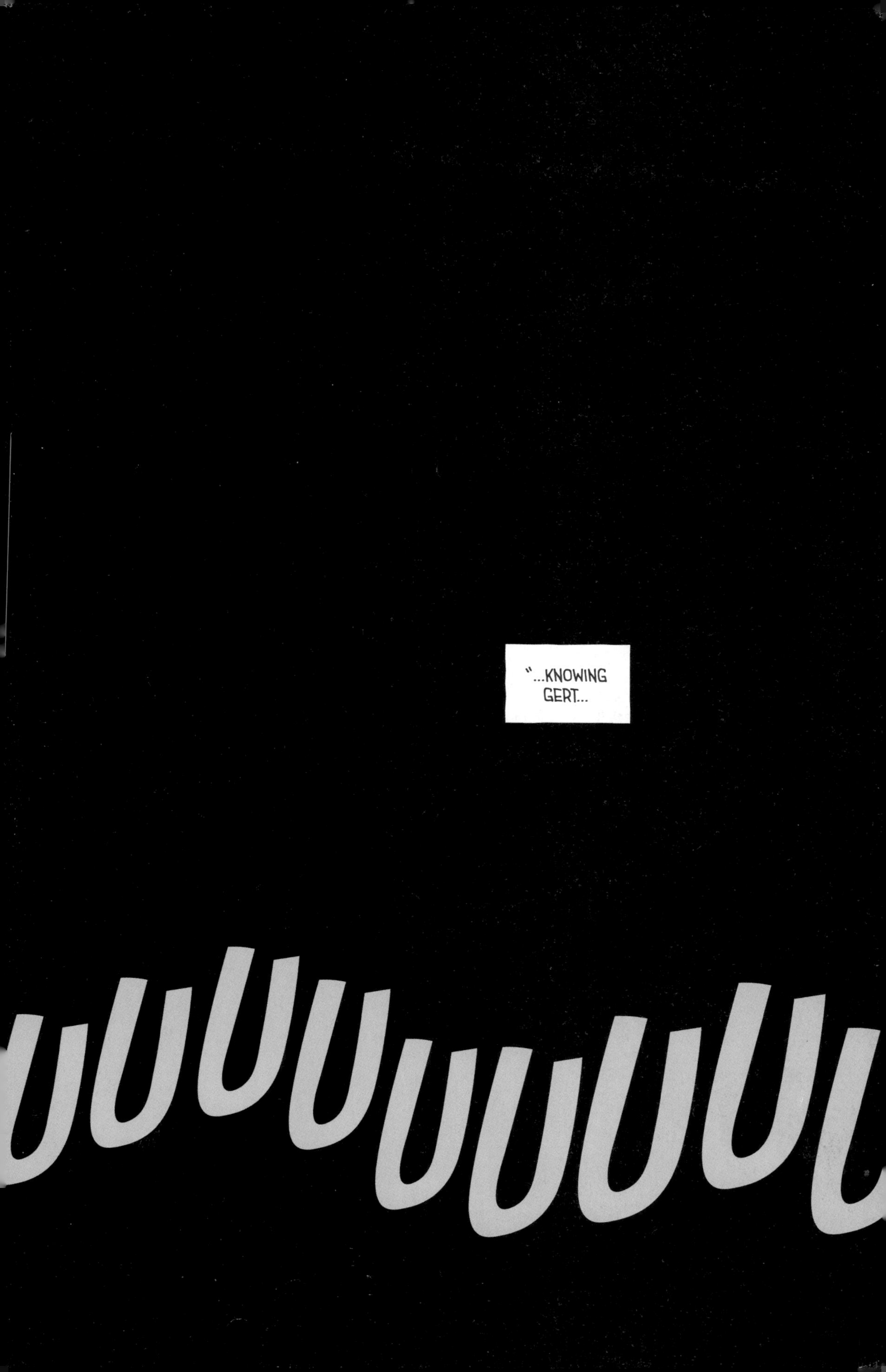
"...KNOWING GERT...

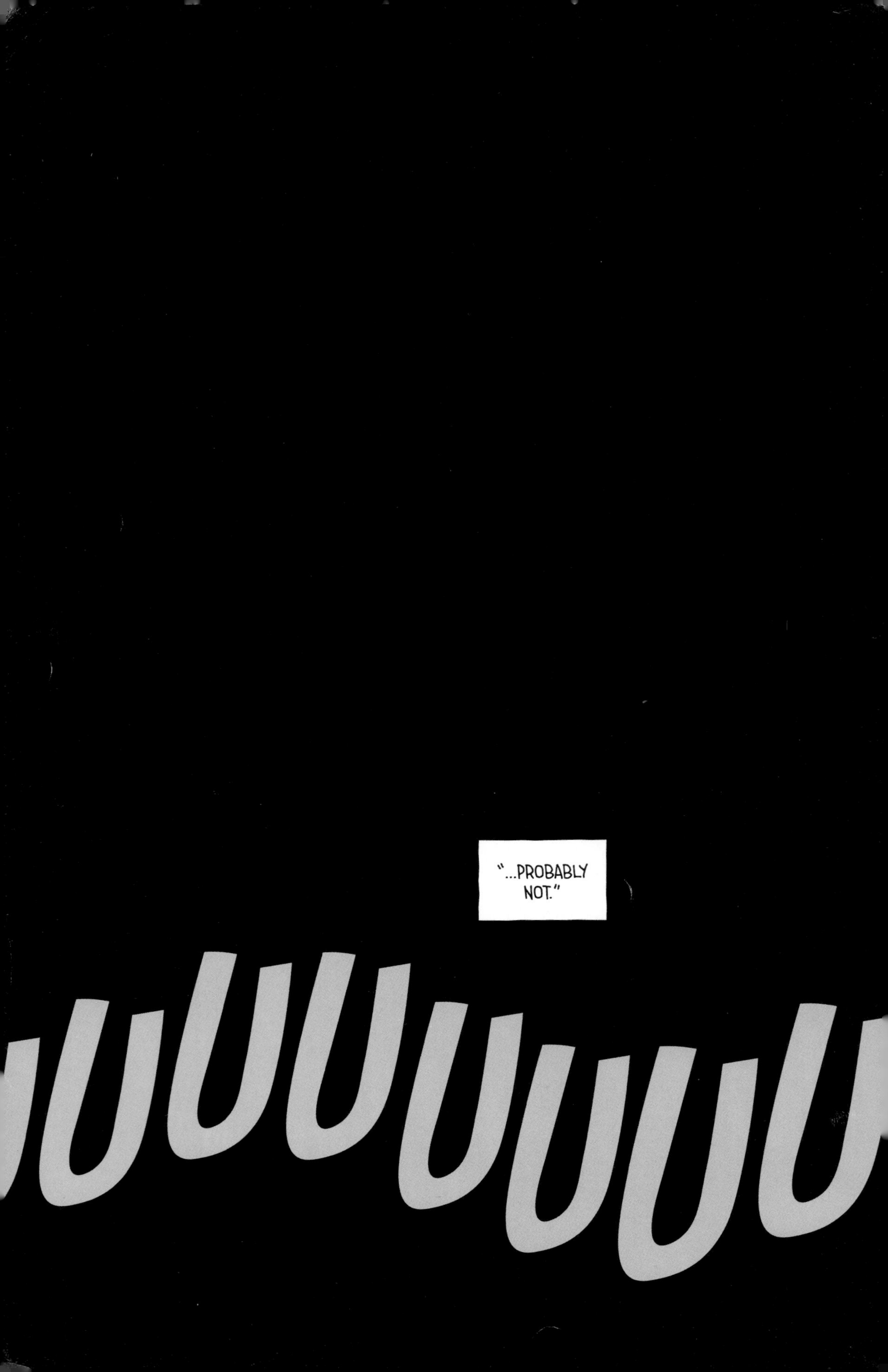
"...PROBABLY NOT."

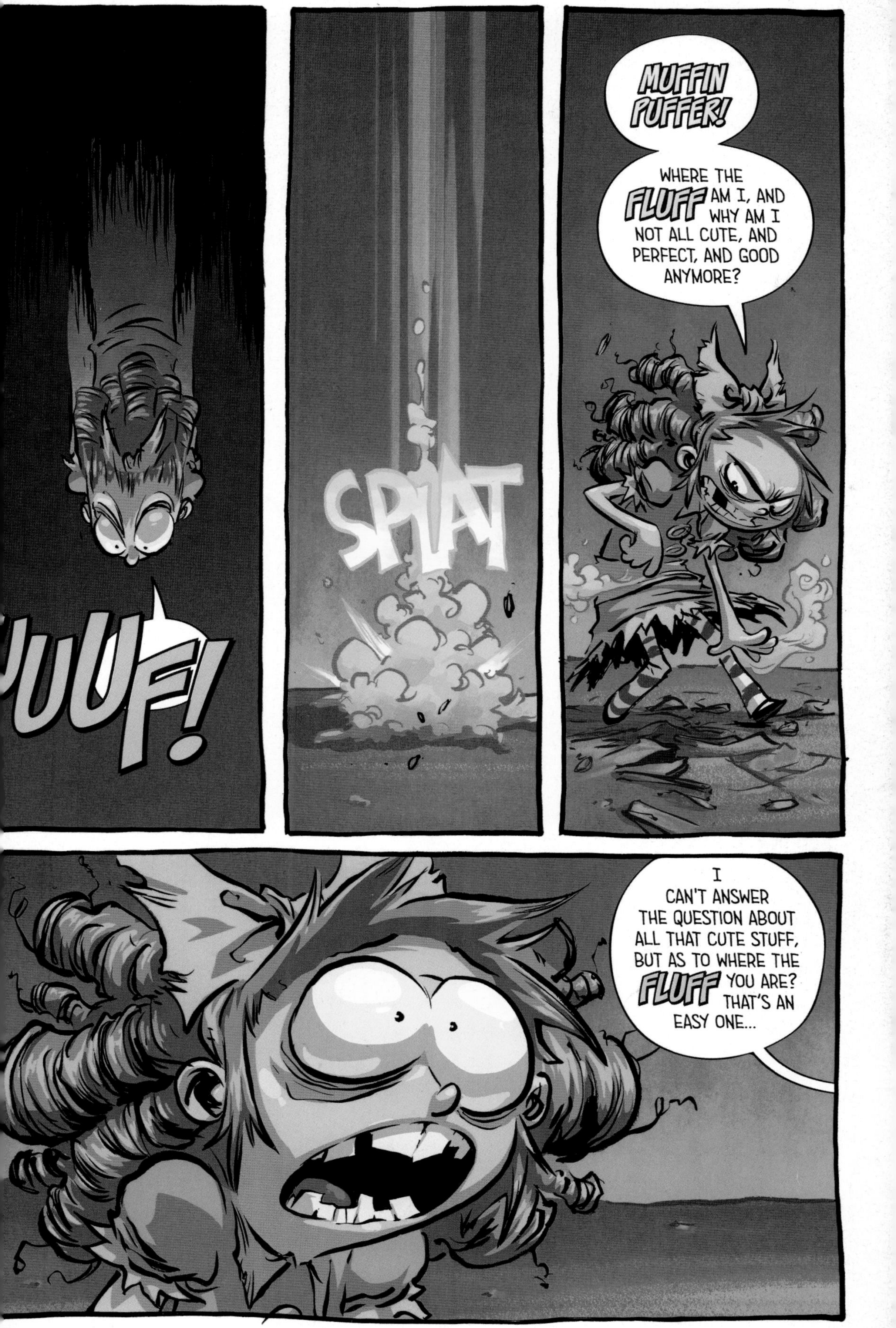

UUUF!
SPLAT
MUFFIN PUFFER!
WHERE THE FLUFF AM I, AND WHY AM I NOT ALL CUTE, AND PERFECT, AND GOOD ANYMORE?
I CAN'T ANSWER THE QUESTION ABOUT ALL THAT CUTE STUFF, BUT AS TO WHERE THE FLUFF YOU ARE? THAT'S AN EASY ONE...

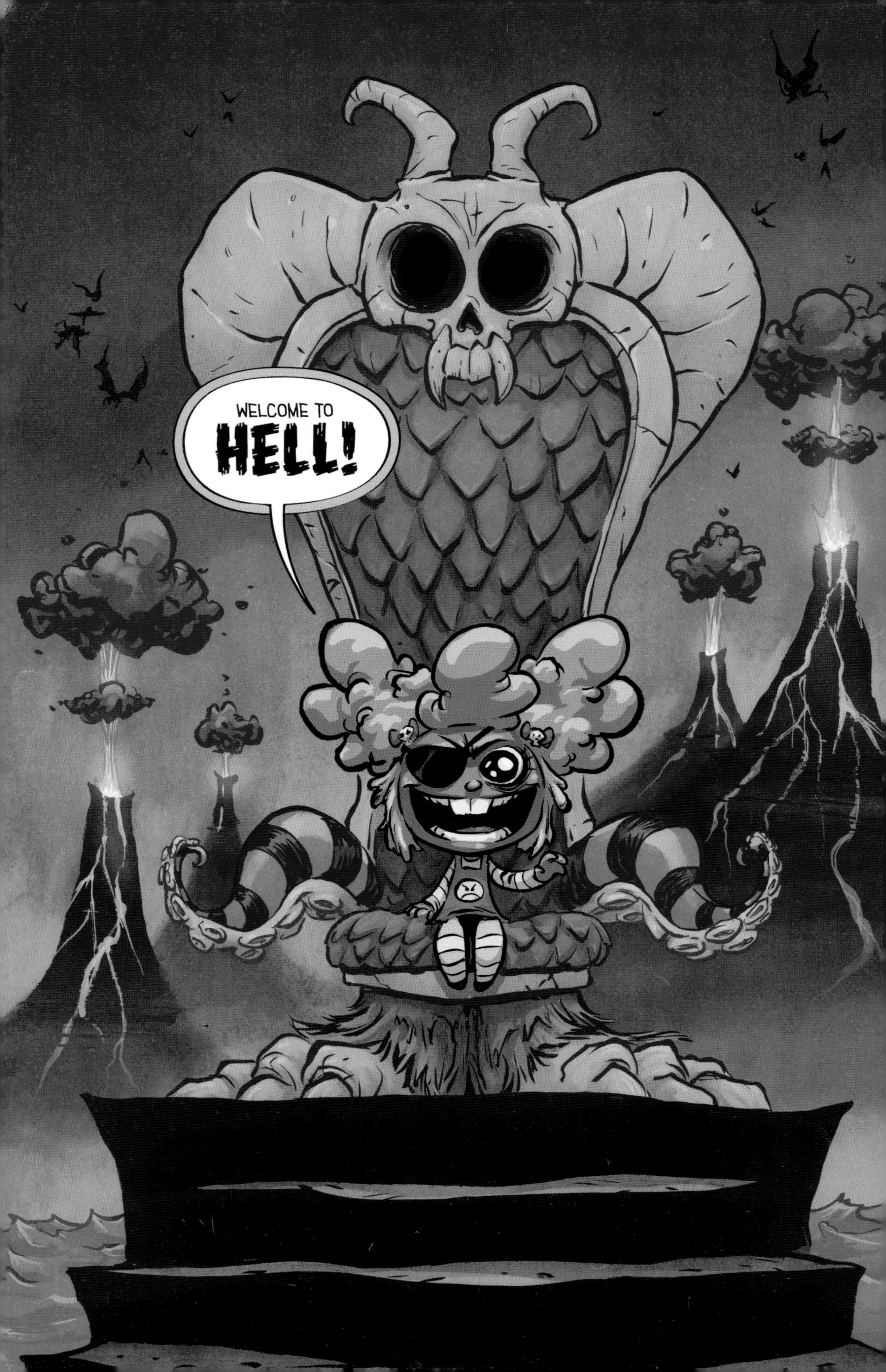
WELCOME TO
HELL!

SKOTTIE YOUNG

...is the New York Times Best Selling cartoonist behi[nd] Marvel's WIZARD OF OZ graphic novel adaptation[s] ROCKET RACCOON and GIANT-SIZE LITTLE MARVEL, as well as illustrating FORTUNATELY, TH[E] MILK with some writer named, NEIL GAIMAN. And in case you have lived in a cave, Skottie has als[o] produced enough Little Marvel variant covers to bui[ld] a small ranch style home out of them. (Though they [are] not waterproof so living in said home is not advised[.) He currently holds the record for most Eisner Award[s] won by anyone born in Fairybury, IL. Skottie lives in Central Illinois with his wife, two sons, and two dogs that drive him crazy. (The dogs, not the humans.)

JEAN-FRANCOIS BEAULIEU

...is the acclaimed colorist behind Marvel's WIZARD OF OZ Graphic Novel adaptations, ROCKET RACCOON, GIANT-SIZE LITTLE MARVEL, NEW WARRIORS, NEW X-MEN, and probably other boo[ks] that Skottie Young didn't draw but since Skottie Young is writing this we'll keep it to mostly Skottie Young books. Okay, fine, INVINCIBLE. Happy? Jea[n] and Skottie have been working together for over a decade. (Which sounds way more epic than saying t[en] years.) Jean is considered one of the industry's top colorists and also holds the record for most people who don't know how to pronounce his last name. H[e] lives somewhere in the Canadian wilderness with hi[s] fiancé, three dogs, nine cats, and an unknown amou[nt] of dope robot model kits.

NATE PIEKOS

...is the founder of BLAMBOT.COM, a company wit[h] a much cooler name than any of us could probably come up with. Good job, Nate! He has created som[e] of the industry's most popular fonts and has used them to letter comic books for Image Comics (HUC[K] Marvel Comics (X-STATIX, X-MEN FIRST CLASS), DC Comics (NEW SUICIDE SQUAD), Dark Horse Comics (FIGHT CLUB 2, UMBRELLA ACADEMY) and all the other companies that end with the word, "Comics". Nate has more guitars in his studio than a[ny] other letterer on the planet. (That was not fact checked, but I'm going with it.) He lives in Rhode Isla[nd] with his wife and the previously mentioned guitars.